Walk in Dread

Walk in Dread

Twelve Classic Eerie Tales

Edited, and with an Introduction, by
DOROTHY TOMLINSON

Taplinger Publishing Company
NEW YORK

First published in the United States in 1972 by
TAPLINGER PUBLISHING CO., INC.
New York, New York

Introduction copyright © 1972 by Dorothy Tomlinson
All rights reserved. Printed in the U.S.A.

Library of Congress Catalog Card Number: 72-2204

ISBN 0-8008-8037-4

The publisher gratefully acknowledges the following for permission
to reproduce:

"The Woman's Ghost Story" by Algernon Blackwood. From the
book *The Listener and Other Stories* by Algernon Blackwood. Published by E. P. Dutton & Co., Inc., and used with their permission.

Introduction

I remember many Christmas Eves ago my father, H. M. Tomlinson, reading to the family just before midnight E. Nesbit's ghost story, "John Charrington's Wedding," so that when I was asked to compile an anthology of ghost stories for Hutchinson a few years after I joined the firm, the first one I thought of was, of course, this particular story.

I have always enjoyed—if one can be said to enjoy—a frightening ghost story, although I don't suppose one has been written that frightens everybody. We each respond in a different way to a particular situation and whereas "things that go bump in the night" may well raise the hair of one person, there will be others who prefer something more subtle.

No collection is ever comprehensive and it is obvious that quite a few big names have been left out of this one, M. R. James and Edgar Allan Poe, for example. Ideally, of course, they should be here as well but within a limit of twelve stories I felt it better to introduce names to you that were either new or better known for other things. Within these limits I have also tried to choose examples of differing types of stories in the hope that at least one will send a shiver down your particular spine. By way of introduction I should like to explain what I feel are the special qualities of each story and why I chose it so that, at least, you won't feel quite so resentful if your own favorite isn't here.

The thing that appeals to me in Cecil Binney's "The Saint and the Vicar" is not only the way it moves from being light-hearted to decidedly sinister in a few pages but also the equivocal position of the vicar. Men of God should, one hopes, be obvious "goodies," but here is one so "good" that even the poor, haunted man cannot decide whether he is his best friend or his worst enemy. Perhaps he imagined himself a sort of St. Anthony figure but that you will have to decide for yourself.

The Walter Scott story is an example of the unexpected from an author who, marvelous novelist though he is, is rarely direct. Yet here is a story that wastes few words and the very title, "The Tapestried Chamber," has the air of a classic story.

In "The Old Nurse's Story" the pace is much more leisurely, yet there is a very strong narrative sense and it is a real story to be read out loud by the fireside. Children, snow, mysterious organ music and a decaying country house are all the right ingredients and Mrs. Gaskell cooks them perfectly.

In some ways, particularly at the beginning, "The Haunted and the Haunters" verges on the edge of parody. It is almost as if Lord Lytton has set out to write the ultimate ghost story by putting in every kind of horror, both physical and mental. Perhaps he *has* written the perfect story as it succeeds beautifully and the ending is both unexpected and sinister.

"Eveline's Visitant" by Miss Braddon has a certain predictability, it is true, in that the reader must guess long before poor Hector what is wrong with his wife. But I chose it because the atmosphere and the image of the spiritual *homme-fatal* with the red hand mark on his face is irresistible.

F. Marion Crawford's story, "Man Overboard," has a marvelously direct opening, and you cannot help reading on. The narrator has buttonholed you like the Ancient Mariner, from which poem the title of this collection comes, and the chatty style leads you painlessly through the saga of the

6

Benton brothers so that the macabre ending is almost a surprise.

I chose "Expiation" because it is typical of E. F. Benson's kind of ghost story. Cornwall is often the setting and the village of Polwithy, inevitably remote, a perfect background. A warm setting and appealing people lure the reader into a cosy feeling of relaxation and then, suddenly, something ruffles the surface and you are off into dark doings from the past with finally an explanation, of sorts. I don't think that I can ever go to Cornwall without expecting a Bensonian happening in every cobbled street!

As with the Marion Crawford story, Algernon Blackwood wastes no time in "The Woman's Ghost Story" in securing his reader. We don't, at the beginning, know who the woman in the corner is, nor do we really care for she has a gripping story to tell, containing that marvelous line that is instantly intriguing and horrifying: "I'm the man who was frightened to death." The slightly moralizing end does not detract from a thoroughly absorbing tale.

"Thurnley Abbey" by Percival Landon sidles in neatly. Continental mail trains aren't common settings for ghost stories, but soon we are back in more familiar surroundings. The conventional framework, though, supports an excellent story with a double twist, leaving behind it two men who would never be the same again after the experience both had shared.

Mrs. Oliphant's "The Library Window" is by far the longest story in the collection but it needs to take its time. This gentle, eerie portrait of a girl and her vision of The Library Window, which seems to exist and yet not to exist, is a masterpiece. It has atmosphere, a sinister old lady and a claustrophobic feeling about it that makes the reader share the girl's obsession with the narrow view from her window.

"The Dream Woman" is a story of obsession, too, but of a very different sort. The landlord's story of his employee,

7

Isaac Scatchard, is a strange one but Wilkie Collins manages to create real sympathy for the poor man possessed with a never-dying vision of his murdering wife.

I have already explained why I chose "John Charrington's Wedding" and although this doesn't have a completely unexpected ending, it is entertainingly written and finishes the collection like a good meal ending with a water ice—lightly but with a cold shiver.

So there it is. Twelve stories of many varied kinds and plenty among them, I hope, to create some uneasiness in all of you. Each is supremely good of its sort and with that I am sure you will agree.

It is sad, I think, that the ghost story has lost so much ground recently to the horror story. People like Roald Dahl and Shirley Jackson have written some marvelously chilling tales, but they lack the essential fireside atmosphere of a good ghost story.

Perhaps the ghost story itself will rise from a literary grave again and successfully chill a new generation. I hope so.

Dorothy Tomlinson

June, 1972

Contents

Like one, that on a lonesome road
Doth walk in fear and dread,
And having once turned round walks on,
And turns no more his head;
Because he knows, a frightful fiend
Doth close behind him tread.

Coleridge, THE ANCIENT MARINER

CECIL BINNEY

The Saint and the Vicar

'AND now,' said the Vicar, 'I must show you our most interesting relic, the shrine of Saint Wilfred of Wilbraham, or rather the ruins of it.'

'I'm afraid I am wasting all your afternoon,' I began.

'Not at all,' said the Vicar, 'I shall enjoy showing it to you.'

Of course he would. There was obviously nothing he enjoyed more than boring casual strangers who permitted him to show them round the parish. Perhaps it would have been a pleasant way of spending the day for anyone who was particularly interested in ecclesiastical architecture, but I am not. I had only gone down to this remote village because an aunt of mine wished me to see about a monument to some of her relations which happened to be in the church, and I could have said everything I needed to say to the Vicar in five minutes. But like a fool I had accepted his offer to show me round, and this was the result. The church did not appear to be particularly old or particularly interesting, but the Vicar had taken nearly three-quarters of an hour to show it to me, and, when I thought my visit was at an end, he insisted on taking me on to the old church.

Apparently the original Wilbraham Church had been burnt down towards the end of the Middle Ages, and instead of rebuilding it they had erected the present church on a completely different site.

That may have constituted an interesting departure from custom but it did not improve the ruins of the old church which consisted, so far as I could see, of a perfectly ordinary Norman Arch and some blocks of rubble overgrown

11

with ivy. And now, having seen that, I was to be taken to see something else of the same description at the opposite end of the village.

'Is it far from here?' I asked. With strangers I have often used my lameness as a pretext to get out of such excursions. But, unfortunately, the Vicar must in our walk through the village have noticed that for practical purposes I was a better walker than he was, and I could think of no other excuse. I could not say I had a train to catch, for the Vicar had seen me driving up in my car.

'About three-quarters of a mile,' he said. 'It is rather a pleasant walk across the meadows. And on the way I can tell you the story, or legend, of the saint.'

With the best intentions in the world, the Vicar was an intolerable bore. He was pedantic rather than learned; as he talked, he gave me the impression of knowing, like a cathedral guide, little beyond what he had learned up in order to tell the story of his parish, and of never having read the books to which he so glibly referred.

'Saint Wilfred of Wilbraham,' he began, rather as though he were preaching at a children's service, 'is our local saint. He has of course nothing to do with the great Saint Wilfred of Ripon. At one time, I believe, it was thought that the parish was called after him, but this theory is frowned upon by modern scholars. He was, as you will have gathered from his name, a Saxon saint; but, unlike most of the Saxon saints, he was an ascetic and a visionary. He came to live here in a cell. In those days the land from here down to the river was marshland and inaccessible.' I felt I could well believe it, for the footpath along which we walked was extremely wet and muddy. 'In it Saint Wilfred lived the life of a hermit, and was afflicted with the terrors of the Nitrian desert. You know the kind of thing which one sees in the grotesque pictures of the temptation of Saint Anthony: there are also very full accounts of them in the various Lives of the saints'—from the way he skipped over these I felt convinced he had no idea where they were to be found—'while in a more rationalist spirit they are described by Gibbon, or perhaps even better by Lecky, in his *History of European Morals*, a work with which you are doubtless familiar.'

'I have never read it.'

'Well, he gives a very good summary of them from an ultra-Protestant point of view, attributing them of course to the effects of loneliness, privation, and religious hallucination. Briefly, one might say that there were two kinds of demon which tormented the saints, those which took on an alluring shape to tempt the ascetic to sin, and those which were merely malevolent, plaguing him in the form of ghosts or hobgoblins or mythological monsters. Saint Wilfred was grievously afflicted by one of the first kind. His biography, which, it must be admitted, dates from two centuries after his supposed death, recounts how a young woman of surpassing beauty and of a charm and intelligence equal to her looks appeared at the door of his cell and asked him in God's name for shelter. She had dark hair and a face like an angel and she wore jewelled rings on her ears and fingers and a marvellous garment of cloth of gold, embroidered with magical letterings—Greek, no doubt. In spite of the saint's tears and protests she continued to live there for many years, trying to ensnare him with temptations of every kind, which the monastic biographer described with great particularity.'

'What did they consist of?'

'Unfortunately,' said the Vicar, 'the details are lost. Saint Wulfstan, thinking they would cause scandal rather than edification, had the pages devoted to them cut out of the manuscript. I believe it is still to be seen in the cathedral library, deliberately mutilated in this manner.'

I felt thoroughly annoyed with the Vicar. I did not believe the story about St. Wulfstan, and thought he had been consciously making fun of me. I showed no particular interest and let him resume his narrative.

'At last the temptation became almost intolerable for the saint to bear; and he prayed that it might pass from him, that, if he was to be tormented by a devil, it should appear

13

rather in its proper hideous shape as the enemy of man or a roaring lion seeking whom it might devour, but that the too beautiful lady might be removed.'

'Most of us would wish exactly the opposite,' I said, rather rudely as my companion was a clergyman.

'He did not wish—he prayed,' said the Vicar, and for the first time I saw a curious look in his eyes. I have often noticed that many elderly clergymen in the country get into a state in which it would not be right to say they are off their heads, but in which they are quite different from the ordinary sane man of the world. I suspected that the Vicar was approaching this condition.

'And his prayer was answered,' he went on, exactly as though he were preaching a sermon. 'The lady no longer pursued him, but instead he suffered from an invisible adversary whose steps he could hear following him when he went in or out of his cell. There were also terrific storms of rain which must have made it uninhabitable. And the saint rejoiced, for he could bear to be torn in pieces by a devil or swept away by the storm, so long as he did not fall into sin. Thus it continued till the end of the year, and then on Saint Sylvester's Day, New Year's Eve, that is, the devil met him face to face, and the saint fled before him, till he reached the river, where, being unable to cross, he plunged into the stream, and perished.'

'Nowadays,' I said 'we should say he went mad from living alone till one day he committed suicide by drowning himself.'

'In the middle ages they thought differently. For hundreds of years he was venerated as a saint and martyr. In particular, the young women of the district made pilgrimages to his shrine which was rebuilt in the thirteenth century—at least the present ruins date from that period. There is no trace of any Saxon work. As in many other matters the Reformation altered things for the worse, and instead of being sacred the shrine was regarded as haunted. No doubt that explains the survival of the steps, which one might have expected to be used for building, for they are of excellent stone, which has evidently been brought from some distance.'

'I am glad to say I am not frightened of ghosts,' I answered.

'Then I hope you will not mind entering the haunted house alone, for I always find that going down into the ruin has a bad effect on my rheumatism. I don't know if it is particularly damp or what.'

'Perhaps it was rheumatism which really drove the saint to despair and death,' I said flippantly.

'Perhaps it was. But I hardly think so.'

The shrine, which we had now reached, was no more worth visiting than the ruins of the old church, for it consisted of little more than a hole in the ground into which descended a flight of well-preserved stone steps. I went down them rather carefully, for they were wet and moss-grown. In spite of his words I could have sworn that the Vicar was following me, till I reached the floor and, looking up, saw him gazing down upon me with a rather mocking expression. I felt sorry if I had annoyed him, for he meant well.

There was nothing particular to look at and I commenced to return up the stairs. Then I realised the cause of my mistake: below ground there was an extraordinarily clear echo, so that every step I took I seemed to hear an invisible person following me. No doubt that explained why the rustics had thought the place haunted. But it was curious that when I made some chance remark to the Vicar my voice did not seem to echo in the same way. I could not resist going once again down the steps and up again.

And then I noticed a very peculiar thing. It was not an echo in the ordinary sense of the word. Having an ear for rhythm, I am acutely conscious of the different sounds made by my own footfalls and by those of a person who does not limp and this is particularly obvious upon a staircase, as I unconsciously descend upon my stronger foot. Yet as I went haltingly, slowly, and cautiously down the

15

stairs, the footsteps echoing behind me were firm and even. It was uncanny. I was quite glad to get back to the surface and the company of the Vicar. I am not superstitious, but I am not at all sure that I should have cared to walk back alone to the village through the gathering dusk, quite apart from the difficulty of finding the way over the muddy fields.

'I hope you will come and have a little tea with me,' said the Vicar. 'Probably you have lost your bearings, but it is actually only a few minutes' walk to the vicarage from here.'

'I really ought to be starting back to London . . .' I began.

'But you must have tea somewhere,' he said, as though the argument was unanswerable. 'Besides, it is coming on to rain and you will not want to start till the shower is over. It rains very heavily in this part of the world when it does rain.'

He gave me permission to put my car in the little vicarage stable, while he went in to make tea. It was as well that I did so, for by the time I had got it safely under cover it was pelting with rain. To avoid being soaked, I had to run across the little yard and along the tiled pathway to the house. And once again I noticed a very peculiar thing. Behind me, as I ran, I could hear footsteps, not the echo of my own steps but the slow measured steps of someone who does not hurry because he knows he must arrive in time. And yet there was nobody: when I got indoors, I found the Vicar placidly boiling a kettle upon a little spirit stove. Everything else seemed to be laid out ready for tea.

I could not help asking him if he was married. He shook his head.

'Do you live all by yourself?'

'Practically so.'

'Don't you find it rather lonely?'

'I have my church to look after and my parishioners.'

This man whom at first I had regarded as a harmless bore seemed now to have taken on a sinister interest, which was increased by the surroundings—the Vicar's study was furnished principally with bookcases and religious pictures, and lighted only by candles, while outside the rain beat upon the lattice windows and the wind howled in the tree-tops. I felt as the great detective in a detective story must feel when he suddenly realises that the harmless lunatic or the old professor, or for that matter why not say 'the Vicar', is leader of the international drug-traffickers and, of course, armed to the teeth.

As far as I remember, he went on telling me about the parish church. I certainly did not feel like asking him any more about St. Wilfred of Wilbraham, and in any case I was far more interested in the man himself than in anything that he said. The more I looked at him the more uncanny and ghostlike he seemed. When I finally went away and the Vicar walked with me to the stable I was quite surprised to find that the only footsteps audible were his and my own. And yet I do not know why I should particularly associate these curious footsteps with the Vicar, for I was never actually in his company when I heard them. But I had evidently worked myself into a queer state of mind, for I just admit, idiotic as it sounds, that when I had got miles away from the vicarage on the main road to Oxford, I could not resist stopping the car for a few minutes to make sure there were not footsteps following me along the road.

.   .   .   .   .

The foregoing account I composed the morning after my return. Indeed, after writing to my aunt, it was the first thing I did—for it happened to be a Sunday morning and I had nothing particular to do. I was determined to put down all the relevant incidents while they were fresh in my mind and as they had struck me at the time, and to tell the story with such artistry as I could command, since I anticipated that it would be the only occasion in my conventional exist-ence when I should be able to tell—what all the world who know no better, desire to tell—a first-hand ghost story. For, of course, I imagined that the story had come to its end. The present record is made in very different circumstances. All attempt at style or narrative skill has vanished. I am merely trying to describe as shortly as I can what I had far rather not have to describe, but what should not in the interest of others remain a secret. At least it is accurate, for I particularly made a note at the time they occurred of the manifestations or symptoms, as I suppose one would call them if, like Lecky, or whoever it was, one regards it as mere insanity.

It was on the Sunday, the very next day after my return, the day I wrote the former narrative, that I realised that the footsteps had not left me. I had been for a short walk, posted the letter to my aunt, and just as it was getting dark I was returning home to tea, when, walking up the stone stairs, I plainly heard behind me the same footsteps, which I had heard before, following me once again with the same insistent slowness and lack of hurry up the four flights of stairs, through the door-way and along the passage to my room. And since then I have never got rid of them. I do not mean they are always there. If they were, it would be better, for I could regard them more easily as a mere nervous affliction like a continual buzzing of the ears. In the broad daylight I do not hear them, nor when I am walking with a companion, but at uncertain times, particularly as I walk about the flat at night, or when I come up the stairs about sunset, they are following me. In the summer it was better, but I was never entirely rid of them: nor is it any use going away from London. They are attached to me, not to any particular place. Once when I was at the seaside and went for a walk along the shore in the evening as it got dark, I could hear them following behind me, crunching down the shingle, never tripping over it as I did, coming on slowly but inevitably.

I do not know that it makes it any better to say it is all an illusion. I admit that I am in some ways a nervous man. At one time, for example, I became excessively apprehensive of burglars, and even bought myself an automatic pistol; until I came to realise there was nothing of sufficient value in my flat to tempt a serious burglar. Perhaps, therefore, my fear of burglars was no more reasonable than a fear of ghosts. Yet there is something, as I realise, absurd in the idea of a supposedly rational business man living in what is surely the most heavily substantial and Victorian block of buildings in the whole of London, unable to walk up the staircase without the sound of these ghostly footsteps following, so slowly yet so firmly, behind me, as though their owner was merely mocking at me, knowing that in the end there could be no escape.

Once I was seized with an idea, and I wrote to the Vicar. I was not sure whether he was my friend or my worst enemy. I did not even know his name but I guessed that, in the eight months that had elapsed, the living would not have changed hands, and I addressed the envelope to 'The Rev. the Vicar of Wilbraham'. I had only one question to ask him: were the footsteps which followed St. Wilfred heard by anyone except himself? And I enclosed a stamped postcard for him to answer.

Of course, the Vicar was incapable of a plain yes or no. He covered the postcard with his unformed finicky little writing. But what he said was something to this effect:

The footsteps were undoubtedly heard (according to the saint's biographer) by many witnesses, so there is no doubt of their reality, but no one but he appreciated their diabolical nature.

With this information I approached my housekeeper, and I asked her without any concealment whether she had noticed the queer way things echoed in the flat, whether in fact it was only my imagination that along with my own footsteps I seemed to hear others as though somebody were following me when there was no other man in the flat. She was a good deal less surprised than I had expected. Perhaps she had read the Vicar's postcard, more likely she had noticed there was something on my mind and thought I was letting myself be bothered by trifles. At any rate, she is an intelligent woman and she gave a rational explanation. She had, she admitted, noticed that one heard strange footsteps in the flat, when there was no one there except ourselves, but it had never worried her as it might have done if she had heard them when I was out, that one did often hear them in old houses, especially on the staircases, and that she had been told it was caused by the boards springing back into position, when they had been trodden upon by someone who walked particularly heavily.

It was exactly the answer I had expected. I did not tell her about the footsteps I had heard coming along the seashore. She could not have explained them away so easily.

.   .   .   .   .

And now I come to write the conclusion of the story, for it is New Year's Eve, St. Sylvester's Day as they seem to have called it in the Middle Ages. I am staying in all alone in my flat—though there is no need to give a reason for staying in with the wind and the rain pouring down outside, but I am staying up, not to see the New Year in—for I shall never see the New Year—but because I know there is something which I may as well stay up for, since in the end I must go to the door and face it. It was on St. Sylvester's Day that St. Wilfred of Wilbraham had at last to turn and see the pursuer that had dogged his footsteps all the year.

Twice already tonight I have heard those same footsteps that he knew so well and that I know so well, not merely following easily behind, but coming up the steps to see me. Twice I have heard a knock upon the door, the way door-knockers sound when there is no real person knocking, and they have gone away again down the stairs. They are not impatient, for they know very well that the third time they come I must go to the door and open it to their knock. Perhaps after all there is nothing mysterious in it, only some caller to ask for a Christmas box or demand payment of a rate—perhaps it is a thief intending to break into the flat, once he is sure it is quite empty, though if it is it will go hardly with him for I shall be armed—but if it is what I know very well that it will be, then I still have my automatic pistol; I shall not have to run like St. Wilfred of Wilbraham for miles till I find a river to hide myself for so long as may be from my pursuers.

SIR WALTER SCOTT

The Tapestried Chamber

ABOUT the end of the American War, when the officers
of Lord Cornwallis's army which surrendered at York-
town, and others, who had been made prisoners during the
impolitic and ill-fated controversy, were returning to their
own country, to relate their adventures and repose themselves after their fatigues, there was amongst them a general
officer of the name of Browne. He was an officer of merit,
as well as a gentleman of high consideration for family
and attainments.

Some business had carried General Browne upon a
tour through the western counties, when, in the conclusion
of a morning stage, he found himself in the vicinity of a
small country town, which presented a scene of uncommon beauty and of a character peculiarly English.

The little town, with its stately old church whose tower
bore testimony to the devotion of ages long past, lay amidst
pasture and corn-fields of small extent, but bounded and
divided with hedge-row timber of great age and size. There
were few marks of modern improvement. The environs of
the place intimated neither the solitude of decay, nor the
bustle of novelty; the houses were old, but in good repair;
and the beautiful little river murmured freely on its way to
the left of the town, neither restrained by a dam, nor bordered by a towing-path.

Upon a gentle eminence, nearly a mile to the southward
of the town, were seen amongst many venerable oaks and
tangled thickets the turrets of a castle, as old as the wars of
York and Lancaster, but which seemed to have received
important alterations during the age of Elizabeth and her

successors. It had not been a place of great size; but what-ever accommodation it formerly afforded, was, it must be supposed, still to be obtained within its walls; at least, such was the inference which General Browne drew from ob-serving the smoke arise merrily from several of the ancient wreathed and carved chimney-stalks. The wall of the park ran alongside of the highway for two or three hundred yards; and through the different points by which the eye found glimpses into the woodland scenery, it seemed to be well stocked. Other points of view opened in succession; now a full one, of the front of the old castle, and now a side glimpse at its particular towers; the former rich in all the bizarrerie of the Elizabethan school, while the simple and solid strength of other parts of the building seemed to show that they had been raised more for defence than ostentation.

Delighted with the partial glimpses which he obtained of the castle through the woods and glades by which this ancient feudal fortress was surrounded, our military tra-veller was determined to inquire whether it might not deserve a nearer view, and whether it contained family pic-tures or other objects of curiosity worthy of a stranger's visit; when, leaving the vicinity of the park, he rolled through a clean and well-paved street, and stopped at the door of a well-frequented inn.

Before ordering horses to proceed on his journey, General Browne made inquiries concerning the proprietor of the château which had so attracted his admiration, and was equally surprised and pleased at hearing in reply a nobleman named whom we shall call Lord Woodville. How fortunate! Much of Browne's early recollections, both at school and at college, had been connected with young Woodville, whom, by a few questions, he now ascertained to be the same with the owner of this fair domain. He had been raised to the peerage by the decease of his father a few months before, and, as the general learned from the landlord, the term of mourning being ended, was now taking possession of his paternal estate in the jovial season

23

of merry autumn, accompanied by a select party of friends to enjoy the sports of a country famous for game.

This was delightful news to our traveller. Frank Woodville had been Richard Browne's fag at Eton, and his chosen intimate at Christ Church; their pleasures and their tasks had been the same; and the honest soldier's heart warmed to find his early friend in possession of so delightful a residence, and of an estate, as the landlord assured him with a nod and a wink, fully adequate to maintain and add to his dignity. Nothing was more natural than that the traveller should suspend a journey, which there was nothing to render hurried, to pay a visit to an old friend under such agreeable circumstances.

The fresh horses, therefore, had only the brief task of conveying the general's travelling carriage to Woodville Castle. A porter admitted them at a modern Gothic Lodge, built in that style to correspond with the castle itself, and at the same time rang a bell to give warning of the approach of visitors. Apparently the sound of the bell had suspended the separation of the company, bent on the various amusements of the morning; for, on entering the court of the château, several young men were lounging about in their sporting dresses, looking at, and criticising, the dogs which the keepers held in readiness to attend their pastime. As General Browne alighted, the young lord came to the gate of the hall and for an instant gazed as at a stranger, upon the countenance of his friend, on which war, with its fatigues and the wounds, had made a great alteration. But the uncertainty lasted no longer than till the visitor had spoken, and the hearty greeting which followed was such as can only be exchanged betwixt those who have passed together merry days of careless boyhood or early youth.

'If I could have formed a wish, my dear Browne,' said Lord Woodville, 'it would have been to have you here, of all men, upon this occasion, which my friends are good enough to hold as a sort of holiday. Do not think you have been unwatched during the years you have been absent from us. I have traced you through your dangers, your triumphs, your misfortunes, and was delighted to see that, whether in victory or defeat, the name of my old friend was always distinguished with applause.'

The general made a suitable reply, and congratulated his friend on his new dignities, and the possession of a place and domain so beautiful.

'Nay, you have seen nothing of it as yet,' said Lord Woodville, 'and I trust you do not mean to leave us till you are better acquainted with it. It is true, I confess, that my present part is pretty large, and the old house, like other places of the kind, does not possess so much accommodation as the extent of the outward walls appears to promise. But we can give you a comfortable, old-fashioned room; and I venture to suppose that your campaigns have taught you to be glad to worse quarters.'

The general shrugged his shoulders and laughed. 'I presume,' he said, 'the worst apartment in your château is considerably superior to the old tobacco-cask, in which I was fain to take up my night's lodging when I was in the bush, as the Virginians call it, with the light corps. There I lay, like Diogenes himself, so delighted with my covering from the elements, that I made a vain attempt to have it rolled on to my next quarters; but my commander, for the time, would give way to no such luxurious provision, and I took farewell of my beloved cask with tears in my eyes.'

'Well, then, since you do not fear your quarters,' said Lord Woodville, 'you will stay with me a week at least. Of guns, dogs, fishing-rods, flies, and means of sport by sea and land, we have enough and to spare: you cannot pitch on an amusement, but we will pitch on the means of pursuing it. But if you prefer the gun and pointers, I will go with you myself and see whether you have mended your shooting since you have been amongst the Indians of the back settlements.'

The general gladly accepted his friendly host's proposal in all its points. After a morning of manly exercise, the company met at dinner, where it was the delight of Lord

Woodville to conduce to the display of the high properties of his recovered friend, so as to recommend him to his guests, most of whom were persons of distinction. He led General Browne to speak of the scenes he had witnessed; and as every word marked alike the brave officer and the sensible man, who retained possession of his cool judgment under the most imminent dangers, the company looked upon the soldier with general respect, as on one who had proved himself possessed of an uncommon portion of personal courage—that attribute, of all others, of which everybody desires to be thought possessed.

The day at Woodville Castle ended as usual in such mansions. The hospitality stopped within the limits of good order; music, in which the young lord was a proficient, succeeded to the circulation of the bottle: cards and billiards, for those who preferred such amusements, were in readiness: but the exercise of the morning required early hours, and not long after eleven o'clock the guests began to retire to their several apartments.

The young lord himself conducted his friend, General Browne, to the chamber destined for him, which answered the description he had given of it, being comfortable, but old-fashioned. The bed was of the massive form used in the end of the seventeenth century, and the curtains of faded silk heavily trimmed with tarnished gold. But then the sheets, pillows, and blankets looked delightful to the campaigner, when he thought of his mansion: the cask. There was an air of gloom in the tapestry hangings, which, with their worn-out graces, curtained the walls of the little chamber, and gently undulated as the autumnal breeze found its way through the ancient lattice window, which pattered and whistled as the air gained entrance. The toilet, too, with its mirror, turbaned, after the manner of the beginning of the century, with a coiffure of murrey-coloured silk, and its hundred strange-shaped boxes, providing for arrangements which had been obsolete for more than fifty years, had an antique and in so far a melancholy aspect. But nothing could blaze more brightly and cheerfully than the two large wax candles; or if aught could rival them, it was the flaming, bickering faggots in the chimney, that sent at once their gleam and their warmth through the snug apartment; which, notwithstanding the general antiquity of its appearance, was not wanting in the least convenience that modern habits rendered either necessary or desirable.

'This is an old-fashioned sleeping-apartment, General,' said the young lord; 'but I hope you will find nothing that makes you envy your old tobacco-cask.'

'I am not particular respecting my lodgings,' replied the general; 'yet were I to make any choice, I would prefer this chamber, by many degrees, to the gayer and more modern rooms of your family mansion. Believe me that when I unite its modern air of comfort with its venerable antiquity, and recollect that it is your lordship's property, I shall feel in better quarters here than if I were in the best hotel London could afford.'

'I trust—I have no doubt—that you will find yourself as comfortable as I wish you, my dear General,' said the young nobleman; and once more bidding his guest good night, he shook him by the hand and withdrew.

The general again looked round him, and internally congratulating himself on his return to peaceful life, the comforts of which were endeared by the recollection of the hardships and dangers he had lately sustained, undressed himself, and prepared himself for a luxurious night's rest.

Here, contrary to the custom of this species of tale, we leave the general in possession of his apartment until the next morning.

The company assembled for breakfast at an early hour, but without the appearance of General Browne, who seemed the guest that Lord Woodville was desirous of honouring above all whom his hospitality had assembled around him. He more than once expressed surprise at the general's absence, and at length sent a servant to make inquiry after him. The man brought back information that General Browne had been walking abroad since an early hour of the morning, in defiance of the weather, which was misty and ungenial.

'The custom of a soldier,' said the young nobleman to his friends. 'Many of them acquire habitual vigilance, and cannot sleep after the early hour at which their duty usually commands them to be alert.'

Yet the explanation which Lord Woodville thus offered to the company seemed hardly satisfactory to his own mind, and it was in a fit of silence and abstraction that he awaited the return of the general. It took place near an hour after the breakfast bell had rung. He looked fatigued and feverish. His hair—the powdering and arrangement of which was at this time one of the most important occupations of a man's whole day, and marked his fashion as much as, in the present time, the tying of a cravat or the want of one—was dishevelled, uncurled, void of powder, and dank with dew. His clothes were huddled on with a careless negligence, remarkable in a military man, whose real or supposed duties are usually held to include some attention to the toilet; and his looks were haggard and ghastly in a peculiar degree.

'So you have stolen a march upon us this morning, my dear General,' said Lord Woodville; 'or you have not found your bed so much to your mind as I had hoped and you seemed to expect. How did you rest last night?'

'Oh, excellently well! remarkably well! Never better in my life,' said General Browne rapidly, and yet with an air of embarrassment which was obvious to his friend. He then hastily swallowed a cup of tea, and neglecting or refusing whatever else was offered, seemed to fall into a fit of abstraction.

'You will take the gun today, General,' said his friend and host, but had to repeat the question twice ere he received the abrupt answer: 'No, my lord; I am sorry I cannot have the honour of spending another day with your lordship; my post-horses are ordered, and will be here directly.'

All who were present showed surprise, and Lord Woodville immediately replied. 'Post-horses, my good friend! What can you possibly want with them when you promised to stay with me quietly for at least a week?'

'I believe,' said the general, obviously much embarrassed, 'that I might, in the pleasure of my first meeting with your lordship, have said something about stopping here a few days; but I have since found it altogether impossible.'

'That is very extraordinary,' answered the young nobleman. 'You seemed quite disengaged yesterday, and you cannot have had a summons today; for our post has not come up from the town, and therefore you cannot have received any letters.'

General Browne, without giving any further explanation, muttered something of indispensable business, and insisted on the absolute necessity of his departure in a manner which silenced all opposition on the part of his host—who saw that his resolution was taken, and forbore further importunity.

'At least, however,' he said, 'permit me, my dear Browne, since go you will, or must, to show you the view from the terrace, which the mist that is now rising will soon display.'

He threw open a sash window, and stepped down upon the terrace as he spoke. The general followed him mechanically, but seemed little to attend to what his host was saying, as, looking across an extended and rich prospect, he pointed out the different objects worthy of observation. Thus they moved on till Lord Woodville had attained his purpose of drawing his guest entirely apart from the rest of the company, when, turning round upon him with an air of great solemnity, he addressed him thus:

'Richard Browne, my old and very dear friend, we are now alone. Let me conjure you to answer me upon the word of a friend, and the honour of a soldier. How did you in reality rest during last night?'

'Most wretchedly indeed, my lord,' answered the general, in the same tone of solemnity; 'so miserably that

I would not run the risk of such a second night, not only for all the lands belonging to this castle, but for all the country which I see from this elevated point of view.'

'This is most extraordinary,' said the young lord, as if speaking to himself, 'then there must be something in the reports concerning that apartment.' Again turning to the general, he said, 'For God's sake, my dear friend, be candid with me, and let me know the disagreeable particulars which have befallen you under a roof where, with consent of the owner, you should have met nothing save comfort.'

The general seemed distressed by this appeal, and paused a moment before he replied. 'My dear lord,' he at length said, 'what happened to me last night is of nature so peculiar and so unpleasant, that I could hardly bring myself to detail it even to your lordship, were it not that, independent of my wish to gratify any request of yours, I think that sincerity on my part may lead to some explanation about a circumstance equally painful and mysterious. To others, the communications I am about to make, might place me in the light of a weak-minded, superstitious fool who suffered his own imagination to delude and bewilder him; but you have known me in childhood and youth, and will not suspect me of having adopted in manhood the feelings and frailties from which my early years were free.' Here he paused, and his friend replied :

'Do not doubt my perfect confidence in the truth of your communication, however strange it may be,' replied Lord Woodville, 'I know your firmness of disposition too well to suspect you could be made the object of imposition, and am aware that your honour and your friendship will equally deter you from exaggerating whatever you may have witnessed.'

'Well, then,' said the general, 'I will proceed with my story as well as I can, relying upon your candour; and yet distinctly feeling that I would rather face a battery than recall to my mind the odious recollections of last night.'

He paused a second time, and then, perceiving that Lord Woodville remained silent and in an attitude of attention, he commenced, though not without obvious reluctance, the history of his night's adventures in the Tapestried Chamber.

'I undressed and went to bed so soon as your lordship left me yesterday evening; but the wood in the chimney, which nearly fronted my bed, blazed brightly and cheerfully, and, aided by a hundred exciting recollections of my childhood and youth which had been recalled by the unexpected pleasure of meeting your lordship, prevented me from falling immediately asleep. I ought, however, to say that these reflections were all of a pleasant and agreeable kind, grounded on a sense of having for a time exchanged the labour, fatigues, and dangers of my profession, for the enjoyments of a peaceful life, and the reunion of those friendly and affectionate ties which I had torn asunder at the rude summons of war.

'While such pleasing reflections were stealing over my mind, and gradually lulling me to slumber, I was suddenly aroused by a sound like that of the rustling of a silken gown and the tapping of a pair of high-heeled shoes, as if a woman were walking in the apartment. Ere I could draw the curtain to see what the matter was, the figure of a little woman passed between the bed and the fire. The back of this form was turned to me, and I could observe, from the shoulders and neck, it was that of an old woman whose dress was an old-fashioned gown which, I think, ladies call a sacque; that is, a sort of robe, completely loose in the body, but gathered into broad plaits upon the neck and shoulders, which fall down to the ground and terminate in a species of train.

'I thought the intrusion singular enough, but never harboured for a moment the idea that what I saw was anything more than the mortal form of some old woman about the establishment who had a fancy to dress like her grandmother, and who, having perhaps (as your lordship mentioned that you were rather straitened for room) being dislodged from her chamber for my accommodation, had forgotten the circumstance, and returned by twelve to her old haunt. Under this persuasion I moved myself in bed and coughed a little to make the intruder sensible of my being in possession of the premises. She turned slowly round, but gracious Heaven! my lord, what a countenance did she display to me! There was no longer any question what she was, or any thought of her being a living being. Upon a face which wore the fixed features of a corpse, were imprinted the traces of the vilest and most hideous passions which had animated her while she lived. The body of some atrocious criminal seemed to have been given up from the grave, and the soul restored from the penal fire, in order to form, for a space, a union with the ancient accomplice of its guilt. I started up in bed, and sat upright, supporting myself on my palms, as I gazed on this horrible spectre. The hag made, as it seemed, a single and swift stride to the bed where I lay, and squatted herself down upon it, in precisely the same attitude which I had assumed in the extremity of horror, advancing her diabolical countenance within half a yard of mine, with a grin which seemed to intimate the malice and the derision of an incarnate fiend.'

Here General Browne stopped and wiped from his brow the cold perspiration with which the recollection of his horrible vision had covered it.

'My lord,' he said, 'I am no coward. I have been in all the mortal dangers incidental to my profession, and I may truly boast that no man ever knew Richard Browne dishonour the sword he wears; but in these horrible circumstances, under the eyes, and, as it seemed, almost in the grasp of an incarnation of an evil spirit, all firmness forsook me, all manhood melted from me like wax in the furnace, and I felt my hair individually bristle. The current of my life-blood ceased to flow, and I sank back in a swoon, a victim to panic terror as ever was a village girl or a child of ten years old. How long I lay in this condition I cannot pretend to guess.

'But I was roused by the castle clock striking one, so loud that it seemed as if it were in the very room. It was some time before I dared open my eyes lest they should again encounter the horrible spectacle. When, however, I summoned courage to look up, she was no longer visible. My first idea was to pull my bell, wake the servants, and remove to a garret or a hay-loft, to be ensured against a second visitation. Nay, I will confess the truth, that my resolution was altered, not by the shame of exposing myself, but by the very fear that, as the bell-cord hung by the chimney, I might, in making my way to it, be again crossed by the fiendish hag, who, I figured to myself, might be still lurking about some corner of the apartment.

'I will not pretend to describe what hot and cold fever fits tormented me for the rest of the night, through broken sleep, weary vigils, and that dubious state which forms the neutral ground between them. A hundred terrible objects appeared to haunt me; but there was the great difference betwixt the vision which I have described and those which followed, that I knew the last to be deceptions of my own fancy and over-excited nerves.

'Day at last appeared, and I rose from my bed ill in health, and humiliated in mind. I was ashamed of myself as a man and a soldier, and still more so at feeling my own extreme desire to escape from the haunted apartment, which, however, conquered all other considerations; so that, huddling on my clothes with the most careless haste, I made my escape from your lordship's mansion, to seek in the open air some relief to my nervous system, shaken as it was by this horrible encounter with a visitant, for such I must believe her, from the other world. Your lordship has now heard the cause of my discomposure, and of my sudden desire to leave your hospitable castle. In other places I trust we may often meet; but God protect me from ever spending a second night under that roof!'

Strange as the general's tale was, he spoke with such a deep air of conviction that it cut short all the usual commentaries which are made on such stories. Lord Woodville never once asked him if he was sure he did not dream of the apparition, or suggested any of the possibilities by which it is fashionable to explain supernatural appearances as wild vagaries of the fancy or deceptions of the optic nerves. On the contrary he seemed deeply impressed with the truth and reality of what he had heard; and, after a considerable pause, regretted, with much appearance of sincerity, that his early friend should in his house have suffered so severely.

'I am the more sorry for your pain, my dear Browne,' he continued, 'that it is the unhappy, though most unexpected, result of an experiment of my own! You must know, that for my father and grandfather's time, at least, the apartment which was assigned to you last night had been shut on account of reports that it was disturbed by supernatural sights and noises. When I came, a few weeks since, into possession of the estate, I thought the accommodation which the castle afforded for my friends was not extensive enough to permit the inhabitants of the invisible world to retain possession of a comfortable sleeping-apartment. I therefore caused the Tapestried Chamber, as we call it, to be opened; and without destroying its air of antiquity, I had such new articles of furniture placed in it as became the modern times. Yet as the opinion that the room was haunted very strongly prevailed among the domestics, and was also known in the neighbourhood and to many of my friends, I feared some prejudice might be entertained by the first occupant of the Tapestried Chamber, which might tend to revive the evil report which it had laboured under, and so disappoint my purpose of rendering it a useful part of the house. I must confess, my dear Browne, that your arrival yesterday, agreeable to me for a thousand reasons besides, seemed the most favourable opportunity of removing the unpleasant rumours which attached to the room, since your courage was indubitable and your mind free of any preoccupation on the subject. I could not, therefore, have chosen a more fitting subject for my experiment.'

34

'Upon my life!' said General Browne, somewhat hastily, 'I am infinitely obliged to your lordship—very particularly indebted indeed. I am likely to remember for some time the consequences of the experiment, as your lordship is pleased to call it.'

'Nay, now you are unjust, my dear friend,' said Lord Woodville. 'You have only to reflect for a single moment in order to be convinced that I could not augur the possibility of the pain to which you have been so unhappily exposed. I was yesterday morning a complete sceptic on the subject of supernatural appearances. Nay, I am sure that had I told you what was said about that room, those very reports would have induced you, by your own choice, to select it for your accommodation. It was my misfortune, perhaps my error, but really cannot be termed my fault, that you have been afflicted so strangely.'

'Strangely indeed!' said the general, resuming his good temper, 'and I acknowledge that I have no right to be offended with your lordship for treating me like what I used to think myself—a man of some firmness and courage. But I see my post-horses are arrived, and I must not detain your lordship from your amusement.'

'Nay, my old friend,' said Lord Woodville, 'since you cannot stay with us another day, which, indeed, I can no longer urge, give me at least half an hour more. You used to love pictures, and I have a gallery of portraits, some of them by Vandyke, representing ancestry to whom the property and castle formerly belonged. I think that several of them will strike you as possessing merit.'

General Browne accepted the invitation, though somewhat unwillingly. It was evident he was not to breathe freely or at ease until he left Woodville Castle far behind him. He could not refuse his friend's invitation, however; and the less so, that he was a little ashamed of the peevishness which he had displayed towards his well-meaning entertainer.

The general, therefore, followed Lord Woodville through

35

several rooms, into a long gallery hung with pictures, which the latter pointed out to his guest, telling the names, and giving some account of the personages whose portraits presented themselves in progression. General Browne was but little interested in the details which these accounts conveyed to him. They were, indeed, of the kind which are usually found in the old family gallery. Here was a cavalier who had ruined the estate in the royal cause; there a fine lady who had reinstated it by contracting a match with a wealthy Roundhead. There hung a gallant who had been in danger for corresponding with the exiled Court of St. Germain's; here one who had taken arms for William at the Revolution; and there a third that had thrown his weight alternately into the scale of Whig and Tory.

While Lord Woodville was cramming these words into his guest's ear, 'against the stomach of his sense', they gained the middle of the gallery, when he beheld General Browne suddenly start, and assume an attitude of the utmost surprise, not unmixed with fear, as his eyes were caught and suddenly riveted by a portrait of an old lady in a sacque, the fashionable dress of the end of the seventeenth century.

'There she is!' he exclaimed. 'There she is, in form and features, though inferior in demoniac expression to the accursed hag who visited me last night!'

'If that be the case,' said the young nobleman, 'there can remain no longer any doubt of the horrible reality of your apparition. That is the picture of a wretched ancestress of mine, of whose crimes a black and fearful catalogue is recorded in a family history in my charter-chest. The recital of them would be too horrible; it is enough to say, that in yon fatal apartment incest and unnatural murder were committed. I will restore it to the solitude to which the better judgment of those who preceded me had consigned it; and never shall anyone, so long as I can prevent it, be exposed to a repetition of the supernatural horrors which could shake such courage as yours.'

Thus the friends, who had met with such glee, parted in a very different mood; Lord Woodville to command the Tapestried Chamber to be unmantled and the door built up; and General Browne to seek in some less beautiful country, and with some less dignified friend, forgetfulness of the painful night which he had passed in Woodville Castle.

MRS. GASKELL

The Old Nurse's Story

You know, my dears, that your mother was an orphan, and an only child; and I dare say you have heard that your grandfather was a clergyman up in Westmorland, where I come from. I was just a girl in the village school, when, one day, your grandmother came in to ask the mistress if there was any scholar there who would do for a nurse-maid; and mighty proud I was, I can tell ye, when the mistress called me up, and spoke to my being a good girl at my needle, and a steady, honest girl, and one whose parents were very respectable, though they might be poor. I thought I should like nothing better than to serve the pretty young lady, who was blushing as deep as I was as she spoke of the coming baby, and what I should have to do with it. However, I see you don't care so much for this part of my story as for what you think is to come, so I'll tell you at once. I was engaged and settled at the parsonage before Miss Rosamond (that was the baby, who is now your mother) was born. To be sure, I had little enough to do with her when she came, for she was never out of her mother's arms, and slept by her all night long; and proud enough was I sometimes when missis trusted her to me.

There never was such a baby before or since, though you've all of you been fine enough in your turns; but for sweet, winning ways, you've none of you come up to your mother. She took after her mother, who was a real lady born; a Miss Furnivall, a grand-daughter of Lord Furnivall's, in Northumberland. I believe she had neither brother nor sister, and had been brought up in my lord's family till she had married your grandfather, who was just a curate, son to a shopkeeper in Carlisle—but a clever, fine gentleman as ever was—and one who was a right-down hard worker in his parish, which was very wide, and scattered all abroad over the Westmorland Fells. When your mother, little Miss Rosamond, was about four or five years old, both her parents died in a fortnight—one after the other. Ah! that was a sad time. My pretty young mistress and me was looking for another baby, when my master came home from one of his long rides, wet and tired, and took the fever he died of; and then she never held up her head again, but just lived to see her dead baby, and have it laid on her breast before she sighed away her life. My mistress had asked me, on her death-bed, never to leave Miss Rosamond; but if she had never spoken a word, I would have gone with the little child to the end of the world.

The next thing, and before we had well stilled our sobs, the executors and guardians came to settle the affairs. They were my poor young mistress's own cousin, Lord Furnivall, and Mr. Esthwaite, my master's brother, a shopkeeper in Manchester; not so well-to-do then as he was afterwards, and with a large family rising about him. Well! I don't know if it were their settling, or because of a letter my mistress wrote on her death-bed to her cousin, my lord; but somehow it was settled that Miss Rosamond and me were to go to Furnivall Manor House, in Northumberland, and my lord spoke as if it had been her mother's wish that she should live with his family, and as if he had no objections, for that one or two more or less could make no difference in so grand a household. So though that was not the way in which I should have wished the coming of my bright and pretty pet to have been looked at—who was like a sunbeam to any family, be it never so grand—I was well pleased that all the folks in the Dale should stare and admire when they heard I was going to be young lady's maid at my Lord Furnivall's at Furnivall Manor.

But I made a mistake in thinking we were to go and live where my lord did. It turned out that the family had left Furnivall Manor House fifty years or more. I could not hear that my poor young mistress had ever been there, though she had been brought up in the family; and I was sorry for that, for I should have liked Miss Rosamond's youth to have passed where her mother's had been.

My lord's gentleman, from whom I asked so many questions as I durst, said that the Manor House was at the foot of the Cumberland Fells, and a very grand place; that an old Miss Furnivall, a great-aunt of my lord's, lived there, with only a few servants; but that it was a very healthy place, and my lord had thought that it would suit Miss Rosamond very well for a few years, and that her being there might perhaps amuse his old aunt.

I was bidden by my lord to have Miss Rosamond's things ready by a certain day. He was a stern, proud man, as they say all the Lords Furnivall were; and he never spoke a word more than was necessary. Folk did say he had loved my young mistress; but that, because she knew that his father would object, she would never listen to him, and married Mr. Esthwaite; but I don't know. He never married, at any rate. But he never took much notice of Miss Rosamond; which I thought he might have done if he had cared for her dead mother. He sent his gentleman with us to Manor House, telling him to join him at New-castle that same evening; so there was no great length of time for him to make us known to all the strangers before he, too, shook us off; and we were left, two lonely young things (I was not eighteen), in the great, old Manor House.

It seems like yesterday that we drove there. We had left our own dear parsonage very early, and we had both cried as if our hearts would break, though we were travel-ling in my lord's carriage, which I thought so much of once. And now it was long past noon on a September day, and we stopped to change horses for the last time at a little smoky town all full of colliers and miners. Miss Rosamond had fallen asleep, but Mr. Henry told me to waken her, that she might see the park and the Manor House as we drove up. I thought it rather a pity; but I did what he bade me, for fear he should complain of me to my lord. We had

left all signs of a town, or even a village, and were then
inside the gates of a large wild park—not like the parks
here in the north, but with rocks, and the noise of running
water, and gnarled thorn-trees, and old oaks, all white
and peeled with age.

The road went up about two miles, and then we saw a
great and stately house, with many trees close around it,
so close that in some places their branches dragged against
the walls when the wind blew; and some hung broken
down; for no one seemed to take much charge of the place;
to lop the wood, or to keep the moss-covered carriage-way
in order. Only in front of the house all was clear. The great
oval drive was without a weed; and neither tree nor creeper
was allowed to grow over the long, many-windowed front;
at both sides of which a wing projected, which were each
the ends of other side fronts; for the house, although it
was so desolate, was even grander than I expected. Behind it rose the Fells, which seemed unenclosed and bare
enough; and on the left-hand of the house, as you stood
facing it, was a little, old-fashioned flower-garden, as I
found out afterwards. A door opened out upon it from
the west front; it had been scooped out of the thick dark
wood for some old Lady Furnivall; but the branches of the
great forest trees had grown and overshadowed it again,
and there were very few flowers that would live there at
that time.

When we drove up to the great front entrance, and went
into the hall I thought we should be lost—it was so large,
and vast, and grand. There was a chandelier, all of bronze,
hung down from the middle of the ceiling; and I had never
seen one before, and looked at it all in amaze. Then, at
one end of the hall, was a great fire-place, as large as the
sides of the houses in my country, with massy andirons
and dogs to hold the wood; and by it were heavy, old-
fashioned sofas. At the opposite end of the hall, to the left
as you went in—on the western side—was an organ built
into the wall, and so large that it filled up the best part of
that end. Beyond it, on the same side, was a door; and

opposite, on each side of the fire-place, were also doors leading to the east front; but those I never went through as long as I stayed in the house, so I can't tell you what lay beyond.

The afternoon was closing in, and the hall, which had no fire lighted in it, looked dark and gloomy, but we did not stay there a moment. The old servant, who had opened the door for us, bowed to Mr. Henry, and took us in through the door at the farther side of the great organ, and led us through several smaller halls and passages into the west drawing-room, where he said that Miss Furnivall was sitting. Poor little Miss Rosamond held very tight to me, as if she were scared and lost in that great place, and as for myself, I was not much better. The west draw-ing-room was very cheerful-looking, with a warm fire in it, and plenty of wood, comfortable furniture about. Miss Furnivall was an old lady not far from eighty, I should think, but I do not know. She was thin and tall, and had a face as full of fine wrinkles as if they had been drawn all over it with a needle's point. Her eyes were very watchful, to make up, I suppose, for her being so deaf as to be obliged to use a trumpet.

Sitting with her, working at the same great piece of tapestry, was Mrs. Stark, her maid and companion, and almost as old as she was. She had lived with Miss Furnivall ever since they were both young, and now she seemed more like a friend than a servant; she looked so cold and grey and stony—as if she had never loved or cared for anyone; and I don't suppose she did care for anyone except her mistress; and, owing to the great deafness of the latter, Mrs. Stark treated her very much as if she were a child. Mr. Henry gave some message from my lord, and then he bowed good-bye to us all—taking no notice of my sweet little Miss Rosamond's outstretched hand—and left us standing there, being looked at by the two old ladies through their spectacles.

I was right glad when they rung for the old footman who had shown us in at first, and told him to take us to our rooms. So we went out of that great drawing-room, and into another sitting-room, and out of that, and then up a great flight of stairs, and along a broad gallery—which was something like a library, having books all down one side and windows and writing-tables all down the other—till we came to our rooms, which I was not sorry to hear were just over the kitchens; for I began to think I should be lost in that wilderness of a house. There was an old nursery that had been used for all the little lords and ladies long ago, with a pleasant fire burning in the grate, and the kettle boiling on the hob, and tea-things spread out on the table; and out of that room was the night-nursery, with a little crib for Miss Rosamond close to my bed. And old James called up Dorothy, his wife, to bid us welcome; and both he and she were so hospitable and kind that by the time tea was over, she was sitting on Dorothy's knee, and chattering away as fast as her little tongue could go.

I soon found out that Dorothy was from Westmorland, and that bound her and me together, as it were; and I would never wish to meet with kinder people than were old James and his wife. James had lived pretty nearly all his life in my lord's family, and thought there was no one so grand as they. He even looked down a little on his wife; because, till he had married her, she had never lived in any but a farmer's household. But he was very fond of her, as well he might be. They had one servant under them, to do all the rough work. Agnes, they called her; and she and me and James and Dorothy, with Miss Furnivall and Mrs. Stark, made up the family; always remembering my sweet little Miss Rosamond. I used to wonder what they had done before she came, they thought so much of her now. Kitchen and drawing-room, it was all the same. The hard, sad Miss Furnivall, and the cold Mrs. Stark, looked pleased when she came fluttering in like a bird, playing and pranking hither and thither, with a continual murmur, and pretty prattle of gladness. I am sure, they were sorry many a time when she flitted away into the kitchen, though they were too proud to ask her to stay with them, and were a little surprised at her taste; though to be sure, as Mrs. Stark said, it was not to be wondered at, remembering what stock her father had come of.

The great, old rambling house was a famous place for little Miss Rosamond. She made expeditions all over it, with me at her heels; all except the east wing, which was never opened, and whither we never thought of going. But in the western and northern part was many a pleasant room; full of things that were curiosities to us, though they might not have been to people who had seen more. The windows were darkened by the sweeping boughs of the trees, and the ivy which had overgrown them: but, in the green gloom, we could manage to see old China jars and carved ivory boxes, and great heavy books, and, above all, the old pictures.

Once, I remember, my darling would have Dorothy go with us to tell us who they all were; for they were all portraits of some of my lord's family, though Dorothy could not tell us the names of every one. We had gone through most of the rooms, when we came to the old state drawing-room over the hall, and there was a picture of Miss Furnivall; or, as she was called in those days, Miss Grace, for she was the younger sister. Such a beauty she must have been! but with such a set, proud look, and such scorn looking out of her handsome eyes, with her eyebrows just a little raised, as if she were wondering how anyone could have the impertinence to look at her; and her lip curled at us, as we stood there gazing. She had a dress on, the like of which I had never seen before, but it was all the fashion when she was young: a hat of some soft white stuff like beaver, pulled a little over her brows, and a beautiful plume of feathers sweeping round it on one side; and her gown of blue satin was open in front to a quilted white stomacher.

'Well, to be sure!' said I, when I had gazed my fill. 'Flesh is grass, they do say; but who would have thought that Miss Furnivall had been such an out-and-out beauty, to see her now?'

'Yes,' said Dorothy. 'Folks change sadly. But if what my master's father used to say was true, Miss Furnivall, the elder sister, was handsomer than Miss Grace. Her picture is here somewhere; but, if I show it you, you must never let on, even to James, that you have seen it. Can the little lady hold her tongue, think you?' asked she.

I was not so sure, for she was such a little sweet, bold, open-spoken child, so I set her to hide herself; and then I helped Dorothy to turn a great picture, that leaned with its face towards the wall, and was not hung up as the others were. To be sure, it beat Miss Grace for beauty; and, I think, for scornful pride too, though in that matter it might be hard to choose. I could have looked at it an hour, but Dorothy seemed half frightened at having shown it to me, and hurried it back again, and bade me run and find Miss Rosamond, for that there were some ugly places about the house, where she should like ill for the child to go. I was a grave, high-spirited girl, and thought little of what the old woman said, for I liked hide-and-seek as well as any child in the parish; so off I ran to find my little one.

As winter drew on, and the days grew shorter, I was sometimes almost certain that I heard a noise as if someone was playing on the great organ in the hall. I did not hear it every evening; but, certainly, I did very often; usually when I was sitting with Miss Rosamond, after I had put her to bed, and keeping quite still and silent in the bedroom. Then I used to hear it booming and swelling away in the distance. The first night, when I went down to my supper, I asked Dorothy who had been playing music, and James said very shortly that I was a gowk to take the wind soughing among the trees for music; but I saw Dorothy look at him very fearfully, and Bessy, the kitchenmaid, said something beneath her breath, and went quite white. I saw they did not like my question, so I held my peace till I was with Dorothy alone, when I knew I could get a good deal out of her.

So, the next day, I watched my time, and I coaxed and asked her who it was that played the organ; for I knew

45

that it was the organ and not the wind well enough, for all I had kept silence before James. But Dorothy had had her lesson, I'll warrant, and never a word could I get from her. So then I tried Bessy, though I had always held my head rather above her, as I was evened to James and Dorothy, and she was little better than their servant. So she said I must never, never tell; and if I ever told, I was never to say *she* had told me; but it was a very strange noise, and she had heard it many a time, but most of all on winter nights, and before storms; and folks did say, it was the old lord playing on the great organ in the hall, just as he used to do when he was alive; but who the old lord was, or why he played, and why he played on stormy winter evenings in particular, she either could not or would not tell me. Well! I told you I had a brave heart; and I thought it was rather pleasant to have that grand music rolling about the house, let who would be the player; for now it rose above the great gusts of wind, and wailed and triumphed just like a living creature, and then it fell to a softness most complete; only it was always music and tunes, so it was nonsense to call it the wind.

I thought at first that it might be Miss Furnivall who played, unknown to Bessy; but one day when I was in the hall by myself, I opened the organ and peeped all about it and around it, as I had done to the organ in Crosthwaite Church once before, and I saw it was all broken and destroyed inside, though it looked so brave and fine; and then though it was noonday, my flesh began to creep a little, and I shut it up, and ran away pretty quickly to my own bright nursery; and I did not like hearing the music for some time after that, any more than James and Dorothy did.

All this time Miss Rosamond was making herself more and more beloved. The old ladies liked her to dine with them at their early dinner; James stood behind Miss Furnivall's chair, and I behind Miss Rosamond's all in state; and, after dinner, she would play about in a corner of the great drawing-room, as still as any mouse, while Miss Furnivall slept, and I had my dinner in the kitchen. But she was glad enough to come to me in the nursery afterwards; for, as she said, Miss Furnivall was so sad, and Mrs. Stark so dull; but she and I were merry enough; and, by and by, I got not to care for that weird, rolling music, which did one no harm, if we did not know where it came from.

That winter was very cold. In the middle of October the frosts began, and lasted many, many weeks. I remember, one day at dinner, Miss Furnivall lifted up her sad, heavy eyes and said to Mrs. Stark, 'I am afraid we shall have a terrible winter,' in a strange kind of meaning way. But Mrs. Stark pretended not to hear, and talked very loud of something else. My little lady and I did not care for the frost; not we! As long as it was dry we climbed up the steep brows, behind the house, and went up on the Fells, which were bleak, and bare enough, and there we ran races in the fresh, sharp air; and once we came down by a new path that took us past the two old gnarled holly trees, which grew about half way down by the east side of the house.

But the days grew shorter and shorter; and the old lord —if it was he—played more and more stormily and sadly on the great organ. One Sunday afternoon—it must have been towards the end of November—I asked Dorothy to take charge of little Missy when she came out of the drawing-room, after Miss Furnivall had had her nap; for it was too cold to take her with me to church, and yet I wanted to go. And Dorothy was glad enough to promise, and was so fond of the child that all seemed well; and Bessy and I set off briskly, though the sky hung heavy and black over the white earth, as if the night had never fully gone away; and the air, though still, was very biting and keen.

'We shall have a fall of snow,' said Bessy to me. And sure enough, even while we were in church, it came down thick, in great, large flakes, so thick it almost darkened the windows. It had stopped snowing before we came out, but it lay soft, thick, and deep beneath our feet as we tramped home. Before we got to the hall the moon rose, and I think it was lighter then—what with the moon, and what with the white dazzling snow—than it had been when we went to church, between two and three o'clock. I have not told you that Miss Furnivall and Mrs. Stark never went to church; they used to read the prayers together, in their quiet, gloomy way; they seemed to feel the Sunday very long with their tapestry-work to be busy at.

So when I went to Dorothy in the kitchen, to fetch Miss Rosamond and take her upstairs with me, I did not much wonder when the old woman told me that the ladies had kept the child with them, and that she had never come to the kitchen, as I had bidden her when she was tired of behaving pretty in the drawing-room. So I took off my things and went to find her, and bring her to her supper in the nursery. But when I went into the best drawing-room there sat the two old ladies, very still and quiet, dropping out a word now and then but looking as if nothing so bright and merry as Miss Rosamond had ever been near them. Still I thought she might be hiding from me; it was one of her pretty ways; and that she had persuaded them to look as if they knew nothing about her; so I went softly peeping under this sofa, and behind that chair, making believe I was sadly frightened at not finding her.

'What's the matter, Hester?' said Mrs. Stark sharply. I don't know if Miss Furnivall had seen me, for, as I told you, she was very deaf, and she sat quite still, idly staring into the fire, with her hopeless face. 'I'm only looking for my little Rosy-Posy,' I replied, still thinking that the child was there, and near me, though I could not see her.

'Miss Rosamond is not here,' said Mrs. Stark. 'She went away more than an hour ago to find Dorothy.' And she too turned and went on looking into the fire.

My heart sank at this, and I began to wish I had never left my darling. I went back to Dorothy and told her. James was gone out for the day, but she and me and Bessy took lights and went up into the nursery first, and then we roamed over the great large house, calling and entreating Miss Rosamond to come out of her hiding-place, and not fright-

en us to death in that way. But there was no answer; no
sound.

'Oh!' said I at last. 'Can she have got into the east wing
and hidden there?'

But Dorothy said it was not possible, for that she herself had never been there; that the doors were always
locked, and my lord's steward had the keys, she believed;
at any rate, neither she nor James had ever seen them. So
I said I would go back and see if, after all, she was not
hidden in the drawing-room, unknown to the old ladies;
and if I found her there I said I would whip her well for
the fright she had given me; but I never meant to do it.
Well, I went back to the west drawing-room, and I told
Mrs. Stark we could not find her anywhere, and asked
for leave to look all about the furniture there, for I thought
now, that she might have fallen asleep in some warm hidden corner; but no! we looked, Miss Furnivall got up and
looked, trembling all over, and she was nowhere there;
then we set off again, everyone in the house, and looked
in all the places we had searched before, but we could not
find her. Miss Furnivall shivered and shook so much that
Mrs. Stark took her back into the warm drawing-room;
but not before they had made me promise to bring her to
them when she was found. Welladay! I began to think she
never would be found, when I bethought me to look out
into the great front court, all covered with snow.

I was upstairs when I looked out; but it was such clear
moonlight I could see, quite plain, two little footprints,
which might be traced from the hall door and round the
corner of the east wing. I don't know how I got down, but
I tugged open the great, stiff hall door; and, throwing the
skirt of my gown over my head for a cloak, I ran out. I
turned the east corner, and there a black shadow fell on
the snow; but when I came again into the moonlight, there
were the little foot-marks going up—up to the Fells. It
was bitter cold; so cold that the air almost took the skin
off my face as I ran, but I ran on, crying to think how my
poor little darling must be perished and frightened. I was

within sight of the holly trees when I saw a shepherd coming down the hill, bearing something in his arms wrapped in his maud. He shouted to me, and asked me if I had lost a bairn; and, when I could not speak for crying, he bore towards me, and I saw my wee bairnie lying still, and white, and stiff, in his arms, as if she had been dead. He told me he had been up the Fells to gather in his sheep, before the deep cold of night came on, and that under the holly trees (black marks on the hill-side, where no other bush was for miles around) he had found my little lady—my lamb—my queen—my darling—stiff and cold, in the terrible sleep which is frost-begotten.

Oh! the joy, and the tears of having her in my arms once again! for I would not let him carry her; but took her, maud and all, into my own arms, and held her near my own warm neck and heart, and felt the life stealing slowly back again into her little gentle limbs. But she was still insensible when we reached the hall, and I had no breath for speech. We went in by the kitchen door.

'Bring the warming-pan,' said I; and I carried her upstairs, and began undressing her by the nursery fire, which Bessy had kept up. I called my little lammie all the sweet and playful names I could think of—even while my eyes were blinded by my tears; and at last, oh! at length she opened her large, blue eyes. Then I put her into her warm bed, and sent Dorothy down to tell Miss Furnivall that all was well; and I made up my mind to sit by my darling's bedside the livelong night. She fell away into a soft sleep as soon as her pretty head had touched the pillow, and I watched by her until morning light; when she wakened up bright and clear—or so I thought at first—and, my dears, so I think now.

She said that she had fancied that she should like to go to Dorothy, for that both the old ladies were asleep, and it was very dull in the drawing-room; and that, as she was going through the west lobby, she saw the snow through the high window falling—falling—soft and steady. But she wanted to see it lying pretty and white on the ground;

so she made her way into the great hall; and then, going to the window, she saw it bright and soft upon the drive; but while she stood there, she saw a little girl, not so old as she was, 'but so pretty,' said my darling, 'and this little girl beckoned to me to come out; and oh, she was so pretty and so sweet, I could not choose but go.' And then this other little girl had taken her by the hand, and side by side the two had gone round the east corner.

'Now you are a naughty little girl, and telling stories,' said I. 'What would your good mamma, that is in heaven, and never told a story in her life, say to her little Rosamond, if she heard her—and I dare say she does—telling stories!'

'Indeed, Hester,' sobbed out my child, 'I'm telling you true. Indeed I am.'

'Don't tell me!' said I, very stern. 'I tracked you by your foot-marks through the snow; there were only yours to be seen; and if you had had a little girl to go hand in hand with you up the hill, don't you think the footprints would have gone along with yours?'

'I can't help it, dear, dear Hester,' said she, crying, 'if they did not. I never looked at her feet, but she held my hand fast and tight in her little one, and it was very, very cold. She took me up the Fell path, up to the holly trees; and there I saw a lady weeping and crying; but when she saw me, she hushed her weeping, and smiled very proud and grand, and took me on her knee, and began to lull me to sleep; and that's all, Hester—but that is true; and my dear mamma knows it is,' said she, crying. So I thought the child was in a fever, and pretended to believe her, as she went over her story—over and over again, and always the same. At last Dorothy knocked at the door with Miss Rosamond's breakfast; and she told me the old ladies were down in the eating-parlour, and that they wanted to speak to me. They had both been into the night-nursery the evening before, but it was after Miss Rosamond was asleep; so they had only looked at her—not asked me any questions.

'I shall catch it,' thought I to myself, as I went along the north gallery. 'And yet,' I thought, taking courage, 'it was in their charge I left her; and it's they that's to blame for letting her steal away unknown and unwatched.' So I went in boldly, and told my story. I told it all to Miss Furnivall, shouting it close to her ear; but when I came to the mention of the other little girl out in the snow, coaxing and tempting her out, and wiling her up to the grand and beautiful lady by the holly tree, she threw her arms up—her old and withered arms—and cried aloud, 'Oh! Heaven, forgive! Have mercy!'

Mrs. Stark took hold of her; roughly enough, I thought; but she was past Mrs. Stark's management, and spoke to me, in a kind of wild warning and authority.

'Hester, keep her from that child! It will lure her to her death! That evil child! Tell her it is a wicked, naughty child.' Then Mrs. Stark hurried me out of the room; where, indeed, I was glad enough to go; but Miss Furnivall kept shrieking out, 'Oh! have mercy! Wilt Thou never forgive! It is many a long year ago ...'

I was very uneasy in my mind after that. I durst never leave Miss Rosamond, night or day, for fear lest she might slip off again, after some fancy or other; and all the more because I thought I could make out that Miss Furnivall was crazy, from their odd ways about her; and I was afraid lest something of the same kind (which might be in the family, you know) hung over my darling. And the great frost never ceased all this time; and whenever it was a more stormy night than usual, between the gusts, and through the wind, we heard the old lord playing on the great organ. But, old lord or not, wherever Miss Rosamond went, there I followed; for my love for her, pretty, helpless orphan, was stronger than my fear for the grand and terrible sound. Besides, it rested with me to keep her cheerful and merry, as beseemed her age. So we played together, and wandered together, here and there, and everywhere; for I never dared to lose sight of her again in that large and rambling house. And so it happened, that one afternoon, not long before Christmas Day, we were playing together on the billiard-table in the great hall (not that we knew the way of playing, but she liked to roll the smooth, ivory balls with her pretty hands, and I liked to do whatever she did); and, by and by, without our noticing it, it grew dusk indoors, though it was still light in the open air, and I was thinking of taking her back into the nursery, when, all of a sudden, she cried out:

'Look! Hester, look! there is my poor little girl out in the snow!'

I turned towards the long narrow windows, and there, sure enough, I saw a little girl, less than my Miss Rosamond—dressed all unfit to be out of doors such a bitter night—crying, and beating against the window-panes, as if she wanted to be let in. She seemed to sob and wail, till Miss Rosamond could bear it no longer, and was flying to the door to open it, when, all of a sudden, and close up upon us, the great organ pealed out so loud and thundering, it fairly made me tremble; and all the more, when I remembered me that, even in the stillness of that dead-cold weather, I had heard no sound of little battering hands upon the window glass, although the Phantom Child had seemed to put forth all its force; and, although I had seen it wail and cry, no faintest touch of sound had fallen upon my ears. Whether I remembered all this at the very moment, I do not know; the great organ sound had so stunned me into terror; but this I know: I caught up Miss Rosamond before she got the hall door opened, and clutched her, and carried her away, kicking and screaming, into the large bright kitchen, where Dorothy and Agnes were busy with their mince pies.

'What is the matter with my sweet one?' cried Dorothy, as I bore in Miss Rosamond, who was sobbing as if her heart would break.

'She won't let me open the door for my little girl to come in; and she'll die if she is out on the Fells all night. Cruel, naughty Hester,' she said, slapping me; but she might have struck harder, for I had seen a look of ghastly terror on Dorothy's face, which made my very blood run cold.

'Shut the back-kitchen door fast, and bolt it well,' said she to Agnes. She said no more; she gave me raisins and almonds to quiet Miss Rosamond: but she sobbed about the little girl in the snow, and would not touch any of the good things. I was thankful when she cried herself to sleep in bed. Then I stole down to the kitchen, and told Dorothy I had made up my mind. I would carry my darling back to my father's house in Applethwaite; where, if we lived humbly, we lived at peace. I said I had been frightened enough with the old lord's organ-playing; but now that I had seen for myself this little moaning child, all decked out as no child in the neighbourhood could be, beating and battering to get in, yet always without any sound or noise —with the dark wound on her right shoulder; and that Miss Rosamond had known it again for the phantom that had nearly lured her to her death (which Dorothy knew was true); I would stand it no longer.

I saw Dorothy change colour once or twice. When I had done she told me she did not think I could take Miss Rosamond with me, for that she was my lord's ward, and I had no right over her; and she asked me, would I leave the child that I was so fond of just for sounds and sights that could do me no harm; and that they had all had to get used to in their turns? I was all in a hot, trembling passion; and I said it was very well for her to talk, that knew what these sights and noises betokened, and that had, perhaps, had something to do with the Spectre-Child while it was alive. And I taunted her so, that she told me all she knew, at last; and then I wished I had never been told, for it only made me afraid more than ever.

She said she had heard the tale from old neighbours, that were alive when she was first married; when folks used to come to the hall sometimes, before it had got such a bad name on the country-side: it might not be true, or it might, what she had been told.

The old lord was Miss Furnivall's father—Miss Grace

as Dorothy called her, for Miss Maude was the elder, and Miss Furnivall by rights. The old lord was eaten up with pride. Such a proud man was never seen or heard of; and his daughters were like him. No one was good enough to wed them, although they had choice enough; for they were the great beauties of their day, as I had seen by their portraits where they hung in the state drawing-room. But, as the old saying is, 'Pride will have a fall'; and these two haughty beauties fell in love with the same man, and he no better than a foreign musician whom their father had down from London to play music with him at the Manor House. For above all things, next to his pride, the old lord loved music. He could play on nearly every instrument that ever was heard of: and it was a strange thing it did not soften him; but he was a fierce, dour old man, and had broken his poor wife's heart with his cruelty, they said. He was mad after music, and would pay any money for it. So he got this foreigner to come; who made such beautiful music, that they said the very birds on the trees stopped their singing to listen. And, by degrees, this foreign gentleman got such a hold over the old lord that nothing would serve him but that he must come every year; and it was he that had the great organ brought from Holland and built up in the hall, where it stood now. He taught the old lord to play on it; but many and many a time, when Lord Furnivall was thinking of nothing but his fine organ, and his finer music, the dark foreigner was walking abroad in the woods with one of the young ladies; now Miss Maude, and then Miss Grace.

Miss Maude won the day and carried off the prize—such as it was; and he and she were married, all unknown to anyone; and before he made his next yearly visit, she had been confined of a little girl at a farm-house on the Moors, while her father and Miss Grace thought she was away at Doncaster Races. But though she was a wife and a mother she was not a bit softened, but as haughty and as passionate as ever; and perhaps more so, for she was jealous of Miss Grace, to whom her foreign husband paid a deal of court—by way of blinding her—as he told his wife. But Miss Grace triumphed over Miss Maude, and Miss Maude grew fiercer and fiercer, both with her husband and with her sister; and the former—who could easily shake off what was disagreeable, and hide himself in foreign countries— went away a month before his usual time that summer, and half threatened that he would never come back again.

Meanwhile, the little girl was left at the farm-house, and her mother used to have her horse saddled and gallop wildly over the hills to see her once every week at the very least—for where she loved, she loved; and where she hated, she hated. And the old lord went on playing—playing on his organ; and the servants thought the sweet music he made had soothed down his awful temper, of which (Dorothy said) some terrible tales could be told. He grew infirm too, and had to walk with a crutch; and his son— that was the present Lord Furnivall's father—was with the army in America, and the other son at sea; so Miss Maude had it pretty much her own way, and she and Miss Grace grew colder and bitterer to each other every day; till at last they hardly ever spoke, except when the old lord was by. The foreign musician came again the next summer, but it was for the last time; for they led him such a life with their jealousy and their passions that he grew weary, and went away, and never was heard of again. And Miss Maude, who had always meant to have her marriage acknowledged when her father should be dead, was left now a deserted wife—whom nobody knew to have been married—with a child that she dared not own, although she loved it to distraction; living with a father whom she feared, and a sister whom she hated.

When the next summer passed over and the dark foreigner never came, both Miss Maude and Miss Grace grew gloomy and sad; they had a haggard look about them, though they looked handsome as ever. But by and by Miss Maude brightened; for her father grew more and more infirm, and more than ever carried away by his music; and she and Miss Grace lived almost entirely apart, having

56

separate rooms, the one on the west side, Miss Maude on the east—those very rooms which were now shut up. So she thought she might have her little girl with her, and no one need ever know except those who dared not speak about it, and were bound to believe that it was, as she said, a cottager's child she had taken a fancy to. All this, Dorothy said, was pretty well known; but what came afterwards no one knew, except Miss Grace and Mrs. Stark, who was even then her maid, and much more of a friend to her than ever her sister had been. But the servants supposed, from words that were dropped, that Miss Maude had triumphed over Miss Grace, and told her that all the time the dark foreigner had been mocking her with pretended love he was her own husband; the colour left Miss Grace's cheeks and lips that very day for ever, and she was heard to say many a time that sooner or later she would have her revenge; and Mrs. Stark was for ever spying about the east rooms.

One fearful night, just after the New Year had come in, when the snow was lying thick and deep, and the flakes were still falling—fast enough to blind anyone who might be out and abroad—there was a great and violent noise heard, and the old lord's voice above all, cursing and swearing awfully; and the cries of a little child; and the proud defiance of a fierce woman; and the sound of a blow; and a dead stillness; and moans and wailings dying away on the hill-side! Then the old lord summoned all his servants, and told them, with terrible oaths, and words more terrible, that his daughter had disgraced herself, and that he had turned her out of doors—her, and her child—and that if ever they gave her help, or food, or shelter, he prayed that they might never enter heaven. And, all the while, Miss Grace stood by him, white and still as any stone; and when he had ended she heaved a great sigh, as much as to say her work was done, and her end was accomplished. But the old lord never touched his organ again, and died within the year; and no wonder! for, on the morrow of that wild and fearful night, the shepherds, coming down the

Fell side, found Miss Maude sitting, all crazy and smiling, under the holly trees, nursing a dead child—with a terrible mark on its right shoulder. 'But that was not what killed it,' said Dorothy; 'it was the frost and the cold. Every wild creature was in its hole, and every beast in its fold—while the child and its mother were turned out to wander on the Fells! And now you know all, and I wonder if you are less frightened now?'

I was more frightened than ever; but I said I was not. I wished Miss Rosamond and myself well out of that dreadful house for ever; but I would not leave her, and I dared not take her away. But oh! how I watched her, and guarded her! We bolted the doors and shut the window-shutters fast, and an hour or more before dark rather than leave them open five minutes too late. But my little lady still heard the weird child crying and mourning; and not all we could do or say could keep her from wanting to go to her, and let her in from the cruel wind and the snow. All this time, I kept away from Miss Furnivall and Mrs. Stark as much as ever I could; for I feared them—I knew no good could be about them, with their grey, hard faces, and their dreamy eyes looking back into the ghastly years that were gone. But, even in my fear, I had a kind of pity—for Miss Furnivall, at least. Those gone down to the pit can hardly have a more hopeless look than that which was ever on her face. At last I even got so sorry for her—who never said a word but what was quite forced from her—that I prayed for her; and I taught Miss Rosamond to pray for one who had done a deadly sin; but often, when she came to those words, she would listen, and start up from her knees, and say, 'I hear my little girl plaining and cry very sad—Oh! let her in, or she will die!'

One night—just after New Year's Day had come at last, and the long winter had taken a turn, as I hoped—I heard the west drawing-room bell ring three times, which was a signal for me. I would not leave Miss Rosamond alone, for all she was asleep—for the old lord had been playing wilder than ever—and I feared lest my darling should waken to hear the Spectre-Child; see her I knew she could not—I had fastened the windows too well for that. So I took her out of her bed and wrapped her up in such outer clothes as were most handy, and carried her down to the drawing-room, where the old ladies sat at their tapestry-work as usual. They looked up when I came in, and Mrs. Stark asked, quite astounded, 'Why did I bring Miss Rosamond there, out of her warm bed?' I had begun to whisper, 'Because I was afraid of her being tempted out while I was away, by the wild child in the snow,' when she stopped me short (with a glance at Miss Furnivall), and said Miss Furnivall wanted me to undo some work she had done wrong, and which neither of them could see to un-pick. So I laid my pretty dear on the sofa, and sat down on a stool by them, and hardened my heart against them, as I heard the wind rising and howling.

Miss Rosamond slept on sound, for all the wind blew so; and Miss Furnivall said never a word, nor looked round when the gusts shook the windows. All at once she started up to her full height, and put up one hand, as if to bid us listen.

'I hear voices!' said she, 'I hear terrible screams—I hear my father's voice!'

Just at that moment my darling wakened with a sudden start: 'My little girl is crying, oh, how she is crying!' and she tried to get up and go to her, but she got her feet en-tangled in the blanket, and I caught her up; for my flesh had begun to creep at these noises, which they heard while we could catch no sound. In a minute or two the noises came, gathered fast, and filled our ears; we, too, heard voices and screams, and no longer heard the winter's wind that raged abroad. Mrs. Stark looked at me, and I at her, but we dared not speak. Suddenly Miss Furnivall went towards the door, out into the ante-room, through the west lobby, and opened the door into the great hall. Mrs. Stark followed, and I durst not be left, though my heart almost stopped beating for fear. I wrapped my darling tight in my arms and went out with them. In the hall the screams were louder than ever; they sounded to come from the east wing—nearer and nearer—close on the other side of the locked-up doors—close behind them. Then I noticed that the great bronze chandelier seemed all alight, though the hall was dim, and that a fire was blazing in the vast hearth-place, though it gave no heat; and I shuddered up with terror, and folded my darling closer to me. But as I did so, the east door shook, and she, suddenly struggling to get free from me, cried, 'Hester, I must go! My little girl is there; I hear her; she is coming! Hester, I must go!'

I held her tight with all my strength; with a set will, I held her. If I had died my hands would have grasped her still, I was so resolved in my mind. Miss Furnivall stood listening, and paid no regard to my darling, who had got down to the ground and whom I, upon my knees now, was holding with both my arms clasped round her neck; she still striving and crying to get free.

All at once the east door gave way with a thundering crash, as if torn open in a violent passion, and there came into that broad and mysterious light, the figure of a tall old man, with grey hair and gleaming eyes. He drove before him, with many a relentless gesture of abhorrence, a stern and beautiful woman, with a little child clinging to her dress.

'Oh, Hester! Hester!' cried Miss Rosamond. 'It's the lady! the lady below the holly trees; and my little girl is with her. Hester! Hester! let me go to her; they are draw-ing me to them. I feel them, I feel them. I must go!'

Again she was almost convulsed by her efforts to get away; but I held her tighter and tighter, till I feared I should do her a hurt; but rather that than let her go towards those terrible phantoms. They passed along towards the great hall door, where the winds howled and ravened for their prey; but before they reached that, the lady turned; and I could see that she defied the old man with a fierce and proud defiance; but then she quailed—and then she threw up her arms wildly and piteously to save her child—her little child—from a blow from his uplifted crutch.

And Miss Rosamond was torn as by a power stronger than mine, and writhed in my arms, and sobbed (for by this time the poor darling was growing faint).

'They want me to go with them on to the Fells—they are drawing me to them. Oh, my little girl! I would come, but cruel, wicked Hester holds me very tight.' But when she saw the uplifted crutch she swooned away, and I thanked God for it. Just at this moment—when the tall old man, his hair streaming as in the blast of a furnace, was going to strike the little shrinking child—Miss Furnivall, the old woman by my side cried out, 'Oh, Father! Father! spare the little innocent child!' But just then I saw —we all saw—another phantom shape itself, and grow clear out of the blue and misty light that filled the hall; we had not seen her till now, for it was another lady who stood by the old man, with a look of relentless hate and triumphant scorn. That figure was very beautiful to look upon, with a soft white hat drawn down over the proud brows and a red and curling lip. It was dressed in an open robe of blue satin. I had seen that figure before. It was the likeness of Miss Furnivall in her youth; and the terrible phantoms moved on, regardless of old Miss Furnivall's wild entreaty—and the uplifted crutch fell on the right shoulder of the little child, and the younger sister looked on, stony and deadly serene. But at that moment the dim lights and the fire that gave no heat went out of themselves, and Miss Furnivall lay at our feet stricken down by the palsy—death stricken.

Yes, she was carried to her bed that night never to rise again. She lay with her face to the wall muttering low but muttering always: 'Alas! alas! what is done in youth can never be undone in age! What is done in youth can never be undone in age!'

SIR EDWARD BULWER-LYTTON
(LORD LYTTON)

The Haunted and the Haunters

A FRIEND of mine, who is a man of letters and a philosopher, said to me one day, as if between jest and earnest: 'Fancy, since we last met I have discovered a haunted house in the midst of London.'

'Really haunted?—and by what?—ghosts?'

'Well, I can't answer these questions—all I know is this —six weeks ago I and my wife were in search of a furnished apartment. Passing a quiet street, we saw on the window of one of the houses a bill, "Apartments—Furnished". The situation suited us: we entered the house—liked the rooms —engaged them by the week—and left them the third day. No power on earth could have reconciled my wife to stay longer, and I don't wonder at it.'

'What did you see?'

'Excuse me—I have no desire to be ridiculed as a superstitious dreamer—nor, on the other hand, could I ask you to accept on my affirmation what you would hold to be incredible without the evidence of your own senses. Let me only say this, it was not so much what we saw or heard (in which you might fairly suppose that we were the dupes of our own excited fancy, or the victims of imposture in others) that drove us away, as it was an undefinable terror which seized both of us whenever we passed by the door of a certain unfurnished room, in which we neither saw nor heard anything. And the strangest marvel of all was, that for once in my life I agreed with my wife—silly woman though she be—and allowed, after the third night, that it was impossible to stay a fourth in that house. Accordingly, on the fourth morning, I summoned the woman who kept

62

the house and attended on us, and told her that the rooms did not quite suit us, and we would not stay out our week. She said dryly: "I know why; you have stayed longer than any other lodger; few ever stayed a second night; none before you, a third. But I take it they have been very kind to you."

' "They—who?" I asked, affecting a smile.

' "Why, they who haunt the house, whoever they are. I don't mind them; I remember them many years ago, when I lived in this house, not as a servant; but I know they will be the death of me some day. I don't care—I'm old, and must die soon, anyhow; and then I shall be with them, and in this house still." The woman spoke with so dreary a calmness, that really it was a sort of awe that prevented my conversing with her further. I paid for my week, and too happy were I and my wife to get off so cheaply.'

'You excite my curiosity,' said I: 'nothing I should like better than to sleep in a haunted house. Pray give me the address of the one which you left so ignominiously.'

My friend gave me the address; and when we parted, I walked straight towards the house thus indicated.

It is situated on the north side of Oxford Street, in a dull but respectable thoroughfare. I found the house shut up—no bill at the window, and no response to my knock. As I was turning away, a beer-boy, collecting pewter pots at the neighbouring areas, said to me: 'Do you want anyone in that house, sir?'

'Yes; I heard it was to let.'

'Let!—why, the woman who kept it is dead—has been dead these three weeks, and no one can be found to stay there, though Mr. J—— offered ever so much. He offered Mother, who chars for him, a pound a week just to open and shut the windows, and she would not.'

'Would not!—and why?'

'The house is haunted; and the old woman who kept it was found dead in her bed, with her eyes wide open. They say the devil strangled her.'

63

'Pooh!—you speak of Mr. J——. Is he the owner of the house?'

'Yes.'

'Where does he live?'

'In G—— Street, No.—.'

'What is he?—in any business?'

'No, sir—nothing particular; a single gentleman.'

I gave the pot-boy the gratuity earned by his liberal information, and proceeded to Mr. J——, in G—— Street, which was close by the street that boasted the haunted house. I was lucky enough to find Mr. J—— at home— an elderly man, with intelligent countenance and prepossessing manners.

I communicated my name and my business frankly. I said I heard the house was considered to be haunted—that I had a strong desire to examine a house with so equivocal a reputation—that I should be greatly obliged if he would allow me to hire it, though only for a night. I was willing to pay for that privilege whatever he might be inclined to ask. 'Sir,' said Mr. J——, with great courtesy, 'the house is at your service for as short or as long a time as you please. Rent is out of the question—the obligation will be on my side should you be able to discover the cause of the strange phenomena which at present deprive it of all value. I cannot let it, for I cannot even get a servant to keep it in order or answer the door. Unluckily the house is haunted, if I may use that expression, not only by night, but by day; though at night the disturbances are of a more unpleasant and sometimes of a more alarming character.

'The poor old woman who died in it three weeks ago was a pauper whom I took out of the workhouse, for in her childhood she had been known to some of my family, and had once been in such good circumstances that she had rented that house of my uncle. She was a woman of superior education and strong mind, and was the only person I could ever induce to remain in the house. Indeed, since her death, which was sudden, and the coroner's inquest, which gave it a notoriety in the neighbourhood, I have so despaired of finding any person to take charge of it, much more a tenant, that I would willingly let it rent-free for a year to anyone who would pay its rates and taxes.'

'How long is it since the house acquired this sinister character?'

'That I can scarcely tell you, but very many years since. The old woman I spoke of said it was haunted when she rented it between thirty and forty years ago. The fact is that my life has been spent in the East Indies and in the civil service of the Company. I returned to England last year on inheriting the fortune of an uncle, amongst whose possessions was the house in question. I found it shut up and uninhabited. I was told that it was haunted, that no one would inhabit it. I smiled at what seemed to me so idle a story. I spent some money in repainting and roofing it—added to its old-fashioned furniture a few modern articles— advertised it, and obtained a lodger for a year. He was a colonel retired on half-pay. He came in with his family, a son and daughter, and four or five servants: they all left the house the next day, and although they deposed that they had all seen something different, that something was equally terrible to all. I really could not in conscience sue, or even blame, the colonel for breach of agreement.

'Then I put in the old woman I have spoken of, and she was empowered to let the house in apartments. I never had one lodger who stayed more than three days. I do not tell you their stories—to no two lodgers have there been exactly the same phenomena repeated. It is better that you should judge for yourself, than enter the house with an imagination influenced by previous narratives; only be prepared to see and hear something or other, and take whatever precautions you yourself, please.'

'Have you never had a curiosity yourself to pass a night in that house?'

'Yes. I passed not a night, but three hours in broad daylight alone in that house. My curiosity is not satisfied, but it is quenched. I have no desire to renew the experiment. You cannot complain, you see, sir, that I am not sufficiently candid; and unless your interest be exceedingly eager and your nerves unusually strong, I honestly advise you *not* to pass a night in that house.'

'My interest *is* exceedingly keen,' said I, 'and though only a coward will boast of his nerves in situations wholly unfamiliar to him, yet my nerves have been seasoned in such variety of danger that I have the right to rely on them —even in a haunted house.'

Mr. J—— said very little more; he took the keys of the house out of his bureau, gave them to me; and, thanking him cordially for his frankness, and his urbane concession to my wish, I carried off my prize.

Impatient for the experiment, as soon as I reached home I summoned my confidential servant, a young man of gay spirits, fearless temper, and as free from superstitious prejudice as anyone I could think of.

'F——,' said I, 'you remember in Germany how disappointed we were at not finding a ghost in that old castle which was said to be haunted by a headless apparition? Well, I have heard of a house in London which, I have reason to hope, is decidedly haunted. I mean to sleep there tonight. From what I hear, there is no doubt that something will allow itself to be seen or to be heard—something, perhaps, excessively horrible. Do you think, if I take you with me, I may rely on your presence of mind, whatever may happen?'

'Oh, sir, pray trust me,' answered F——, grinning with delight.

'Very well—then here are the keys of the house—this is the address. Go now—select for me any bedroom you please; and since the house has not been inhabited for weeks, make up a good fire—air the bed well—see, of course, that there are candles as well as fuel. Take with you my revolver and my dagger—so much for my weapons —arm yourself equally well; and if we are not a match for a dozen ghosts, we shall be but a sorry couple of Englishmen.'

I was engaged for the rest of the day on business so urgent that I had not leisure to think much on the nocturnal adventure to which I had plighted my honour. I dined alone, and very late, and while dining, read, as is my habit. The volume I selected was one of Macaulay's Essays. I thought to myself that I would take the book with me; there was so much of healthfulness in the style, and praccal life in the subjects, that it would serve an antidote against the influence of superstitious fancy.

Accordingly, about half past nine, I put the book into my pocket, and strolled leisurely towards the haunted house. I took with me a favourite dog—an exceedingly sharp, bold, and vigilant bull-terrier—a dog fond of prowling about strange ghostly corners and passages at night in search of rats—a dog of dogs for a ghost.

It was a summer night, but chilly, the sky somewhat gloomy and overcast. Still, there was a moon—faint and sickly, but still a moon, and if the clouds permitted, after midnight it would be brighter.

I reached the house, knocked, and my servant opened with a cheerful smile.

'All right, sir, and very comfortable.'

'Oh!' said I, rather disappointed. 'Have you not seen nor heard anything remarkable?'

'Well, sir I must own I have heard something queer.'

'What—what?'

'The sound of feet pattering behind me; and once or twice small noises like whispers close at my ear—nothing more.'

'You are not at all frightened?'

'I—not a bit of it, sir'; and the man's bold look reassured me on one point—viz. that, happen what might, he would not desert me.

We were in the hall, the street door closed, and my attention was now drawn to my dog. He had at first run in eagerly enough, but had sneaked back to the door, and was scratching and whining to get out. After patting him on the head, and encouraging him gently, the dog seemed to reconcile himself to the situation and followed me and F—— through the house, but keeping close at my heels instead of hurrying inquisitively in advance, which was his usual and normal habit in all strange places. We first visited the subterranean apartments, the kitchen and other offices, and especially the cellars, in which last there were two or three bottles of wine still left in a bin, covered with cobwebs, and evidently, by their appearance, undisturbed for many years. It was clear that the ghosts were not wine-bibbers.

For the rest we discovered nothing of interest. There was a gloomy little backyard, with very high walls. The stones of this yard were very damp—and what with the damp, and what with the dust and smoke-grime on the pavement, our feet left a slight impression where we passed. And now appeared the first strange phenomenon witnessed by myself in this strange abode. I saw, just before me, the print of a foot suddenly form itself, as it were. I stopped, caught hold of my servant, and pointed to it. In advance of that foot-print as suddenly dropped another. We both saw it. I advanced quickly to the place; the footprint kept advancing before me, a small footprint—the foot of a child: the impression was too faint thoroughly to distinguish the shape, but it seemed to us both that it was the print of a naked foot. This phenomenon ceased when we arrived at the opposite wall, nor did it repeat itself on returning.

We remounted the stairs, and entered the rooms on the ground floor—a dining-parlour, a small back-parlour, and a still smaller third room that had been probably appro-priated to a footman—as still as death. We then visited the drawing-rooms, which seemed fresh and new. In the front room I seated myself in an arm-chair. F—— placed on the table the candlestick with which he had lighted us. I told him to shut the door. As he turned to do so, a chair oppo-site to me moved from the wall quickly and noiselessly, and dropped itself about a yard from my own chair, im-mediately fronting it.

'Why, this is better than the turning-tables,' said I, with

a half-laugh—and as I laughed, my dog put back his head and howled.

F——, coming back, had not observed the movement of the chair. He employed himself now in quieting the dog. I continued to gaze on the chair, and fancied I saw on it a pale-blue misty outline of a human figure, but an outline so indistinct that I could only distrust my own vision. The dog now was quiet. 'Put back that chair opposite to me,' said I to F——; 'put it back to the wall.'

F—— obeyed. 'Was that you, sir?' said he, turning abruptly.

'I—what?'

'Why, something struck me. I felt it sharply on the shoulder—just here.'

'No,' said I 'But we have jugglers present, and though we may not discover their tricks, we shall catch *them* before they frighten *us*.'

We did not stay long in the drawing-rooms—in fact, they felt so damp and so chilly that I was glad to get to the fire upstairs. We locked the doors of the drawing-rooms—a precaution which, I should observe, we had taken with all the rooms we had searched below. The bedroom my servant had selected for me was the best on the floor—a large one, with two windows fronting the street. The four-posted bed, which took up no inconsiderable space, was opposite the fire, which burned clear and bright; a door in the wall to the left, between the bed and the window, communicated with the room which my servant appropriated to himself.

This last was a small room with a sofa-bed, and had no communication with the landing-place—no other door but that which conducted to the bedroom I was to occupy. On either side of my fireplace was a cupboard, without locks, flushed with the wall, and covered with the same dull-brown paper. We examined these cupboards—only hooks to suspend female dresses—nothing else; we sounded the walls—evidently solid—the outer walls of the building. Having finished the survey of these apartments, I warmed myself a few moments, and lighted my cigar, I then, still accompanied by F——, went forth to complete my reconnoitre. In the landing-place there was another door; it was closed firmly.

'Sir,' said my servant in surprise, 'I unlocked this door with all the others when I first came; it cannot have got locked from the inside, for it is a ...'

Before he had finished the sentence the door, which neither of us then was touching, opened quietly of itself. We looked at each other a single instant. The same thought seized both—some human agency might be detected here. I rushed in first, my servant followed. A small blank dreary room without furniture—a few empty boxes and hampers in a corner—a small window—the shutters closed—not even a fireplace—no other door but that by which we had entered—no carpet on the floor, and the floor seemed very old, uneven, worm-eaten, mended here and there, as was shown by the whiter patches on the wood; but no living being, and no visible place in which a living being could have hidden. As we stood gazing around, the door by which we had entered closed as quietly as it had before opened: we were imprisoned.

For the first time I felt a creep of undefinable horror. Not so my servant. 'Why, they don't think to trap us, sir; I could break that trumpery door with a kick of my boot.'

'Try first if it will open to your hand,' said I, shaking off the vague apprehension that had seized me, 'while I open the shutters and see what is without.'

I unbarred the shutters—the window looked on the little backyard I have before described; there was no ledge without—nothing but sheer descent. No man getting out of that window would have found any footing till he had fallen on the stones below.

F——, meanwhile, was vainly attempting to open the door. He now turned round to me, and asked my permission to use force. And I should here state, in justice to the servant, that, far from evincing any superstitious terrors, his nerve, composure, and even gaiety amidst circumstances so extraordinary compelled my admiration, and made me congratulate myself on having secured a companion in every way fitted to the occasion. I willingly gave him the permission he required. But though he was a remarkably strong man, his force was as idle as his milder efforts; the door did not even shake to his stoutest kick. Breathless and panting, he desisted. I then tried the door myself, equally in vain.

As I ceased from the effort, again that creep of horror came over me; but this time it was more cold and stubborn. I felt as if some strange and ghastly exhalation were rising up from the chinks of that rugged floor, and filling the atmosphere with a venomous influence hostile to human life. The door now very slowly and quietly opened as of its own accord. We precipitated ourselves into the landing-place. We both saw a large pale light—as large as the human figure, but shapeless and unsubstantial—move before us, and ascend the stairs that led from the landing into the attics. I followed the light, and my servant followed me. It entered, to the right of the landing, a small garret, of which the door stood open. I entered in the same instant. The light then collapsed into a small globule, exceedingly brilliant and vivid, rested a moment on a bed in the corner, quivered, and vanished. We approached the bed and examined it—a half-tester, such as is commonly found in attics devoted to servants. On the drawers that stood near it we perceived an old faded silk kerchief, with the needle still left in a rent half repaired. The kerchief was covered with dust; probably it had belonged to the old woman who had last died in that house, and this might have been her sleeping-room.

I had sufficient curiosity to open the drawers; there were a few odds and ends of female dress, and two letters tied round with a narrow ribbon of faded yellow. I took the liberty to possess myself of the letters. We found nothing else in the room worth noticing—nor did the light reappear; but we distinctly heard, as we turned to go, a pattering footfall on the floor—just before us. We went through the other attics (in all, four), the footfall still preceding us. Nothing to be seen—nothing but the footfall heard. I had the letters in my hand; just as I was descending the stairs I distinctly felt my wrist seized, and a faint, soft effort made to draw the letters from my clasp. I only held them the more tightly, and the effort ceased.

We regained the bed-chamber appropriated to myself, and I then remarked that my dog had not followed us when we had left it. He was thrusting himself close to the fire, and trembling. I was impatient to examine the letters; and while I read them, my servant opened a little box in which he had deposited the weapons I had ordered him to bring, took them out, placed them on a table close at my bed-head, and then occupied himself in soothing the dog, who, however, seemed to heed him very little.

The letters were short; they were dated—the dates exactly thirty-five years ago. They were evidently from a lover to his mistress, or a husband to some young wife. Not only the terms of expression, but a distinct reference to a former voyage indicated the writer to have been a seafarer. The spelling and handwriting were those of a man imperfectly educated, but still the language itself was forcible. In the expressions of endearment there was a kind of rough wild love; but here and there were dark unintelligible hints at some secret not of love—some secret that seemed of crime. 'We ought to love each other,' was one of the sentences I remember, 'for how everyone else would execrate us if all was known.' Again: 'Don't let anyone be in the same room with you at night—you talk in your sleep.' And again: 'What's done can't be undone; and I tell you there's nothing against us unless the dead could come to life.' Here there was underlined in a better handwriting (a female's), 'They do!' At the end of the letter latest in date the same female hand had written these words: 'Lost at sea the 4th of June, the same day as . . .'

I put down the letters, and began to muse over their contents.

Fearing, however, that the train of thought into which I

fell might unsteady my nerves, I fully determined to keep
my mind in a fit state to cope with whatever of marvellous
the advancing night might bring forth. I roused myself—
laid the letters on the table—stirred up the fire, which was
still bright and cheering—and opened my volume of Macaulay. I read quietly enough till about half past eleven.
I then threw myself dressed upon the bed, and told my
servant he might retire to his own room, but must keep
himself awake. I bade him leave open the door between
the two rooms. Thus alone, I kept two candles burning on
the table by my bed-head. I placed my watch beside the
weapons, and calmly resumed my Macaulay.

Opposite me the fire burned clear; and on the hearth-
rug, seemingly asleep, lay the dog. In about twenty minutes
I felt an exceedingly cold air pass by my cheek, like a sudden draught. I fancied the door to my right, communicating with the landing-place, must have got open; but no—it
was closed. I then turned my glance to my left, and saw
the flame of the candles violently swayed as by a wind.
At the same moment the watch beside the revolver softly
slid from the table—softly, softly—no visible hand—it was
gone. I sprang up, seizing the revolver with the one hand,
the dagger with the other; I was not willing that my weapons should share the fate of the watch. Thus armed, I
looked round the floor—no sign of the watch. Three slow,
loud, distinct knocks were now heard at the bed-head. My
servant called out: 'Is that you, sir?'

'No; be on your guard.'

The dog now roused himself and sat on his haunches,
his ears moving quickly backwards and forwards. He kept
his eyes fixed on me with a look so strange that he concentrated all my attention on himself. Slowly he rose up, all
his hair bristling, and stood perfectly rigid, and with the
same wild stare. I had not time, however, to examine the
dog. Presently my servant emerged from his room; and if
ever I saw horror in the human face, it was then. I should
not have recognised him had we met in the streets, so
altered was every lineament. He passed by me quickly,

73

saying in a whisper that seemed scarcely to come from his
lips, 'Run—run, it is after me!' He gained the door to the
landing, pulled it open, and rushed forth. I followed him
into the landing involuntarily, calling him to stop; but,
without heeding me, he bounded down the stairs, clinging
to the balusters, and taking several steps at a time. I heard,
where I stood, the street door open—heard it again clap
to. I was left alone in the haunted house.

It was but for a moment that I remained undecided
whether or not to follow my servant; pride and curiosity
alike forbade so dastardly a flight. I re-entered my room,
closing the door after me, and proceeded cautiously into
the interior chamber. I encountered nothing to justify my
servant's terror. I again carefully examined the walls, to
see if there were any concealed door. I could find no trace
of one—not even a seam in the dull-brown paper with
which the room was hung. How, then, had the Thing,
whatever it was, which had so scared him, obtained ingress
except through my own chamber?

I returned to my room, shut and locked the door that
opened upon the interior one, and stood on the hearth,
expectant and prepared. I now perceived that the dog had
slunk into an angle of the wall, and was pressing himself
close against it, as if literally trying to force his way into it.
I approached the animal and spoke to it; the poor brute
was evidently beside itself with terror. It showed all its
teeth, the saliva dropping from its jaws, and would certainly have bitten me if I had touched it. It did not seem
to recognise me. Whoever has seen at the Zoological Gar-
dens a rabbit fascinated by a serpent, cowering in a corner,
may form some idea of the anguish which the dog exhi-
bited. Finding all efforts to soothe the animal in vain, and
fearing that his bite might be as venomous in that state as
if in the madness of hydrophobia, I left him alone, placed
my weapons on the table beside the fire, seated myself, and
recommenced my Macaulay.

Perhaps in order not to appear seeking credit for a courage, or rather a coolness, which the reader may conceive

I exaggerate, I may be pardoned if I pause to indulge in one or two egotistical remarks.

As I hold presence of mind, or what is called courage, to be precisely proportioned to familiarity with the circumstances that lead to it, so I should say that I had been long sufficiently familiar with all experiments that appertain to the marvellous. I had witnessed many very extraordinary phenomena in various parts of the world—phenomena that would be either totally disbelieved if I stated them or ascribed to supernatural agencies. Now, my theory is that the Supernatural is the Impossible, and that what is called supernatural is only a something in the laws of nature of which we have been hitherto ignorant. Therefore, if a ghost rise before me, I have not the right to say, 'So, then, the supernatural is possible,' but rather, 'So, then, the apparition of a ghost is, contrary to received opinion, within the laws of nature—i.e. not supernatural.'

Now, in all that I had hitherto witnessed, and indeed in all the wonders which the amateurs of mystery in our age record as facts, a material living agency is always required. On the Continent you will still find magicians who assert that they can raise spirits. Assuming for the moment that what they assert is the truth, still the living material form of the magician is present; and he is the material agency by which from some constitutional peculiarities certain strange phenomena are represented to your natural senses.

Accept again, as truthful, the tales of spirit manifestation in America—musical or other sounds—writings on paper, produced by no discernible hand—articles of furniture moved about without apparent human agency—or the actual sight and touch of hands to which no bodies seem to belong—still there must be found the *medium* or living being, with constitutional peculiarities, capable of obtaining these signs. In fine, in all such marvels, supposing even that there is no imposture, there must be a human being like ourselves, by whom, or through whom, the effects presented to human beings are produced. It is so with the now familiar phenomena of mesmerism or electro-biology; the mind of the person operated on is affected through a material living agent. Nor, supposing it true that a mesmerised patient can respond to the will or passes of a mesmeriser a hundred miles distant, is the response less occasioned by a material being; it may be through a material fluid—call it Electric, call it Odic, call it what you will—which had the power of traversing space and passing obstacles, that the material effect is communicated from one to the other.

Hence all that I had hitherto witnessed, or expected to witness, in this strange house, I believed to be occasioned through some agency or medium as mortal as myself; and this idea necessarily prevented the awe with which those who regard as supernatural things that are not within the ordinary operations of nature, might have been impressed by the adventures of that memorable night.

As, then, it was my conjecture that all that was presented, or would be presented, to my senses, must originate in some human being gifted by constitution with the power so to present them, and having some motive so to do, I felt an interest in my theory which, in its way, was rather philosophical than superstitious. And I can sincerely say that I was in as tranquil a temper for observation as any practical experimentalist could be in awaiting the effects of some rare though perhaps perilous chemical combination. Of course, the more I kept my mind detached from fancy, the more the temper fitted for observation would be obtained; and I therefore riveted eye and thought on the strong daylight sense in the page of my Macaulay.

I now became aware that something interposed between the page and the light—the page was over-shadowed; I looked up, and I saw what I shall find it very difficult, perhaps impossible, to describe.

It was a Darkness shaping itself out of the air in very undefined outline. I cannot say it was of a human form, and yet it had more resemblance to a human form, or rather shadow, than anything else. As it stood, wholly part and distinct from the air and the light around it, its dimensions seemed gigantic, the summit nearly touching the ceiling. While I gazed, a feeling of intense cold seized me. An iceberg before me could not more have chilled me; nor could the cold of an iceberg have been more purely physical. I feel convinced that it was not the cold caused by fear. As I continued to gaze, I thought—but this I cannot say with precision—that I distinguished two eyes looking down on me from the height. One moment I seemed to distinguish them clearly, the next they seemed gone; but still two rays of a pale-blue light frequently shot through the darkness, as from the height on which I half believed, half doubted that I had encountered the eyes.

I strove to speak—my voice utterly failed me; I could only think: 'Is this fear? It is *not* fear!' I strove to rise—in vain; I felt as if weighed down by an irresistible force. Indeed, my impression was that of an immense and overwhelming power opposed to my volition; that sense of utter inadequacy to cope with a force beyond men's, which one may feel *physically* in a storm at sea, in a conflagration, or when confronting some terrible wild beast, or rather, perhaps, the shark of the ocean, I felt *morally*. Opposed to my will was another will, as far superior to its strength as storm, fire, and shark are superior in material force to the force of men.

And now, as this impression grew on me, now came, at last, horror—horror to a degree that no words can convey. Still I retained pride, if not courage; and in my own mind I said: 'This is horror, but it is not fear; unless I fear, I cannot be harmed; my reason rejects this thing; it is an illusion—I do not fear.' With a violent effort I succeeded at last in stretching out my hand towards the weapon on the table; as I did so, on the arm and shoulder I received a strange shock, and my arm fell to my side powerless. And now, to add to my horror, the light began slowly to wane from the candles—they were not, as it were, extinguished, but their flame seemed very gradually withdrawn; it was the same with the fire—the light was extracted from the fuel; in a few minutes the room was in utter darkness.

The dread that came over me, to be thus in the dark with that dark Thing, whose power was so intensely felt, brought a reaction of nerve. In fact, terror had reached that climax, that either my senses must have deserted me, or I must have burst through the spell. I did burst through it. I found voice, though the voice was a shriek. I remember that I broke forth with words like these—'I do not fear, my soul does not fear'; and at the same time I found the strength to rise. Still in that profound gloom I rushed to one of the windows—tore aside the curtain—flung open the shutters; my first thought was—LIGHT. And when I saw the moon high, clear, and calm, I felt a joy that almost compensated for the previous terror. There was the moon, there was also the light from the gas-lamps in the deserted slumbrous street. I turned to look back into the room; the moon penetrated its shadow very palely and partially— but still there was light. The dark Thing, whatever it might be, was gone—except that I could yet see a dim shadow which seemed the shadow of that shade, against the opposite wall.

My eye now rested on the table, and from under the table (which was without cloth or cover—an old mahogany round table) there rose a hand, visible as far as the wrist. It was a hand, seemingly, as much of flesh and blood as my own, but the hand of an aged person—lean, wrinkled, small too—a woman's hand.

That hand very softly closed on the two letters that lay on the table: hand and letters both vanished. There then came the same three loud measured knocks I had heard at the bed-head before this extraordinary drama had commenced.

As those sounds slowly ceased, I felt the whole room vibrate sensibly; and at the far end there rose, as from the floor, sparks or globules like bubbles of light, many-coloured—green, yellow, fire-red, azure. Up and down, to and fro, hither, thither, as tiny will-o'-the-wisps, the sparks moved, slow or swift, each at its own caprice. A chair (as in the drawing-room below) was now advanced from the wall without apparent agency, and placed at the opposite side of the table. Suddenly, as forth from the chair, there grew a shape—a woman's shape. It was distinct as a shape of life—ghastly as a shape of death. The face was that of youth, with a strange mournful beauty; the throat and shoulders were bare, the rest of the form in a loose robe of cloudy white. It began sleeking its long yellow hair, which fell over its shoulders; its eyes were not turned towards me, but to the door; it seemed listening, watching, waiting. The shadow of a shade in the background grew darker; and again I thought I beheld the eyes gleaming out from the summit of the shadow—eyes fixed upon that shape.

As if from the door, though it did not open, there grew out another shape equally distinct, equally ghastly—a man's shape—a young man's. It was in the dress of the last century, or rather in a likeness of such dress; for both the male shape and the female, though defined, were evidently unsubstantial, impalpable—simulacra—phantasms; and there was something incongruous, grotesque, yet fearful, in the contrast between the elaborate finery, the courtly precision of that old-fashioned garb, with its ruffles and lace and buckles, and the corpse-like aspect and ghost-like stillness of the flitting wearer. Just as the male shape approached the female, the dark Shadow started from the wall, all three for a moment wrapped in darkness. When the pale light returned, the two phantoms were as if in the grasp of the Shadow that towered between them; and there was a bloodstain on the breast of the female; and the phantom-male was leaning on its phantom sword, and blood seemed trickling fast from the ruffles, from the lace; and the darkness of the intermediate Shadow swallowed them up—they were gone. And again the bubbles of light shot, and sailed, and undulated, growing thicker and thicker and more wildly confused in their movements.

The closet-door to the right of the fireplace now opened,

79

and from the aperture there came the form of a woman,
aged. In her hand she held letters—the very letters over
which I had seen *the* Hand close; and behind her I heard a
footstep. She turned round as if to listen, then she opened
the letters and seemed to read; and over her shoulder I
saw a livid face, the face as of a man long drowned—
bloated, bleached—seaweed tangled in its dripping hair;
and at her feet lay a form as of a corpse and beside the
corpse there cowered a child, a miserable, squalid child,
with famine in its cheeks and fear in its eyes. And as I
looked in the old woman's face, the wrinkles and lines
vanished, and it became a face of youth—hard-eyed, stony,
but still youth; and the Shadow darted forth and darkened
over these phantoms as it had darkened over the last.

Nothing now was left but the Shadow, and on that my
eyes were intently fixed, till again eyes grew out of the
Shadow—malignant serpent eyes. And the bubbles of
light again rose and fell, and in their disordered, irregular,
turbulent maze, mingled with the wan moonlight. And now
from these globules themselves as from the shell of an egg,
monstrous things burst out; the air grew filled with them;
larvae so bloodless and so hideous that I can in no way
describe them except to remind the reader of the swarming
life which the solar microscope brings before his eyes in a
drop of water—things transparent, supple, agile, chasing
each other, devouring each other—forms like naught ever
beheld by the naked eye. As the shapes were without sym-
metry, so their movements were without order. In their
very vagrancies there was no sport; they came round me
and round, thicker and faster and swifter, swarming over
my head, crawling over my right arm, which was outstretched in involuntary command against all evil beings.

Sometimes I felt myself touched, but not by them; invisible hands touched me. Once I felt the clutch as of cold
soft fingers at my throat. I was still equally conscious that
if I gave way to fear I should be in bodily peril; and I concentrated all my faculties in the single focus of resisting,
stubborn will. And I turned my sight from the Shadow—

above all, from those strange serpent eyes—eyes that had now become distinctly visible. For there, though in naught else around me, I was aware that there was a *will*, and a will of intense, creative, working evil, which might crush down my own.

The pale atmosphere in the room began now to redden as if in the air of some near conflagration. The larvae grew lurid as things that live in fire. Again the room vibrated; again were heard the three measured knocks; and again all things were swallowed up in the darkness of the dark Shadow, as if out of that darkness all had come, into that darkness all returned.

As the gloom receded, the Shadow was wholly gone. Slowly as it had been withdrawn, the flame grew again into the candles on the table, again into the fuel in the grate. The whole room came once more calmly, healthfully into sight.

The two doors were still closed, the door communicating with the servants' room still locked. In the corner of the wall, into which he had so convulsively niched himself, lay the dog. I called to him—no movement; I approached —the animal was dead; his eyes protruded; his tongue out of his mouth; the froth gathered round his jaws. I took him in my arms; I brought him to the fire; I felt acute grief for the loss of my poor favourite—acute self-reproach; I accused myself of his death; I imagined he had died of fright. But what was my surprise on finding that his neck was actually broken—actually twisted out of the vertebrae. Had this been done in the dark?—must it not have been by a hand human as mine?—must there not have been a human agency all the while in that room? Good cause to suspect it. I cannot tell. I cannot do more than state the fact fairly; the reader may draw his own inference.

Another surprising circumstance—my watch was restored to the table from which it had been so mysteriously withdrawn; but it had stopped at the very moment it was so withdrawn; nor, despite all the skill of the watchmaker, has it ever gone since—that is, it will go in a strange erratic way for a few hours, and then comes to a dead stop—it is worthless.

Nothing more chanced for the rest of the night. Nor, indeed, had I long to wait before the dawn broke. Not till it was broad daylight did I quit the haunted house. Before I did so, I revisited the little blind room in which my servant and myself had been for a time imprisoned. I had a strong impression—for which I could not account—that from that room had originated the mechanism of the phenomena—if I may use the term—which had been experienced in my chamber. And though I entered it now in the clear day, with the sun peering through the filmy window, I still felt, as I stood on its floor, the creep of the horror which I had first there experienced the night before, and which had been so aggravated by what had passed in my own chamber. I could not, indeed, bear to stay more than half a minute within those walls. I descended the stairs, and again I heard the footfall before me; and when I opened the street door, I thought I could distinguish a very low laugh, I gained my own home, expecting to find my runaway servant there. But he had not presented himself; nor did I hear more of him for three days, when I received a letter from him, dated from Liverpool, to this effect:

Honoured Sir,

I humbly entreat your pardon, though I can scarcely hope that you will think I deserve it, unless—which heaven forbid!—you saw what I did. I feel that it will be years before I can recover myself; and as to being fit for service, it is out of the question. I am therefore going to my brother-in-law at Melbourne. The ship sails tomorrow. Perhaps the long voyage will set me up. I do nothing but start and tremble, and fancy It is behind me. I humbly beg you, honoured sir, to order my clothes, and whatever wages are due to me, to be sent to my mother's, at Walworth—John knows her address.

The letter ended with additional apologies, somewhat incoherent, and explanatory details as to effects that had been under the writer's charge.

This flight may perhaps warrant a suspicion that the man wished to go to Australia, and had been somehow or other fraudulently mixed up with the events of the night. I say nothing in refutation of that conjecture; rather, I suggest it as one that would seem to many persons the most probable solution of improbable occurrences. My own theory remained unshaken. I returned in the evening to the house, to bring away in a hack-cab the things I had left there, with my poor dog's body. In this task I was not disturbed, nor did any incident worth note befall me, except that again, on ascending and descending the stairs I heard the same footfalls in advance. On leaving the house, I went to Mr. J——'s. He was at home. I returned him the keys, told him that my curiosity was sufficiently gratified, and was about to relate quickly what had passed, when he stopped me, and said, though with much politeness, that he had no longer any interest in the mystery which none had ever solved.

I determined at least to tell him of the two letters I had read, as well as of the extraordinary manner in which they had disappeared, and I then inquired if he thought they had been addressed to the woman who had died in the house, and if there were anything in her early history which could possibly confirm the dark suspicions to which the letters gave rise. Mr. J—— seemed startled, and, after musing a few moments, answered: 'I know but little of the woman's earlier history, except, as I before told you, that her family were known to mine. But you revive some vague reminiscences to her prejudice. I will make inquiries, and inform you of their result. Still, even if we could admit the popular superstition that a person who had been either the perpetrator or the victim of dark crimes in life could revisit, as a restless spirit, the scene in which those crimes had been committed, I should observe that the house was

infested by strange sights and sounds before the old woman
died . . . You smile—what would you say?'

'I would say this: that I am convinced, if we could get
to the bottom of these mysteries, we should find a living
human agency.'

'What, you believe it is all an imposture? For what
object?'

'Not an imposture in the ordinary sense of the word.
If suddenly I were to sink into a deep sleep, from which
you could not awake me, but in that sleep could answer
questions with an accuracy which I could not pretend to
when awake—tell you what money you had in your pocket
—nay, describe your very thoughts—it is not necessarily
an imposture, any more than it is necessarily supernatural.
I should be, unconsciously to myself, under a mesmeric
influence conveyed to me from a distance by a human
being who had acquired power over me by previous
rapport.'

'Granting mesmerism, so far carried, to be a fact, you
are right. And you would infer from this that a mesmeriser
might produce the extraordinary efforts you and others
have witnessed over inanimate objects—fill the air with
sights and sounds?'

'Or impress our senses with the belief in them—we never
having been *en rapport* with the person acting on us? No.
What is commonly called mesmerism could not do this;
but there may be a power akin to mesmerism, and superior
to it—the power that in the old days was called Magic.
That such a power may extend to all inanimate objects of
matter, I do not say; but if so, it would not be against
nature, only a rare power in nature which might be given
to constitutions with certain peculiarities, and cultivated
by practice to an extraordinary degree. That such a power
might extend over the dead—that is, over certain thoughts
and memories that the dead may still retain—and compel,
not that which ought properly to be called the *soul*, and
which is far beyond human reach, but rather a phantom
of what has been most earthstained on earth, to make it-

self apparent to our senses—is a very ancient though obsolete theory, upon which I will hazard no opinion. But I do not conceive the power would be supernatural.

'Let me illustrate what I mean from an experiment which Paracelsus describes as not difficult, and which the author of the *Curiosities of Literature* cites as credible: A flower perishes; you burn it. Whatever were the elements of that flower while it lived are gone, dispersed, you know not whither; you can never discover nor re-collect them. But you can, by chemistry, out of the burnt dust of that flower, raise a spectrum of the flower, just as it seemed in life. It may be the same with the human being. The soul has so much escaped you as the essence or elements of the flower. Still you may make a spectrum of it. And this phantom, though in the popular superstition it is held to be the soul of the departed, must not be confounded with the true soul; it is but the eidolon of the dead form.

'Hence, like the best-attested stories of ghosts or spirits, the thing that most strikes us is the absence of what we hold to be soul—that is, of superior emancipated intelligence. They come for little or no object—they seldom speak, if they do come; they utter no ideas above that of an ordinary person on earth. These American spirit-seers have published volumes of communications in prose and verse, which they assert to be given in the names of the most illustrious dead—Shakespeare, Bacon—heaven knows whom. Those communications, taking the best, are certainly not a whit of higher order than would be communications from living persons of fair talent and education; they are wondrously inferior to what Bacon, Shakespeare, and Plato said and wrote when on earth.

'Now, what is more notable, do they ever contain an idea that was not on the earth before. Wonderful, therefore, as such phenomena may be (granting them to be truthful), I see much that philosophy may question, nothing that it is incumbent on philosophy to deny—viz. nothing supernatural. They are but ideas conveyed somehow or other (we have not yet discovered the means) from one

85

mortal brain to another. Whether, in so doing, tables walk of their own accord, or fiend-like shapes appear in a magic circle, or bodiless hands rise and remove material objects, or a Thing of Darkness, such as presented itself to me, freeze our blood—still am I persuaded that these are but agencies conveyed, as by electric wires, to my own brain from the brain of another.

'In some constitutions there is a natural chemistry, and those may produce chemic wonders—in others a natural fluid, call it electricity, and these produce electric wonders. But they differ in this from Normal Science—they are alike objectless, purposeless, puerile, frivolous. They lead on to no grand results; and therefore the world does not heed, and true sages have not cultivated them. But sure I am, that of all I saw or heard, a man, human as myself, was the remote originator; and I believe unconsciously to himself as to the exact effects produced, for this reason: no two persons, you say, have ever told you that they experienced exactly the same thing. Well, observe, no two persons ever experience exactly the same dream. If this were an ordinary imposture, the machinery would be arranged for results that would but little vary; if it were a supernatural agency permitted by the Almighty, it would surely be for some definite end.

'These phenomena belong to neither class; my persuasion is that they originate in some brain now far distant; that that brain had no distinct volition in anything that oc-curred; that what does occur reflects but its devious, mot-ley, ever-shifting, half-formed thoughts; in short, that it has been but the dreams of such a brain put into action and invested with a semi-substance. That this brain is of im-mense power, that it can set matter into movement, that it is malignant and destructive, I believe: some material force must have killed my dog; it might, for aught I know, have sufficed to kill myself, had I been as subjugated by terror as the dog—had my intellect or my spirit given me no countervailing resistance in my will.'

'It killed your dog! That is fearful! Indeed, it is strange

that no animal can be induced to stay in that house; not even a cat. Rats and mice are never found in it.'

'The instincts of the brute creation detect influences deadly to their existence. Man's reason has a sense less subtle, because it has a resisting power more supreme. But enough; do you comprehend my theory?'

'Yes, though imperfectly—and I accept any crotchet (pardon the word), however odd, rather than embrace at once the notion of ghosts and hobgoblins we imbibed in our nurseries. Still, to my unfortunate house the evil is the same. What on earth can I do with the house?'

'I will tell you what I would do. I am convinced from my own internal feelings that the small unfurnished room at right angles to the door of the bedroom which I occupied, forms a starting point or receptacle for the influences which haunt the house; and I strongly advise you to have the walls opened, the floor removed—nay, the whole room pulled down. I observe that it is detached from the body of the house, built over the small back-yard, and could be removed without injury to the rest of the building.'

'And you think if I did that . . .'

'You would cut off the telegraph wires. Try it. I am so persuaded that I am right, that I will pay half the expense if you will allow me to direct the operations.'

'Nay, I am well able to afford the cost; for the rest, allow me to write to you.'

About ten days afterwards I received a letter from Mr. J——, telling me that he had visited the house since I had seen him; that he had found the two letters I had described, replaced in the drawer from which I had taken them; that he had read them with misgivings like my own; that he had instituted a cautious inquiry about the woman to whom I rightly conjectured they had been written. It seemed that thirty-six years ago (a year before the date of the letters), she had married, against the wish of her relatives, an American of very suspicious character; in fact, he was generally believed to have been a pirate. She herself was the daughter of very respectable tradespeople, and had

served in the capacity of a nursery governess before her
marriage. She had a brother, a widower, who was considered wealthy, and who had one child of about six years
old. A month after the marriage, the body of this brother
was found in the Thames, near London Bridge; there
seemed some marks of violence about his throat, but they
were not deemed sufficient to warrant the inquest in any
verdict other than that of 'found drowned'.

The American and his wife took charge of the little boy,
the deceased brother having by his will left his sister the
guardian of his only child—and in the event of the child's
death, the sister inherited. The child died about six months
afterwards—it was supposed to have been neglected and
ill-treated. The neighbours deposed to have heard it shriek
at night. The surgeon who had examined it after death, said
that it was emaciated as if from want of nourishment, and
the body was covered with livid bruises. It seemed that
one winter night the child had sought to escape—crept out
into the back-yard—tried to scale the wall—fallen back
exhausted, and been found at morning on the stones in a
dying state. But though there was some evidence of cruelty,
there was none of murder; and the aunt and her husband
had sought to palliate cruelty by alleging the exceeding
stubbornness and perversity of the child, who was declared
to be half-witted. Be that as it may, at the orphan's death
the aunt inherited her brother's fortune.

Before the first wedded year was out, the American
quitted England abruptly, and never returned to it. He
obtained a cruising vessel, which was lost in the Atlantic
two years afterwards. The widow was left in affluence;
but reverses of various kinds had befallen her: a bank
broke—an investment failed—she went into a small business and became insolvent—then she entered into service,
sinking lower and lower, from housekeeper down to maid-
of-all-work—never long retaining a place, though nothing
peculiar against her character was ever alleged. She was
considered sober, honest, and peculiarly quiet in her ways;
still nothing prospered with her. And so she had dropped

into the workhouse, from which Mr. J—— had taken her, to be placed in charge of the very house which she had rented as mistress in the first year of her wedded life.

Mr. J—— added that he had passed an hour alone in the unfurnished room which I had urged him to destroy, and that his impressions of dread while there were so great, though he had neither heard nor seen anything, that he was eager to have the walls bared and the floors removed as I had suggested. He had engaged persons for the work, and would commence any day I would name.

The day was accordingly fixed. I repaired to the haunted house—we went into the blind dreary room, took up the skirting, and then the floors. Under the rafters, covered with rubbish, was found a trap-door, quite large enough to admit a man. It was closely nailed down with clamps and rivets of iron. On removing these we descended into a room below, the existence of which had never been suspected. In this room there had been a window and a flue, but they had been bricked over, evidently for many years. By the help of candles we examined this place; it still retained some mouldering furniture—three chairs, an oak settee, a table—all of the fashion of about eighty years ago. There was a chest-of-drawers against the wall, in which we found, half rotted away, old-fashioned articles of a man's dress, such as might have been worn eighty or a hundred years ago by a gentleman of some rank—costly steel buckles and buttons, like those yet worn in court dresses—a handsome court sword. In a waistcoat which had once been rich with gold lace, but which was now blackened and foul with damp, we found five guineas, a few silver coins, and an ivory ticket, probably for some entertainment long since passed away. But our main discovery was in a kind of iron safe fixed to the wall, the lock of which it cost us much trouble to get picked.

In this safe were three shelves and two small drawers. Ranged on the shelves were several small bottles of crystal, hermetically stopped. They contained colourless volatile essences, of what nature I shall say no more than that they were not poisons—phosphor and ammonia entered into some of them. There were also some very curious glass tubes, and a small pointed rod of iron, with a large lump of rock-crystal, and another of amber—also a lodestone of great power.

In one of the drawers we found a miniature portrait set in gold, and retaining the freshness of its colours most remarkably, considering the length of time it had probably been there. The portrait was that of a man who might be somewhat advanced in middle life, perhaps forty-seven or forty-eight.

It was a most peculiar face—a most impressive face. If you could fancy some mighty serpent transformed into man, preserving in the human lineaments the old serpent type, you would have a better idea of that countenance than long descriptions can convey: the width and flatness of frontal—the tapering elegance of contour disguising the strength of the deadly jaw—the long, large, terrible eye, glittering and green as the emerald—and withal a certain ruthless calm, as if from the consciousness of an immense power. The strange thing was this—the instant I saw the miniature I recognised a startling likeness to one of the rarest portraits in the world—the portrait of a man of a rank only below that of royalty, who in his own day had made a considerable noise. History says little or nothing of him; but search the correspondence of his contemporaries, and you find reference to his wild daring, his bold profligacy, his restless spirit, his taste for the occult sciences. While still in the meridian of life he died and was buried, so say the chronicles, in a foreign land. He died in time to escape the grasp of the law, for he was accused of crimes which would have given him to the headsman.

After his death, the portraits of him, which had been numerous, for he had been a munificent encourager of art, were bought up and destroyed—it was supposed by his heirs, who might have been glad could they have razed his very name from their splendid line. He had enjoyed a vast wealth; a large portion of this was believed to have

been embezzled by a favourite astrologer or soothsayer—
at all events, it had unaccountably vanished at the time
of his death. One portrait alone of him was supposed to
have escaped the general destruction; I had seen it in the
house of a collector some months before. It had made on
me a wonderful impression, as it does on all who behold
it—a face never to be forgotten; and there was that face in
the miniature that lay within my hand. True, that in the
miniature the man was a few years older than in the portrait I had seen, or than the original was even at the time
of his death. But a few years!—why, between the date in
which flourished that direful noble, and the date in which
the miniature was evidently painted, there was an interval
of more than two centuries. While I was thus gazing, silent
and wondering, Mr. J—— said:

'But is it possible? I have known this man.'

'How—where?' I cried.

'In India. He was high in the confidence of the Rajah
of ——, and wellnigh drew him into a revolt which would
have lost the Rajah his dominions. The man was a Frenchman—his name de V——, clever, bold, lawless. We insisted on his dismissal and banishment: it must be the same
man—no two faces like his—yet this miniature seems nearly
a hundred years old.'

Mechanically I turned round the miniature to examine
the back of it, and on the back was engraved a pentacle;
in the middle of the pentacle a ladder, and the third step
of the ladder was formed by the date 1765. Examining
still more minutely, I detected a spring; this, on being
pressed, opened the back of the miniature as a lid. Within-
side the lid was engraved 'Mariana to thee—Be faithful in
life and in death to——.' Here follows a name that I will
not mention, but it was not unfamiliar to me. I had heard
it spoken of by old men in my childhood as the name borne
by a dazzling charlatan who had made a great sensation in
London for a year or so, and had fled the country on the
charge of a double murder within his own house—that of

his mistress and his rival. I said nothing of this to Mr. J——, to whom reluctantly I resigned the miniature.

We had found no difficulty in opening the first drawer within the iron safe; we found great difficulty in opening the second: it was not locked, but it resisted all efforts till we inserted in the chinks the edge of a chisel. When we had thus drawn it forth, we found a very singular apparatus in the nicest order. Upon a small thin book, or rather tablet, was placed a saucer of crystal; this saucer was filled with a clear liquid—on that liquid floated a kind of compass, with a needle shifting rapidly round, but instead of the usual points of a compass were seven strange characters, not very unlike those used by astrologers to denote the planets. A very peculiar, but not strong nor displeasing odour came from this drawer, which was lined with a wood that we afterwards discovered to be hazel. Whatever the cause of this odour, it produced a material effect on the nerves. We all felt it, even the two workmen who were in the room— a creeping tingling sensation from the tips of the fingers to the roots of the hair. Impatient to examine the tablet, I removed the saucer. As I did so the needle of the compass went round and round with exceeding swiftness, and I felt a shock that ran through my whole frame, so that I dropped the saucer on the floor. The liquid was spilt—the saucer was broken—the compass rolled to the end of the room—and at that instant the walls shook to and fro, as if a giant had swayed and rocked them.

The two workmen were so frightened that they ran up the ladder by which we had descended from the trap-door; but seeing that nothing more happened, they were easily induced to return.

Meanwhile I had opened the tablet: it was bound in a plain red leather, with a silver clasp; it contained but one sheet of thick vellum, and on that sheet were inscribed, within a double pentacle, words in old monkish Latin, which are literally to be translated thus: 'On all that it can reach within these walls—sentient or inanimate, living or dead—as moves the needle, so work my will! Accursed be the house, and restless be the dwellers therein.'

We found no more. Mr. J—— burnt the tablet and its anathema. He razed to the foundations the part of the building containing the secret room with the chamber over it. He had then the courage to inhabit the house himself for a month, and a quieter, better-conditioned house could not be found in all London. Subsequently he let it to advantage, and his tenant has made no complaints. But my story is not yet done. A few days after Mr. J—— had removed into the house, I paid him a visit. We were standing by the open window and conversing. A van containing some articles of furniture which he was moving from his former house was at the door. I had just urged on him my theory that all those phenomena regarded as supermundane had emanated from a human brain; adducing the charm, or rather curse, we had found and destroyed in support of my philosophy. Mr. J—— was observing in reply, 'That even if mesmerism, or whatever analogous power it might be called, could really thus work in the absence of the operator, and produce effects so extraordinary, still could those effects continue when the operator himself was dead? And if the spell had been wrought, and, indeed, the room walled up, more than seventy years ago, the probability was, that the operator had long since departed this life.' Mr. J——, I say, was thus answering, when I caught hold of his arm and pointed to the street below.

A well-dressed man had crossed from the opposite side, and was accosting the carrier in charge of the van. His face, as he stood, was exactly fronting our window. It was the face of the miniature we had discovered; it was the face of the portrait of the noble three centuries ago.

'Good heavens!' cried Mr. J——, 'that is the face of de V——, and scarcely a day older than when I saw it in the rajah's court in my youth!'

Seized by the same thought, we both hastened downstairs. I was first in the street; but the man had already gone. I caught sight of him, however, not many yards in advance, and in another moment I was by his side.

I had now resolved to speak to him, but when I looked into his face I felt as if it were impossible to do so. That eye—the eye of the serpent—fixed and held me spellbound. And withal, about the man's whole person there was a dignity, an air of pride and station and superiority, that would have made anyone, habituated to the usages of the world, hesitate long before venturing upon a liberty or impertinence. And what could I say? What was it I would ask? Thus ashamed of my first impulse, I fell a few paces back, still, however, following the stranger, undecided what else to do. Meanwhile he turned the corner of the street; a plain carriage was in waiting, with a servant out of livery, dressed like a *valet-de-place*, at the carriage door. In another moment he had stepped into the carriage, and it drove off. I returned to the house. Mr. J—— was still at the street-door. He had asked the carrier what the stranger had said to him.

'Merely asked whom that house now belonged to.'

The same evening I happened to go with a friend to a place in town called the Cosmopolitan Club, a place open to men of all countries, all opinions, all degrees. One orders one's coffee, smokes one's cigar. One is always sure to meet agreeable, sometimes remarkable, persons.

I had not been two minutes in the room before I beheld at a table, conversing with an acquaintance of mine, whom I will designate by the initial G——, the man—the Original of the Miniature. He was now without his hat, and the likeness was yet more startling, only I observed that while he was conversing there was less severity in the countenance; there was even a smile, though a very quiet and very cold one. The dignity of mien I had acknowledged in the street was also more striking; a dignity akin to that which invests some prince of the East—conveying the idea of supreme indifference and habitual, indisputable, indolent, but resistless power.

G—— soon after left the stranger, who then took up a

scientific journal, which seemed to absorb his attention.

I drew G—— aside. 'Who and what is that gentleman?'

'That? Oh, a very remarkable man indeed. I met him last year amidst the caves of Petra—the scriptural Edom. He is the best Oriental scholar I know. We joined company, had an adventure with robbers, in which he showed a coolness that saved our lives; afterwards he invited me to spend a day with him in a house he had bought at Damascus—a house buried amongst almond blossoms and roses—the most beautiful thing! He had lived there for some years, quite as an Oriental, in grand style. I half suspect he is a renegade, immensely rich, very odd; by the by, a great mesmeriser. I have seen him with my own eyes produce an effect on inanimate things. If you take a letter from your pocket and throw it to the other end of the room, he will order it to come to his feet, and you will see the letter wriggle itself along the floor till it has obeyed his command. 'Pon my honour, 'tis true: I have seen him affect even the weather, disperse or collect clouds, by means of a glass tube or wand. But he does not like talking of these matters to strangers. He has only just arrived in England; says he has not been for a great many years. Let me introduce him to you.'

'Certainly! He is English, then? What is his name?'

'Oh!—a very homely one—Richards.'

'And what is his birth—his family?'

'How do I know? What does it signify? No doubt some *parvenu*, but rich—so infernally rich!'

G—— drew me up to the stranger, and the introduction was effected. The manners of Mr. Richards were not those of an adventurous traveller. Travellers are in general constitutionally gifted with high animal spirits: they are talkative, eager, imperious. Mr. Richards was calm and subdued in tone, with manners which were made distant by the loftiness of punctilious courtesy—the manners of a former age. I observed that the English he spoke was not exactly of our day. I should even have said that the accent was slightly foreign. But then Mr. Richards remarked that he had been little in the habit for many years of speaking in his native tongue. The conversation fell upon the changes in the aspect of London since he had last visited our metropolis. G—— then glanced off to the moral changes—literary, social, political—the great men who were removed from the stage within the last twenty years—the new great men who were coming on. In all this Mr. Richards evinced no interest. He had evidently read none of our living authors, and seemed scarcely acquainted by name with our younger statesmen. Once and only once he laughed; it was when G—— asked him whether he had any thought of getting into Parliament. And the laugh was inward—sarcastic—sinister—a sneer raised into a laugh. After a few minutes G—— left us to talk to some other acquaintances who had just lounged into the room, and I then said quietly:

'I have seen a miniature of you, Mr. Richards, in the house you once inhabited, and perhaps built, if not wholly, at least in part, in —— Street. You passed by that house this morning.'

Not till I had finished did I raise my eyes to his, and then his fixed my gaze so steadfastly that I could not withdraw it—those fascinating serpent eyes. But involuntarily, and as if the words that translated my thought were dragged from me, I added in a low whisper: 'I have been a student in the mysteries of life and nature; of those mysteries I have known the occult professors. I have the right to speak to you thus.' And I uttered a certain pass-word.

'Well,' said he, dryly, 'I concede the right—what would you ask?'

'To what extent human will in certain temperaments can extend?'

'To what extent can thought extend? Think, and before you draw breath you are in China.'

'True. But my thought has no power in China.'

'Give it expression, and it may have: you may write down a thought which, sooner or later, may alter the whole condition of China. What is a law but a thought? Therefore thought is infinite—therefore thought has power; not in proportion to its value—a bad thought may make a bad law as potent as a good thought can make a good one.'

'Yes; what you say confirms my own theory. Through invisible currents one human brain may transmit its ideas to other human brains with the same rapidity as a thought promulgated by visible means. And as thought is imperishable—as it leaves its stamp behind it in the natural world even when the thinker has passed out of this world—so the thought of the living may have power to rouse up and revive the thoughts of the dead—such as those thoughts *were in life*—though the thought of the living cannot reach the thoughts which the dead *now* may entertain. Is it not so?'

'I decline to answer, if, in my judgment, thought has the limit you would fix to it; but proceed. You have a special question you wish to put.'

'Intense malignity in an intense will, engendered in a peculiar temperament, and aided by natural means within the reach of science, may produce effects like those ascribed of old to evil magic. It might thus haunt the walls of a human habitation with spectral revivals of all guilty thoughts and guilty deeds once conceived and done within those walls; all, in short, with which the evil will claims *rapport* and affinity—imperfect, incoherent, fragmentary snatches at the old dramas acted therein years ago. Thoughts thus crossing each other haphazard, as in the nightmare of a vision, growing up into phantom sights and sounds, and all serving to create horror, not because those sights and sounds are really visitations from a world without, but that they are ghastly monstrous renewals of what have been in this world itself, set into malignant play by a malignant mortal.

'And it is through the material agency of that human brain that these things would acquire even a human power —would strike as with the shock of electricity, and might kill, if the thought of the person assailed did not rise superior to the dignity of the original assailer—might kill the most powerful animal if unnerved by fear, but not injure the feeblest man, if, while his flesh crept, his mind stood out fearless. Thus, when in old stories we read of a magician rent to pieces by the fiends he had evoked—or still more, in Eastern legends, that one magician succeeds by arts in destroying another—there may be so far truth, that a material being has clothed, from its own evil propensities, certain elements and fluids, usually quiescent or harmless, with awful shape and terrific force—just as the lightning that had lain hidden and innocent in the cloud becomes by natural law suddenly visible, takes a distinct shape to the eye, and can strike destruction on the object to which it is attracted.'

'You are not without glimpses of a very mighty secret,' said Mr. Richards composedly. 'According to your view, could a mortal obtain the power you speak of, he would necessarily be a malignant and evil being.'

'If the power were exercised as I have said, most malignant and most evil—though I believe in the ancient traditions that he could not injure the good. His will could only injure those with whom it has established an affinity, or over whom it forces unresisted sway. I will now imagine an example that may be within the laws of nature, yet seem wild as the fables of a bewildered monk.

'You will remember that Albertus Magnus, after describing minutely the process by which spirits may be invoked and commanded, adds emphatically that the process will instruct and avail only to the few—that a *man must be born a magician*!—that is, born with a peculiar physical temperament, as a man is born a poet. Rarely are men in whose constitution lurks this occult power of the highest order of intellect—usually in the intellect there is some twist, perversity, or disease. But, on the other hand, they must possess, to an astonishing degree, the faculty that we call *will*. Therefore, though their intellect be not sound, it is exceedingly forcible for the attainment of what it desires.

'I will imagine such a person pre-eminently gifted with this constitution and its concomitant forces. I will place

98

him in the loftier grades of society. I will suppose his desires emphatically those of the sensualist—he has, therefore, a strong love of life. He is an absolute egotist—his
will is concentrated in himself—he has fierce passions—
he knows no enduring, no holy affections, but he can covet
eagerly what for the moment he desires—he can hate im-
placably what opposes itself to his objects—he can commit
fearful crimes, yet feel small remorse—he resorts rather
to curses upon others than to penitence for his misdeeds.
Circumstances, to which his constitution guides him, lead
him to a rare knowledge of the natural secrets which may
serve his egotism. He is a close observer where his passions
encourage observation, he is a minute calculator, not from
love of truth, but where love of self sharpens his faculties—
therefore he can be a man of science.

'I suppose such a being, having by experience learned
the power of his arts over others, trying what may be the
power of will over his own frame, and studying all that in
natural philosophy may increase that power. He loves life,
he dreads death; he *wills to live on.* He cannot restore himself to youth, he cannot entirely stay the progress of death,
he cannot make himself immortal in the flesh and blood;
but he may arrest for a time so prolonged as to appear
incredible, if I said it—that hardening of the parts which
constitutes old age. A year may age him no more than an
hour ages another. His intense will, scientifically trained
into system, operates, in short, over the wear and tear of
his own frame. He lives on. That he may not seem a por-
tent and a miracle, he *dies* from time to time, seemingly,
to certain persons. Having schemed the transfer of a wealth
that suffices to his wants, he disappears from one corner
of the world, and contrives that his obsequies shall be
celebrated. He reappears at another corner of the world,
where he resides undetected, and does not revisit the scenes
of his former career till all who could remember his features are no more. He would be profoundly miserable if he
had affections—he has none but for himself. No good man

would accept his longevity, and to no men, good or bad, would he or could he communicate its true secret.

'Such a man might exist; such a man as I have described I see now before me!—Duke of——, in the court of ——, dividing time between lust and brawl, alchemists and wizards. Again, in the last century, charlatan and criminal, with name less noble, domiciled in the house at which you gazed today, and flying from the law you had outraged, none knew whither; traveller once more revisiting London, with the same earthly passions which filled your heart when races now no more walked through yonder streets; outlaw from the school of all the nobler and diviner mystics; execrable Image of Life in Death and Death in Life, I warn you back from the cities and homes of healthful men; back to the ruins of departed empires; back to the deserts of nature unredeemed!'

There answered me a whisper so musical, so potently musical, that it seemed to enter into my whole being, and subdue me despite myself. Thus it said:

'I have sought one like you for the last hundred years. Now I have found you, we part not till I know what I desire. The vision that sees through the Past, and cleaves through the veil of the Future, is in you at this hour; never before, never to come again. The vision of no puling fantastic girl, of no sick-bed somnambule, but of a strong man, with a vigorous brain. Soar and look forth!'

As he spoke I felt as if I rose out of myself upon eagle wings. All the weight seemed gone from air—roofless the room, roofless the dome of space. I was not in the body—where I knew not—but aloft over time, over earth.

Again I heard the melodious whisper—'You say right. I have mastered great secrets by the power of Will; true, by Will and by Science I can retard the process of years: but death comes not by age alone. Can I frustrate the accidents which bring death upon the young?'

'No; every accident is a providence. Before a providence snaps every human will.'

'Shall I die at last, ages and ages hence, by the slow,

though inevitable, growth of time or by the cause that I call accident?'

'By a cause you call accident.'

'Is not the end still remote?' asked the whisper with a slight tremor.

'Regarded as my life regards time, it is still remote.'

'And shall I, before then, mix with the world of men as I did ere I learned these secrets, resume eager interest in their strife and their trouble—battle with ambition, and use the power of the sage to win the power that belongs to kings?'

'You will yet play a part on the earth that will fill earth with commotion and amaze. For wondrous designs have you, a wonder yourself, been permitted to live on through the centuries. All the secrets you have stored will then have their uses—all that now makes you a stranger amidst the generations will contribute then to make you their lord. As the trees and the straws are drawn into a whirlpool— as they spin round, are sucked to the deep, and again tossed aloft by the eddies, so shall races and thrones be plucked into the charm of your vortex. Awful Destroyer—but in destroying, made, against your own will, a Constructor!'

'And that date, too, is far off?'

'Far off; when it comes, think your end in this world is at hand!'

'How and what is the end! Look east, west, south, and north.'

'In the north, where you never yet trod, towards the point whence your instincts have warned you, there a spectre will seize you. 'Tis Death! I see a ship—it is haunted— 'tis chased—it sails on. Baffled navies sail after that ship. It enters the regions of ice. It passes a sky red with meteors. Two moons stand on high, over ice-reefs. I see the ship locked between white defiles—they are ice-rocks. I see the dead strew the decks—stark and livid, green mould on their limbs. All are dead, but one man—it is you! But years, though so slowly they come, have then scathed you. There is the coming of age on your brow, and the will is relaxed in the cells of the brain. Still that will, though enfeebled,

exceeds all that man knew before you; through the will
you live on, gnawed with famine; and nature no longer
obeys you in that death-spreading region; the sky is a sky
of iron, and the air has iron clamps, and the ice-rocks
wedge in the ship. Hark how it cracks and groans. Ice will
imbed it as amber imbeds a straw. And a man has gone
forth, living yet, from the ship and its dead; and he has
clambered up the spikes of an iceberg, and the two moons
gaze down on his form. That man is yourself; and terror is
on you—terror; and terror has swallowed your will. And
I see swarming up the steep ice-rock, grey grisly things.
The bears of the north have scented their quarry—they
come near you and nearer, shambling and rolling their
bulk. And in that day every moment shall seem to you
longer than the centuries through which you have passed.
And heed this—after life, moments continued make the
bliss or the hell of eternity.'

'Hush,' said the whisper; 'but the day, you assure me, is
far off—very far! I go back to the almond and rose of
Damascus!—sleep!'

The room swam before my eyes. I became insensible.
When I recovered, I found G—— holding my hand and
smiling. He said: 'You who have always declared yourself proof against mesmerism have succumbed at last to
my friend Richards.'

'Where is Mr. Richards?'

'Gone, when you passed into a trance—saying quietly
to me, "Your friend will not wake for an hour." '

I asked, as collectedly as I could, where Mr. Richards
lodged.

'At the Trafalgar Hotel.'

'Give me your arm,' said I to G——; 'let us call on him;
I have something to say.'

When we arrived at the hotel, we were told that Mr.
Richards had returned twenty minutes before, paid his
bill, left directions with his servant (a Greek) to pack his
effects and proceed to Malta by the steamer that should
leave Southampton the next day. Mr. Richards had merely

said of his own movements that he had visits to pay in the neighbourhood of London, and it was uncertain whether he should be able to reach Southampton in time for that steamer; if not, he should follow in the next one.

The waiter asked me my name. On my informing him, he gave me a note that Mr. Richards had left for me, in case I called.

The note was as follows:

I wished you to utter what was in your mind. You obeyed. I have therefore established power over you. For three months from this day you can communicate to no living man what has passed between us—you cannot even show this note to the friend by your side. During three months, silence complete as to me and mine. Do you doubt my power to lay on you this command?—try to disobey me. At the end of the third month, the spell is raised. For the rest I spare you. I shall visit your grave a year and a day after it has received you.

So ends this strange story, which I ask no one to believe. I write it down exactly three months after I received the above note. I could not write it before, nor could I show to G——, in spite of his urgent request, the note which I read under the gas-lamp by his side.

MISS BRADDON

Eveline's Visitant

It was at a masked ball at the Palais Royal that my fatal quarrel with my first cousin André de Brissac began. The quarrel was about a woman. The women who followed the footsteps of Philip of Orleans were the causes of many such disputes; and there was scarcely one fair head in all that glittering throng which, to a man versed in social histories and mysteries, might not have seemed bedabbled with blood.

I shall not record the name of her for love of whom André de Brissac and I crossed one of the bridges, in the dim August dawn on our way to the waste ground beyond the church of Saint-Germain des Prés.

There were many beautiful vipers in those days, and she was one of them. I can feel the chill breath of that August morning blowing in my face, as I sit in my dismal chamber at my château of Puy Verdun tonight, alone in the stillness, writing the strange story of my life. I can see the white mist rising from the river, the grim outline of the Châtelet, and the square towers of Notre Dame black against the pale-grey sky. Even more vividly can I recall André's fair young face, as he stood opposite to me with his two friends— scoundrels both, and alike eager for that unnatural fray. We were a strange group to be seen in a summer sunrise, all of us fresh from the heat and clamour of the Regent's saloons—André in a quaint hunting-dress copied from a family portrait at Puy Verdun, I costumed as one of Law's Mississippi Indians; the other men in like garish frippery, adorned with broideries and jewels that looked wan in the pale light of dawn.

Our quarrel had been a fierce one—a quarrel which could have but one result, and that the direst. I had struck him; and the welt raised by my open hand was crimson upon his fair, womanish face as he stood opposite to me. The eastern sun shone on the face presently, and dyed the cruel mark with a deeper red; but the sting of my own wrongs was fresh, and I had not yet learned to despise myself for that brutal outrage.

To André de Brissac such an insult was most terrible. He was the favourite of Fortune, the favourite of women; and I was nothing—a rough soldier who had done my country good service, but in the boudoir of a Parabère a mannerless boor.

We fought, and I wounded him mortally. Life had been very sweet for him; and I think that a frenzy of despair took possession of him when he felt the life-blood ebbing away. He beckoned me to him as he lay on the ground. I went, and knelt at his side.

'Forgive me, André!' I murmured.

He took no more heed of my words than if that piteous entreaty had been the idle ripple of the river near at hand.

'Listen to me, Hector de Brissac,' he said. 'I am not one who believes that a man has done with earth because his eyes glaze and his jaw stiffens. They will bury me in the old vault at Puy Verdun; and you will be master of the château. Ah, I know how lightly they take things in these days, and how Dubois will laugh when he hears that *Ça* has been killed in a duel. They will bury me, and sing masses for my soul; but you and I have not finished our affair yet, my cousin. I will be with you when you least look to see me—I, with this ugly scar upon the face that women have praised and loved. I will come to you when your life seems brightest. I will come between you and all that you hold fairest and dearest. My ghostly hand shall drop a poison in your cup of joy. My shadowy form shall shut the sunlight from your life. Men with such iron will as mine can do what they please, Hector de Brissac. It is my will to haunt you when I am dead.'

All this in short broken sentences he whispered into my ear. I had need to bend my ear close to his dying lips; but the iron will of André de Brissac was strong enough to do battle with Death, and I believe he said all he wished to say before his head fell back upon the velvet cloak they had spread beneath him, never to be lifted again.

As he lay there, you would have fancied him a fragile stripling, too fair and frail for the struggle called life; but there are those who remember the brief manhood of André de Brissac, and who can bear witness to the terrible force of that proud nature.

I stood looking down at the young face with that foul mark upon it, and God knows I was sorry for what I had done.

Of those blasphemous threats which he had whispered in my ear I took no heed. I was a soldier, and a believer. There was nothing absolutely dreadful to me in the thought that I had killed this man. I had killed many men on the battlefield; and this one had done me cruel wrong.

My friends would have had me cross the frontier to escape the consequences of my act; but I was ready to face those consequences, and I remained in France. I kept aloof from the court, and receive a hint that I had best confine myself to my own province. Many masses were chanted in the little chapel of Puy Verdun for the soul of my dead cousin, and his coffin filled a niche in the vault of our ancestors.

His death had made me a rich man; and the thought that it was so made my newly acquired wealth very hateful to me. I lived a lonely existence in the old château, where I rarely held converse with any but the servants of the household, all of whom had served my cousin, and none of whom liked me.

It was a hard and bitter life. It galled me, when I rode through the village, to see the peasant children shrink away from me. I have seen old women cross themselves stealthily as I passed them by. Strange reports had gone forth about me; and there were those who whispered that I had given my soul to the Evil One as the price of my cousin's heritage. From my boyhood I had been dark of visage and stern of manner; and hence, perhaps, no woman's love had ever been mine. I remembered my mother's face in all its changes of expression; but I can remember no look of affection that ever shone on me. That other woman, beneath whose feet I laid my heart, was pleased to accept my homage, but she never loved me; and the end was treachery.

I had grown hateful to myself, and had well-nigh begun to hate my fellow-creatures, when a feverish desire seized upon me, and I pined to be back in the press and throng of the busy world once again. I went back to Paris, where I kept myself aloof from the court, and where an angel took compassion upon me.

She was the daughter of an old comrade, a man whose merits had been neglected, whose achievements had been ignored, and who sulked in his shabby lodging like a rat in a hole, while all Paris went mad with the Scotch Financier, and gentleman and lackeys were trampling one another to death in the Rue Quincampoix. The only child of this little cross-grained old captain of dragoons was an incarnate sunbeam, whose mortal name was Eveline Duchalet.

She loved me. The richest blessings of our lives are often those which cost us least. I wasted the best years of my youth in the worship of a wicked woman, who jilted and cheated me at last. I gave this meek angel but a few courteous words—a little fraternal tenderness—and lo, she loved me. The life which had been so dark and desolate grew bright beneath her influence; and I went back to Puy Verdun with a fair young bride for my companion.

Ah, how sweet a change there was in my life and in my home! The village children no longer shrank appalled as the dark horseman rode by, the village crones no longer crossed themselves; for a woman rode by his side—a woman whose charities had won the love of all those ignorant creatures, and whose companionship had transformed the gloomy lord of the château into a loving hus-

band and a gentle master. The old retainers forgot the
untimely fate of my cousin, and served me with cordial
willingness, for love of their young mistress.

There are no words which can tell the pure and perfect
happiness of that time. I felt like a traveller who had traversed the frozen seas of an arctic region, remote from
human love or human companionship, to find himself on a
sudden in the bosom of a verdant valley, in the sweet atmosphere of home. The change seemed too bright to be real;
and I strove in vain to put away from my mind the vague
suspicion that my new life was but some fantastic dream.

So brief were those halcyon hours, that, looking back on
them now, it is scarcely strange if I am still half inclined to
fancy the first days of my married life could have been no
more than a dream.

Neither in my days of gloom nor in my days of happiness
had I been troubled by the recollection of André's blasphemous oath. The words which with his last breath he had
whispered in my ear were vain and meaningless to me. He
had vented his rage in those idle threats, as he might have
vented it in idle execrations. That he will haunt the footsteps of his enemy after death is the one revenge which a
dying man can promise himself; and if men had power
thus to avenge themselves the earth would be peopled with
phantoms.

I had lived for three years at Puy Verdun; sitting alone
in the solemn midnight by the hearth where he had sat,
pacing the corridors that had echoed his footfall; and in all
that time my fancy had never so played me false as to
shape the shadow of the dead. Is it strange, then, if I had
forgotten André's horrible promise?

.   .   .   .   .

There was no portrait of my cousin at Puy Verdun. It
was the age of boudoir art, and a miniature set in the lid of
a gold bonbonnière, or hidden artfully in a massive bracelet, was more fashionable than a clumsy life-size image, fit

108

only to hang on the gloomy walls of a provincial château rarely visited by its owner. My cousin's fair face had adorned more than one bonbonnière, and had been concealed in more than one bracelet; but it was not among the faces that looked down from the panelled walls of Puy Verdun.

In the library I found a picture which awoke painful associations. It was the portrait of a de Brissac, who had flourished in the time of Francis the First; and it was from this picture that my cousin André had copied the quaint hunting-dress he wore at the Regent's ball. The library was a room in which I spent a good deal of my life; and I ordered a curtain to be hung before this picture.

.　　.　　.　　.　　.

We had been married three months, when Eveline one day asked: 'Who is the lord of the château nearest to this?'

I looked at her in astonishment.

'My dearest,' I answered, 'do you not know that there is no other château within forty miles of Puy Verdun?'

'Indeed!' she said. 'That is strange.'

I asked her why the fact seemed strange to her; and after much entreaty I obtained from her the reason of her surprise.

In her walks about the park and woods during the last month she had met a man who, by his dress and bearing, was obviously of noble rank. She had imagined that he occupied some château near at hand, and that his estate adjoined ours. I was at a loss to imagine who this stranger could be; for my estate of Puy Verdun lay in the heart of a desolate region, and unless when some traveller's coach went lumbering and jingling through the village, one had little more chance of encountering a gentleman than of meeting a demigod.

'Have you seen this man often, Eveline?' I asked.

She answered, in a tone which had a touch of sadness: 'I see him every day.'

'Where, dearest?'

'Sometimes in the park, sometimes in the wood. You know the little cascade, Hector, where there is some old neglected rock-work that forms a kind of cavern. I have taken a fancy to that spot, and have spent many mornings there reading. Of late I have seen the stranger there every morning.'

'He has never dared to address you?'

'Never. I have looked up from my book, and have seen him standing at a little distance, watching me silently. I have continued reading; and when I have raised my eyes again I have found him gone. He must approach and depart with a stealthy tread, for I never hear his footfall. Sometimes I have almost wished that he would speak to me. It is so terrible to see him standing silently there.'

'He is some insolent peasant who seeks to frighten you.'

My wife shook her head.

'He is no peasant,' she answered. 'It is not by his dress alone I judge, for that is strange to me. He has an air of nobility which it is impossible to mistake.'

'Is he young or old?'

'He is young and handsome.'

I was much disturbed by the idea of this stranger's intrusion on my wife's solitude; and I went straight to the village to enquire if any stranger had been seen there. I could hear of no one. I questioned the servants closely, but without result. Then I determined to accompany my wife in her walks, and to judge for myself of the rank of the stranger.

For a week I devoted all my mornings to rustic rambles with Eveline in the park and woods; and in all that week we saw no one but an occasional peasant in *sabos*, or one of our own household returning from a neighbouring farm.

I was a man of studious habits, and those summer rambles disturbed the even current of my life. My wife perceived this, and entreated me to trouble myself no further.

'I will spend my mornings in the pleasaunce, Hector,' she said; 'the stranger cannot intrude upon me there.'

'I began to think the stranger is only a phantasm of your own romantic brain,' I replied, smiling at the earnest face lifted to mine. 'A châtelaine who is always reading romances may well meet handsome cavaliers in the woodlands. I dare say I have Mademoiselle Scuderi to thank for this noble stranger, and that he is only the great Cyrus in modern costume.'

'Ah, that is the point which mystifies me, Hector,' she said. 'The stranger's costume is not modern. He looks as an old picture might look if it could descend from its frame.'

Her words pained me, for they reminded me of that hidden picture in the library, and the quaint hunting costume of orange and purple, which André de Brissac wore at the Regent's ball.

After this my wife confined her walks to the pleasaunce; and for many weeks I heard no more of the nameless stranger. I dismissed all thought of him from my mind, for a graver and heavier care had come upon me. My wife's health began to droop. The change in her was so gradual as to be almost imperceptible to those who watched her day by day. It was only when she put on a rich gala dress which she had not worn for months that I saw how wasted the form must be on which the embroidered bodice hung so loosely, and how wan and dim were the eyes which had once been brilliant as the jewels she wore in her hair.

I sent a messenger to Paris to summon one of the court physicians; but I knew that many days must needs elapse before he could arrive at Puy Verdun.

In the interval I watched my wife with unutterable fear.

It was not her health only that had declined. The change was more painful to behold than any physical alteration. The bright and sunny spirit had vanished, and in the place of my joyous young bride I beheld a woman weighed down by rooted melancholy. In vain I sought to fathom the cause of my darling's sadness. She assured me that she had no

111

reason for sorrow or discontent, and that if she seemed
sad without a motive, I must forgive her sadness, and consider it as a misfortune rather than a fault.

I told her that the court physician would speedily find
some cure for her despondency, which must needs arise
from physical causes, since she had no real ground for sorrow. But although she said nothing, I could see she had
no hope or belief in the healing powers of medicine.

.   .   .   .   .

One day, when I wished to beguile her from that pen-
sive silence in which she was wont to sit an hour at a time,
I told her, laughing, that she appeared to have forgotten
her mysterious cavalier of the wood, and it seemed also as
if he had forgotten her.

To my wonderment, her pale face became a sudden
crimson; and from crimson changed to pale again in a
breath.

'You have never seen him since you deserted your woodland grotto?' I said.

She turned to me with a heart-rending look.

'Hector,' she cried, 'I see him every day; and it is that
which is killing me.'

She burst into a passion of tears when she had said this.
I took her in my arms as if she had been a frightened child,
and tried to comfort her.

'My darling, this is madness,' I said. 'You know that
no stranger can come to you in the pleasaunce. The moat is
ten feet wide and always full of water, and the gates are
kept locked day and night by old Massou. The châtelaine
of a medieval fortress need fear no intruder in her antique
garden.'

My wife shook her head sadly.

'I see him every day,' she said.

On this I believed that my wife was mad. I shrank from
questioning her more closely concerning her mysterious
visitant. It would be ill, I thought, to give a form and sub-

stance to the shadow that tormented her by too close inquiry about its looks and manner, its coming and going.

I took care to assure myself that no stranger to the household could by any possibility penetrate to the pleasaunce.
Having done this, I was fain to await the coming of the
physician.

He came at last. I revealed to him the conviction which
was my misery. I told him that I believed my wife to be
mad. He saw her—spent an hour alone with her, and then
came to me. To my unspeakable relief he assured me of her
sanity.

'It is just possible that she may be affected by one delusion,' he said; 'but she is so reasonable upon all other
points that I can scarcely bring myself to believe her the
subject of a monomania. I am rather inclined to think that
she really sees the person of whom she speaks. She described him to me with a perfect minuteness. The descriptions of scenes or individuals given by patients afflicted
with monomania are always more or less disjointed; but
your wife spoke to me as clearly and calmly as I am now
speaking to you. Are you sure there is no one who can
approach her in that garden where she walks?'

'I am quite sure.'

'Is there any kinsman of your steward, or hanger-on of
your household—a young man with a fair, womanish face,
very pale and rendered remarkable by a crimson scar,
which looks like the mark of a blow?'

'My God!' I cried, as the light broke in upon me all at
once. 'And the dress—the strange, old-fashioned dress?'

'The man wears a hunting costume of purple and
orange,' answered the doctor.

I knew then that André de Brissac had kept his word,
and that in the hour when my life was brightest his shadow
had come between me and happiness.

.   .   .   .   .

I showed my wife the picture in the library, for I would

fain assure myself that there was some error in my fancy about my cousin. She shook like a leaf when she beheld it, and clung to me convulsively.

'This is witchcraft, Hector,' she said. 'The dress in that picture is the dress of the man I see in the pleasaunce; but the face is not his.'

Then she described to me the face of the stranger; and it was my cousin's face line for line—André de Brissac, whom she had never seen in the flesh. Most vividly of all did she describe the cruel mark upon his face, the trace of a fierce blow from an open hand.

.   .   .   .   .

After this I carried my wife away from Puy Verdun. We wandered far—through the southern provinces, and into the very heart of Switzerland. I thought to distance the ghastly phantom, and I fondly hoped that change of scene would bring peace to my wife.

It was not so. Go where we would, the ghost of André de Brissac followed us. To my eyes that fatal shadow never revealed itself. *That* would have been too poor a vengeance. It was my wife's innocent heart which André made the instrument of his revenge. The unholy presence destroyed her life. My constant companionship could not shield her from the horrible intruder. In vain did I watch her; in vain did I strive to comfort her.

'He will not let me be at peace,' she said. 'He comes between us, Hector. He is standing between us now. I can see his face with the red mark upon it plainer than I see yours.'

.   .   .   .   .

One fair moonlight night, when we were together in a mountain village in the Tyrol, my wife cast herself at my feet, and told me she was the worst and vilest of women. 'I have confessed all to my Director,' she said; 'from the first I have not hidden my sin from heaven. But I feel that death is near me; and before I die I would fain reveal my sin to you.'

'What sin, my sweet one?'

'When first the stranger came to me in the forest, his presence bewildered and distressed me, and I shrank from him as from something strange and terrible. He came again and again; by and by I found myself thinking of him, and watching for his coming. His image haunted me perpetually; I strove in vain to shut his face out of my mind. Then followed an interval in which I did not see him; and, to my shame and anguish, I found that life seemed dreary and desolate without him. After that came the time in which he haunted the pleasaunce; and—oh, Hector, kill me if you will, for I deserve no mercy at your hands!—I grew in those days to count the hours that must elapse before his coming, to take no pleasure save in the sight of that pale face with the red brand upon it. He plucked all old familiar joys out of my heart, and left in it but one weird, unholy pleasure—the delight of his presence. For a year I have lived but to see him. And now curse me, Hector; for this is my sin. Whether it comes of the baseness of my own heart, or is the work of witchcraft, I know not; but I know that I have striven against this wickedness in vain.'

.   .   .   .   .

I took my wife to my breast, and forgave her. In sooth, what had I to forgive? Was the fatality that overshadowed us any work of hers? On the next night she died, with her hand in mine; and at the very last she told me, sobbing and affrighted, that *he* was by her side.

F. MARION CRAWFORD

Man Overboard

YES—I have heard 'Man overboard!' a good many times since I was a boy, and once or twice I have seen the man go. There are more men lost in that way than passengers on ocean steamers ever learn of. I have stood looking over the rail on a dark night, when there was a step beside me, and something flew past my head like a big black bat—and then there was a splash! Stokers often go like that. They go mad with the heat, and they slip up on deck and are gone before anybody can stop them, often without being seen or heard.

Now and then a passenger will do it, but he generally has what he thinks a pretty good reason. I have seen a man empty his revolver into a crowd of emigrants forward, and then go over like a rocket. Of course, any officer who respects himself will do what he can to pick a man up, if the weather is not so heavy that he would have to risk his ship; but I don't think I remember seeing a man come back when he was once fairly gone more than two or three times in all my life, though we have often picked up the life-buoys and sometimes the fellow's cap. Stokers and passengers jump over; I never knew a sailor to do that, drunk or sober. Yes, they say it has happened on hard ships, but I never knew a case myself. Once in a long time a man is fished out when it is just too late, and dies in the boat before you can get him aboard, and—well, I don't know that I ever told that story since it happened—I knew a fellow who went over, and came back dead. I didn't see him after he came back; only one of us did, but we all knew he was there.

No, I am not giving you 'sharks'. There isn't a shark

in this story, and I don't know that I would tell it at all if
we weren't alone, just you and I. But you and I have seen
things in various parts, and maybe you will understand.
Anyhow, you know that I am telling what I know about,
and nothing else; and it has been on my mind to tell you
ever since it happened, only there hasn't been a chance.

It's a long story, and it took some time to happen; and
it began a good many years ago, in October, as well as I
can remember. I was mate then; I passed the local Marine
Board for master about three years later. She was the *Helen
B. Jackson*, of New York, with lumber for the West Indies,
four-masted schooner, Captain Hackstaff. She was an old-
fashioned one, even then—no steam donkey, and all to do
by hand.

There were still sailors in the coasting trade in those
days, you remember. She wasn't a hard ship, for the Old
Man was better than most of them, though he kept to himself and had a face like a monkey-wrench. We were thir-
teen, all told, in the ship's company; and some of them
afterwards thought that might have had something to do
with it, but I had all that nonsense knocked out of me when
I was a boy. I don't mean to say that I like to go to sea on a
Friday, but I *have* gone to sea on a Friday, and nothing
has happened; and twice before that we have been thir-
teen, because one of the hands didn't turn up at the last
minute, and nothing ever happened either—nothing worse
than the loss of a light spar or two, or a little canvas. Whenever I have been wrecked, we had sailed as cheerily as you
please—no thirteens, no Fridays, no dead men in the hold.
I believe it generally happens that way.

I dare say you remember those two Benton boys that
were so much alike? It's no wonder, for they were twin
brothers. They shipped with us as boys on the old *Boston
Belle*, when you were mate and I was before the mast. I
never was quite sure which was which of those two, even
then; and when they both had beards it was harder than
ever to tell them apart. One was Jim, and the other was
Jack; James Benton and John Benton. The only difference

I ever could see was, that one seemed to be rather more cheerful and inclined to talk than the other; but one couldn't even be sure of that. Perhaps they had moods. Anyhow, there was one of them that used to whistle when he was alone. He only knew one tune, and that was 'Nancy Lee', and the other didn't know any tune at all; but I may be mistaken about that, too. Perhaps they both knew it.

Well, those two Benton boys turned up on board the *Helen B. Jackson*. They had been on half a dozen ships since the *Boston Belle*, and they had grown up and were good seamen. They had reddish beards and bright blue eyes and freckled faces; and they were quiet fellows, good workmen on rigging, pretty willing, and both good men at the wheel. They managed to be in the same watch—it was the port watch on the *Helen B.*, and that was mine, and I had great confidence in them both. If there was any job aloft that needed two hands, they were always the first to jump into the rigging; but that doesn't often happen on a fore-and-aft schooner. If it breezed up, and the jibtopsail was to be taken in, they never minded a wetting, and they would be out at the bowsprit end before there was a hand at the down-haul. The men liked them for that, and because they didn't blow about what they could do.

I remember one day in a reefing job, the downhaul parted and came down on deck from the peak of the spanker. When the weather moderated, and we shook the reefs out, the downhaul was forgotten, until we happened to think we might soon need it again. There was some sea on, and the boom was off and the gaff was slamming. One of those Benton boys was at the wheel, and before I knew what he was doing, the other was out on the gaff with the end of the new downhaul, trying to reeve it through its block. The one who was steering watched him, and got as white as cheese. The other one was swinging about on the gaff end, and every time she rolled to leeward he brought up with a jerk that would have sent anything but a monkey flying into space. But he didn't leave it until he had rove the new rope, and he got back all right. I think it was Jack at the wheel; the one that seemed more cheerful, the one that whistled 'Nancy Lee'. He had rather have been doing the job himself than watch his brother do it, and he had a scared look; but he kept her as steady as he could in the swell, and he drew a long breath when Jim had worked his way back to the peak-halliard block, and had something to hold on to. I think it was Jim.

They had good togs, too, and they were neat and clean men in the forecastle. I knew they had nobody belonging to them ashore—no mother, no sisters, and no wives; but somehow they both looked as if a woman overhauled them now and then. I remember that they had one ditty bag between them, and they had a woman's thimble in it. One of the men said something about it to them and they looked at each other; and one smiled, but the other didn't. Most of their clothes were alike, but they had one red guernsey between them. For some time I used to think it was always the same one that wore it, and I thought that might be a way to tell them apart. But then I heard one asking the other for it, and saying that the other had worn it last. So that was no sign either.

The cook was a West India man, called James Lawley; his father had been hanged for putting lights in coconut trees where they didn't belong. But he was a good cook, and knew his business; and it wasn't soup-and-bully and dog's-body every Sunday. That's what I meant to say. On Sunday the cook called both those boys Jim, and on week-days he called them Jack. He used to say he must be right sometimes if he did that, because even the hands on a painted clock point right twice a day.

What started me trying for some way of telling the Bentons apart was this. I heard them talking about a girl. It was at night, in our watch, and the wind had headed us off a little rather suddenly, and when we had flattened in the jibs, we clewed down the topsails, while the two Benton boys got the spanker sheet aft. One of them was at the helm. I coiled down the mizzen-topsail downhaul myself, and was going aft to see how she headed up, when I stopped

119

to look at a light, and leaned against the deck-house. While I was standing there I heard the two boys talking. It sounded as if they had talked of the same thing before, and as far as I could tell, the voice I heard first belonged to the one who wasn't quite so cheerful as the other—the one who was Jim when one knew which he was.

'Does Mamie know?' Jim asked.

'Not yet,' Jack answered quietly. He was at the wheel. 'I mean to tell her next time we get home.'

'All right.'

That was all I heard, because I didn't care to stand there listening while they were talking about their own affairs; so I went aft to look into the binnacle, and I told the one at the wheel to keep her so as long as she had way on her, for I thought the wind would back up again before long, and there was land to leeward. When he answered, his voice, somehow, didn't sound like the cheerful one. Perhaps his brother had relieved the wheel while they had been speaking, but what I had heard set me wondering which of them it was that had a girl at home. There's lots of time for wondering on a schooner in fair weather.

After that I thought I noticed that the two brothers were more silent when they were together. Perhaps they guessed that I had overheard something that night, and kept quiet when I was about. Some men would have amused themselves by trying to chaff them separately about the girl at home, and I suppose whichever one it was would have let the cat out of the bag if I had done that. But, somehow, I didn't like to. Yes, I was thinking of getting married myself at that time, so I had a sort of fellow-feeling for whichever one it was, that made me not want to chaff him.

They didn't talk much, it seemed to me; but in fair weather when there was nothing to do at night, and one was steering, the other was everlastingly hanging round as if he were waiting to relieve the wheel, though he might have been enjoying a quiet nap for all I cared in such weather. Or else, when one was taking his turn at the lookout, the other would be sitting on an anchor beside him.

120

I noticed that. They were fond of sitting on that anchor, and they generally tucked away their pipes under it, for the *Helen B.* was a dry boat in most weather, and like most fore-and-afters was better on a wind than going free. With a beam sea we sometimes shipped a little water aft. We were by the stern, anyhow, on that voyage, and that is one reason why we lost the man.

We fell in with a southerly gale, south-east at first; and then the barometer began to fall while you could watch it, and a long swell began to come up from the south'ard. A couple of months earlier we might have been in for a cyclone, but it's 'October all over' in those waters, as you know better than I. It was just going to blow, and then it was going to rain, that was all; and we had plenty of time to make everything snug before it breezed up much. It blew harder after sunset, and by the time it was quite dark it was a full gale. We had shortened sail for it, but as we were by the stern we were carrying the spanker close reefed instead of the storm trysail. She steered better so, as long as we didn't have to heave to. I had the first watch with the Benton boys, and we had not been on deck an hour when a child might have seen that the weather meant business.

The Old Man came up on deck and looked round, and in less than a minute he told us to give her the trysail. That meant heaving to, and I was glad of it; for though the *Helen B.* was a good vessel enough, she wasn't a new ship by a long way, and it did her no good to drive her in that weather. I asked whether I should call all hands, but just then the cook came aft, and the Old Man said he thought we could manage the job without waking the sleepers, and the trysail was handy on deck already, for we hadn't been expecting anything better. We were all in oilskins, of course, and the night was as black as a coal mine, with only a ray of light from the slit in the binnacle shield, and you couldn't tell one man from another except by his voice.

The Old Man took the wheel; we got the boom amidships, and he jammed her into the wind until she had hardly any way. It was blowing now, and it was all that I and two

others could do to get in the slack of the downhaul, while
the others lowered away at the peak and throat, and we
had our hands full to get a couple of turns round the wet
sail. It's all child's play on a fore-and-after compared with
reefing topsails in anything like weather, but the gear of a
schooner sometimes does unhandy things that you don't
expect, and those everlasting long halliards get foul of
everything if they get adrift. I remember thinking how unhandy that particular job was. Somebody unhooked the
throat-halliard block, and thought he had hooked it into
the head-cringle of the trysail, and sang out to hoist away,
but he had missed it in the dark, and the heavy block went
flying into the lee rigging, and nearly killed him when it
swung back with the weather roll. Then the Old Man got
her up in the wind until the jib was shaking like thunder;
then he held her off, and she went off as soon as the head-
sails filled, and he couldn't get her back again with the
spanker.

Then the *Helen B.* did her favourite trick, and before we
had time to say much we had a sea over the quarter and
were up to our waists, with the parrels of the trysail only
half becketed round the mast, and the deck so full of gear
that you couldn't put your foot on a plank, and the spanker
beginning to get adrift again, being badly stopped, and the
general confusion and hell's delight that you can only
have on a fore-and-after when there's nothing really serious
the matter. Of course, I don't mean to say that the Old
Man couldn't have steered his trick as well as you or I or
any other seaman; but I don't believe he had ever been on
board the *Helen B.* before, or had his hand on her wheel
till then; and he didn't know her ways. I don't mean to
say that what happened was his fault. I don't know
whose fault it was. Perhaps nobody was to blame. But I
know something happened somewhere on board when we
shipped that sea, and you'll never get it out of my head.
I hadn't any spare time myself, for I was becketing the
rest of the trysail to the mast. We were on the starboard
tack, and the throat-halliard came down to port as usual,

and I suppose there were at least three men at it, hoisting away, while I was at the beckets.

Now I am going to tell you something. You have known me, man and boy, several voyages; and you are older than I am; and you have always been a good friend to me. Now, do you think I am the sort of man to think I hear things when there isn't anything to hear, or to think I see things when there is nothing to see? No, you don't. Thank you.

Well now, I had passed the last becket, and I sang out to the men to sway away, and I was standing on the jaws of the spanker-gaff, with my left hand on the bolt-rope of the trysail, so that I could feel when it was board taut, and I wasn't thinking of anything except being glad the job was over, and that we were going to heave her to. It was as black as a coal-pocket, except that you could see the streaks on the seas as they went by, and abaft the deck-house I could see the ray of light from the binnacle on the captain's yellow oilskin as he stood at the wheel—or, rather, I might have seen it if I had looked round at that minute. But I didn't look round. I heard a man whistling. It was 'Nancy Lee', and I could have sworn that the man was right over my head in the crosstrees. Only somehow I knew very well that if anybody could have been up there, and could have whistled a tune, there were no living ears sharp enough to hear it on deck then. I heard it distinctly, and at the same time I heard the real whistling of the wind in the weather rigging, sharp and clear as the steam-whistle on a dago's peanut-cart in New York. That was all right, that was as it should be; but the other wasn't right; and I felt queer and stiff, as if I couldn't move, and my hair was curling against the flannel lining of my sou'-wester, and I thought somebody had dropped a lump of ice down my back.

I said that the noise of the wind in the rigging was real, as if the other wasn't, for I felt that it wasn't, though I heard it. But it was, all the same; for the captain heard it too. When I came to relieve the wheel, while the men were clearing up decks, he was swearing. He was a quiet man,

123

and I hadn't heard him swear before, and I don't think I did again, though several queer things happened after that. Perhaps he said all he had to say then; I don't see how he could have said anything more. I used to think nobody could swear like a Dane, except a Neapolitan or a South American; but when I had heard the Old Man I changed my mind. There's nothing afloat or ashore that can beat one of your quiet American skippers, if he gets off on that tack. I didn't need to ask him what was the matter, for I knew he had heard 'Nancy Lee', as I had, only it affected us differently.

He did not give me the wheel, but told me to go forward and get the second bonnet off the staysail, so as to keep her up better. As we tailed on to the sheet when it was done, the man next me knocked his sou'wester off against my shoulder, and his face came so close to me that I could see it in the dark. It must have been very white for me to see it, but I only thought of that afterwards. I don't see how any light could have fallen upon it, but I knew it was one of the Benton boys. I don't know what made me speak to him. 'Hullo, Jim! Is that you?' I asked. I don't know why I said Jim, rather than Jack.

'I am Jack,' he answered.

We made all fast, and things were much quieter.

'The Old Man heard whistling "Nancy Lee" just now,' I said, 'and he didn't like it.'

It was as if there were a white light inside his face, and it was ghastly. I know his teeth chattered. But he didn't say anything, and the next minute he was somewhere in the dark trying to find his sou'wester at the foot of the mast.

When all was quiet, and she was hove to, coming to and falling off her four points as regularly as a pendulum, and the helm lashed a little to the lee, the Old Man turned in again, and I managed to light a pipe in the lee of the deck-house, for there was nothing more to be done till the gale chose to moderate, and the ship was as easy as a baby in its cradle. Of course the cook had gone below, as he might have done an hour earlier; so there were supposed to be four of us in the watch. There was a man at the lookout, and there was a hand by the wheel, though there was no steeping to be done, and I was having my pipe in the lee of the deck-house, and the fourth man was somewhere about decks, probably having a smoke too. I thought some skippers I have sailed with would have called the watch aft, and given them a drink after that job; but it wasn't cold, and I guessed that our Old Man wouldn't be particularly generous in that way. My hands and feet were red-hot, and it would be time enough to get into dry clothes when it was my watch below; so I stayed where I was, and smoked. But by and by, things being so quiet, I began to wonder why nobody moved on deck; just that sort of restless wanting to know where every man is that one sometimes feels in a gale of wind on a dark night.

So when I had finished my pipe I began to move about. I went aft, and there was a man leaning over the wheel, with his legs apart and both hands hanging down in the light from the binnacle, and his sou'wester over his eyes. Then I went forward, and there was a man at the lookout, with his back against the foremast, getting what shelter he could from the staysail. I knew by his small height that he was not one of the Benton boys. Then I went round by the weather side, and poked about in the dark, for I began to wonder where the other man was. But I couldn't find him, though I searched the decks until I got right aft again. It was certainly one of the Benton boys that was missing, but it wasn't like either of them to go below to change his clothes in such warm weather. The man at the wheel was the other, of course. I spoke to him.

'Jim, what's become of your brother?'

'I am Jack, sir.'

'Well, then, Jack, where's Jim? He's not on deck.'

'I don't know, sir.'

When I had come up to him he had stood up from force of instinct, and had laid his hands on the spokes as if he were steering, though the wheel was lashed; but he still bent his face down, and it was half hidden by the edge of

125

his sou'wester, while he seemed to be staring at the compass. He spoke in a very low voice, but that was natural, for the captain had left his door open when he turned in, as it was a warm night in spite of the storm, and there was no fear of shipping any more water now.

'What put it into your head to whistle like that, Jack? You've been at sea long enough to know better.'

He said something, but I couldn't hear the words: it sounded as if he were denying the charge.

'Somebody whistled,' I said.

He didn't answer, and then, I don't know why, perhaps because the Old Man hadn't given us a drink, I cut half an inch off the plug of tobacco I had in my oilskin pocket, and gave it to him. He knew my tobacco was good, and he shoved it into his mouth with a word of thanks. I was on the weather side of the wheel.

'Go forward and see if you can find Jim,' I said.

He started a little, and then stepped back and passed behind me, and was going along the weather side. Maybe his silence about the whistling had irritated me, and his taking it for granted that because we were hove to, and it was a dark night, he might go forward any way he pleased. Anyhow, I stopped him, though I spoke good-naturedly enough.

'Pass to leeward, Jack,' I said.

He didn't answer, but crossed the deck between the binnacle and the deck-house to the lee side. She was only falling off and coming to, and riding the big seas as easily as possible, but the man was not steady on his feet and reeled against the corner of the deck-house and then against the lee rail. I was quite sure he couldn't have had anything to drink, for neither of the brothers were the kind to hide rum from their shipmates, if they had any, and the only spirits that were aboard were locked up in the captain's cabin. I wondered whether he had been hit by the throat-halliard block and was hurt.

I left the wheel and went after him, but when I got to the corner of the deck-house I saw that he was on a full run forward, so I went back. I watched the compass for a while, to see how far she went off, and she must have come to again half a dozen times before I heard voices, more than three or four, forward; and then I heard the little West Indies cook's voice. high and shrill above the rest:

'Man overboard!'

There wasn't anything to be done, with the ship hove to and the wheel lashed. If there was a man overboard, he must be in the water right alongside. I couldn't imagine how it could have happened, but I ran forward instinctively. I came upon the cook first, half dressed in his shirt and trousers, just as he had tumbled out of his bunk. He was jumping into the main rigging, evidently hoping to see the man, as if anyone could have seen anything on such a night, except the foam-streaks on the black water, and now and then the curl of a breaking sea as it went away to leeward. Several of the men were peering over the rail into the dark. I caught the cook by the foot, and asked who was gone.

'It's Jim Benton,' he shouted down to me. 'He's not aboard this ship!'

There was no doubt about that. Jim Benton was gone; and I knew in a flash that he had been taken off by that sea when we were setting the storm trysail. It was nearly half an hour since then; she had run like wild for a few minutes until we got her hove to, and no swimmer that ever swam could have lived as long as that in such a sea. The men knew it as well as I, but still they stared into the foam as if they had any chance of seeing the lost man. I let the cook get into the rigging, and joined the men, and asked if they had made a thorough search on board, though I knew they had and that it could not take long, for he wasn't on deck, and there was only the forecastle below.

'That sea took him over, sir, as sure as you're born,' said one of the men close beside me.

We had no boat that could have lived in that sea, of course, and we all knew it. I offered to put one over, and let her drift astern two or three cables'-lengths by a line,

F. MARION CRAWFORD

if the men thought they could haul me aboard again; but
none of them would listen to that, and I should probably
have been drowned if I had tried it, even with a life-belt;
for it was breaking sea. Besides, they all knew as well as
I did that the man could not be right in our wake. I don't
know why I spoke again.

'Jack Benton, are you there? Will you go if I will?'

'No, sir,' answered a voice; and that was all.

By that time the Old Man was on deck, and I felt his
hand on my shoulder rather roughly, as if he meant to shake
me.

'I'd reckoned you had more sense, Mr. Torkeldsen,' he
said. 'God knows I would risk my ship to look for him, if
it were any use; but he must have gone half an hour ago.'

He was a quiet man, and the men knew he was right,
and that they had seen the last of Jim Benton when they
were bending the trysail—if anybody had seen him then.
The captain went below again, and for some time the men
stood around Jack, quite near him, without saying anything, as sailors do when they are sorry for a man and can't
help him; and then the watch below turned in again, and
we were three on deck.

Nobody can understand that there can be much consolation in a funeral, unless he has felt that blank feeling there
is when a man's gone overboard whom everybody likes. I
suppose landsmen think it would be easier if they didn't
have to bury their fathers and mothers and friends; but it
wouldn't be. Somehow the funeral keeps up the idea of
something beyond. You may believe in that something
just the same; but a man who has gone in the dark, between two seas, without a cry, seems much more beyond
reach than if he were still lying on his bed, and had only
just stopped breathing. Perhaps Jim Benton knew that,
and wanted to come back to us. I don't know, and I am
only telling you what happened, and you may think what
you like.

Jack stuck by the wheel that night until the watch was
over. I don't know whether he slept afterwards, but when

I came on deck four hours later, there he was again, in his oilskins, with his sou'wester over his eyes, staring into the binnacle. We saw that he would rather stand there, and we left him alone. Perhaps it was some consolation to him to get that ray of light when everything was so dark.

It began to rain, too, as it can when a southerly gale is going to break up, and we got every bucket and tub on board, and set them under the booms to catch the fresh water for washing our clothes. The rain made it very thick, and I went and stood under the lee of the staysail, looking out. I could tell that day was breaking, because the foam was whiter in the dark where the seas crested, and little by little the black rain grew grey and steamy, and I couldn't see the red glare of the port light on the water when she went off and rolled to leeward. The gale had moderated considerably, and in another hour we should be under way again. I was still standing there when Jack Benton came forward. He stood still a few minutes near me. The rain came down in a solid sheet, and I could see his wet beard and a corner of his cheek, too, grey in the dawn. Then he stooped down and began feeling under the anchor for his pipe. We had hardly shipped any water forward, and I suppose he had some way of tucking the pipe in so that the rain hadn't floated it off.

Presently he got on his legs again, and I saw that he had two pipes in his hand. One of them had belonged to his brother, and after looking at them a moment I suppose he recognised his own, for he put it in his mouth, dripping with water. Then he looked at the other fully a minute without moving. When he had made up his mind, I suppose, he quietly chucked it over the lee rail, without even looking round to see whether I was watching him. I thought it was a pity, for it was a good wooden pipe, with a nickel ferrule, and somebody would have been glad to have it. But I didn't like to make any remark, for he had a right to do what he pleased with what had belonged to his dead brother.

He blew the water out of his own pipe, and dried it against his jacket; putting his hand inside his oilskin, he filled it, standing under the lee of the foremast, got a light after wasting two or three matches, and turned the pipe upside down in his teeth, to keep the rain out of the bowl. I don't know why I noticed everything he did, and remember it now; but somehow I felt sorry for him, and I kept wondering whether there was anything I could say that would make him feel better. But I didn't think of anything, and as it was broad daylight I went aft again, for I guessed the Old Man would turn out before long and order the spanker set and the helm up. But he didn't turn out before seven bells, just as the clouds broke and showed blue sky to leeward—'the Frenchman's barometer', you used to call it.

Some people don't seem to be so dead, when they are dead, as others are. Jim Benton was like that. He had been on my watch, and I couldn't get used to the idea that he wasn't about decks with me. I was always expecting to see him, and his brother was so exactly like him that I often felt as if I did see him and forgot he was dead, and made the mistake of calling Jack by his name; though I tried not to, because I knew it must hurt. If ever Jack had been the cheerful one of the two, as I had always supposed he had been, he had changed very much, for he grew to be more silent than Jim had ever been.

One fine afternoon I was sitting on the main-hatch, over-hauling the clockwork of the taffrail-log, which hadn't been registering very well of late, and I had got the cook to bring me a coffee-cup to hold the small screws as I took them out, and a saucer for the sperm oil I was going to use. I noticed that he didn't go away, but hung round without exactly watching what I was doing, as if he wanted to say something to me. I thought if it were worth much he would say it anyhow, so I didn't ask him questions; and sure enough he began of his own accord before long. There was nobody on deck but the man at the wheel, and the other man away forward.

'Mr. Torkeldsen,' the cook began, and then stopped.

I supposed he was going to ask me to let the watch break out a barrel of flour, or some salt horse.

'Well, doctor?' I asked, as he didn't go on.

'Well, Mr. Torkeldsen,' he answered, 'I somehow want to ask you whether you think I am giving satisfaction on this ship, or not?'

'So far as I know you are, doctor. I haven't heard any complaints from the forecastle, and the captain has said nothing, and I think you know your business, and the cabin-boy is bursting out of his clothes. That looks as if you are giving satisfaction. What makes you think you are not?'

I am not good at giving you that West Indies talk, and shan't try; but the doctor beat about the bush awhile, and then he told me he thought the men were beginning to play tricks on him, and he didn't like it, and thought he hadn't deserved it, and would like his discharge at our next port. I told him he was a d——d fool, of course, to begin with; and that men were more apt to try a joke with a chap they liked than with anybody they wanted to get rid of; unless it was a bad joke, like flooding his bunk, or filling his boots with tar. But it wasn't that kind of practical joke. The doctor said that the men were trying to frighten him, and he didn't like it, and that they put things in his way that frightened him. So I told him he was a d——d fool to be frightened, anyway, and I wanted to know what things they put in his way. He gave me a queer answer. He said they were spoons and forks, and odd plates, and a cup now and then, and such things.

I set down the taffrail log on the bit of canvas I had put under it, and looked at the doctor. He was uneasy, and his eyes had a sort of hunted look, and his yellow face looked grey. He wasn't trying to make trouble. He was in trouble. So I asked him questions.

He said he could count as well as anybody, and do sums without using his fingers, but that when he couldn't count any other way he did use his fingers, and it always came

131

out the same. He said that when he and the cabin-boy
cleared up after the men's meals there were more things
to wash than he had given out. There'd be a fork more,
or there'd be a spoon more, and sometimes there'd be a
spoon and a fork, and there was always a plate more. It
wasn't that he complained of that. Before poor Jim Benton
was lost they had a man more to feed, and his gear to wash
up after meals, and that was in the contract, the doctor
said. It would have been if there were twenty in the ship's
company; but he didn't think it was right for the men to
play tricks like that. He kept his things in good order, and
he counted them, and he was responsible for them, and
it wasn't right that the men should take more things than
they needed when his back was turned, and just soil them
and mix them up with their own, so as to make him
think . . .

He stopped there, and looked at me, and I looked at
him. I didn't know what he thought, but I began to guess.
I wasn't going to humour any such nonsense as that, so I
told him to speak to the men himself, and not come bother-
ing me about such things.

'Count the plates and forks and spoons before them
when they sit down to table, and tell them that's all they'll
get; and when they have finished, count the things again,
and if the count isn't right, find out who did it. You know
it must be one of them. You're not a green hand; you've
been going to sea ten or eleven years, and don't want any
lessons about how to behave if the boys play a trick on
you.'

'If I could catch him,' said the cook, 'I'd have a knife
into him before he could say his prayers.'

Those West India men are always talking about knives,
especially when they are badly frightened. I knew what he
meant, and didn't ask him, but went on cleaning the brass
cog-wheels of the patent log and oiling the bearings with a
feather.

'Wouldn't it be better to wash it out with boiling water,
sir?' asked the cook, in an insinuating tone. He knew that

132

he had made a fool of himself, and was anxious to make it right again.

I heard no more about the odd platter and gear for two or three days, though I thought about his story a good deal. The doctor evidently believed that Jim Benton had come back, though he didn't quite like to say so. His story had sounded silly enough on a bright afternoon, in fair weather, when the sun was on the water, and every rag was drawing in the breeze, and the sea looked as pleasant and harmless as a cat that has just eaten a canary. But when it was toward the end of the first watch, and the waning moon had not risen yet, and the water was like still oil, and the jibs hung down flat and helpless like the wings of a dead bird—it wasn't the same then. More than once I have started then, and looked round when a fish jumped, expecting to see a face sticking up out of the water with its eyes shut. I think we all felt something like that at the time.

One afternoon we were putting a fresh service on the jib-sheet-pennant. It wasn't my watch, but I was standing by looking on. Just then Jack Benton came up from below, and went to look for his pipe under the anchor. His face was hard and drawn, and his eyes were cold like steel balls. He hardly ever spoke now, but he did his duty as usual, and nobody had to complain of him, though we were all beginning to wonder how long his grief for his dead brother was going to last like that. I watched him as he crouched down and ran his hand into the hiding-place for the pipe. When he stood up he had two pipes in his hand.

Now, I remembered very well seeing him throw one of those pipes away, early in the morning after the gale; and it came to me now, and I didn't suppose we kept a stock of them under the anchor. I caught sight of his face, and it was greenish-white, like the foam on shallow water, and he stood a long time looking at the two pipes. He wasn't looking to see which was his, for I wasn't five yards from him as he stood, and one of those pipes had been smoked that day, and was shiny where his hand had rubbed it, and

133

the bone mouthpiece was chafed white where his teeth had bitten it. The other was waterlogged. It was swelled and cracking with wet, and it looked to me as if there were a little green weed on it.

Jack Benton turned his head rather stealthily as I looked away, and then he hid the thing in his trousers pocket, and went aft on the lee side, out of sight. The men had got the sheet-pennant on a stretch to serve it, but I ducked under it and stood where I could see what Jack did, just under the fore-staysail. He couldn't see me, and he was looking about for something. His hand shook as he picked up a bit of half-bent iron rod, about a foot long, that had been used for turning an eye-bolt, and had been left on the main-hatch. His hand shook as he got a piece of marline out of his pocket and made the waterlogged pipe fast to the iron. He didn't mean it to get adrift either, for he took his turns carefully, and hove them taut and then rode them, so that they couldn't slip, and made the end fast with two half-hitches round the iron, and hitched it back on itself. Then he tried it with his hands, and looked up and down the deck furtively, and then quietly dropped the pipe and iron over the rail, so that I didn't even hear the splash. If anybody was playing tricks on board, they weren't meant for the cook.

I asked some questions about Jack Benton, and one of the men told me that he was off his feed, and hardly ate anything, and swallowed all the coffee he could lay his hands on, and had used up all his own tobacco and had begun on what his brother had left.

'The doctor says it ain't so, sir,' said the man, looking at me shyly, as if he didn't expect to be believed; 'the doctor says there's as much eaten from breakfast to breakfast as there was before Jim fell overboard, though there's a mouth less and another that eats nothing. I says it's the cabin-boy that gets it. He's bu'sting.'

I told him that if the cabin-boy ate more than his share, he must work more than his share, so as to balance things. But the man laughed queerly, and looked at me again.

'I only said that, sir, just like that. We all know it ain't
so.'

'Well, how is it?'

'How is it?' asked the man, half angry all at once. 'I
don't know how it is, but there's a hand on board that's
getting his whack along with us as regular as the bells.'

'Does he use tobacco?' I asked, meaning to laugh it out
of him, but as I spoke I remembered the waterlogged pipe.

'I guess he's using his own still,' the man answered, in a
queer, low voice. 'Perhaps he'll take someone else's when
his is all gone.'

It was about nine o'clock in the morning, I remember,
for just then the captain called to me to stand by the chronometer while he took his fore observation. Captain Hackstaff wasn't one of those old skippers who do everything
themselves with a pocket watch, and keep the key of the
chronometer in their waistcoat pocket, and won't tell the
mate how far the dead reckoning is out. He was rather the
other way, and I was glad of it, for he generally let me
work the sights he took, and just ran his eye over my figures
afterwards. I am bound to say his eye was pretty good, for
he would pick out a mistake in logarithm, or tell me that
I had worked the 'Equation of Time' with the wrong sign,
before it seemed to me that he could have got as far as 'half
the sum, minus the altitude'. He was always right, too,
and besides he knew a lot about iron ships and local de-
viation, and adjusting the compass, and all that sort of
thing.

I don't know how he came to be in command of a fore-
and-aft schooner. He never talked about himself, and
maybe he had just been mate on one of those big steel
square-riggers, and something had put him back. Perhaps
he had been captain, and had got his ship aground, through
no particular fault of his, and had to begin over again.
Sometimes he talked just like you and me, and sometimes
he would speak more like books do, or some of those
Boston people I have heard. I don't know. We have all

been shipmates now and then with men who have seen
better days.

Perhaps he had been in the Navy, but what makes me
think he couldn't have been, was that he was a thorough
good seaman, a regular old wind-jammer, and understood
sail, which those Navy chaps rarely do. Why, you and I
have sailed with men before the mast who had their master's
certificates in their pockets—English Board of Trade certificates, too—who could work a double altitude if you
would lend them a sextant and give them a look at the
chronometer, as well as many a man who commands a big
square-rigger. Navigation ain't everything, nor seamanship
either. You've got to have it in you, if you mean to get
there.

I don't know how our captain heard that there was
trouble forward. The cabin-boy may have told him, or the
men may have talked outside his door when they relieved
the wheel at night. Anyhow, he got wind of it, and when
he had got his sight that morning he had all hands aft, and
gave them a lecture. It was just the kind of talk you might
have expected from him. He said he hadn't any complaint
to make, and that so far as he knew everybody on board
was doing his duty, and that he was given to understand
that the men got their whack, and were satisfied. He said
his ship was never a hard ship, and that he liked quiet,
and that was the reason he didn't mean to have any nonsense, and the men might just as well understand that
too. We'd had a great misfortune, he said, and it was nobody's fault. We had lost a man we all liked and respected,
and he felt that everybody in the ship ought to be sorry
for the man's brother, who was left behind, and that it
was rotten lubberly childishness, and unjust and unmanly
and cowardly, to be playing schoolboy tricks with forks
and spoons and pipes, and that sort of gear. He said it
had got to stop right now, and that was all, and the men
might go forward. And so they did.

It got worse after that, and the men watched the cook,
and the cook watched the men, as if they were trying to

catch each other; but I think everybody felt that there was something else. One evening, at supper-time, I was on deck, and Jack came aft to relieve the wheel while the man who was steering got his supper. He hadn't got past the main-hatch on the lee side, when I heard a man running in slippers that slapped on the deck, and there was a sort of a yell and I saw the coloured cook going for Jack, with a carving-knife in his hand. I jumped to get between them, and Jack turned round short, and put out his hand. I was too far to reach them, and the cook jabbed out with his knife. But the blade didn't get anywhere near Benton. The cook seemed to be jabbing it into the air again and again, at least four feet short of the mark. Then he dropped his right hand, and I saw the whites of his eyes in the dusk, and he reeled up against the pin-rail, and caught hold of a belaying-pin with his left. I had reached him by that time, and grabbed hold of his knife-hand and the other too, for I thought he was going to use the pin, but Jack Benton was standing staring stupidly at him as if he didn't understand. But instead, the cook was holding on because he couldn't stand, and his teeth were chattering, and he let go of the knife, and the point stuck into the deck.

'He's crazy!' said Jack Benton, and that was all he said; and he went aft.

When he was gone, the cook began to come to, and he spoke quite low, near my ear.

'There were two of them! So help me God, there were two of them!'

I don't know why I didn't take him by the collar and give him a good shaking; but I didn't. I just picked up the knife and gave it to him and told him to go back to his galley, and not to make a fool of himself. You see, he hadn't struck at Jack, but at something he thought he saw, and I knew what it was, and I felt that same thing, like a lump of ice sliding down my back, that I felt that night when we were bending the trysail.

When the men had seen him running aft, they jumped up after him, but they held off when they saw that I had

137

caught him. By and by, the man who had spoken to me before told me what had happened. He was a stocky little chap, with a red head.

'Well,' he said, 'there isn't much to tell. Jack Benton had been eating his supper with the rest of us. He always sits at the after corner of the table, on the port side. His brother used to sit at the end, next him. The doctor gave him a thundering big piece of pie to finish up with, and when he had finished he didn't stop for a smoke, but went off quick to relieve the wheel. Just as he had gone, the doctor came in from the galley, and when he saw Jack's empty plate he stood stock still staring at it; and we all wondered what was the matter, till we looked at the plate. There were two forks in it, sir, lying side by side. Then the doctor grabbed his knife, and flew up through the hatch like a rocket. The other fork was there all right, Mr. Torkeldsen, for we all saw it and handled it; and we all had our own. That's all I know.'

I didn't feel that I wanted to laugh when he told me that story; but I hoped the Old Man wouldn't hear it, for I knew he wouldn't believe it, and no captain that ever sailed likes to have stories like that going round about his ship. It gives her a bad name. But that was all anybody ever saw except the cook, and he isn't the first man who has thought he saw things without having any drink in him. I think, if the doctor had been weak in the head as he was afterwards, he might have done something foolish again, and there might have been serious trouble. But he didn't. Only, two or three times I saw him looking at Jack Benton in a queer, scared way, and once I heard him talking to himself.

'There's two of them! So help me God, there's two of them!'

He didn't say anything more about asking for his discharge, but I knew well enough that if he got ashore at the next port we should never see him again, if he had to leave his kit behind him, and his money too. He was scared all through, for good and all; and he wouldn't be right again

138

till he got another ship. It's no use to talk to a man when
he gets like that, any more than it is to send a boy to the
main truck when he has lost his nerve.

Jack Benton never spoke of what happened that evening. I don't know whether he knew about the two forks, or
not; or whether he understood what the trouble was. Whatever he knew from the other men, he was evidently living
under a hard strain. He was quiet enough, and too quiet;
but his face was set, and sometimes it twitched oddly when
he was at the wheel, and he would turn his head round
sharp to look behind him. A man doesn't do that naturally, unless there's a vessel that he thinks is creeping up on
the quarter. When that happens, if the man at the wheel
takes a pride in his ship, he will almost always keep glanc-
ing over his shoulder to see whether the other fellow is
gaining. But Jack Benton used to look round when there
was nothing there; and what is curious, the other men
seemed to catch the trick when they were steering. One day
the Old Man turned out just as the man at the wheel looked
behind him.

'What are you looking at?' asked the captain.

'Nothing, sir,' answered the man.

'Then keep your eye on the mizzen-royal,' said the
Old Man, as if he were forgetting that we weren't a square-
rigger.

'Ay, ay, sir,' said the man.

The captain told me to go below and work up the lati-
tude from the dead-reckoning, and he went forward of the
deck-house and sat down to read, as he often did. When I
came up, the man at the wheel was looking round again,
and I stood beside him and just asked him quietly what
everybody was looking at, for it was getting to be a general
habit. He wouldn't say anything at first, but just answered
that it was nothing. But when he saw that I didn't seem to
care, and just stood there as if there were nothing more to
be said, he naturally began to talk.

He said that it wasn't that he saw anything, because
there wasn't anything to see except the spanker sheet just

139

straining a little, and working in the sheaves of the blocks as the schooner rose to the short seas. There wasn't anything to be seen, but it seemed to him that the sheet made a queer noise in the blocks. It was a new manilla sheet; and in dry weather it did make a little noise, something between a creak and a wheeze. I looked at it and looked at the man, and said nothing; and presently he went on. He asked me if I didn't notice anything peculiar about the noise. I listened a while, and said I didn't notice anything. Then he looked rather sheepish, but said he didn't think it could be his own ears, because every man who steered his trick heard the same thing now and then— sometimes once in a day, sometimes once in a night, sometimes it would go on a whole hour.

'It sounds like sawing wood,' I said, just like that.

'To us it sounds a good deal more like a man whistling "Nancy Lee". He started nervously as he spoke the last words. 'There, sir, don't you hear it?' he asked suddenly.

I heard nothing but the creaking of the manilla sheet. It was getting near noon, and fine, clear weather in southern waters—just the sort of day and the time when you would least expect to feel creepy. But I remembered how I had heard that same tune overhead at night in a gale of wind a fortnight earlier, and I am not ashamed to say that the same sensation came over me now, and I wished myself well out of the *Helen B.*, and aboard of any old cargo-dragger, with a windmill on deck, and an eighty-nine forty-eighter for captain, and a fresh leak whenever it breezed up.

Little by little during the next few days, life on board that vessel came to be about as unbearable as you can imagine. It wasn't that there was much talk, for I think the men were shy even of speaking to each other freely about what they thought. The whole ship's company grew silent, until one hardly ever heard a voice, except giving an order and the answer. The men didn't sit over their meals when their watch was below, but either turned in at once or sat about on the forecastle smoking their pipes without saying a word. We were all thinking of the same thing. We all felt as if there were a hand on board, sometimes below, sometimes about decks, sometimes aloft, sometimes on the boom end; taking his full share of what the others got, but doing no work for it. We didn't only feel it, we knew it. He took up no room, he cast no shadow, and we never heard his footfall on deck; but he took his whack with the rest as regular as the bells, and—he whistled 'Nancy Lee'. It was like the worst sort of dream you can imagine; and I dare say a good many of us tried to believe it was nothing else sometimes, when we stood looking over the weather rail in fine weather with the breeze in our faces; but if we happened to turn round and look into each other's eyes, we knew it was something worse than any dream could be; and we would turn away from each other with a queer, sick feeling, wishing that we could just for once see somebody who didn't know what we knew.

There's not much more to tell about the *Helen B. Jackson* so far as I am concerned. We were more like a shipload of lunatics than anything else when we ran in under Morro Castle and anchored in Havana. The cook had brain fever, and was raving mad in his delirium; and the rest of the men weren't far from the same state. The last three or four days had been awful, and we had been as near to having a mutiny on board as I ever want to be. The men didn't want to hurt anybody; but they wanted to get away out of that ship, if they had to swim for it; to get away from that whistling, from that dead shipmate who had come back, and who filled the ship with his unseen self! I know that if the Old Man and I hadn't kept a sharp lookout the men would have put a boat over quietly on one of those calm nights, and pulled away, leaving the captain and me and the mad cook to work the schooner into harbour. We should have done it somehow, of course, for we hadn't far to run if we could get a breeze; and once or twice I found myself wishing that the crew were really gone, for the awful state of fright in which they lived was beginning to work on me too. You see, I partly believed

141

and partly didn't; but, anyhow, I didn't mean to let the thing get the better of me, whatever it was. I turned crusty, too, and kept the men at work on all sorts of jobs, and drove them to it until they wished I was overboard too. It wasn't that the Old Man and I were trying to drive them to desert without their pay, as I am sorry to say a good many skippers and mates do, even now.

Captain Hackstaff was as straight as a string, and I didn't mean those poor fellows should be cheated out of a single cent; and I didn't blame them for wanting to leave the ship, but it seemed to me that the only chance to keep everybody sane through those last days was to work the men till they dropped. When they were dead tired they slept a little, and forgot the thing until they had to tumble up on deck and face it again.

That was a good many years ago. Do you believe that I can't hear 'Nancy Lee' now without feeling cold down my back? For I heard it too, now and then, after the man had explained why he was always looking over his shoulder. Perhaps it was imagination. I don't know. When I look back it seems to me that I only remember a long fight against something I couldn't see, against an appalling presence, against something worse than cholera or yellow Jack or the plague—and, goodness knows, the mildest of them is bad enough when it breaks out at sea. The men got as white as chalk, and wouldn't go about decks alone at night, no matter what I said to them. With the cook raving in his bunk the forecastle would have been a perfect hell, and there wasn't a spare cabin on board. There never is on a fore-and-after. So I put him into mine, and he was more quiet there, and at last fell into a sort of stupor as if he were going to die. I don't know what became of him, for we put him ashore alive and left him in the hospital.

The men came aft in a body, quiet enough, and asked the captain if he wouldn't pay them off, and let them go ashore. Some men wouldn't have done it, for they had shipped for the voyage, and had signed articles. But the captain knew that when sailors get an idea into their heads they're no better than children; and if he forced them to stay aboard he wouldn't get much work out of them, and couldn't rely on them in a difficulty. So he paid them off, and let them go. When they had gone forward to get their kits, he asked me whether I wanted to go too, and for a minute I had a sort of weak feeling that I might just as well. But I didn't, and he was a good friend to me afterwards. Perhaps he was grateful to me for sticking to him.

When the men went off he didn't come on deck; but it was my duty to stand by while they left the ship. They owed me a grudge for making them work during the last few days, and most of them dropped into the boat without so much as a word or a look, as sailors will. Jack Benton was the last to go over the side, and he stood still a minute and looked at me, and his white face twitched. I thought he wanted to say something.

'Take care of yourself, Jack,' said I. 'So long!'

It seemed as if he couldn't speak for two or three seconds; then his words came thick.

'It wasn't my fault, Mr. Torkeldsen. I swear it wasn't my fault!'

That was all; and he dropped over the side, leaving me to wonder what he meant.

The captain and I stayed on board, and the ship-chandler got a West India boy to cook for us.

That evening, before turning in, we were standing by the rail having a quiet smoke, watching the lights of the city, a quarter of a mile off, reflected in the still water. There was music of some sort ashore, in a sailors' dance-house, I dare say; and I had no doubt that most of the men who had left the ship were there, and already full of jiggy-jiggy. The music played a lot of sailors' tunes that ran into each other, and we could hear the men's voices in the chorus now and then. One followed another, and then it was 'Nancy Lee' loud and clear, and the men singing 'Yo-ho, heave-ho!'

'I have no ear for music,' said Captain Hackstaff, 'but it appears to me that's the tune that man was whistling the night we lost the man overboard. I don't know why it has stuck in my head, and of course it's all nonsense: but it seems to me that I have heard it all the rest of the trip.'

I didn't say anything to that, but I wondered just how much the Old Man had understood. Then we turned in, and I slept ten hours without opening my eyes.

I stuck to the *Helen B. Jackson* after that as long as I could stand a fore-and-after; but that night when we lay in Havana was the last time I ever heard 'Nancy Lee' on board of her. The spare hand had gone ashore with the rest, and he never came back, and he took his tune with him, but all those things are just as clear in my memory as if they had happened yesterday.

After that I was in deep water for a year or more, and after I came home I got my certificate, and what with having friends and having saved a little money, and having had a small legacy from an uncle in Norway, I got the command of a coastwise vessel, with a small share in her. I was at home three weeks before going to sea, and Jack Benton saw my name in the local papers, and wrote to me.

He said that he had left the sea, and was trying farming, and he was going to be married, and he asked if I wouldn't come over for that, for it wasn't more than forty minutes by train; and he and Mamie would be proud to have me at the wedding. I remembered how I had heard one brother ask the other whether Mamie knew. That meant, whether she knew he wanted to marry her, I suppose. She had taken her time about it, for it was pretty nearly three years then since we had lost Jim Benton overboard.

I had nothing particular to do while we were getting ready for sea; nothing to prevent me from going over for a day, I mean; and I thought I'd like to see Jack Benton, and have a look at the girl he was going to marry. I wondered whether he had grown cheerful again, and had got rid of that drawn look he had when he told me it wasn't his fault. How could it have been his fault, anyhow? So I wrote to Jack that I would come down and see him married; and when the day came I took the train, and got there about

ten o'clock in the morning. I wish I hadn't. Jack met me at
the station, and he told me that the wedding was to be late
in the afternoon, and that they weren't going off on any silly
wedding trip, he and Mamie, but were just going to walk
home from her mother's house to his cottage. That was
good enough for him, he said. I looked at him hard for a
minute after we met. When we had parted I had a sort
of idea that he might take to drink, but he hadn't. He
looked very respectable and well-to-do in his black coat
and high city collar; but he was thinner and bonier than
when I had known him, and there were lines in his face, and
I thought his eyes had a queer look in them, half shifty,
half scared. He needn't have been afraid of me, for I didn't
mean to talk to his bride about the *Helen B. Jackson*.

He took me to his cottage first, and I could see that he
was proud of it. It wasn't above a cable's-length from high-
water mark, but the tide was running out, and there was
already a broad stretch of hard, wet sand on the other side
of the beach road. Jack's bit of land ran back behind the
cottage about a quarter of a mile, and he said that some of
the trees we saw were his. The fences were neat and well
kept, and there was a fair-sized barn a little way from the
cottage, and I saw some nice-looking cattle in the meadows; but it didn't look to me to be much of a farm, and I
thought that before long Jack would have to leave his wife
to take care of it and go to sea again. But I said it was a
nice farm, so as to seem pleasant, and as I don't know
much about these things I dare say it was, all the same. I
never saw it but that once. Jack told me that he and his
brother had been born in the cottage, and that when their
father and mother died they leased the land to Mamie's
father, but had kept the cottage to live in when they came
home from sea for a spell.

It was as neat a little place as you would care to see: the
floors as clean as the decks of a yacht, and the paint as
fresh as a man-o'-war. Jack always was a good painter.
There was a nice parlour on the ground floor, and Jack
had papered it and had hung the walls with photographs

145

of ships and foreign ports, and with things he had brought
home from his voyages: a boomerang, a South Sea club,
Japanese straw hats, and a Gibraltar fan with a bull-
fight on it, and all that sort of gear. It looked to me as if
Miss Mamie had taken a hand in arranging it. There was a
brand-new polished iron Franklin stove set into the old
fireplace, and a red table-cloth from Alexandria embroidered with those outlandish Egyptian letters.

It was all as bright and homelike as possible, and he
showed me everything, and was proud of everything, and
I liked him the better for it. But I wished that his voice
would sound more cheerful, as it did when we first sailed in
the *Helen B.*, and that the drawn look would go out of his
face for a minute. Jack showed me everything, and took
me upstairs, and it was all the same: bright and fresh and
ready for the bride. But on the upper landing there was a
door that Jack didn't open. When we came out of the bedroom I noticed that it was ajar, and Jack shut it quickly
and turned the key.

'That lock's no good,' he said, half to himself. 'The
door is always open.'

I didn't pay much attention to what he said, but as we
went down the short stairs, freshly painted and varnished
so that I was almost afraid to step on them, he spoke again.

'That was his room, sir. I have made a sort of store-
room of it.'

'You may be wanting it in a year or so,' I said, wishing
be pleasant.

'I guess we won't use his room for that.' Jack answered
in a low voice.

Then he offered me a cigar from a fresh box in the parlour, and he took one, and we lit them, and went out; and
as we opened the front door there was Mamie Brewster
standing in the path as if she were waiting for us. She was a
fine-looking girl, and I didn't wonder that Jack had been
willing to wait three years for her. I could see that she
hadn't been brought up on steam heat and cold storage,

but had grown into a woman by the seashore. She had brown eyes and fine brown hair and a good figure.

'This is Captain Torkeldsen,' said Jack. 'This is Miss Brewster, Captain, and she is glad to see you.'

'Well, I am,' said Miss Mamie, 'for Jack has often talked to us about you, Captain.'

She put out her hand and took mine and shook it heartily, and I suppose I said something, but I didn't say much.

The front door to the cottage looked towards the sea, and there was a straight path leading to the gate on the beach road. There was another path from the steps of the cottage that turned to the right, broad enough for two people to walk easily, and it led straight across the fields through gates to a larger house about a quarter of a mile away. That was where Mamie's mother lived, and the wedding was to be there. Jack asked me whether I would like to look round the farm before dinner, but I told him I didn't know much about farms. Then he said he just wanted to look round himself a bit, as he mightn't have much more chance that day, and he smiled and Mamie laughed.

'Show the captain the way to the house, Mamie,' he said. 'I'll be along in a minute.'

So Mamie and I began to walk along the path and Jack went up towards the barn.

'It was sweet of you to come, Captain,' Miss Mamie began, 'for I have always wanted to see you.'

'Yes,' I said, expecting something more.

'You see, I always knew them both,' she went on. 'They used to take me out in a dory to catch cod-fish when I was a little girl, and I liked them both,' she added thoughtfully. 'Jack doesn't care to talk about his brother now. That's natural. But you won't mind telling me how it happened, will you? I should so much like to know.'

Well, I told her about the voyage and what happened that night when we fell in with a gale of wind, and that it hadn't been anybody's fault, for I wasn't going to admit that it was my old captain's, if it was. But I didn't tell her anything about what happened afterwards. As she didn't speak, I just went on talking about the two brothers, and how alike they had been and how when poor Jim was drowned and Jack left, I took Jack for him. I told her that none of us had ever been sure which was which.

'I wasn't always sure myself,' she said, 'unless they were together. Leastways, not for a day or two after they came home from sea. And now it seems to me that Jack is more like poor Jim, as I remembered him, than he ever was, for Jim was always more quiet, as if he were thinking.'

I told her I thought so, too. We passed the gate and went into the next field, walking side by side. Then she turned her head to look for Jack, but he wasn't in sight. I shan't forget what she said next.

'Are you sure now?' she asked.

I stood stock-still and she went on a step, and then turned and looked at me. We must have looked at each other while you could count five or six.

'I know it's silly,' she went on, 'it's silly and it's awful, too, and I have got no right to think it, but sometimes I can't help it. You see, it was always Jack I meant to marry.'

'Yes,' I said stupidly, 'I suppose so.'

She waited a minute and began walking on slowly before she went on again.

'I am talking to you as if you were an old friend, Captain, and I have only known you five minutes. It was Jack I meant to marry, but now he is so like the other one.'

When a woman gets a wrong idea into her head there is only one way to make her tired of it, and that is to agree with her. That's what I did, and she went on talking the same way for a little while and I kept on agreeing and agreeing until she turned round on me.

'You know you don't believe what you say,' she said, and laughed. 'You know that Jack is Jack, right enough, and it's Jack I am going to marry.'

Of course I said so, for I didn't care whether she thought me a weak creature or not. I wasn't going to say a word that could interfere with her happiness, and I didn't intend to go back on Jack Benton; but I remembered what he had said when he left the ship in Havana: that it wasn't his fault.

'All the same,' Miss Mamie went on, as a woman will, without realising what she was saying, 'all the same, I wish I had seen it happen. Then I should know.'

Next minute she knew that she didn't mean that and was afraid that I would think her heartless, and began to explain that she would really rather have died herself than have seen poor Jim go overboard. Women haven't got much sense anyhow. All the same, I wondered how she could marry Jack if she had a doubt that he might be Jim after all. I suppose she had really got used to him since he had given up the sea and had stayed ashore, and she cared for him.

Before long we heard Jack coming up behind us, for we had walked very slowly to wait for him.

'Promise not to tell anybody what I said, Captain,' said Mamie, as girls do as soon as they have told their secrets.

Anyhow, I know I never did tell anyone but you. This is the first time I have talked of all that, the first time since I took the train from that place. I am not going to tell you all about the day. Miss Mamie introduced me to her mother, who was a quiet, hard-faced old New England farmer's widow, and to her cousins and relations, and there were plenty of them, too, at dinner, and there was the parson besides. He was what they call a Hard-shell Baptist in those parts, with a long, shaven upper lip and a whacking appetite, and a sort of superior look, as if he didn't expect to see many of us hereafter—the way a New York pilot looks round and orders things about when he boards an Italian cargo-dragger, as if the ship weren't up to much anyway, though it was his business to see that she didn't get aground. That's the way a good many parsons look, I think. He said grace as if he were ordering the men to sheet home the top-gallant-sail and get the helm up.

After dinner we went out on the piazza, for it was warm autumn weather, and the young folks went off in pairs along the beach road, and the tide had turned and was beginning to come in. The morning had been clear and fine, but by four o'clock it began to look like a fog, and the damp came up out of the sea and settled on everything. Jack said he's go down to his cottage and have a last look, for the wedding was to be at five o'clock, or soon after, and he wanted to light the lights, so as to have things look cheerful.

'I will just take a last look,' he said again, as we reached the house. We went in and he offered me another cigar, and I lit it and sat down in the parlour. I could hear him moving about, first in the kitchen and then upstairs, and then I heard him in the kitchen again, and then before I knew anything I heard somebody moving upstairs again. I knew he couldn't have got up those stairs as quick as that. He came into the parlour and he took a cigar himself and, while he was lighting it, I heard those steps again overhead. His hand shook and he dropped the match.

'Have you got in somebody to help?' I asked.

'No,' Jack answered sharply, and struck another match.

'There's somebody upstairs, Jack,' I said. 'Don't you hear footsteps?'

'It's the wind, Captain,' Jack answered, but I could see he was trembling.

'That isn't any wind, Jack,' I said; 'it's still and foggy. I'm sure there's somebody upstairs.'

'If you are so sure of it, you'd better go and see for yourself, Captain,' Jack answered, almost angrily.

He was angry because he was frightened. I left him before the fireplace and went upstairs. There was no power on earth that could make me believe I hadn't heard a man's footsteps overhead. I knew there was somebody there. But there wasn't. I went into the bedroom and it was all quiet, and the evening light was streaming in, reddish through the foggy air, and I went out on the landing and looked in the little back room that was meant for a servant-girl or a child. And as I came back again I saw that the door of the other room was wide open, though I knew Jack had locked it. He had said the lock was no good.

I looked in. It was a room as big as the bedroom, but almost dark, for it had shutters and they were closed.

There was a musty smell, as of old gear, and I could make out that the floor was littered with sea-chests and that there were oilskins and such stuff piled on the bed. But I still believed that there was somebody upstairs, and I went in and struck a match and looked round. I could see the four walls and the shabby old paper, an iron bed and a cracked looking-glass, and the stuff on the floor. But there was nobody there. So I put out the match and came out and shut the door and turned the key. Now, what I am telling you is the truth. When I had turned the key, I heard footsteps walking away from the door inside the room. Then I felt queer for a minute and when I went downstairs I looked behind me, as the men at the wheel used to look behind them on board the *Helen B.*

Jack was already outside on the steps, smoking. I have an idea that he didn't like to stay inside alone.

'Well?' he asked, trying to seem careless.

'I didn't find anybody,' I answered, 'but I heard somebody moving about.'

'I told you it was the wind,' said Jack contemptuously. 'I ought to know, for I live here and I hear it often.'

There was nothing to be said to that, so we began to walk down towards the beach. Jack said there wasn't any hurry, as it would take Miss Mamie some time to dress for the wedding. So we strolled along and the sun was setting through the fog, and the tide was coming in. I knew the moon was full, and that when she rose the fog would roll away from the land, as it does sometimes. I felt that Jack didn't like my having heard that noise, so I talked of other things and asked him about his prospects, and before long we were chatting as pleasantly as possible.

I haven't been at many weddings in my life and I don't suppose you have, but that one seemed to me to be all right until it was pretty near over, and then, I don't know whether it was part of the ceremony or not, but Jack put out his hand and took Mamie's and held it a minute and looked at her, while the parson was still speaking.

Mamie turned as white as a sheet and screamed. It wasn't a loud scream, but just a sort of stifled little shriek, as if she were half frightened to death, and the parson stopped and asked her what was the matter, and the family gathered round.

'Your hand's like ice,' said Mamie to Jack, 'and it's all wet!'

She kept looking at it, as she got hold of herself again.

'It don't feel cold to me,' said Jack, and he held the back of his hand against his cheek. 'Try it again.'

Mamie held out hers and touched the back of his hand, timidly at first, and then took hold of it.

'Why, that's funny,' she said.

'She's been as nervous as a witch all day,' said Mrs. Brewster severely.

'It is natural,' said the parson, 'that young Mrs. Benton should experience a little agitation at such a moment.'

Most of the bride's relations lived at a distance and were busy people, so it had been arranged that the dinner we'd had in the middle of the day was to take the place of a dinner afterwards, and that we should just have a bite after the wedding was over, and then that everybody should go home, and the young couple would walk down to the cottage by themselves. When I looked out I could see the light burning brightly in Jack's cottage, a quarter of a mile away. I said I didn't think I could get any train to take me back before half past nine, but Mrs. Brewster begged me to stay until it was time, as she said her daughter would want to take off her wedding-dress before she went home, for she had put on something white with a wreath, that was very pretty, and she couldn't walk home like that, could she?

So when we had all had a little supper the party began to break up, and when they were all gone Mrs. Brewster and Mamie went upstairs, and Jack and I went on the piazza to have a smoke, as the old lady didn't like tobacco in the house.

The full moon had risen now and it was behind me as I looked down towards Jack's cottage, so that everything was clear and white, and there was only the light burning in the window. The fog had rolled down to the water's edge and a little beyond, for the tide was high, or nearly, and was lapping up over the last reach of sand within fifty feet of the beach road.

Jack didn't say much as we sat smoking, but he thanked me for coming to his wedding, and I told him I hoped he would be happy, and so I did. I dare say both of us were thinking of those footsteps upstairs just then, and that the house wouldn't seem so lonely with a woman in it. By and by we heard Mamie's voice talking to her mother on the stairs, and in a minute she was ready to go. She had put on again the dress she had worn in the morning.

Well, they were ready to go now. It was all very quiet after the day's excitement, and I knew they would like to walk down that path alone now that they were man and wife at last. I bade them good night, although Jack made a show of pressing me to go with them by the path as far as the cottage, instead of going to the station by the beach road. It was all very quiet, and it seemed to me a sensible way of getting married, and when Mamie kissed her mother good night I just looked the other way, and knocked my ashes over the rail of the piazza. So they started down the straight path to Jack's cottage, and I waited a minute with Mrs. Brewster, looking after them, before taking my hat to go. They walked side by side, a little shyly at first, and then I saw Jack put his arm round her waist. As I looked he was on her left and I saw the outline of the two figures very distinctly against the moonlight on the path, and the shadow on Mamie's right was broad and black as ink, and it moved along, lengthening and shortening with the unevenness of the ground beside the path.

I thanked Mrs. Brewster and bade her good night, and though she was a hard New England woman her voice trembled a little as she answered, but being a sensible person she went in and shut the door behind her as I stepped out on the path. I looked after the couple in the distance a last time, meaning to go down to the road, so as not to overtake them; but when I had made a few steps I stopped and looked again, for I knew I had seen something queer, though I had only realised it afterwards. I looked again, and it was plain enough now, and I stood stock-still, staring at what I saw. Mamie was walking between two men. The second man was just the same height as Jack, both being about a half a head taller than she; Jack on her left in his black tail-coat and round hat, and the other man on her right—well, he was a sailor-man in wet oilskins. I could see the moonlight shining on the water than ran down him, and on the little puddle that had settled where the flap of his sou'wester was turned up behind—and one of his wet shiny arms was round Mamie's waist, just above Jack's. I was fast to the spot where I stood, and for a minute I thought I was crazy. We'd had nothing but some cider for dinner and tea in the evening, otherwise I'd have thought something had got into my head, though I was never drunk in my life. It was more like a bad dream after that.

I was glad Mrs. Brewster had gone in. As for me, I couldn't help following the three, in a sort of wonder to see what would happen, to see whether the sailor-man in his wet togs would just melt away into the moonshine. But he didn't.

I moved slowly, and I remembered afterwards that I walked on the grass, instead of on the path, as if I were afraid they might hear me coming. I suppose it all happened in less than five minutes after that, but it seemed as if it must have taken an hour. Neither Jack nor Mamie seemed to notice the sailor. She didn't seem to know that his wet arm was round her, and little by little they got near the cotage, and I wasn't a hundred yards from them when they reached the door. Something made me stand still then. Perhaps it was fright, for I saw everything that happened just as I see you now.

Mamie set her foot on the step to go up, and as she went forward I saw the sailor slowly lock his arm in Jack's, and Jack didn't move to go up. Then Mamie turned round on the step, and they all three stood that way for a second or two. She cried out then—I heard a man cry like that once, when his arm was taken off by a steam-crane—and she fell back in a heap on the little piazza.

I tried to jump forward, but I couldn't move, and I felt my hair rising under my hat. The sailor turned slowly where he stood, and swung Jack round by the arm steadily and easily, and began to walk him down the pathway from the house. He walked him straight down that path, as steadily as Fate, and all the time I saw the moonlight shining on his wet oilskins. He walked him through the gate and across the beach road and out upon the wet sand, where the tide was high. Then I got my breath with a gulp and ran for them across the grass and vaulted over the fence and stumbled across the road. But when I felt the sand under my feet, the two were at the water's edge; and when I reached the water they were far out and up to their waists; and I saw that Jack Benton's head had fallen forward on his breast, and his free arm hung limp beside him, while his dead brother steadily marched him to his death. The moonlight was on the dark water, but the fog-bank was white beyond, and I saw them against it, and they went slowly and steadily down. The water was up to their armpits and then up to their shoulders, and then I saw it rise up to the black rim of Jack's hat. But they never wavered; and the two heads went straight on, straight on, till they were under, and there was just a ripple in the moonlight where Jack had been.

It has been on my mind to tell you that story, whenever I got a chance. You have known me, man and boy, a good many years, and I thought I would like to hear your opinion. Yes, that's what I always thought. It wasn't Jim that went overboard, it was Jack, and Jim just let him go when he might have saved him; and then Jim passed himself off for Jack with us, and with the girl. If that's what hap-

155

pened, he got what he deserved. People said the next day that Mamie found it out as they reached the house, and that her husband just walked out into the sea and drowned himself—and they would have blamed me for not stopping him if they'd known that I was there. But I never told what I had seen, for they wouldn't have believed me. I just let them think I had come too late.

When I reached the cottage and lifted Mamie up, she was raving mad. She got better afterwards, but she was never right in her head again.

Oh, you want to know if they found Jack's body? I don't know whether it was his, but I read in a paper at a Southern port where I was with my new ship that two dead bodies had come ashore in a gale down East, in pretty bad shape. They were locked together, and one was a skeleton in oilskins.

E. F. BENSON

Expiation

PHILIP STUART and I, unattached and middle-aged persons, had for the last four or five years been accustomed to spend a month or six weeks together in the summer, taking a furnished house in some part of the country, which, by an absence of attractive pursuits, was not likely to be overrun by gregarious holiday-makers. When, as the season for getting out of London draws near, and we scan the advertisement columns which set forth the charms and the cheapness of residences to be let for August, and see the mention of tennis-clubs and esplanades and admirable golf-links within a stone's throw of the proposed front door, our offended and disgusted eyes instantly wander to the next item.

For the point of a holiday, according to our private heresy, is not to be entertained and occupied and jostled by glad crowds, but to have nothing to do, and no temptation which might lead to any unseasonable activity. London has held employments and diversion enough; we want to be without both. But vicinity to the sea is desirable, because it is easier to do nothing by the sea than anywhere else, and because bathing and basking on the shore cannot be considered an employment but only an apotheosis of loafing. A garden also is a requisite, for that tranquillises any fidgety notion of going for a walk.

In pursuance of this sensible policy we had this year taken a house on the south coast of Cornwall, for a re- laxing climate conduces to laziness. It was too far off for us to make any personal inspection of it, but a perusal of the modestly worded advertisement carried conviction.

It was close to the sea; the village Polwithy, outside which it was situated, was remote and, as far as we knew, unknown; it had a garden; and there was attached to it a cook-housekeeper who made for simplification. No mention of golf-links or attractive resorts in the neighbourhood defiled the bald and terse specification, and though there was a tennis-court in the garden, there was no clause that bound the tenants to use it. The owner was a Mrs. Herne, who had been living abroad, and our business was transacted with a house-agent in Falmouth.

To make our household complete, Philip sent down a parlour-maid and I a housemaid, and after leaving them a day in which to settle in, we followed. There was a six miles drive from the station across high uplands, and at the end a long steady descent into a narrow valley, cloven between the hills, that grew ever more luxuriant in verdure as we descended. Great trees of fuchsia spread up to the eaves of the thatched cottages which stood by the wayside, and a stream, embowered in green thickets, ran babbling through the centre of it. Presently we came to the village, no more than a dozen houses, built of the grey stone of the district, and on a shelf just above it a tiny church with parsonage adjoining. High above us now flamed the gorse-clad slopes of the hills on each side, and now the valley opened out at its lower end, and the still, warm air was spiced and renovated by the breeze that drew up it from the sea. Then round a sharp angle of the road we came alongside a stretch of brick wall, and stopped at an iron gate above which flowed a riot of rambler rose.

It seemed hardly credible that it was this of which that terse and laconic advertisement had spoken. I had pictured something of villa-ish kind, yellow bricked, perhaps, with a roof of purplish slate, a sitting-room one side of the entrance, a dining-room the other; with a tiled hall and a pitch-pine staircase, and instead, here was this little gem of an early Georgian manor-house, mellow and gracious, with mullioned windows and a roof of stone slabs. In front of it was a paved terrace, below which blossomed a herbaceous border, tangled and tropical, with no inch of earth visible through its luxuriance. Inside, too, was fulfilment of this fair exterior: a broad-balustered staircase led up from the odiously entitled 'lounge hall', which I had pictured as a medley of Benares ware and saddle-bagged sofas, but which proved to be cool, broad, and panelled, with a door opposite that through which we entered, leading on to the farther area of garden at the back.

There was the advertised but innocuous tennis-court, bordered on the length of its far side by a steep grass bank, along which was planted a row of limes, once pollarded, but now allowed to develop at will. Thick boughs, some fourteen or fifteen feet from the ground, interlaced with one another, forming an arcaded row; above them, where Nature had been permitted to go her own way, the trees broke into feathered and honey-scented branches. Beyond lay a small orchard climbing upwards, above that the hillside rose more steeply, in broad spaces of short-cropped turf and ablaze with gorse, the Cornish gorse that flowers all the year round, and spreads its sunshine from January to December.

There was time for a stroll through this perfect little domain before dinner, and for a short interview with the housekeeper, a quiet, capable-looking woman, slightly aloof—as is the habit of her race—from strangers and foreigners, for so the Cornish account the English, but who proved herself at the repast that followed to be as capable as she appeared. The evening closed in hot and still, and after dinner we took chairs out on to the terrace in front of the house.

'Far the best place we've struck yet,' observed Philip. 'Why did not one say Polwithy before?'

'Because nobody had ever heard of it, luckily,' said I.

'Well, I'm a Polwithian. At least I am in spirit. But how aware Mrs.—Mrs. Criddle made me feel that I wasn't really.'

Philip's profession, a doctor of obscure nervous diseases, has made him preternaturally acute in the diagnosis of

E. F. BENSON

what other people feel, and for some reason, quite undefined, I wanted to know what exactly he meant by this. I was in sympathy with his feeling, but I could not analyse it.

'Describe your symptoms,' I said.

'I have. When she came up and talked to us, and hoped we should be comfortable, and told us that she would do her best, she was just gossiping. Probably it was perfectly true gossip. But it wasn't she. However, as that's all that matters, there's no reasons why we should probe further.'

'Which means that you have,' I said.

'No; it means that I tried to and couldn't. She gave me an extraordinary sense of her being aware of something which we knew nothing of; of being on a plane which we couldn't imagine. I constantly meet such people; they aren't very rare. I don't mean that there's anything the least uncanny about them, or that they know things that are uncanny. They are simply aloof, as hard to understand as your dog or your cat. She would find us equally aloof if she succeeded in analysing her sensations about us, but like a sensible woman she probably feels not the smallest interest in us. She is there to bake and to boil, and we are there to eat her bakings and appreciate her boilings.'

The subject dropped, and we sat on in the dusk that was rapidly deepening into night. The door into the hall was open at our backs, and a panel of light from the lamps within was cast out on to the terrace. Wandering moths, invisible in the darkness, suddenly became manifest as they fluttered into this illumination, and vanished again as they passed out of it. One moment they were there, living things with life and motion of their own, the next they had quite disappeared. How inexplicable that would be, I thought, if one did not know from long familiarity, that light of the appropriate sort and strength is needed to make material objects visible.

Philip must have been following precisely the same train of thought, for his voice broke in, carrying it a little further.

'Look at that moth,' he said, 'and even while you look

160

it has gone like a ghost, even as like a ghost it appeared. Light made it visible. And there are other sorts of light, interior psychical light which similarly makes visible the beings which people the darkness of our blindness.'

Just as he spoke I thought for the moment that I heard the tinkle of a telephone bell. It sounded very faintly, and I could not have sworn that I had actually heard it. At the most it gave one staccato little summons and was silent again.

'Is there a telephone in the house?' I asked. 'I haven't noticed one.'

'Yes, by the door into the back garden,' said he. 'Do you want to telephone?'

'No, but I thought I heard it ring. Didn't you?'

He shook his head; then smiled.

'Ah, that was it,' he said.

Certainly now there was the clink of glass, rather bell-like, as the parlour-maid came out of the dining-room with a tray of syphon and decanter, and my reasonable mind was quite content to accept this very probable explanation. But behind that, quite unreasonably, some little obstinate denizen of my consciousness rejected it. It told me that what I had heard was like the moth that came out of darkness and went on into darkness again. . . .

My room was at the back of the house, overlooking the lawn-tennis court, and presently I went up to bed. The moon had risen, and the lawn lay in bright illumination. bordered by a strip of dark shadow below the pollarded limes. Somewhere along the hillside an owl was foraging, softly hooting, and presently it swept whitely across the lawn. No sound is so intensely rural, yet none, to my mind, so suggests a signal. But it seemed to signal nothing, and, tired with the long hot journey, and soothed by the deep tranquillity of the place, I was soon asleep. But often during the night I woke, though never to more than a doz-ing dreamy consciousness of where I was, and each time I had the notion that some slight noise had roused me, and each time I found myself listening to hear whether

161

the tinkle of a telephone bell was the cause of my disturbance. There came no repetition of it, and again I slept, and again I woke with drowsy attention for the sound which I felt I expected, but never heard.

Daylight banished these imaginations, but though I must have slept many hours all told, for these wakings had been only brief and partial, I was aware of a certain weariness, as if though my bodily senses had been rested, some part of me had been wakeful and watching all night. This was fanciful enough to disregard, and certainly during the day I forgot it altogether.

Soon after breakfast we went down to the sea, and a short ramble along a shingly shore brought us to a sandy cove framed in promontories of rock that went down into deep water. The most fastidious connoisseur in bathing could have pictured no more ideal scene for his operations, for with hot sand to bask on and rocks to plunge from, and a limpid ocean and a cloudless sky, there was indeed no lacuna in perfection.

All morning we loafed here, swimming and sunning ourselves, and for the afternoon there was the shade of the garden, and a stroll later on up through the orchard and to the gorse-clad hillside. We came back through the churchyard, looked into the church, and coming out, Philip pointed to a tombstone which, from its newness among its dusky and moss-grown companions, easily struck the eye. It recorded, without pious or scriptural reflection, the date of the birth and death of George Hearne; the latter event had taken place close on two years ago, and we were within a week of the exact anniversary. Other tombstones near were monuments to those of the same name, and dated back for a couple of centuries and more.

'Local family,' said I, and strolling on we came to our own gate in the long brick wall. It was opened from inside just as we arrived at it, and there came out a brisk, middle-aged man in clergyman's dress, obviously our vicar.

He very civilly introduced himself.

'I heard that Mrs. Hearne's house had been taken and

that the tenants had come,' he said, 'and I ventured to leave my card.'

We performed our part of the ceremony, and in answer to his inquiry professed our satisfaction with our quarters and our neighbourhood.

'That is good news,' said Mr. Stephens, 'I hope you will continue to enjoy your holiday. I am Cornish myself, and like all natives think there is no place like Cornwall!'

Philip pointed with his stick towards the churchyard. 'We noticed that the Hearnes are people of the place,' he said. Quite suddenly I found myself understanding what he had meant by the aloofness of the race. Something between reserve and suspicion came into Mr. Stephens' face.

'Yes, yes, an old family here,' he said; 'and large land-owners. But now some remote cousin . . . The house, however, belongs to Mrs. Hearne for life.'

He stopped, and by that reticence confirmed the impression he had made. In consequence, for there is something in the breast of the most incurious, which, when treated with reserve, becomes inquisitive, Philip proceeded to ask a direct question.

'Then I take it that the George Hearne who, as I have just seen, died two years ago, was the husband of Mrs. Hearne, from whom we took the house?'

'Yes, he was buried in the churchyard,' said Mr. Stephens quickly. Then, for no reason at all, he added:

'Naturally he was buried in the churchyard here.'

Now my impression at that moment was that Mr. Stephens had said something he did not mean to say, and had corrected it by saying the same thing again. He went on his way, back to the vicarage, with an amiably expressed desire to do anything that was in his power for us in the way of local information, and we went in through the gate. The post had just arrived; there was the London morning paper and a letter for Philip which cost him two perusals before he folded it up and put it into his pocket. But he made no comment, and presently, as dinner-time was near, I went up to my room.

Here in this deep valley, with the great westerly hill towering above us, it was already dark, and the lawn lay beneath a twilight as of deep clear water. Quite idly as I brushed my hair in front of the glass on the table in the window, of which the blinds were not yet drawn, I looked out, and saw that on the bank along which grew the pollarded limes, there was a ladder. It was just a shade odd that it should be there, but the oddity of it was quite accounted for by the supposition that the gardener had had business among the trees in the orchard, and had left it there for the completion of his labours tomorrow. It was just as odd as that, and no odder, just worth a twitch of the imagination to account for it, but now completely accounted for.

I went downstairs, and passing Philip's door heard the swish of ablutions, which implied he was not quite ready, and in the most loafer-like manner I strolled round the corner of the house. The kitchen window which looked on to the tennis-court was open, and there was a good smell, I remember, coming from it. And still without thought of the ladder I had just seen, I mounted the slope of the grass on to the tennis-court. Just across it was the bank where the pollarded limes grew, but there was no ladder lying there. Of course, the gardener must have remembered he had left it, and had returned to remove it exactly as I came downstairs. There was nothing singular about that, and I could not imagine why the thing interested me at all. But for some inexplicable reason I found myself saying: 'But I did see the ladder just now.'

A bell—no telephone bell, but a welcome harbinger to a hungry man—sounded from inside the house, and I went back on to the terrace, just as Philip got downstairs. At dinner our speech rambled pleasantly over the accomplishments of today, and the prospects of tomorrow, and in due course we came to the consideration of Mr. Stephens. We settled that he was an aloof fellow, and then Philip said:

'I wonder why he hastened to tell us that George Hearne

was buried in the churchyard, and then added that naturally he was!'

'It's the natural place to be buried in,' said I.

'Quite. That's just why it was hardly worth mentioning.'

I felt then, just momentarily, just vaguely, as if my mind was regarding stray pieces of a jig-saw puzzle. The fancied ringing of the telephone bell last night was one of them, this burial of George Hearne in the churchyard was another, and, even more inexplicably, the ladder I had seen under the trees was a third. Consciously I made nothing whatever out of them, and did not feel the least inclination to devote any ingenuity to so fortuitous a collection of pieces. Why shouldn't I add, for that matter, our morning's bathe, or the gorse on the hillside? But I had the sensation that, though my conscious brain was presently occupied with piquet, and was rapidly growing sleepy with the day of sun and sea, some sort of mole inside it was digging passages and connecting corridors below the soil.

Five eventless days succeeded, there were no more ladders, no more phantom telephone bells, and emphatically no more Mr. Stephens. Once or twice we met him in the village street and got from him the curtest salutation possible short of a direct cut. And yet somehow he seemed charged with information, so we lazily concluded, and he made for us a field of imaginative speculation. I remembered that I constructed a highly fanciful romance, which postulated that George Hearne was not dead at all, but that Mr. Stephens had murdered some inconvenient blackmailer, whom he had buried with the rites of the church. Or—these romances always broke down under cross-examination from Philip—Mr. Stephens himself was George Hearne, who had fled from justice, and was supposed to have died. Or Mrs. Hearne was really George Hearne, and our admirable housekeeper was the real Mrs. Hearne. From such indications you may judge how the intoxication of the sun and the sea had overpowered us.

But there was one explanation of why Mr. Stephens had so hastily assured us that George Hearne was buried in the churchyard, which never passed our lips. It was just because Philip and I really believed it to be the true one that we did not mention it. But just as if it were some fever or plague, we both knew that we were sickening with it. And then these fanciful romances stopped because we knew that the Real Thing was approaching. There had been faint glimpses of it before, like distant sheet-lightning; now the noise of it, authentic and audible, began to rumble.

There came a day of hot, overclouded weather. We had bathed in the morning, and loafed in the afternoon, but Philip, after tea, had refused to come for our usual ramble, and I set out alone. That morning Mrs. Criddle had rather peremptorily told me that a room in the front of the house would prove much cooler for me, for it caught the sea-breeze, and though I objected that it would also catch the southerly sun, she had clearly made up her mind that I was to move from the bedroom overlooking the tennis-court and the pollarded limes, and there was no resisting so polite and yet determined a woman.

When I set out for my ramble after tea, the change had already been effected, and my brain nosed slowly about as I strolled sniffing for her reason; for no self-respecting brain could accept the one she gave. But in this hot, drowsy air I entirely lacked nimbleness, and when I came back, the question had become a mere silly, unanswerable riddle. I returned through the churchyard, and saw that in a couple of days we should arrive at the anniversary of George Hearne's death.

Philip was not on the terrace in front of the house, and I went in at the door of the hall, expecting to find him there or in the back garden. Exactly as I entered my eye told me that there he was, a black silhouette against the glass door at the end of the hall, which was open, and led through into the back garden. He did not turn round at the sound of my entry, but took a step or two in the direction of the far door, still framed in the oblong of it. I glanced at the table where the post lay, found letters both for me and him, and looked up again. There was no one there.

He had hastened his steps, I supposed, but simultaneously I thought how odd it was that he had not taken his
letters, if he was in the hall, and that he had not turned
when I entered. However, I should find him just round the
corner, and with his post and mine in my hand, I went
towards the far door. As I approached it I felt a sudden
cold stir of air, rather unaccountable, for the day was no-
tably sultry, and went out. He was sitting at the far end of
the tennis-court.

I went up to him with his letters.

'I thought I saw you just now in the hall,' I said. But I
knew already that I had not seen him in the hall.

He looked up quickly.

'And have you only just come in?' he said.

'Yes; this moment. Why?'

'Because half an hour ago I went in to see if the post
had come, and thought I saw you in the hall.'

'And what did I do?' I asked.

'You went out on to the terrace. But I didn't find you
there.'

There was a short pause as he opened his letters.

'Damned interesting,' he observed. 'Because there's
someone here who isn't you or me.'

'Anything else?' I asked.

He laughed, pointing at the row of trees.

'Yes, something too silly for words,' he said. 'Just now
I saw a piece of rope dangling from the big branch of that
pollarded lime. I saw it quite distinctly. And then there
wasn't any rope there at all, any more than there is now.'

.   .   .   .   .

Philosophers have argued about the strongest emotion
known to man. Some say 'love', others 'hate', others 'fear'.
I am disposed to put 'curiosity' on a level, at least, with
these august sensations, just mere, simple inquisitiveness.
Certainly at the moment it rivalled fear in my mind, and
there was a hint of that.

167

As he spoke the parlour-maid came out into the garden with a telegram in her hand. She gave it to Philip, who, without a word, scribbled a line on the reply-paid form inside it, and handed it back to her.

'Dreadful nuisance,' he said, 'but there's no help for it. A few days ago I got a letter which made me think I might have to go up to town, and this telegram makes it certain. There's an operation possible on a patient of mine, which I hoped might have been avoided, but my locum tenens won't take the responsibility of deciding whether it is necessary or not.'

He looked at his watch.

'I can catch the night train,' he said, 'and I ought to be able to catch the night train back from town tomorrow. I shall be back, that is to say, the day after tomorrow in the morning. There's no help for it. Ha! That telephone of yours will come in useful. I can get a taxi from Falmouth, and needn't start till after dinner.'

He went into the house, and I heard him rattling and tapping at the telephone. Soon he called for Mrs. Criddle, and presently came out again.

'We're not on the telephone service,' he said. 'It was cut off a year ago, only they haven't removed the apparatus. But I can get a trap in the village, Mrs. Criddle says, and she's sent for it. If I start at once I shall easily be in time. Spicer's packing a bag for me, and I'll take a sandwich.'

He looked sharply towards the pollarded trees.

'Yes, just there,' he said. 'I saw it plainly, and equally plainly I saw it not. And then there's that telephone of yours.'

I told him now about the ladder I had seen below the tree where he saw the dangling rope.

'Interesting,' he said, 'because it's so silly and unexpected. It is really tragic that I should be called away just now, for it looks as if the—well, the matter were coming out of the darkness into a shaft of light. But I'll be back, I hope, in thirty-six hours. Meantime, do observe very carefully, and whatever you do, don't make a theory. Darwin says somewhere that you can't observe without a theory, but to make a theory is a great danger to an observer. It can't help influencing your imagination; you tend to see or hear what falls in with your hypothesis. So just observe; be as mechanical as a phonograph and a photographic lens.'

Presently the dog-cart arrived and I went down to the gate with him. 'Whatever it is that is coming through, is coming through in bits,' he said. 'You heard a telephone; I saw a rope. We both saw a figure, but not simultaneously nor in the same place. I wish I didn't have to go.'

I found myself sympathising strongly with this wish, when after dinner I found myself with a solitary evening in front of me, and the pledge to 'observe' binding me. It was not mainly a scientific ardour that prompted this sympathy and the desire for independent combination, but, quite emphatically, fear of what might be coming out of the huge darkness which lies on all sides of human experience. I could no longer fail to connect together the fancied telephone bell, the rope, and the ladder, for what made the chain between them was the figure that both Philip and I had seen. Already my mind was seething with conjectural theory, but I would not let the ferment of it ascend to my surface consciousness; my business was not to aid but rather stifle my imagination.

I occupied myself, therefore, with the ordinary devices of a solitary man, sitting on the terrace, and subsequently coming into the house, for a few spots of rain began to fall. But though nothing disturbed the outward tranquillity of the evening, the quietness administered no opiate to that seething mixture of fear and curiosity that obsessed me. I heard the servants creep bedwards up the back stairs and presently I followed them. Then, forgetting for the moment that my room had been changed, I tried the handle of the door of that which I had previously occupied. It was locked.

Now here, beyond doubt, was the sign of a human agency, and at once I was determined to get into the room.

The key, I could see, was not in the door, which must therefore have been locked from outside. I therefore searched the usual cache for keys along the top of the door-frame, found it and entered.

The room was quite empty, the blinds not drawn, and after looking round it I walked across to the window. The moon was up, and, though obscured behind clouds, gave sufficient light to enable me to see objects outside with tolerable distinctness. There was the row of pollarded limes, and then, with a sudden intake of my breath, I saw that a foot or two below one of the boughs there was suspended something whitish and oval which oscillated as it hung there. In the dimness I could see nothing more than that, but now conjecture crashed into my conscious brain. But even as I looked it was gone again; there was nothing there but deep shadow, the trees steadfast in the windless air. Simultaneously I knew that I was not alone in the room.

I turned swiftly about, but my eyes gave no endorsement of that conviction, and yet their evidence that there was no one here except myself failed to shake it. The presence, somewhere close to me, needed no such evidence; it was self-evident though invisible, and I knew that then my forehead was streaming with the abject sweat of terror. Somehow I knew that the presence was that of the figure both Philip and I had seen that evening in the hall, and, credit it or not as you will, the fact that it was invisible made it infinitely the more terrible. I knew, too, that though my eyes were blind to it, it had got into closer touch with me; I knew more of its nature now, it had had tragic and awful commerce with evil and despair.

Some sort of catalepsy was on me while it thus obsessed me; presently, minutes afterwards or perhaps mere seconds, the grip and clutch of its power was relaxed, and with shaking knees I crossed the room and went out, and again locked the door. Even as I turned the key I smiled at the futility of that. With my emergence the terror completely passed; I went across the passage leading to my room, got into bed, and was soon asleep. But I had no more need to question myself as to why Mrs. Criddle made the change. Another guest, she knew, would come to occupy it as the season arrived when George Hearne died and was buried in the churchyard.

The night passed quietly and then succeeded a day hot and still and sultry beyond belief. The very sea had lost its coolness and vitality, and I came in from my swim tired and enervated instead of refreshed. No breeze stirred; the trees stood motionless as if cast in iron, and from horizon to horizon the sky was overlaid by an ever-thickening pall of cloud. The cohorts of storm and thunder were gathering in the stillness, and all day I felt that power, other than that of these natural forces, was being stored for some imminent manifestation.

As I came near to the house the horror deepened, and after dinner I had a mind to drop into the vicarage, according to Mr. Stephens' general invitation, and get through an hour or two with other company than my own. But I delayed till it was past any reasonable time for such an informal visit, and ten o'clock still saw me on the terrace in front of the house. My nerves were all on edge, a stir or step in the house was sufficient to make me turn round in apprehension of seeing I knew not what; but presently it grew still. One lamp burned in the hall behind me; by it stood the candle which would light me to bed.

I went indoors soon after, meaning to go up to bed, then, suddenly ashamed of this craven imbecility of mind, took the fancy to walk round the house for the purpose of convincing myself that all was tranquil and normal, and that my fear, that nameless, indefinable load of my spirit, was but a product of this close and thundery night. The tension of the weather could not last much longer; soon the storm must break and the relief come, but it would be something to know that there was nothing more than that. Accordingly I went out again on to the terrace, traversed it and turned the corner of the house where lay the tennis-lawn.

Tonight the moon had not yet risen, and the darkness was

such that I could barely distinguish the outline of the house, and that of the pollarded limes, but through the glass door that led from this side of the house into the hall, there shone the light of the lamp that stood there. All was absolutely quiet, and half reassured I traversed the lawn, and turned to go back. Just as I came opposite the lit door, I heard a sound very close at hand from under the deep shadow of the pollarded limes. It was as if some heavy object had fallen with a thump and rebound on the grass, and with it there came the noise of a creaking bough suddenly strained by some weight. Then interpretation came upon me with the unreasoning force of conviction, though in the blackness I could see nothing. But at the sound a horror such as I have never felt laid hold on me. It was scarcely physical at all, it came from some deep-seated region of the soul.

The heavens were rent, a stream of blinding light shot forth, and straight in front of my eyes, a few yards from where I stood, I saw. The noise had been of a ladder thrown down on the grass, and from the bough of the pollarded lime, there was the figure of a man, white-faced against the blackness, oscillating and twisting on the rope that strangled him. Just that I saw before the stillness was torn to atoms by the roar of thunder, and, as from a hose, the rain descended. Once again, even before that first appalling riot had died, the clouds were shredded again by the lightning, and my eyes which had not moved from the place saw only the framed shadow of the trees and their upper branches bowed by the pelting rain. All night the storm raged and bellowed making sleep impossible, and for an hour at least, between the peals of thunder, I heard the ringing of the telephone bell.

.   .   .   .   .

Next morning Philip returned, to whom I told exactly what is written here, but watch and observe as we might, neither of us, in the three further weeks which we spent at Polwithy, heard or saw anything that could interest the

172

student of the occult. Pleasant lazy days succeeded one another, we bathed and rambled and played piquet of an evening, and incidentally we made friends with the vicar. He was an interesting man, full of curious lore concerning local legends and superstitions, and one night, when in our ripened acquaintanceship he had dined with us, he asked Philip directly whether either of us had experienced anything unusual during our tenancy.

Philip nodded towards me.

'My friend saw most,' he said.

'May I hear it?' asked the vicar.

When I had finished, he was silent awhile.

'I think the—shall we call it explanation?—is yours by right,' he said. 'I will give it you if you care to hear it.'

Our silence, I suppose, answered him.

'I remember meeting you two on the day after your arrival here,' he said, 'and you inquired about the tombstone in the churchyard erected to the memory of George Hearne. I did not want to say more of him then, for a reason that you will presently know. I told you, I recollect, perhaps rather hurriedly, that it was Mrs. Hearne's husband who was buried there. Already, I imagine, you guess that I concealed something. You may even have guessed it at the time.'

He did not wait for any confirmation or repudiation of this. Sitting out on the terrace in the deep dusk, his communication was very impersonal. It was just a narrating voice, without identity: an anonymous chronicle.

'George Hearne succeeded to the property here, which is considerable, only two years before his death. He was married shortly after he succeeded. According to any decent standard, his life both before and after his marriage was vile. I think—God forgive me if I wrong him—he made evil his god; he liked evil for its own sake. But out of the middle of the mire of his own soul there sprang a flower: he was devoted to his wife. And he was capable of shame.

'A fortnight before his—his death, she got to know what

173

his life was like, and what he was in himself. I need not tell you what the particular disclosure that came to her knowledge; it is sufficient to say that it was revolting. She was here at the time; he was coming down from London that night. When he arrived he found a note from her saying that she had left him and could never come back. She told him that he must give her opportunity for her to divorce him, and threatened him with exposure if he did not.

'He and I had been friends, and that night he came to me with her letter, acknowledged the justice of it, but asked me to intervene. He said that the only thing that could save him from utter damnation was she, and I believe that there he spoke sincerely. But, speaking as a clergyman, I should not have called him penitent. He did not hate his sin, but only the consequences of it. But it seemed to me that if she came back to him, he might have a chance, and next day I went to her. Nothing that I could say moved her one atom, and after a fruitless day I came back, and told him of the uselessness of my mission.

'Now, according to my view, no man who deliberately prefers evil to good just for the sake of wickedness is sane, and this refusal of hers to have anything more to do with him, I fully believe, upset the unstable balance of his soul altogether. There was just his devotion to her which might conceivably have restored it, but she refused—and I can quite understand her refusal—to come near him. If you knew what I know, you could not blame her. But the effect of it on him was portentous and disastrous, and three days afterwards I wrote to her again, saying quite simply that the damnation of his soul would be on her head unless, leaving her personal feelings altogether out of the question, she came back. She got that letter the next evening, and already it was too late.

'That afternoon, two years ago, on the 15th of August, there was washed up in the harbour here a dead body, and that night George Hearne took a ladder from the fruit-wall in the kitchen garden and hanged himself. He climbed into one of the pollarded limes, tied the rope to a bough, and made a slip-knot at the other end of it. Then he kicked the ladder away.

'Mrs. Hearne meantime had received my letter. For a couple of hours she wrestled with her own repugnance and then decided to come to him. She rang him up on the telephone, but the housekeeper here, Mrs. Criddle, could only tell her that he had gone out after dinner. She continued ringing him up for a couple of hours, but there was always the same reply.

'Eventually she decided to waste no more time, and motored over from her mother's house where she was staying at the north end of the county. By then the moon had risen, and looking out from his bedroom window she saw him.'

He paused.

'There was an inquest,' he said, 'and I could truthfully testify that I believed him to be insane. The verdict of suicide during temporary insanity was brought in, and he was buried in the churchyard. The rope was burned, and the ladder was burned.'

The parlour-maid brought out drinks, and we sat in silence till she had gone again.

'And what about the telephone my friend heard?' asked Philip.

He thought a moment.

'Don't you think that great emotion like that of Mrs. Hearne's may make some sort of record,' he asked, 'so that if the needle of a sensitive temperament comes in contact with it, a reproduction takes place? And it is the same, perhaps, about that poor fellow who hanged himself. One can hardly believe that his spirit is bound to visit and re-visit the scene of his follies and his crimes year by year.'

'Year by year?' I asked.

'Apparently. I saw him myself last year, Mrs. Criddle did also.'

He got up.

'How can one tell?' he said. 'Expiation, perhaps. Who knows?'

The Woman's Ghost Story

'YES,' she said, from her seat in the dark corner, 'I'll tell you an experience if you care to listen. And, what's more, I'll tell it briefly, without trimmings—I mean without unessentials. That's a thing story-tellers never do, you know,' she laughed. 'They drag in all the unessentials and leave their listeners to disentangle; but I'll give you just the essentials, and you can make of it what you please. But on one condition: that at the end you ask no questions, because I can't explain it and have no wish to.'

We agreed. We were all serious. After listening to a dozen prolix stories from people who merely wished to 'talk' but had nothing to tell, we wanted 'essentials'.

'In those days,' she began, feeling from the quality of our silence that we were with her, 'in those days I was interested in psychic things, and had arranged to sit up alone in a haunted house in the middle of London. It was a cheap and dingy lodging-house in a mean street, unfurnished. I had already made a preliminary examination in daylight that afternoon, and the keys from the caretaker, who lived next door, were in my pocket. The story was a good one—satisfied me, at any rate, that it was worth investigating; and I won't weary you with details as to the woman's murder and all the tiresome elaboration as to *why* the place was *alive*. Enough that it was.

'I was a good deal bored, therefore, to see a man, whom I took to be the talkative old caretaker, waiting for me on the steps when I went in at 11 p.m., for I had sufficiently explained that I wished to be there alone for the night.

'"I wished to show you *the* room," he mumbled, and,

of course, I couldn't exactly refuse, having tipped him for the temporary loan of a chair and table.

' "Come in, then, and let's be quick," I said.

'We went in, he shuffling after me through the unlighted hall up to the first floor where the murder had taken place, and I prepared myself to hear his inevitable account before turning him out with the half-crown his persistence had earned. After lighting the gas I sat down in the armchair he had provided—a faded, brown plush arm-chair —and turned for the first time to face him and get through with the performance as quickly as possible. And it was in that instant I got my first shock. The man was *not* the caretaker. It was not the old fool, Carey, I had interviewed earlier in the day and made my plans with. My heart gave a horrid jump.

' "Now who are *you*, pray?" I said. "You're not Carey, the man I arranged with this afternoon. Who are you?"

'I felt very uncomfortable, as you may imagine. I was a "psychical researcher", and a young woman of new tendencies, and proud of my liberty, but I did not care to find myself in an empty house with a stranger. Something of my confidence left me. Confidence with women, you know, is all humbug after a certain point. Or perhaps you don't know, for most of you are men. But anyhow, my pluck ebbed in a quick rush, and I felt afraid.

' "Who are you?" I repeated quickly and nervously. The fellow was well dressed, youngish and good-looking, but with a face of great sadness. I myself was barely thirty. I am giving you essentials, or I would not mention it. Out of quite ordinary things comes this story. I think that's why it has value.

' "No," he said; "I'm the man who was frightened to death."

'His voice and his words ran through me like a knife, and I felt ready to drop. In my pocket was the book I had bought to make notes in. I felt the pencil sticking in the socket. I felt, too, the extra warm things I had put on to sit up in, as no bed or sofa was available—a hundred things dashed through my mind, foolishly and without sequence or meaning, as the way is when one is really frightened. Unessentials leaped up and puzzled me, and I thought of what the papers might say if it came out, and what my "smart" brother-in-law would think, and whether it would be told that I had cigarettes in my pocket, and was a free-thinker.'

' "The man who was frightened to death!" I repeated, aghast.

' "That's me," he said stupidly.

'I stared at him just as you would have done—anyone of you men now listening to me—and felt my life ebbing and flowing like a sort of hot fluid. You needn't laugh! That's how I felt. Small things, you know, touch the mind with great earnestness when terror is there—*real terror*. But I might have been at a middle-class tea-party, for all the ideas I had: they were so ordinary!

' ""But I thought you were the caretaker I tipped this afternoon to let me sleep here!" I gasped. "Did—did Carey send you to meet me?"

' "No," he replied in a voice that touched my boots somehow. "I am the man who was frightened to death. And what is more, I am frightened *now*!'

' "So am I," I managed to utter, speaking instinctively. "I'm simply terrified."

' "Yes," he replied in that same odd voice that seemed to sound within me. "But you are still in the flesh, and I—*am not!*'

'I felt the need for vigorous self-assertion. I stood up in that empty, unfurnished room, digging the nails into my palms and clenching my teeth. I was determined to assert my individuality and my courage as a new woman and a free soul.

' "You mean to say you are not in the flesh!' I gasped. "What in the world are you talking about?"

'The silence of the night swallowed up my voice. For the first time I realised that darkness was over the city; that dust lay upon the stairs; that the floor above was un-

tenanted and the floor below empty. I was alone in an un-
occupied and haunted house, unprotected, and a woman.
I chilled. I heard the wind round the house, and knew the
stars were hidden. My thoughts rushed to policemen and
omnibuses, and everything that was useful and comforting.
I suddenly realised what a fool I was to come to such a
house alone. I was icily afraid. I thought the end of my life
had come. I was an utter fool to go in for psychical research
when I had not the necessary nerve.

' "Good God!" I gasped. "If you're not Carey, the man
I arranged with, who are you?"

'I was really stiff with terror. The man moved slowly
towards me across the empty room. I held out my arm to
stop him, getting up out of my chair at the same moment,
and he came to a halt just opposite me, a smile on his worn,
sad face.

' "I told you who I am," he repeated quietly with a sigh,
looking at me with the saddest eyes I have ever seen, "and
I am frightened *still*."

'By this time I was convinced that I was entertaining
either a rogue or a madman, and I cursed my stupidity in
bringing the man in without having seen his face. My mind
was quickly made up, and I knew what to do. Ghosts
and psychic phenomena flew to the winds. If I angered
the creature my life might pay the price. I must humour
him till I got to the door, and race for the street. I stood
bolt upright and faced him. We were about of a height, and
I was a strong, athletic woman who played hockey in winter and climbed Alps in summer. My hand itched for a
stick, but I had none.

' "Now, of course, I remember," said I with a sort of
stiff smile that was very hard to force. "Now I remember
your case and the wonderful way you behaved."

'The man stared at me stupidly, turning his head to
watch me as I backed more and more quickly to the door.
But when his face broke into a smile I could control myself
no longer. I reached the door in a run, and shot out on to
the landing. Like a fool, I turned the wrong way, and stum-

179

bled over the stairs leading to the new storey. But it was too late to change. The man was after me, I was sure, though no sound of footsteps came; and I dashed up the next flight, tearing my skirt and banging my ribs in the darkness, and rushed headlong into the first room I came to. Luckily the door stood ajar, and, still more fortunate, there was a key in the lock. In a second I had slammed the door, flung my whole weight against it, and turned the key.

'I was safe, but my heart was beating like a drum. A second later it seemed to stop altogether, for I saw that there was someone else in the room besides myself. A man's figure stood between me and the windows, where the street lamps gave just enough light to outline his shape against the glass. I'm a plucky woman, you know, for even then I didn't give up hope, but I may tell you that I have never felt so vilely frightened in all my born days. I had locked myself in with him!

'The man leaned against the window, watching me where I lay in a collapsed heap upon the floor. So there were two men in the house with me, I reflected. Perhaps other rooms were occupied too! What could it all mean? But, as I stared, something changed in the room, or in me—hard to say which—and I realised my mistake, so that my fear, which had so far been physical, at once altered its character and became *psychical*. I became afraid in my soul instead of in my heart, and I knew immediately who this man was.

' "How in the world did you get up here?" I stammered to him across the empty room, amazement momentarily stemming my fear.

' "Now, let me tell you," he began, in that odd, far-away voice of his that went down my spine like a knife. "I'm in different space, for one thing, and you'd find me in any room you went into; for according to your way of measuring, I'm *all over the house*. Space is a bodily condition, but I am out of the body, and am not affected by space. It's my condition that keeps me here. I want some-

THE WOMAN'S GHOST STORY

thing to change my condition for me, for then I could get away. What I want is sympathy. Or, really, more than sympathy; I want affection—I want *love*!"

'While he was speaking I gathered myself slowly upon my feet. I wanted to scream and cry and laugh all at once, but I only succeeded in sighing, for my emotion was exhausted and a numbness was coming over me. I felt for the matches in my pocket and made a movement towards the gas-jet.

' "I should be much happier if you didn't light the gas," he said at once, "for the vibrations of your light hurt me a good deal. You need not be afraid that I shall injure you. I can't touch your body to begin with, for there's a great gulf fixed, you know; and really this half-light suits me best. Now, let me continue what I was trying to say before. You know, so many people have come to this house to see me, and most of them have seen me, and one and all have been terrified. If only, oh, if only someone would be *not* terrified, but kind and loving to me! Then, you see, I might be able to change my condition and get away."

'His voice was so sad that I felt tears start somewhere at the back of my eyes; but fear kept all else in check, and I stood shaking and cold as I listened to him.

' "Who are you, then? Of course Carey didn't send you, I know now," I managed to utter. My thoughts scattered dreadfully and I could think of nothing to say. I was afraid of a stroke.

' "I know nothing about Carey, or who he is," continued the man quietly, "and the name my body had I have forgotten, thank God; but I am the man who was frightened to death in this house ten years ago, and have been frightened ever since, and am frightened still; for the succession of cruel and curious people who come to this house to see the ghost, and thus keep alive its atmosphere of terror, only helps to render my condition worse. If only someone would be kind to me—*laugh*, speak gently and rationally with me, cry if they like, pity, comfort, soothe me—anything but come here in curiosity and tremble as

181

you are now doing in that corner. Now, madam, won't you take pity on me?" His voice rose to a dreadful cry. "Won't you step out into the middle of the room and try to love me a little?"

'A horrible laughter came gurgling up in my throat as I heard him, but the sense of pity was stronger than the laughter, and I found myself actually leaving the support of the wall and approaching the centre of the floor.

' "By God!" he cried, at once straightening up against the window, "you have done a kind act. That's the first attempt at sympathy that has been shown me since I died, and I feel better already. In life, you know, I was a misanthrope. Everything went wrong with me, and I came to hate my fellow men so much that I couldn't bear to see them even. Of course, like begets like, and this hate was returned. Finally I suffered from horrible delusions, and my room became haunted with demons that laughed and grimaced, and one night I ran into a whole cluster of them near the bed—and the fright stopped my heart and killed me. It's hate and remorse, as much as terror, that clogs me so thickly and keeps me here. If only someone could feel pity, and sympathy, and perhaps a little love for me, I could get away and be happy. When you came this afternoon to see over the house I watched you, and a little hope came to me for the first time. I saw you had courage, originality, resource—*love*. If only I could perhaps tap that love you have stored up in your being there, and thus borrow the wings for my escape!"

'Now I must confess my heart began to ache a little, as fear left me and the man's words sank their sad meaning into me. Still, the whole affair was so incredible, and so touched with unholy quality, and the story of a woman's murder I had come to investigate had so obviously nothing to do with this thing, that I felt myself in a kind of wild dream that seemed likely to stop at any moment and leave me somewhere in bed after a nightmare.

'Moreover, his words possessed me to such an extent that I found it impossible to reflect upon anything else at

182

all, or to consider adequately any ways and means of action or escape.

'I moved a little nearer to him in the gloom, horribly frightened, of course, but with the beginnings of a strange determination in my heart.

' "You women," he continued, his voice plainly thrilling at my approach, "you wonderful women, to whom life often brings no opportunity of spending your great love, oh, if you only could know how many of *us* simply yearn for it! It would save our souls, if you but knew. Few might find the chance that you now have, but if you only spend your love freely, without definite object, just letting it flow openly for all who need, you would reach hundreds and thousands of souls like me, and *release us*! Oh, madam, I ask you again to feel with me, to be kind and gentle—and if you can to love me a little!"

'My heart did leap within me and this time the tears did come, for I could not restrain them. I laughed too, for the way he called me "madam" sounded so odd, here in this empty room at midnight in a London street, but my laughter stopped dead and emerged in a flood of weeping when I saw how my change of feeling affected him. He had left his place by the window and was kneeling on the floor at my feet, his hands stretched out towards me, and the first signs of a kind of glory about his head.

' "Put your arms round me and kiss me, for the love of God!" he cried. "Kiss me, oh, kiss me, and I shall be freed! You have done so much already—now do this!"

'I stuck there, hesitating, shaking, my determination on the verge of action, yet not quite able to compass it. But the terror had almost gone.

' "Forget that I'm a man and you're a woman," he continued in the most beseeching voice I ever heard. "Forget that I'm a ghost, and come out boldly and press me to you with a great kiss, and let your love flow into me. Forget yourself just for one minute and do a brave thing! Oh, love me, *love me*, LOVE ME! and I shall be free!"

'The words, or the deep force they somehow released in the centre of my being, stirred me profoundly, and an emotion infinitely greater than fear surged up over me and carried me with it across the edge of action. Without hesitation I took two steps forward towards him where he knelt, and held out my arms. Pity and love were in my heart at that moment, genuine pity, I swear, and genuine love. I forgot myself and my little tremblings in a great desire to help another soul.

'"I love you, poor, aching, unhappy thing! I love you," I cried through hot tears; "and I am not the least bit afraid in the world."

'The man uttered a curious sound, like laughter, yet not laughter, and turned his face up to me. The light from the street below fell on it, but there was another light, too, shining all round it that seemed to come from the eyes and skin. He rose to his feet and met me, and in that second I folded him to my breast and kissed him full on the lips again and again.'

.   .   .   .   .

All our pipes had gone out, and not even a skirt rustled in that dark studio as the story-teller paused a moment to steady her voice, and put a hand softly up to her eyes before going on again.

.   .   .   .   .

'Now, what can I say, and how can I describe to you, all you sceptical men sitting there with pipes in your mouths, the amazing sensation I experienced of holding an intangible, impalpable thing so closely to my heart that it touched my body with equal pressure all the way down, and then melted away somewhere into my very being? For it was like seizing a rush of cool wind and feeling a touch of burning fire the moment it had struck its swift blow and passed on. A series of shocks ran all over and all through

184

me; a momentary ecstasy of flaming sweetness and wonder thrilled down into me; my heart gave another great leap— and then I was alone.

'The room was empty. I turned on the gas and struck a match to prove it. All fear had left me, and something was singing round me in the air and in my heart like the joy of a spring morning in youth. Not all the devils or shadows or hauntings in the world could then have caused me a single tremor.

'I unlocked the door and went over all the dark house, even to kitchen and cellar and up among the ghostly attics. But the house was empty. Something had left it. I lingered a short hour, analysing, thinking, wondering—you can guess what and how, perhaps, but I won't detail, for I promised only essentials, remember—and then went out to sleep the remainder of the night in my own flat, locking the door behind me upon a house no longer haunted.

'But my uncle, Sir Henry, the owner of the house, required an account of my adventure, and, of course, I was in duty bound to give him some kind of story. Before I could begin, however, he held up his hand to stop me.

' "First," he said, "I wish to tell you a little deception I ventured to practise on you. So many people have been to that house and seen the ghost that I came to think the story acted on their imaginations, and I wished to make a better test. So I invented for their benefit another story, with the idea that if you did see anything I could be sure it was not due merely to an excited imagination."

' "Then what you told me about a woman having been murdered, and all that, was not the true story of the haunting?"

' "It was not. The true story is that a cousin of mine went mad in the house, and killed himself in a fit of morbid terror following upon years of miserable hypochondriasis. It is his figure that investigators see."

' "That explains, then," I gasped ...

' "Explains what?"

185

'I thought of that poor struggling soul, longing all these years for escape, and determined to keep my story for the present to myself.

' "Explains, I mean, why I did not see the ghost of the murdered woman," I concluded.

' "Precisely," said Sir Henry, "and why, if you had seen anything, it would have had value, inasmuch as it could not have been caused by the imagination working upon a story you already knew." '

PERCIVAL LANDON

Thurnley Abbey

THREE years ago I was on my way out to the East, and
as an extra day in London was of some importance I took
the Friday evening mail-train to Brindisi instead of the
usual Thursday morning Marseilles express. Many people
shrink from the long forty-eight-hour train journey through
Europe, and the subsequent rush across the Mediterranean
on the nineteen-knot *Isis* or *Osiris*; but there is really very
little discomfort on either the train or the mail-boat, and,
unless there is actually nothing for me to do, I always like
to save the extra day and a half in London before I say
good-bye to her for one of my longer tramps.

This time—it was early, I remember, in the shipping
season, probably about the beginning of September—there
were few passengers, and I had a compartment in the
P. & O. Indian express to myself all the way from Calais.
All Sunday I watched the blue waves dimpling the Adri-
atic, and the pale rosemary along the cuttings; the plain
white towns, with their flat roofs and their bold *duomos*,
and the grey-green, gnarled, olive orchards of Apulia. The
journey was just like any other. We ate in the dining-car
as often and as long as we decently could. We slept after
luncheon; we dawdled the afternoon away with yellow-
backed novels; sometimes we exchanged platitudes in the
smoking-room, and it was there that I met Alastair Colvin.

Colvin was a man of middle height, with a resolute, well-
cut jaw; his hair was turning grey; his moustache was sun-
whitened, otherwise he was clean-shaven—obviously a
gentleman, and obviously also a pre-occupied man. He
had no great wit. When spoken to, he made the usual re-

marks in the right way, and I dare say he refrained from banalities only because he spoke less than the rest of us; most of the time he buried himself in the Wagon-lit Company's time-table, but seemed unable to concentrate his attention on any one page of it. He found that I had been over the Siberian railway, and for a quarter of an hour he discussed it with me. Then he lost interest in it, and rose to go to his compartment. But he came back again very soon, and seemed glad to pick up the conversation again.

Of course this did not seem to me to be of any importance. Most travellers by train become a trifle infirm of purpose after thirty-six hours' rattling. But Colvin's restless way I noticed in somewhat marked contrast with the man's personal importance and dignity; especially ill-suited was it to his finely made, large hand with its strong, broad, regular nails and its few lines. As I looked at his hand I noticed a long, deep, and recent scar of ragged shape. However, it is absurd to pretend that I thought anything was unusual. I went off at five o'clock on Sunday afternoon to sleep away the hour or two that had still to be got through before we arrived at Brindisi.

Once there, we few passengers transhipped our hand baggage, verified our berths—there were only a score of us in all—and then, after an aimless ramble of half an hour in Brindisi, we returned to dinner at the Hotel International, not wholly surprised that the town had been the death of Virgil. If I remember rightly, there is a gaily painted hall at the International—I do not wish to advertise anything, but there is no other place in Brindisi at which to await the coming of the mails—and after dinner I was looking with awe at a trellis overgrown with blue vines, when Colvin moved across the room to my table. He picked up *Il Secolo*, but almost immediately gave up the pretence of reading it. He turned squarely to me and said:

'Would you do me a favour?'

One doesn't do favours to stray acquaintances on Continental expresses without knowing something more of them than I knew of Colvin. But I smiled in a non-committal way, and asked him what he wanted. I wasn't wrong in part of my estimate of him; he said bluntly:

'Will you let me sleep in your cabin on the *Osiris*?' And he coloured a little as he said it.

Now, there is nothing more tiresome than having to put up with a stable-companion at sea, and I asked him rather pointedly:

'Surely there is room for all of us?' I thought that perhaps he had been partnered off with some mangy Levantine, and wanted to escape from him at all hazards.

Colvin, still somewhat confused, said: 'Yes, I am in a cabin by myself. But you would do me the greatest favour if you would allow me to share yours.'

This was all very well, but, besides the fact that I always sleep better when alone, there had been some recent thefts on board English liners, and I hesitated, frank and honest and self-conscious as Colvin was. Just then the mail-train came in with a clatter and a rush of escaping steam, and I asked him to see me again about it on the boat when we started. He answered me curtly—I suppose he saw the mistrust in my manner—'I am a member of White's.' I smiled to myself as he said it, but I remembered in a moment that the man—if he were really what he claimed to be, and I make no doubt that he was—must have been sorely put to it before he urged the fact as a guarantee of his respectability to a total stranger at a Brindisi hotel.

That evening, as we cleared the red and green harbour-lights of Brindisi, Colvin explained. This is his story in his own words.

. . . . .

'When I was travelling in India some years ago, I made the acquaintance of a youngish man in the Woods and Forests. We camped out together for a week, and I found him a pleasant companion. John Broughton was a light-hearted soul when off duty, but a steady and capable man in any of the small emergencies that continually arise in that department. He was liked and trusted by the natives, and, though a trifle over-pleased with himself when he escaped to civilisation at Simla or Calcutta, Broughton's future was well assured in Government service when a fair-sized estate was unexpectedly left to him, and he joyfully shook the dust of the Indian plains from his feet and returned to England.

'For five years he drifted about London. I saw him now and then. We dined together about every eighteen months, and I could trace pretty exactly the gradual sickening of Broughton with a merely idle life. He then set out on a couple of long voyages, returned as restless as before, and at last told me that he had decided to marry and settle down at his place, Thurnley Abbey, which had long been empty. He spoke about looking after the property and standing for his constituency in the usual way. Vivien Wilde, his *fiancée*, had, I suppose, begun to take him in hand. She was a pretty girl with a deal of fair hair and rather an exclusive manner; deeply religious in a narrow school, she was still kindly and high-spirited, and I thought that Broughton was in luck. He was quite happy and full of information about his future.

'Among other things, I asked him about Thurnley Abbey. He confessed that he hardly knew the place. The last tenant, a man called Clarke, had lived in one wing for fifteen years and seen no one. He had been a miser and a hermit. It was the rarest thing for a light to be seen at the Abbey after dark. Only the barest necessities of life were ordered, and the tenant himself received them at the side-door. His one half-caste manservant, after a month's stay in the house, had abruptly left without warning, and had returned to the Southern States.

'One thing Broughton complained bitterly about: Clarke had wilfully spread the rumour among the villagers that the Abbey was haunted, and had even condescended to play childish tricks with spirit-lamps and salt in order to scare trespassers away at night. He had been detected in the act of this tomfoolery, but the story spread, and no one,

said Broughton, would venture near the house, except in
broad daylight. The hauntedness of Thurnley Abbey was
now, he said with a grin, part of the gospel of the country-
side, but he and his young wife were going to change all
that. Would I propose myself any time I liked? I, of course,
said I would, and equally, of course, intended to do nothing of the sort without a definite invitation.

'The house was put in thorough repair, though not a
stick of the old furniture and tapestry was removed. Floors
and ceilings were relaid; the roof was made water-tight
again, and the dust of half a century was scoured out. He
showed me some photographs of the place. It was called
an Abbey, though as a matter of fact it had been only the
infirmary of the long-vanished Abbey of Closter some five
miles away. The larger part of this building remained as it
had been in pre-Reformation days, but a wing had been
added in Jacobean times, and that part of the house had
been kept in something like repair by Mr. Clarke. He had
in both the ground and first floors set a heavy timber door,
strongly barred with iron, in the passage between the earlier
and the Jacobean parts of the house, and had entirely neglected the former. So there had been a good deal of work
to be done.

'Broughton, whom I saw in London two or three times
about this period, made a deal of fun over the positive refusal of the workmen to remain after sundown. Even after
the electric light had been put into every room, nothing
would induce them to remain, though, as Broughton
observed, electric light was death on ghosts. The legend of
the Abbey's ghosts had gone far and wide, and the men
would take no risks. They went home in batches of five
and six, and even during the daylight hours there was an
inordinate amount of talking between one and another, if
either happened to be out of sight of his companion. On
the whole, though nothing of any sort or kind had been
conjured up even by their heated imaginations during their
five months' work upon the Abbey, the belief in the ghosts
was rather strengthened than otherwise in Thurnley be-

191

cause of the men's confessed nervousness, and local tradi-
tion declared itself in favour of the ghost of an immured
nun.

' "Good old nun!" said Broughton.

'I asked him whether in general he believed in the possibility of ghosts, and, rather to my surprise, he said that he
couldn't say he entirely disbelieved in them. A man in
India had told him one morning in camp that he believed
that his mother was dead in England, as her vision had
come to his tent the night before. He had not been alarmed,
but had said nothing, and the figure vanished again. As a
matter of fact, the next possible *dak-walla* brought on a
telegram announcing the mother's death. "There the thing
was," said Broughton. But at Thurnley he was practical
enough. He roundly cursed the idiotic selfishness of Clarke,
whose silly antics had caused all the inconvenience. At the
same time, he couldn't refuse to sympathise to some extent
with the ignorant workmen. "My own idea," said he, "is
that if a ghost ever does come in one's way, one ought to
speak to it."

'I agreed. Little as I knew of the ghost world and its
conventions, I had always remembered that a spook was
in honour bound to wait to be spoken to. It didn't seem
much to do, and I felt that the sound of one's own voice
would at any rate reassure oneself as to one's wakefulness. But there are few ghosts outside Europe—few, that
is, that a white man can see—and I had never been troubled
with any. However, as I have said, I told Broughton that
I agreed.

'So the wedding took place, and I went to it in a tall hat
which I bought for the occasion, and the new Mrs.
Broughton smiled very nicely at me afterwards. As it had
to happen, I took the Orient Express that evening and was
not in England again for nearly six months. Just before I
came back I got a letter from Broughton. He asked if I
could see him in London or come to Thurnley, as he
thought I should be better able to help him than anyone
else he knew. His wife sent a nice message to me at the

end, so I was reassured about at least one thing. I wrote from Budapest that I would come and see him at Thurnley two days after my arrival in London, and as I sauntered out of the Pannonia into the Kerepesi Utcza to post my letters, I wondered of what earthly service I could be to Broughton. I had been out with him after tiger on foot, and I could imagine few men better able at a pinch to manage their own business. However, I had nothing to do, so after dealing with some small accumulations of business during my absence, I packed a kit-bag and departed to Euston.

'I was met by Broughton's great limousine at Thurnley Road station, and after a drive of nearly seven miles we echoed through the sleepy streets of Thurnley village, into which the main gates of the park thrust themselves, splendid with pillars and spread-eagles and tom-cats rampant atop of them. I never was a herald, but I know that the Broughtons have the right to supporters—heaven knows why! From the gates a quadruple avenue of beech-trees led inwards for a quarter of a mile. Beneath them a neat strip of fine turf edged the road and ran back until the poison of the dead beech leaves killed it under the trees. There were many wheel tracks on the road, and a comfortable little pony trap jogged past me laden with a country parson and his wife and daughter. Evidently there was some garden-party going on at the Abbey. The road dropped away to the right at the end of the avenue, and I could see the Abbey across a wide pasturage and a broad lawn thickly dotted with guests.

'The end of the building was plain. It must have been almost mercilessly austere when it was first built, but time had crumbled the edges and toned the stone down to an orange-lichened grey wherever it showed behind its curtain of magnolia, jasmine, and ivy. Farther on was the three-storied Jacobean house, tall and handsome. There had not been the slightest attempt to adapt the one to the other, but the kindly ivy had glossed over the touching point. There was a tall *flèche* in the middle of the building, surmounting a small bell tower. Behind the house there rose the mountainous verdure of Spanish chestnuts all the way up the hill.

'Broughton had seen me coming from afar, and walked across from his other guests to welcome me before turning me over to the butler's care. This man was sandy-haired and rather inclined to be talkative. He could, however, answer hardly any questions about the house; he had, he said, been there only three weeks. Mindful of what Broughton had told me, I made no inquiries about ghosts, though the room into which I was shown might have justified anything. It was a very large, low room with oak beams projecting from the white ceiling. Every inch of the walls, including the doors, was covered with tapestry, and a remarkably fine Italian four-post bedstead, heavily draped, added to the darkness and dignity of the place. All the furniture was old, well made, and dark. Underfoot there was a plain green pile carpet, the only new thing about the room except the electric light fittings and the jugs and basins. Even the looking-glass on the dressing-table was an old pyramidal Venetian glass set in heavy repoussé frame of tarnished silver.

'After a few minutes' cleaning up, I went downstairs and out upon the lawn, where I greeted my hostess. The people gathered there were of the usual country type, all anxious to be pleased and roundly curious as to the new master of the Abbey. Rather to my surprise, and quite to my pleasure, I rediscovered Glenham, whom I had known well in old days in Barotseland; he lived quite close, as, he remarked with a grin, I ought to have known. "But," he added, "I don't live in a place like this." He swept his hand to the long, low lines of the Abbey in obvious admiration, and then, to my intense interest, muttered beneath his breath: "Thank God!" He saw that I had overheard him, and turning to me said decidedly: "Yes, 'thank God' I said, and I meant it. I wouldn't live at the Abbey for all Broughton's money."

' "But surely," I demurred, "you know that old Clarke

was discovered in the very act of setting light to his bug-a-boos?"

'Glenham shrugged his shoulders. "Yes, I know about that. But there is something wrong with the place still. All I can say is that Broughton is a different man since he has lived here. I don't believe that he will remain much longer. But—you're staying here?—well, you'll hear all about it tonight. There's a big dinner, I understand." The conversation turned off to old reminiscences, and Glenham soon after had to go.

'Before I went to dress that evening I had twenty minutes' talk with Broughton in his library. There was no doubt that the man was altered, gravely altered. He was nervous and fidgety, and I found him looking at me only when my eye was off him. I naturally asked him what he wanted of me. I told him I would do anything I could, but that I couldn't conceive what he lacked that I could provide. He said with a lustreless smile that there was, however, something, and that he would tell me the following morning. It struck me that he was somehow ashamed of himself, and perhaps ashamed of the part he was asking me to play. However, I dismissed the subject from my mind and went up to dress in my palatial room. As I shut the door a draught blew out the Queen of Sheba from the wall, and I noticed that the tapestries were not fastened to the wall at the bottom. I have always held very practical views about spooks, and it has often seemed to me that the slow waving in firelight of loose tapestry upon a wall would account for ninety-nine per cent of the stories one hears. Certainly the dignified undulation of this lady with her attendants and huntsmen—one of whom was untidily cutting the throat of a fallow deer upon the very steps on which King Solomon, a grey-faced Flemish nobleman with the order of the Golden Fleece, awaited his fair visitor—gave colour to my hypothesis.

'Nothing much happened at dinner. The people were very much like those of the garden-party. A young woman next me seemed anxious to know what was being read in

London. As she was far more familiar than I with the most recent magazines and literary supplements, I found salvation in being myself instructed in the tendencies of modern fiction. All true art, she said, was shot through and through with melancholy. How vulgar were the attempts at wit that marked so many modern books! From the beginning of literature it had always been tragedy that embodied the highest attainment of every age. To call such works morbid merely begged the question. No thoughtful man—she looked sternly at me through the steel rim of her glasses—could fail to agree with her.

'Of course, as one would, I immediately and properly said that I slept with Pett Ridge and Jacobs under my pillow at night, and that if *Jorrocks* weren't quite so large and cornery, I would add him to the company. She hadn't read any of them, so I was saved—for a time. But I remember grimly that she said that the dearest wish of her life was to be in some awful and soul-freezing situation of horror, and I remember that she dealt hardly with the hero of Nat Paynter's vampire story, between nibbles at her brown-bread ice. She was a cheerless soul, and I couldn't help thinking that if there were many such in the neighbourhood it was not surprising that old Glenham had been stuffed with some nonsense or other about the Abbey. Yet nothing could well have been less creepy than the glitter of silver and glass, and the subdued lights and cackle of conversation all round the dinner-table.

'After the ladies had gone I found myself talking to the rural dean. He was a thin, earnest man, who at once turned the conversation to old Clarke's buffooneries. But, he said, Mr. Broughton had introduced such a new and cheerful spirit, not only into the Abbey but, he might say, into the whole neighbourhood, that he had great hopes that the ignorant superstitions of the past were from henceforth destined to oblivion. Thereupon his other neighbour, a portly gentleman of independent means and position, audibly remarked "Amen", which damped the rural dean, and we talked of partridges past, partridges present, and pheasants to come. At the other end of the table Broughton sat with a couple of his friends, red-faced hunting men. Once I noticed that they were discussing me, but I paid no attention to it at the time. I remembered it a few hours later.

'By eleven all the guests were gone, and Broughton, his wife, and I were alone together under the fine plaster ceiling of the Jacobean drawing-room. Mrs. Broughton talked about one or two of the neighbours, and then, with a smile, said that she knew I would excuse her, shook hands with me, and went off to bed. I am not very good at analysing things, but I felt that she talked a little uncomfortably and with a suspicion of effort, smiled rather conventionally, and was obviously glad to go. These things seem trifling enough to repeat, but I had throughout the faint feeling that everything was not square. Under the circumstances, this was enough to set me wondering what on earth the service could be that I was to render—wondering also whether the whole business were not some ill-advised jest in order to make me come down from London for a mere shooting-party.

'Broughton said little after she had gone. But he was evidently labouring to bring the conversation round to the so-called haunting of the Abbey. As soon as I saw this, of course, I asked him directly about it. He then seemed at once to lose interest in the matter. There was no doubt about it: Broughton was somehow a changed man, and to my mind he had changed in no way for the better. Mrs. Broughton seemed no sufficient cause. He was clearly very fond of her, and she of him. I reminded him that he was going to tell me what I could do for him in the morning, pleaded my journey, lighted a candle, and went upstairs with him. At the end of the passage leading into the old house he grinned weakly and said: "Mind, if you see a ghost, do talk to it; you said you would." He stood irresolutely a moment and then turned away. At the door of his dressing-room he paused once more: "I'm here," he called out, "if you should want anything. Good night," and he shut his door.

197

'I went along the passage to my room, undressed, switched on a lamp beside my bed, read a few pages of the *Jungle Book*, and then, more than ready for sleep, turned the light off and went fast asleep.

. . . . .

'Three hours later I woke up. There was not a breath of wind outside. There was not even a flicker of light from the fireplace. As I lay there, an ash tinkled slightly as it cooled, but there was hardly a gleam of the dullest red in the grate. An owl cried among the silent Spanish chestnuts on the slope outside. I idly reviewed the events of the day, hoping that I should fall off to sleep again before I reached dinner. But at the end I seemed as wakeful as ever. There was no help for it. I must read my *Jungle Book* again till I felt ready to go off, so I fumbled for the pear at the end of the cord that hung down inside the bed, and I switched on the bedside lamp. The sudden glory dazzled me for a moment. I felt under my pillow for my book with half-shut eyes. Then, growing used to the light, I happened to look down to the foot of my bed.

'I can never tell you really what happened then. Nothing I could ever confess in the most abject words could even faintly picture to you what I felt. I know that my heart stopped dead, and my throat shut automatically. In one instinctive movement I crouched back up against the headboards of the bed, staring at the horror. The movement set my heart going again, and the sweat dripped from every pore. I am not a particularly religious man, but I had always believed that God would never allow any supernatural appearance to present itself to man in such a guise and in such circumstances that harm, either bodily or mental, could result to him. I can only tell you that at that moment both my life and my reason rocked unsteadily on their seats.'

. . . . .

The other *Osiris* passengers had gone to bed. Only he and I remained leaning over the starboard railing, which rattled uneasily now and then under the fierce vibration of the over-engined mail-boat. Far over, there were the lights of a few fishing-smacks riding out the night, and a great rush of white combing and seething water fell out and away from us overside.

At last Colvin went on:

.   .   .   .   .

'Leaning over the foot of my bed, looking at me, was a figure swathed in a rotten and tattered veiling. This shroud passed over the head, but left both eyes and the right side of the face bare. It then followed the line of the arm down to where the hand grasped the bed-end. The face was not entirely that of a skull, though the eyes and the flesh of the face were totally gone. There was a thin, dry skin drawn tightly over the features, and there was some skin left on the hand. One wisp of hair crossed the forehead. It was perfectly still. I looked at it, and it looked at me, and my brains turned dry and hot in my head. I had still got the pear of the electric lamp in my hand, and I played idly with it; only I dared not turn the light out again. I shut my eyes only to open them in a hideous terror the same second. The thing had not moved. My heart was thumping, and the sweat cooled me as it evaporated. Another cinder tinkled in the gate, and a panel creaked in the wall.

'My reason failed me. For twenty minutes, or twenty seconds, I was able to think of nothing else but this awful figure, till there came, hurtling through the empty channels of my senses, the remembrance that Broughton and his friends had discussed me furtively at dinner. The dim possibility of its being a hoax stole gratefully into my unhappy mind, and once there, one's pluck came creeping back along a thousand tiny veins. My first sensation was one of blind, unreasoning thankfulness that my brain was going to stand the trial. I am not a timid man, but the best of us needs some human handle to steady him in time of extremity, and in this faint but growing hope that after all it might be only a brutal hoax, I found the fulcrum that I needed. At last I moved.

'How I managed to do it I cannot tell you, but with one spring towards the foot of the bed I got within arm's length and struck out one fearful blow with my fist at the thing. It crumbled under it, and my hand was cut to the bone. With a sickening revulsion after my terror, I dropped half-fainting across the end of the bed. So it was merely a foul trick after all. No doubt the trick had been played many a time before: no doubt Broughton and his friends had had some large bet among themselves as to what I should do when I discovered the gruesome thing. From my state of abject terror I found myself transported into an insensate anger. I shouted curses upon Broughton. I dived rather than climbed over the bed-end on to the sofa. I tore at the robed skeleton—how well the whole thing had been carried out, I thought—I broke the skull against the floor, and stamped upon its dry bones. I flung the head away under the bed, and rent the brittle bones of the trunk in pieces. I snapped the thin thigh-bones across my knee, and flung them in different directions. The shin-bones I set up against a stool and broke with my heel. I raged like a Berserker against the loathly thing, and stripped the ribs from the backbone and slung the breastbone against the cupboard. My fury increased as the work of destruction went on. I tore the frail, rotten veil into twenty pieces, and the dust went up over everything, over the clean blotting-paper and the silver inkstand.

'At last my work was done. There was but a raffle of broken bones and strips of parchment and crumbling wool. Then, picking up a piece of the skull—it was the cheek and temple bone of the right side, I remember—I opened the door and went down the passage to Broughton's dressing-room. I remember still how my sweat-dripping pyjamas clung to me as I walked. At the door I kicked and entered.

'Broughton was in bed. He had already turned the light

on and seemed shrunken and horrified. For a moment he could hardly pull himself together. Then I spoke. I don't know what I said. I only know that from a heart full and over-full with hatred and contempt, spurred on by shame of my own recent cowardice, I let my tongue run on. He answered nothing. I was amazed at my own fluency. My hair still clung lanky to my wet temples, my hand was bleeding profusely, and I must have looked a strange sight. Broughton huddled himself up at the head of the bed just as I had. Still he made no answer, no defence. He seemed pre-occupied with something beside my reproaches, and once or twice moistened his lips with his tongue. But he could say nothing, though he moved his hands now and then, just as a baby who cannot speak moves its hands.

'At last the door into Mrs. Broughton's room opened and she came in, white and terrified. "What is it? What is it? Oh, in God's name, what is it?" she cried again and again, and then she went up to her husband and sat on the bed in her night-dress, and the two faced me. I told her what the matter was. I spared her husband not a word for her presence there. Yet he seemed hardly to understand. I told the pair that I had spoiled their cowardly joke for them. Broughton looked up.

' "I have smashed the foul thing into a hundred pieces," I said. Broughton licked his lips again and his mouth worked. "By God!" I shouted, "it would serve you right if I thrashed you within an inch of your life. I will take care that no decent man or woman of my acquaintance ever speaks to you again. And there," I added, throwing the broken piece of the skull upon the floor beside his bed— "there is a souvenir for you of your damned work tonight!"

'Broughton saw the bone, and in a moment it was his turn to frighten me. He squealed like a hare caught in a trap. He screamed and screamed till Mrs. Broughton, almost as bewildered as myself, held on to him and coaxed him like a child to be quiet. But Broughton—and as he moved I thought that ten minutes ago I perhaps looked as terribly ill as he did—thrust her from him, and scrambled

out of the bed on to the floor, and still screaming put out
his hand to the bone. It had blood on it from my hand.
He paid no attention to me whatever. In truth I said nothing. This was a new turn indeed to the horrors of the evening. He rose from the floor with the bone in his hand and
stood silent. He seemed to be listening. "Time, time, perhaps," he muttered, and almost at the same moment fell
at full length on the carpet, cutting his head against the
fender. The bone flew from his hand and came to rest near
the door. I picked Broughton up, haggard and broken,
with blood over his face. He whispered hoarsely and
quickly: "Listen, listen!" We listened.

'After ten seconds' quiet, I seemed to hear something.
I could not be sure, but at last there was no doubt. There
was a quiet sound as of one moving along the passage.
Little regular steps came towards us over the hard oak
flooring. Broughton moved to where his wife sat, white and
speechless, on the bed, and pressed her face into his
shoulder.

'Then, the last thing that I could see as he turned the
light out, he fell forward with his own head pressed into
the pillow of the bed. Something in their company, something in their cowardice, helped me, and I faced the open
doorway of the room which was outlined fairly clearly
against the dimly lighted passage. I put out one hand and
touched Mrs. Broughton's shoulder in the darkness. But
at the last moment I too failed. I sank on my knees and put
my face in the bed. Only we all heard. The footsteps came
to the door, and there they stopped. The piece of bone was
lying a yard inside the door. There was a rustle of moving
stuff, and the thing was in the room. Mrs. Broughton was
silent; I could hear Broughton's voice praying, muffled in
the pillow; I was cursing my own cowardice. Then the
steps moved out again on the oak boards of the passage,
and I heard the sounds dying away. In a flash of remorse
I went to the door and looked out. At the end of the cor-
ridor I thought I saw something that moved away. A moment later the passage was empty. I stood with my forehead

against the jamb of the door almost physically sick.

' "You can turn the light on," I said, and there was an answering flare. There was no bone at my feet. Mrs. Broughton had fainted. Broughton was almost useless, and it took me ten minutes to bring her to. Broughton only said one thing worth remembering. For the most part he went on muttering prayers. But I was glad afterwards to recollect that he had said that thing. He said in a colourless voice, half as a question, half as a reproach: "You didn't speak to her."

'We spent the remainder of the night together. Mrs. Broughton actually fell off into a kind of sleep before dawn, but she suffered so horribly in her dreams that I shook her into consciousness again. Never was dawn so long in coming. Three or four times Broughton spoke to himself. Mrs. Broughton would then just tighten her hold on his arm, but she could say nothing. As for me, I can honestly say that I grew worse as the hours passed and the light strengthened. The two violent reactions had battered down my steadiness of view, and I felt that the foundations of my life had been built upon the sand. I said nothing, and after binding up my hand with a towel I did not move. It was better so. They helped me and I helped them, and we all three knew that our reason had gone very near to ruin that night.

'At last, when the light came in pretty strongly, and the birds outside were chattering and singing, we felt that we must do something. Yet we never moved. You might have thought that we should particularly dislike being found as we were by the servants: yet nothing of that kind mattered a straw, and an overpowering listnessness found us as we sat, until Chapman, Broughton's man, actually knocked and opened the door. None of us moved. Broughton, speaking hardly and stiffly, said: "Chapman, you can come back in five minutes." Chapman was a discreet man, but it would have made no difference to us if he had carried his news to the "room" at once.

'We looked at one another and I said I must go back. I

meant to wait outside until Chapman returned. I simply dared not re-enter my bedroom alone. Broughton roused himself and said that he would come with me. Mrs. Broughton agreed to remain in her own room for five minutes if the blinds were drawn up and all the doors left open.

'So Broughton and I, leaning stiffly one against the other, went down to my room. By the morning light that filtered past the blinds we could see our way, and I released the blinds. There was nothing wrong in the room from end to end, except smears of my own blood on the end of the bed, on the sofa, and on the carpet where I had torn the thing to pieces.'

.   .   .   .   .

Colvin had finished his story. There was nothing to say. Seven bells stuttered out from the fo'c'sle, and the answering cry wailed through the darkness. I took him downstairs.

'Of course I am much better now, but it is a kindness of you to let me sleep in your cabin.'

MRS. OLIPHANT

The Library Window

From STORIES OF THE SEEN AND THE UNSEEN

I

I WAS not aware at first of the many discussions which had gone on about that window. It was almost opposite one of the windows of the large, old-fashioned drawing-room of the house in which I spent that summer, which was of so much importance in my life. Our house and the library were on opposite sides of the broad High Street of St. Rule's, which is a fine street, wide and ample, and very quiet, as strangers think who come from noisier places; but in a summer evening there is much coming and going, and the stillness is full of sound—the sound of footsteps and pleasant voices, softened by the summer air.

There are even exceptional moments when it is noisy: the time of the fair, and on Saturday night sometimes, and when there are excursion trains. Then even the softest sunny air of the evening will not smooth the harsh tones and the stumbling steps; but at these unlovely moments we shut the windows, and even I, who am so fond of that deep recess where I can take refuge from all that is going on inside, and make myself a spectator of all the varied story out of doors, withdraw from my watch-tower. To tell the truth, there never was very much going on inside.

The house belonged to my aunt, to whom (she says, 'Thank God!') nothing ever happens. I believe that many things have happened to her in her time; but that was all over at the period of which I am speaking, and she was old, and very quiet. Her life went on in a routine never broken. She got up at the same hour every day, and did the same things in the same rotation, day by day the same. She said that this was the greatest support in the world, and that routine is a kind of salvation. It may be so; but it is a very dull salvation, and I used to feel that I would rather have incident, whatever kind of incident it might be. But then at that time I was not old, which makes all the difference.

At the time of which I speak the deep recess of the drawing-room window was a great comfort to me. Though she was an old lady (perhaps because she was so old she was very tolerant, and had a kind of feeling for me. She never said a word, but often gave me a smile when she saw how I had built myself up, with my books and my basket of work.

I did very little work, I fear—now and then a few stitches when the spirit moved me, or when I had got well afloat in a dream, and was more tempted to follow it out than to read my books, as sometimes happened. At other times, and if the book were interesting, I used to get through volume after volume sitting there, paying no attention to anybody. And yet I did pay a kind of attention. Aunt Mary's old ladies came in to call, and I heard them talk, though I very seldom listened; but for all that, if they had anything to say that was interesting, it is curious how I found it in my mind afterwards, as if the air had blown it to me. They came and went, and I had the sensation of their old bonnets gliding in and out, and their dresses rustling; and now and then had to jump up and shake hands with someone who knew me, and asked after my papa and mamma. Then Aunt Mary would give me a little smile again, and I slipped back to my window. She never seemed to mind.

My mother would not have let me do it, I know. She would have remembered dozens of things there were to do. She would have sent me upstairs to fetch something which I was quite sure she did not want, or downstairs to

206

carry some quite unnecessary message to the housemaid.
She liked to keep me running about. Perhaps that was one
reason why I was so fond of Aunt Mary's drawing-room,
and the deep recess of the window, and the curtain that
fell half over it, and the broad window-seat where one
could collect so many things without being found fault
with for untidiness. Whenever we had anything the matter with us in these days, we were sent to St. Rule's to get
up our strength. And this was my case at the time of which
I am going to speak.

Everybody had said, since ever I learned to speak, that
I was fantastic and fanciful and dreamy, and all the other
words with which a girl who may happen to like poetry,
and to be fond of thinking, is so often made uncomfortable. People don't know what they mean when they say fantastic. It wounds like Madge Wildfire, or something of
that sort. My mother thought I should always be busy, to
keep nonsense out of my head. But really I was not at all
fond of nonsense. I was rather serious than otherwise. I
would have been no trouble to anybody if I had been left
to myself. It was only that I had a sort of second sight, and
was conscious of things to which I paid no attention.

Even when reading the most interesting book, the things
that were being talked about blew in to me; and I heard
what the people were saying in the streets as they passed
under the window. Aunt Mary always said I could do
two or indeed three things at once—both read and listen and
see. I am sure that I did not listen much, and seldom looked
out—of set purpose—as some people do who notice what
bonnets the ladies in the street have on. But I did hear what
I couldn't help hearing, even when I was reading my book,
and I did see all sorts of things, though often for a whole
half-hour I might never lift my eyes.

This does not explain what I said at the beginning, that
there were many discussions about that window. It was,
and still is, the last window in the row of the College
Library, which is opposite my aunt's house in the High
Street. Yet it is not exactly opposite, but a little to the west,

so that I could see it best from the left side of my recess. I took it calmly for granted that it was a window like any other till I first heard the talk about it which was going on in the drawing-room. 'Have you never made up your mind, Mrs. Balcarres,' said old Mr. Pitmilly, 'whether that window opposite is a window or not?' He said Mistress Balcarres—and he was always called Mr. Pitmilly Morton: which was the name of his place.

'I am never sure of it, to tell the truth,' said Aunt Mary, 'all these years.'

'Bless me!' said one of the old ladies. 'And what window may that be?'

Mr. Pitmilly had a way of laughing as he spoke, which did not please me; but it was true that he was not perhaps desirous of pleasing me. He said: 'Oh, just the window opposite,' with his laugh running through his words; 'our friend can never make up her mind about it, though she has been living opposite it since . . .'

'You need never mind the date,' said another; 'the leebrary window! Dear me, what should it be but a window? Up at that height it could not be a door.'

'The question is,' said my aunt, 'if it is a real window with glass in it, or if it is merely painted, or if it once was a window and has been built up. And the oftener people look at it, the less they are able to say.'

'Let me see this window,' said old Lady Carnbee, who was very active and strong-minded; and then they all came crowding upon me—three or four old ladies, very eager, and Mr. Pitmilly's white hair appearing over their heads, and my aunt sitting quiet and smiling behind.

'I mind the window very well,' said Lady Carnbee; 'ay, and so do more than me. But in its present appearance it is just like any other window; but has not been cleaned, I should say, in the memory of man.'

'I see what ye mean,' said one of the others. 'It is just a very dead thing without any reflection in it; but I've seen as bad before.'

'Ay, it's dead enough,' said another, 'but that's no rule; for these huzzies of women-servants in this ill age . . .'

'Nay, the women are well enough,' said the softest voice of all, which was Aunt Mary's. 'I will never let them risk their lives cleaning the outside of mine. And there are no women-servants in the old library: there is maybe something more in it than that.'

They were all pressing into my recess, pressing upon me, a row of old faces, peering into something they could not understand. I had a sense in my mind how curious it was the wall of old ladies in their old satin gowns all glazed with age, Lady Carnbee with her lace about her head. Nobody was looking at me or thinking of me; but I felt unconsciously the contrast of my youngness to their oldness, and stared at them as they stared over my head at the library window. I had given it no attention up to this time. I was more taken up with the old ladies than with the thing they were looking at.

'The framework is all right at least, I can see that, and pented black . . .'

'And the panes are pented black too. It's no window, Mrs. Balcarres. It has been filled in, in the days of the window duties: you will mind, Leddy Carnbee.'

'Mind!' said that oldest lady. 'I mind when your mother was marriet, Jeanie: and that's neither the day nor yester-day. But as for the window, it's just a delusion; and that is my opinion of the matter, if you ask me.'

'There's a great want of light in that muckle room at the college,' said another. 'If it was a window, the leebrary would have more light.'

'One thing is clear,' said one of the younger ones: 'it cannot be a window to see through. It may be filled in or it may be built up, but it is not a window to give light.'

'And whoever heard of a window that was no' to see through?' Lady Carnbee said. I was fascinated by the look on her face, which was a curious, scornful look as of one who knew more than she chose to say; and then my wandering fancy was caught by her hand as she held it up, throwing back the lace that drooped over it. Lady Carnbee's lace was the chief thing about her—heavy, black, Spanish lace with large flowers. Everything she wore was trimmed with it. A large veil of it hung over her old bonnet. But her hand coming out of this heavy lace was a curious thing to see.

She had very long fingers, very tapered, which had been much admired in her youth; and her hand was very white, or rather more than white: pale, bleached, and bloodless, with large blue veins standing up upon the back; and she wore some fine rings, among others a big diamond in an ugly old claw setting. They were too big for her and were wound round and round with yellow silk to make them keep on: and this little cushion of silk, turned brown with long wearing, had twisted round so that it was more conspicuous than the jewels; while the big diamond blazed underneath in the hollow of her hand, like some dangerous thing hiding and sending out darts of light. The hand, which seemed to come almost to a point, with this strange ornament underneath, clutched at my half-terrified imagination. It too seemed to mean far more than was said. I felt as if it might clutch me with sharp claws, and the lurking, dazzling creature bite—with a sting that would go to the heart.

Presently, however, the circle of the old faces broke up, the old ladies returned to their seats, and Mr. Pitmilly, small but very erect, stood up in the midst of them, talking with mild authority like a little oracle among the ladies. Only Lady Carnbee always contradicted the neat, little old gentleman. She gesticulated when she talked, like a Frenchwoman, and darted forth that hand of hers with the lace hanging over it, so that I always caught a glimpse of the lurking diamond. I thought she looked like a witch among the comfortable little group which gave such attention to everything Mr. Pitmilly said.

'For my part, it is my opinion there is no window there at all,' he said. 'It's very like the thing that's called in scienteefic language an optical illusion. It arises generally, if I

may use such a word in the presence of ladies, from a liver
that is not just in the perfitt order and balance that organ
demands—and then you will see things—a blue dog, I remember, was the thing in one case, and in another . . .'

'The man has gane gyte,' said Lady Carnbee; 'I mind
the windows in the auld leebrary as long as I mind anything. Is the leebrary itself an optical illusion too?'

'Na, na,' and 'No, no,' said the old ladies. 'A blue dogue
would be a strange vagary; but the library we have all
kent from our youth,' said one. 'And I mind when the
Assemblies were held there one year when the Town Hall
was building,' another said.

'It is just a great divert to me,' said Aunt Mary; but
what was strange was that she paused there, and said in a
low tone, 'now', and then went on again, 'For whoever
comes to my house, there are aye discussions about that
window. I have never just made up my mind about it myself. Sometimes I think it's a case of these wicked window
duties, as you said, Miss Jeanie, when half the windows in
our houses were blocked up to save the tax. And then I
think it may be due to that blank kind of building like the
great new buildings on the Earthen Mound in Edinburgh,
where the windows are just ornaments. And then wiles I
am ˜sure I can see the glass shining when the sun catches
it in the afternoon.'

'You could so easily satisfy yourself, Mrs. Balcarres, if
you were to . . .'

'Give a laddie a penny to cast a stone, and see what
happens,' said Lady Carnbee.

'But I am not sure that I have any desire to satisfy myself,' Aunt Mary said. And then there was a stir in the
room, and I had to come out from my recess and open the
door for the old ladies and see them downstairs as they
all went away following one another. Mr. Pitmilly gave his
arm to Lady Carnbee, though she was always contradicting
him; and so the tea-party dispersed. Aunt Mary came to
the head of the stairs with her guests in an old-fashioned
gracious way, while I went down with them to see that the

maid was ready at the door. When I came back Aunt Mary was still standing in the recess looking out. Returning to my seat she said, with a kind of wistful look, 'Well, honey, and what is your opinion?'

'I have no opinion. I was reading my book all the time,' I said.

'And so you were, honey, and no' very civil; but all the same I ken well you heard every word we said.'

II

It was a night in June; dinner was long over, and had it been winter the maids would have been shutting up the house, and my Aunt Mary preparing to go upstairs to her room. But it was still clear daylight, that daylight out of which the sun has been long gone, and which has no longer any rose reflections, but all has sunk into a pearly, neutral tint—a light which is daylight yet is not day. We had taken a turn in the garden after dinner, and now we had returned to what we called our usual occupations. My aunt was reading. The English post had come in, and she had got her *Times*, which was her great diversion. The *Scotsman* was her morning reading, but she liked her *Times* at night.

As for me, I too was at my usual occupation, which at that time was doing nothing. I had a book as usual, and was absorbed in it; but I was conscious of all that was going on all the same. The people strolled along the broad pavement, making remarks as they passed under the open window, which came up into my story or my dream, and sometimes made me laugh. The tone and the faint singsong, or rather chant, of the accent, which was 'a wee Fifish', was novel to me, and associated with holiday, and pleasant; and sometimes they said to each other something that was amusing, and often something that suggested a whole story; but presently they began to drop off, the footsteps slackened, the voices died away. It was getting late, though the clear, soft daylight went on and on.

All through the lingering evening, which seemed to consist of interminable hours, long but not weary, drawn out as if the spell of the light and the outdoor life might never end, I had now and then, quite unawares, cast a glance at the mysterious window which my aunt and her friends had discussed, as I felt, though I dared not say it even to myself, rather foolishly. It caught my eye without any intention on my part, as I paused, as it were, to take breath, in the flowing and current of undistinguishable thoughts and things from without and within which carried me along.

First it occurred to me, with a little sensation of discovery, how absurd to say it was not a window, a living window, one to see through! Why, then, had they never *seen* it, these old folk? I saw as I looked up suddenly the faint greyness as of visible space within—a room behind, certainly—dim, as it was natural a room should be on the other side of the street—quite indefinite; yet so clear that if someone were to come to the window there would be nothing surprising in it. For certainly there was a feeling of space behind the panes which these old half-blind ladies had disputed about whether they were glass or only fictitious panes marked on the wall. How silly, when eyes that could see could make it out in a minute! It was only a greyness at present, but it was unmistakable: a space that went back into gloom, as every room does when you look into it across a street.

There were no curtains to show whether it was inhabited or not; but a room—oh, as distinctly as ever room was! I was pleased with myself, but said nothing, while Aunt Mary rustled her paper, waiting for a favourable moment to announce a discovery which settled her problem at once. Then I was carried away upon the stream again, and forgot the window, till somebody threw, unawares, a word from the outer world, 'I'm goin' hame; it'll soon be dark.' Dark! what was the fool thinking of? it never would be dark if one waited out, wandering in the soft air for hours

MRS. OLIPHANT

longer; and then my eyes, acquiring easily that new habit, looked across the way again.

Ah, now! nobody indeed had come to the window; and no light had been lighted, seeing it was still beautiful to read by—a still, clear, colourless light; but the room inside had certainly widened. I could see the grey space and air a little deeper, and a sort of vision, very dim, of a wall, and something against it—something dark, with the blackness that a solid article, however indistinctly seen, takes in the lighter darkness that is only space: a large, black, dark thing coming out into the grey. I looked more intently, and made sure it was a piece of furniture, either a writing-table or perhaps a large bookcase. No doubt it must be the last, since this was part of the old library. I never visited the old College Library, but I had seen such places before, and I could well imagine it to myself. How curious that for all the time these old people had looked at it they had never seen this before!

It was more silent now, and my eyes, I suppose, had grown dim with gazing, doing my best to make it out, when suddenly Aunt Mary said: 'Will you ring the bell, my dear? I must have my lamp.'

'Your lamp?' I cried, 'when it is still daylight.' But then I gave another look at my window, and perceived with a start that the light had indeed changed: for now I saw nothing. It was still light, but there was so much change in the light that my room, with the grey space and the large shadowy bookcase, had gone out, and I saw them no more; for even a Scotch night in June, though it looks as if it would never end, does darken at the last. I had almost cried out, but checked myself, and rang the bell for Aunt Mary, and made up my mind I would say nothing till next morning, when, to be sure, naturally, it would be more clear.

Next morning I rather think I forgot all about it, or was busy, or was more idle than usual—the two things meant nearly the same. At all events I thought no more of the window, though I still sat in my own, opposite to it, but occupied with some other fancy. Aunt Mary's visitors came as usual in the afternoon; but their talk was of other things, and for a day or two nothing at all happened to bring back my thoughts into this channel.

It might be nearly a week before the subject came back, and once more it was old Lady Carnbee who set me thinking. Not that she said anything upon that particular theme, but she was the last of my aunt's afternoon guests to go away, and when she rose to leave she threw up her hands, with those lively gesticulations which so many old Scotch ladies have. 'My faith!' said she, 'there is that bairn there still like a dream. Is the creature bewitched. Mary Balcarres? and is she bound to sit there by night and by day for the rest of her days? You should mind that there's things about, uncanny for women of our blood.'

I was too much startled at first to recognise that it was of me she was speaking. She was like a figure in a picture, with her pale face the colour of ashes, and the big pattern of the Spanish lace hanging half over it, and her hand held up, with the big diamond blazing at me from the inside of her uplifted palm. It was held up in surprise, but it looked as if it were raised in malediction; and the diamond threw out darts of light, and glared and twinkled at me. If it had been in its right place it would not have mattered; but there, in the open of the hand! I started up, half in terror, half in wrath. And then the old lady laughed, and her hand dropped.

'I've wakened you to life, and broke the spell,' she said, nodding her old head at me, while the large black silk flowers of the lace waved and threatened. And she took my arm to go downstairs, laughing and bidding me be steady, and no' tremble and shake like a broken reed. 'You should be as steady as a rock at your age. I was like a young tree,' she said, leaning so heavily that my willowy girlish frame quivered. 'I was a support to virtue, like Pamela, in my time.'

'Aunt Mary, Lady Carnbee is a witch!' I cried, when I came back.

'Is that what you think, honey? well, maybe she once was,' said Aunt Mary, whom nothing surprised.

And it was that night once more after dinner, and after the post came in, and *The Times*, that I suddenly saw the library window again. I had seen it every day—and noticed nothing; but tonight, still in a little tumult of mind over Lady Carnbee and her wicked diamond which wished me harm, and her lace which waved threats and warnings at me, I looked across the street, and there I saw quite plainly the room opposite, far more clear than before.

I saw dimly that it must be a large room, and that the big piece of furniture against the wall was a writing-desk. That in a moment, when first my eyes rested upon it, was quite clear: a large, old-fashioned escritoire, standing out into the room: and I knew by the shape of it that it had a great many pigeon-holes and little drawers in the back, and a large table for writing. There was one just like it in my father's library at home. It was such a surprise to see it all so clearly that I closed my eyes, for the moment almost giddy, wondering how papa's desk could have come here —and then when I reminded myself that this was nonsense and that there were many such writing-tables besides papa's, and looked again—lo! it had all become quite vague and indistinct as it was at first; and I saw nothing but the blank window of which the old ladies could never be certain whether it was filled up to avoid the window-tax, or whether it had ever been a window at all.

This occupied my mind very much, and yet I did not say anything to Aunt Mary. For one thing, I rarely saw anything at all in the early part of the day; but, then, that is natural: you can never see into a place from outside, whether it is an empty room or a looking-glass or people's eyes or anything else that is mysterious, in the day. It has, I suppose, something to do with the light. But in the evening in June in Scotland—then is the time to see. For it is daylight, yet it is not day, and there is a quality in it which I cannot describe, it is so clear, as if every object was a reflection of itself.

I used to see more and more of the room as the days went on. The large escritoire stood out more and more into the space: with sometimes white glimmering things, which looked like papers, lying on it: and once or twice I was sure I saw a pile of books on the floor close to the writing-table, as if they had gilding upon them in broken specks, like old books. It was always about the time when the lads in the street began to call to one another that they were going home, and sometimes a shriller voice would come from one of the doors, bidding somebody to 'cry upon the laddies' to come back to their suppers. That was always the time I saw best, though it was close upon the moment when the veil seemed to fall and the clear radiance became less living, and all the sounds died out of the street, and Aunt Mary said in her soft voice, 'Honey, will you ring for the lamp?' She said honey as people say darling; and I think it is a prettier word.

Then, finally, while I sat one evening with my book in my hand, looking straight across the street, not distracted by anything, I saw a little movement within. It was not anyone visible—but everybody must know what it is to see the stir in the air, the little disturbance—you cannot tell what it is, but that it indicates someone there, even though you can see no one. Perhaps it is a shadow making just one flicker in the still place. You may look at an empty room and the furniture in it for hours, and then suddenly there will be the flicker, and you know that something has come into it. It might only be a dog or a cat; it might be, if that were possible, a bird flying across; but it is someone, something living, which is so different, so completely different, in a moment from the things that are not living. It seemed to strike right through me, and I gave a little cry. Then Aunt Mary stirred a little, and put down the huge newspaper that almost covered her from sight, and said, 'What is it, honey?' I cried, 'Nothing,' with a little gasp, quickly, for I did not want to be disturbed just at this moment when somebody was coming! But I suppose she was not satisfied, for she got up and stood behind to see what it was, putting her hand on my shoulder. It was the softest touch in the world, but I could have flung it off angrily: for that moment everything was still again, and the place grew grey and I saw no more.

'Nothing,' I repeated, but I was so vexed I could have cried. 'I told you it was nothing, Aunt Mary. Don't you believe me, that you come to look—and spoil it all!'

I did not mean, of course, to say these last words; they were forced out of me. I was so much annoyed to see it all melt away like a dream: for it was no dream, but as real as—as real as—myself or anything I ever saw.

She gave my shoulder a little pat with her hand. 'Honey,' she said, 'were you looking at something? Is't that? is't that?' 'is it what?' I wanted to say, shaking off her hand, but something in me stopped me: for I said nothing at all, and she went quietly back to her place. I suppose she must have rung the bell herself, for immediately I felt the soft flood of the light behind me, and the evening outside dimmed down, as it did every night, and I saw nothing more.

It was next day, I think, in the afternoon that I spoke. It was brought on by something she said about her fine work. 'I get a mist before my eyes,' she said; 'you will have to learn my old lace stitches, honey, for I soon will not see to draw the threads.'

'Oh, I hope you will keep your sight,' I cried, without thinking what I was saying. I was then young and very matter of fact. I had not found out that one may mean something, yet not half or a hundredth part of what one seems to mean: and even then probably hoping to be contradicted if it is anyhow against one's self.

'My sight!' she said, looking up at me with a look that was almost angry; 'there is no question of losing my sight—on the contrary, my eyes are very strong. I may not see to draw fine threads, but I see at a distance as well as ever I did—as well as you do.'

'I did not mean any harm, Aunt Mary,' I said. 'I thought you said . . . But how can your sight be as good as

ever when you are in doubt about that window? I can see
into the room as clear as . . .' My voice wavered, for I had
just looked up and across the street, and I could have sworn
that there was no window at all, but only a false image of
one painted on the wall.

'Ah!' she said, with a little tone of keenness and of
surprise; and she half rose up, throwing down her work
hastily, as if she meant to come to me. Then, perhaps seeing
the bewildered look on my face, she paused and hesitated.
'Ay, honey!' she said, 'have you got so far ben as that?'

What did she mean? Of course I knew all the Scotch
phrases as well as I knew myself; but it is a comfort to take
refuge in a little ignorance, and I know I pretended not to
understand whenever I was put out. 'I don't know what
you mean by "far ben",' I cried out, very impatient. I
don't know what might have followed, but someone just
then came to call, and she could only give me a look before
she went forward, putting out her hand to her visitor. It
was a very soft look, but anxious, and as if she did not
know what to do: and she shook her head a very little, and
I thought, though there was a smile on her face, there was
something wet about her eyes. I retired into my recess, and
nothing more was said.

But it was very tantalising that it should fluctuate so;
for sometimes I saw that room quite plain and clear—quite
as clear as I could see papa's library, for example, when I
shut my eyes. I compared it naturally to my father's study,
because of the shape of the writing-table, which, as I tell
you, was the same as his. At times I saw the papers on the
table quite plain, just as I had seen his papers many a day.
And the little pile of books on the floor at the foot—not
ranged regularly in order, but put down one above the
other, with all their angles going different ways, and a speck
of the old gilding shining here and there. And then again
at other times I saw nothing, absolutely nothing, and was
no better than the old ladies who had peered over my head,
drawing their eyelids together, and arguing that the window had been shut up because of the old, long-abolished

window tax, or else that it had never been a window at all. It annoyed me very much at those dull moments to feel that I too puckered up my eyelids and saw no better than they.

Aunt Mary's old ladies came and went day after day while June went on. I was to go back in July, and I felt that I should be very unwilling indeed to leave until I had quite cleared up—as I was indeed in the way of doing— the mystery of that window which changed so strangely and appeared quite a different thing, not only to different people, but to the same eyes at different times. 'Of course,' I said to myself, 'it must simply be an effect of the light.' And yet I did not quite like that explanation either, but would have been better pleased to make out to myself that it was some superiority in me which made it so clear to me, if it were only the great superiority of young eyes over old —though that was not quite enough to satisfy me, seeing it was a superiority which I shared with every little lass and lad in the street. I rather wanted, I believe, to think that there was some particular insight in me which gave clearness to my sight—which was a most impertinent assumption, but really did not mean half the harm it seems to mean when it is put down here in black and white. I had several times again, however, seen the room quite plain, and made out that it was a large room, with a great picture in a dim gilded frame hanging on the farther wall, and many other pieces of solid furniture making a blackness here and there, besides the great escritoire against the wall, which had evidently been placed near the window for the sake of the light. One thing became visible to me after another, till I almost thought I should end by being able to read the old lettering on one of the big volumes which projected from the others and caught the light; but this was all preliminary to the great event which happened about Midsummer Day—the day of St. John, which was once so much thought of as a festival, but now means nothing at all in Scotland any more than any other of the saints' days: which I shall always think a great pity and loss to Scotland, whatever Aunt Mary may say.

III

It was about midsummer, I cannot say exactly to a day when, but near that time, when the great event happened. I had grown very well acquainted by this time with that large, dim room. Not only the escritoire, which was very plain to me now, with the papers upon it, and the books at its foot, but the great picture that hung against the farther wall, and various other shadowy pieces of furniture, especially a chair which one evening I saw had been moved into the space before the escritoire—a little change which made my heart beat, for it spoke so distinctly of someone who must have been there, the someone who had already made me start, two or three times before, by some vague shadow of him or thrill of him which made a sort of movement in the silent space : a movement which made me sure that next minute I must see something or hear something which would explain the whole—if it were not that something always happened outside to stop it, at the very moment of its accomplishment.

I had no warning this time of movement or shadow. I had been looking into the room very attentively a little while before, and had made out everything almost clearer than ever; and then had bent my attention again on my book, and read a chapter or two at a most exciting period of the story: and consequently had quite left St. Rule's, and the High Street, and the College Library, and was really in a South American forest, almost throttled by the flowery creepers, and treading softly lest I should put my foot on a scorpion or a dangerous snake. At this moment something suddenly called my attention to the outside. I looked across, and then, with a start, sprang up, for I could not contain myself. I don't know what I said, but enough to startle the people in the room, one of whom was old Mr. Pitmilly. They all looked round upon me to ask what was the matter. And when I gave my usual answer of 'Nothing', sitting down again, shamefaced but very much excited, Mr. Pitmilly got up and came forward, and looked out, apparently to see what was the cause. He saw nothing, for he went back again, and I could hear him telling Aunt Mary not to be alarmed, for Missy had fallen into a doze with the heat, and had startled herself waking up, at which they all laughed: another time I could have killed him for his impertinence, but my mind was too much taken up now to pay any attention. My head was throbbing and my heart beating. I was in such high excitement, however, that to restrain myself completely, to be perfectly silent, was more easy to me then than at any other time of my life. I waited until the old gentlemen had taken his seat again, and then I looked back. Yes, there he was. I had not been deceived. I knew then, when I looked across, that this was what I had been looking for all the time—that I had known he was there, and had been waiting for him, every time there was that flicker of movement in the room—him and no one else. And there at last, just as I had expected, he was. I don't know that in reality I ever had expected him, or anyone: but this was what I felt when, suddenly looking into that curious dim room, I saw him there.

He was sitting in the chair, which he must have placed for himself, or which someone else in the dead of night when nobody was looking must have set for him, in front of the escritoire—with the back of his head towards me—writing. The light fell upon him from the left hand, and therefore upon his shoulders and the side of his head, which, however, was too much turned away to show anything of his face. Oh, how strange that there should be someone staring at him as I was doing, and he never to turn his head, to make a movement! If anyone stood and looked at me, were I in the soundest sleep that ever was, I would wake, I would jump up, I would feel it through everything. But there he sat and never moved. You are not to suppose, though I said the light fell upon him from the left hand, that there was very much light. There never is in a room you are looking into like that across the street; but there was enough to see him by—the outline of his figure, dark and solid, seated in the chair, and the fairness of his head visible faintly, a clear spot against the dimness. I saw this outline against the dim gilding of the frame of the large picture which hung on the farther wall.

I sat, all the time the visitors were there, in a sort of rapture, gazing at this figure. I knew no reason why I should be so much moved. In an ordinary way, to see a student at an opposite window quietly doing his work might have interested me a little, but certainly it would not have moved me in any such way. It is always interesting to have a glimpse like this of an unknown life—to see so much and yet know so little, and to wonder, perhaps, what the man is doing, and why he never turns his head. One would go to the window—but not too close, lest he should see you and think you were spying upon him—and one would ask, 'Is he still there? Is he writing, writing always? I wonder what he is writing!' And it would be a great amusement: but no more. This was not my feeling at all in the present case. It was a sort of breathless watch, an absorption. I did not feel that I had eyes for anything else, or any room in my mind for another thought. I no longer heard, as I generally did, the stories and the wise remarks (or foolish) of Aunt Mary's old ladies or Mr. Pitmilly. I heard only a murmur behind me, the interchange of voices, one softer, one sharper; but it was not as in the time when I sat reading and heard every word, till the story in my book and the stories they were telling (what they said almost always shaped into stories), were all mingled into one another, and the hero in the novel became somehow the hero (or more likely heroine) of them all. But I took no notice of what they were saying now. And it was not that there was anything very interesting to look at, except the fact that he was there. He did nothing to keep up the absorption of my thoughts. He moved just so much as a man will do when he is very busily writing, thinking of nothing else.

There was a faint turn of his head as he went from one

side to another of the page he was writing; but it appeared
to be a long, long page which never wanted turning. Just a
little outward, inclination when he was at the end of the
line, and then a little inclination inward when he began
the next. That was little enough to keep one gazing. But I
suppose it was the gradual course of events leading up to
this, the finding out of one thing after another as the eyes
got accustomed to the vague light: first the room itself, and
then the writing-table, and then the other furniture, and
last of all the human inhabitant who gave it all meaning.
This was all so interesting that it was like a country which
one had discovered. And then the extraordinary blindness
of the other people who disputed among themselves whether
it was a window at all! I did not, I am sure, wish to be dis-
respectful, and I was very fond of my Aunt Mary, and I
liked Mr. Pitmilly well enough, and I was afraid of Lady
Carnbee. But yet to think of the—I know I ought not to
say stupidity—the blindness of them, the foolishness, the
insensibility! discussing it as if a thing that your eyes could
see was a thing to discuss! It would have been unkind to
think it was because they were old and their faculties
dimmed. It is so sad to think that the faculties grow dim,
that such a woman as my Aunt Mary should fail in seeing,
or hearing, or feeling, that I would not have dwelt on it
for a moment, it would have seemed so cruel! And then
such a clever old lady as Lady Carnbee—who could see
through a millstone, people said—and Mr. Pitmilly, such
an old man of the world. It did indeed bring tears to my
eyes to think that all those clever people, solely by reason
of being no longer young as I was, should have the simplest
things shut out from them; and for all their wisdom and
their knowledge be unable to see what a girl like me could
see so easily. I was too much grieved for them to dwell
upon that thought, and half ashamed, though perhaps half
proud too, to be so much better off than they.

All those thoughts flitted through my mind as I sat and
gazed across the street. And I felt there was so much going
on in that room across the street! He was so absorbed in

his writing, never looked up, never paused for a word, never turned round in his chair, or got up and walked about the room as my father did. Papa is a great writer, everybody says: but he would have come to the window and looked out, he would have drummed with his fingers on the pane, he would have watched a fly and helped it over a difficulty, and played with the fringe of the curtain, and done a dozen other nice, pleasant, foolish things, till the next sentence took shape.

'My dear, I am waiting for a word,' he would say to my mother when she looked at him, with a question why he was so idle, in her eyes; and then he would laugh, and go back again to his writing-table. But He over there never stopped at all. It was like a fascination. I could not take my eyes from him and that little scarcely perceptible movement he made, turning his head. I trembled with impatience to see him turn the page, or perhaps throw down his finished sheet on the floor, as somebody looking into a window like me once saw Sir Walter do, sheet after sheet.

I should have cried out if this Unknown had done that. I should not have been able to help myself, whoever had been present; and gradually I got into such a state of suspense waiting for it to be done that my head grew hot and my hands cold. And then, just when there was a little movement of his elbow, as if he were about to do this, to be called away by Aunt Mary to see Lady Carnbee to the door! I believe I did not hear her till she had called me three times, and then I stumbled up, all flushed and hot, and nearly crying. When I came out from the recess to give the old lady my arm (Mr. Pitmilly had gone away some time before) she put up her hand and stroked my cheek. 'What ails the bairn?' she said; 'she's fevered. You must not let her sit her lane in the window, Mary Balcarres. You and me know what comes of that.' Her old fingers had a strange touch, cold like something not living, and I felt that dreadful diamond sting me on the cheek.

I do not say that this was not just a part of my excitement and suspense; and I know it is enough to make anyone laugh when the excitement was all about an unknown man writing in a room on the other side of the way, and my impatience because he never came to an end of the page. If you think I was not quite as well aware of this as anyone could be! But the worst was that this dreadful old lady felt my heart beating against her arm that was within mine. 'You are just in a dream,' she said to me, with her old voice close at my ear as we went downstairs. 'I don't know who it is about, but it's bound to be some man that is not worth it. If you were wise you would think of him no more.'

'I am thinking of no man!' I said, half crying. 'It is very unkind and dreadful of you to say so, Lady Carnbee. I never thought of—any man, in all my life!' I cried in a passion of indignation. The old lady clung tighter to my arm, and pressed it to her, not unkindly.

'Poor little bird,' she said, 'how it's strugglin' and flutterin'! I'm not saying but what it's more dangerous when it's all for a dream.'

She was not at all unkind; but I was very angry and excited, and would scarcely shake that old pale hand which she put out to me from her carriage window when I had helped her in. I was angry with her, and I was afraid of the diamond, which looked up from under her finger as if it saw through and through me; and whether you believe me or not, I am certain that it stung me again—a sharp, malignant prick, oh, full of meaning! She never wore gloves, but only black lace mittens, through which that horrible diamond gleamed. I ran upstairs—she had been the last to go—and Aunt Mary too had gone to get ready for dinner, for it was late. I hurried to my place, and looked across, with my heart beating more than ever. I made quite sure I should see the finished sheet lying white upon the floor. But what I gazed at was only the dim blank of that window which they said was no window.

The light had changed in some wonderful way during that five minutes I had been gone, and there was nothing, nothing, not a reflection, not a glimmer. It looked exactly as they all said, the blank form of a window painted on the wall. It was too much: I sat down in my excitement and cried as if my heart would break. I felt that they had done something to it, that it was not natural, that I could not bear their unkindness—even Aunt Mary. They thought it not good for me! not good for me! and they had done something—even Aunt Mary herself—and that wicked diamond that hid itself in Lady Carnbee's hand.

Of course I knew all this was ridiculous as well as you could tell me; but I was exasperated by the disappointment and the sudden stop to all my excited feelings, and I could not bear it. It was more strong than I.

I was late for dinner, and naturally there were some traces in my eyes that I had been crying when I came into the full light in the dining-room, where Aunt Mary could look at me at her pleasure, and I could not run away. She said, 'Honey, you have been shedding tears. I'm loth, loth that a bairn of your mother's should be made to shed tears in my house.'

'I have not been made to shed tears,' cried I; and then, to save myself another fit of crying, I burst out laughing and said, 'I am afraid of that dreadful diamond on old Lady Carnbee's hand. It bites—I am sure it bites! Aunt Mary, look here.'

'You foolish lassie,' Aunt Mary said; but she looked at my cheek under the light of the lamp, and then she gave it a little pat with her soft hand. 'Go away with you, you silly bairn. There is no bite; but a flushed cheek, my honey, and a wet eye. You must just read out my paper to me after dinner when the post is in; and we'll have no more thinking and no more dreaming for tonight.'

'Yes, Aunt Mary,' said I. But I knew what would happen; for when she opens up her *Times*, all full of the news of the world, and the speeches and things which she takes an interest in—though I cannot tell why—she forgets. And as I kept very quiet and made not a sound, she forgot to-night what she had said, and the curtain hung a little more over me than usual, and I sat down in my recess as if I had been a hundred miles away.

And my heart gave a great jump, as if it would have come out of my breast; for he was there. But not as he had been in the morning—I suppose the light, perhaps, was not good enough to go on with his work without a lamp or candles—for he had turned away from the table and was fronting the window, sitting leaning back in his chair, and turning his head to me. Not to me—he knew nothing about me. I thought he was not looking at anything; but with his face turned my way.

My heart was in my mouth: it was so unexpected, so strange! Though why it should have seemed strange I know not, for there was no communication between him and me that it should have moved me; and what could be more natural than that a man, wearied of his work, and feeling the want, perhaps, of more light, and yet that it was not dark enough to light a lamp, should turn round in his own chair, and rest a little, and think—perhaps of nothing at all? Papa always says he is thinking of nothing at all. He says things blow through his mind as if the doors were open, and he has no responsibility. What sort of things were blowing through this man's mind? Or was he thinking, still thinking, of what he had been writing and going on with it still?

The thing that troubled me most was that I could not make out his face. It is very difficult to do so when you see a person only through two windows, your own and his. I wanted very much to recognise him afterwards if I should chance to meet him in the street. If he had only stood up and moved about the room I should have made out the rest of his figure, and then I should have known him again; or if he had only come to the window (as papa always did), then I should have seen his face clearly enough to have recognised him.

But to be sure, he did not see any need to do anything in order that I might recognise him, for he did not know I existed; and probably if he had known I was watching him, he would have been annoyed and gone away.

But he was as immovable there, facing the window, as

he had been seated at the desk. Sometimes he made a little
faint stir with a hand or a foot, and I held my breath,
hoping he was about to rise from his chair—but he never
did it. And with all the efforts I made I could not be sure
of his face. I puckered my eyelids together, as old Miss
Jeanie did who was shortsighted, and I put my hands on
each side of my face to concentrate the light on him: but
it was all in vain. Either the face changed as I sat staring, or
else it was the light that was not good enough, or I don't
know what it was.

His hair seemed to me light—certainly there was no
dark line about his head, as there would have been had it
been very dark—and I saw, where it came across the old
gilt frame on the wall behind, that it must be fair: and I am
almost sure he had no beard. Indeed I am sure that he had
no beard, for the outline of his face was distinct enough;
and the daylight was still quite clear out of doors, so that
I recognised perfectly a baker's boy who was on the pavement opposite, and whom I should have known again
whenever I had met him: as if it were of the least importance to recognise a baker's boy!

There was one thing, however, rather curious about this
boy. He had been throwing stones at something or somebody. In St. Rule's they have a great way of throwing stones
at one another, and I suppose there had been a battle. I
suppose also that he had one stone in his hand left over
from the battle, and his roving eye took in all the incidents
of the street to judge where he could throw it with most
effect and mischief. But apparently he found nothing
worthy of it in the street, for he suddenly turned round
with a flick under his leg to show his cleverness, and aimed
it straight at the window.

I remarked without remarking that it struck with a hard
sound and without any breaking of glass, and fell straight
down on the pavement. But I took no notice of this even
in my mind, so intently was I watching the figure within,
which moved not nor took the slightest notice, and remained
just as dimly clear, as perfectly seen, yet as undistinguish-

able, as before. And then the light began to fail a little, not diminishing the prospect within, but making it still less distinct than it had been.

Then I jumped up, feeling Aunt Mary's hand upon my shoulder. 'Honey,' she said, 'I asked you twice to ring the bell; but you did not hear me.'

'Oh, Aunt Mary!' I cried in great penitence, but turned again to the window in spite of myself.

'You must come away from there; you must come away from there,' she said, almost as if she were angry: and then her soft voice grew softer, and she gave me a kiss. 'Never mind about the lamp, honey; I have rung myself, and it is coming; but, silly bairn, you must not aye be dreaming— your little head will turn.'

All the answer I made, for I could scarcely speak, was to give a little wave with my hand to the window on the other side of the street.

She stood there patting me softly on the shoulder for a whole minute or more, murmuring something that sounded like, 'She must go away, she must go away.' Then she said, always with her hand soft on my shoulder, 'Like a dream when one awaketh.' And when I looked again I saw the blank of an opaque surface and nothing more.

Aunt Mary asked me no more questions. She made me come into the room and sit in the light and read something to her. But I did not know what I was reading, for there suddenly came into my mind and took possession of it, the thud of the stone upon the window, and its descent straight down, as if from some hard substance that threw it off: though I had myself seen it strike upon the glass of the panes across the way.

IV

I am afraid I continued in a state of great exaltation and commotion of mind for some time. I used to hurry through the day till the evening came, when I could watch my neigh-

bour through the window opposite. I did not talk much to
anyone, and I never said a word about my own questions
and wonderings. I wondered who he was, what he was
doing, and why he never came till the evening (or very
rarely); and I also wondered much to what house the room
belonged in which he sat. It seemed to form a portion of
the old College Library, as I have often said.

The window was one of the line of windows which, I
understood, lighted the large hall; but whether this room
belonged to the library itself, or how its occupant gained
access to it, I could not tell. I made up my mind that it
must open out of the hall, and that the gentleman must be
the librarian or one of his assistants, perhaps kept busy all
the day in his official duties, and only able to get to his desk
and do his own private work in the evening. One had heard
of so many things like that—a man who had to take up
some other kind of work for his living, and then when his
leisure time came, gave it all up to something he really
loved—some study or some book he was writing.

My father himself at one time had been like that. He had
been in the Treasury all day, and then in the evening wrote
his books, which made him famous. His daughter, however little she might know of other things, could not but
know that! But it discouraged me very much when somebody pointed out to me one day in the street an old gentleman who wore a wig and took a great deal of snuff, and
said, 'That's the librarian of the old college.' It gave me
a great shock for a moment; but then I remembered that
an old gentleman has generally assistants, and that it must
be one of them.

Gradually I became quite sure of this. There was another small window above, which twinkled very much when
the sun shone, and looked a very kindly, bright little window, above that dullness of the other which hid so much.
I made up my mind this was the window of his other room,
and that these two chambers at the end of the beautiful hall
were really beautiful for him to live in, so near all the
books, and so retired and quiet, that nobody knew of them.

What a fine thing for him! and you could see what use he
made of his good fortune as he sat there, so constant at his
writing for hours together.

Was it a book he was writing, or could it be perhaps
poems? This was a thought which made my heart beat;
but I concluded with much regret that it could not be
poems, because no one could possibly write poems like
that, straight off, without pausing for a word or a rhyme.
Had they been poems he must have risen up, he must have
paced about the room or come to the window as papa
did—not that papa wrote poems: he always said, 'I am
not worthy even to speak of such prevailing mysteries,'
shaking his head—which gave me a wonderful admiration
and almost awe of a poet, who thus much greater even than
papa.

But I could not believe that a poet could have kept still
for hours and hours like that. What could it be, then? Perhaps it was history; that is a great thing to work at, but
you would not, perhaps, need to move nor to stride up
and down, or look out upon the sky and the wonderful
light.

He did move now and then, however, though he never
came to the window. Sometimes, as I have said, he would
turn round in his chair and turn his face towards it, and sit
there for a long time musing when the light had begun to
fail, and the world was full of that strange day which was
night, that light without colour, in which everything was
so clearly visible, and there were no shadows. 'It was between the night and the day, when the fairy folk have
power.' This was the after-light of the wonderful, long,
long summer evening, the light without shadows. It had a
spell in it, and sometimes it made me afraid: and all manner of strange thoughts seemed to come in, and I always
felt that if only we had a little more vision in our eyes we
might see beautiful folk walking about in it, who were
not of our world. I thought most likely he saw them, from
the way he sat there looking out: and this made my heart
expand with the most curious sensation, as if of pride that,

though I could not see, he did, and did not even require
to come to the window, as I did, sitting close in the depth
of the recess, with my eyes upon him, and almost seeing
things through his eyes.

I was so much absorbed in these thoughts and in watching him every evening—for now he never missed an evening
but was always there—that people began to remark that I
was looking pale and that I could not be well, for I paid no
attention when they talked to me, and did not care to go
out, nor to join the other girls for their tennis, nor to do
anything that others did. And some said to Aunt Mary
that I was quickly losing all the ground I had gained, and
that she could never send me back to my mother with a
white face like that.

Aunt Mary had begun to look at me anxiously for some
time before that, and, I am sure, held secret consultations
over me, sometimes with the doctor, and sometimes with
her old ladies, who thought they knew more about young
girls than even the doctors. And I could hear them saying
to her that I wanted diversion, that I must be diverted,
and that she must take me out more, and give a party, and
that when the summer visitors began to come there would
perhaps be a ball or two, or Lady Carnbee would get up
a picnic.

'And there's my young lord coming home,' said the old
lady whom they called Miss Jeanie, 'and I never knew
the young lassie yet that would not cock up her bonnet at
the sight of a young lord.'

But Aunt Mary shook her head. 'I would not lippen
much to the young lord,' she said. 'His mother is sore set
upon siller for him; and my poor bit honey has no fortune
to speak of. No, we must not fly so high as the young lord;
but I will gladly take her about the country to see the old
castles and towers. It will perhaps rouse her up a little.'

'And if that does not answer we must think of something else,' the old lady said.

I heard them, perhaps, that day because they were talking of me, which is always so effective a way of making

233

you hear—for latterly I had not been paying any attention to what they were saying; and I thought to myself how little they knew, and how little I cared about even the old castles and curious houses, having something else in my mind. But just about that time Mr. Pitmilly came in, who was always a friend to me, and, when he heard them talking, he managed to stop them and turn the conversation into another channel.

And after a while, when the ladies were gone away, he came up to my recess, and gave a glance right over my head. And then he asked my Aunt Mary if ever she had settled her question about the window opposite 'that you thought was a window sometimes, and then not a window, and many curious things', the old gentleman said.

My Aunt Mary gave me another very wistful look; and then she said, 'Indeed, Mr. Pitmilly, we are just where we were, and I am quite as unsettled as ever; and I think my niece she has taken up my views, for I see her many a time looking across and wondering, and I am not clear now what her opinion is.'

'My opinion!' I said. 'Aunt Mary!' I could not help being a little scornful, as one is when one is very young. 'I have no opinion. There is not only a window but there is a room, and I could show you . . .' I was going to say, 'show you the gentleman who sits and writes in it', but I stopped, not knowing what they might say, and looked from one to another. 'I could tell you—all the furniture that is in it,' I said. And then I felt something like a flame that went over my face, and that all at once my cheeks were burning. I thought they gave a little glance at one another, but that may have been folly. 'There is a great picture, in a big dim frame,' I said, feeling a little breathless, 'on the wall opposite the window . . .'

'Is there so?' said Mr. Pitmilly, with a little laugh. And he said, 'Now I will tell you what we'll do. You know that there is a conversation party, or whatever they call it, in the big room tonight, and it will be all open and lighted up. And it is a handsome room, and two-three things well worth looking at. I will just step along after we have all got our dinner, and take you over to the pairty, madam— Missy and you ...'

'Dear me!' said Aunt Mary. 'I have not gone to a party for more years than I would like to say—and never once to the Library Hall.' Then she gave a little shiver, and said quite low, 'I could not go there.'

'Then you will just begin again tonight, madam,' said Mr. Pitmilly, taking no notice of this, 'and a proud man will I be leading in Mistress Balcarres that was once the pride of the ball.'

'Ah, once!' said Aunt Mary, with a low little laugh and then a sigh. 'And we'll not say how long ago,' and after that she made a pause, looking always at me: and then she said, 'I accept your offer, and we'll put on our braws; and I hope you will have no occasion to think shame of us. But why not take your dinner here?'

That was how it was settled, and the old gentleman went away to dress, looking quite pleased. But I came to Aunt Mary as soon as he was gone, and besought her not to make me go. 'I like the long bonnie night and the light that lasts so long. And I cannot bear to dress up and go out, wasting it all in a stupid party. I hate parties, Aunt Mary!' I cried, 'and I would far rather stay here.'

'My honey,' she said, taking both my hands, 'I know it will maybe be a blow to you—but it's better so.'

'How could it be a blow to me?' I cried; 'but I would far rather not go.'

'You'll just go with me, honey, just this once: it is not often I go out. You will go with me this one night, just this one night, my honey sweet.'

I am sure there were tears in Aunt Mary's eyes, and she kissed me between the words. There was nothing more that I could say; but how I grudged the evening! A mere party, a conversazione (when all the college was away, too, and nobody to make conversation!), instead of my enchanted hour at my window and the soft, strange light, and the dim face looking out, which kept me wondering and wondering what was he thinking of, what was he looking for, who was he? all one wonder and mystery and question, through the long, long, slowly fading night.

It occurred to me, however, when I was dressing—though I was so sure that he would prefer his solitude to everything—that he might perhaps, it was just possible, be there. And when I thought of that, I took out my white frock—though Janet had laid out my blue one—and my little pearl necklace which I had thought was too good to wear. They were not very large pearls, but they were real pearls, and very even and lustrous though they were small; and though I did not think much of my appearance then, there must have been something about me—pale as I was but apt to colour in a moment, with my dress so white, and my pearls so white, and my hair all shadowy—perhaps, that was pleasant to look at: for even old Mr. Pitmilly had a strange look in his eyes, as if he was not only pleased but sorry too, perhaps thinking me a creature that would have troubles in this life, though I was so young and knew them not.

And when Aunt Mary looked at me, there was a little quiver about her mouth. She herself had on her pretty lace and her white hair very nicely done, and looking her best. As for Mr. Pitmilly, he had a beautiful fine French cambric frill to his shirt, plaited in the most minute plaits, and with a diamond pin in it which sparkled as much as Lady Carnbee's ring; but this was a fine, frank, kindly stone that looked you straight in the face and sparkled, with the light dancing in it as if it were pleased to see you, and to be shining on that old gentleman's honest and faithful breast: for he had been one of Aunt Mary's lovers in their early days, and still thought there was nobody like her in the world.

I had got into quite a happy commotion of mind by the time we set out across the street in the soft light of the evening to the Library Hall. Perhaps, after all, I should see him, and see the room which I was so well acquainted with, and find out why he sat there so constantly and never was

seen abroad. I thought I might even hear what he was working at, which would be such a pleasant thing to tell papa
when I went home. A friend of mine at St. Rule's—oh,
far, far more busy than you ever were, papa!—and then
my father would laugh as he always did, and say he was
but an idler and never busy at all.

The room was all light and bright, flowers wherever
flowers could be, and the long lines of the books that went
along the walls on each side, lighting up wherever there was
a line of gilding or an ornament, with a little response. It
dazzled me at first all that light; but I was very eager,
though I kept very quiet, looking round to see if perhaps
in any corner, in the middle of any group, he would be
there. I did not expect to see him among the ladies. He
would not be with them—he was too studious, too silent:
but perhaps among that circle of grey heads at the upper
end of the room—perhaps...

No; I am not sure that it was not half a pleasure to me
to make quite sure that there was not one whom I could
take for him, who was at all like my vague image of him.
No: it was absurd to think that he would be here, amid all
that sound of voices, under the glare of that light. I felt a
little proud to think that he was in his room as usual, doing
his work, or thinking so deeply over it, as when he turned
round in his chair with his face to the light.

I was thus getting a little composed and quiet in my
mind—for now that the expectation of seeing him was
over, though it was a disappointment it was a satisfaction
too—when Mr. Pitmilly came up to me, holding out his
arm. 'Now,' he said, 'I am going to take you to see the
curiosities.' I thought to myself that after I had seen them
and spoken to everybody I knew, Aunt Mary would let
me go home, so I went very willingly, though I did not
care for the curiosities. Something, however, struck me
strangely as we walked up the room. It was the air, rather
fresh and strong, from an open window at the east end of
the hall. How should there be a window there? I hardly

saw what it meant for the first moment, but it blew in my face as if there was some meaning in it, and I felt very uneasy without seeing why.

Then there was another thing that startled me. On that side of the wall which was to the street there seemed no windows at all. A long line of bookcases filled it from end to end. I could not see what that meant either, but it confused me. I was altogether confused. I felt as if I was in a strange country, not knowing where I was going, not knowing what I might find out next. If there were no windows on the wall to the street where was my window? My heart, which had been jumping up and calming down again all the time, gave a great leap at this, as if it would have come out of me—but I did not know what it could mean.

Then we stopped before a glass case, and Mr. Pitmilly showed me some things in it. I could not pay much attention to them. My head was going round and round. I heard his voice going on, and then myself speaking with a queer sound that was hollow in my ears; but I did not know what I was saying or what he was saying.

Then he took me to the very end of the room, the east end, saying something that I caught—that I was pale, that the air would do me good. The air was blowing full on me, lifting the lace of my dress, lifting my hair, almost chilly. The window opened into the pale daylight, into the little lane that ran by the end of the building. Mr. Pitmilly went on talking, but I could not make out a word he said. Then I heard my own voice speaking through it, though I did not seem to be aware that I was speaking. 'Where is my window?—where, then, is my window?' I seemed to be saying, and I turned right round, dragging him with me, still holding his arm. As I did this my eyes fell upon something at last which I knew. It was a large picture in a broad frame, hanging against the farther wall.

What did it mean? Oh, what did it mean? I turned round again to the open window at the east end, and to the daylight, the strange light without any shadow that was all round about this lighted hall, holding it like a bubble that

238

would burst, like something that was not real. The real
place was the room I knew, in which that picture was hanging, where the writing-table was, and where he sat with his
face to the light. But where was the light and the window
through which it came? I think my senses must have left
me. I went up to the picture which I knew, and then
I walked straight across the room, always dragging Mr.
Pitmilly, whose face was pale, but who did not struggle
but allowed me to lead him, straight across to where the
window was—where the window was not—where there
was no sign of it. 'Where is my window? where is my window?' I said. And all the time I was sure that I was in a
dream, and these lights were all some theatrical illusion,
and the people talking; and nothing real but the pale, pale,
watching, lingering day standing by to wait until that foolish bubble should burst.

'My dear,' said Mr. Pitmilly, 'my dear! Mind that you
are in public. Mind where you are. You must not make
an outcry and frighten your Aunt Mary. Come away with
me. Come away, my dear young lady, and you'll take a
seat for a minute or two and compose yourself; and I'll
get you an ice or a little wine.' He kept patting my hand,
which was on his arm, and looking at me very anxiously.
'Bless me! bless me! I never thought it would have this
effect,' he said.

But I would not allow him to take me away in that direction. I went to the picture again and looked at it without
seeing it; and then I went across the room again, with some
kind of wild thought that if I insisted I should find it. 'My
window, my window!' I said.

There was one of the professors standing there, and he
heard me. 'The window!' said he. 'Ah, you've been
taken in with what appears outside. It was put there to be
in uniformity with the window on the stair. But it never
was a real window. It is just behind that bookcase. Many
people are taken in by it,' he said.

His voice seemed to sound from somewhere far away,
and as if it would go on forever; and the hall swam in a

dazzle of shining and of noises round me; and the daylight through the open window grew greyer, waiting till it should be over, and the bubble burst.

V

It was Mr. Pitmilly who took me home: or rather it was I who took him, pushing him on a little in front of me, holding fast by his arm, not waiting for Aunt Mary or anyone. We came out into the daylight again outside, I, without even a cloak or a shawl, with my bare arms, and uncovered head, and the pearls round my neck. There was a rush of the people about, and a baker's boy, that baker's boy, stood right in my way and cried, 'Here's a braw ane!' shouting to the others: the words struck me somehow, as his stone had struck the window, without any reason. But I did not mind the people staring, and hurried across the street, with Mr. Pitmilly half a step in advance.

The door was open, and Janet standing at it, looking out to see what she could see of the ladies in their grand dresses. She gave a shriek when she saw me hurrying across the street; but I brushed past her, and pushed Mr. Pitmilly up the stairs, and took him breathless to the recess, where I threw myself down on the seat, feeling as if I could not have gone another step farther, and waved my hand across to the window. 'There! there!' I cried. Ah! there it was—not that senseless mob—not the theatre and the gas, and the people all in a murmur and clang of talking. Never in all these days had I seen that room so clearly.

There was a faint tone of light behind, as if it might have been a reflection from some of those vulgar lights in the hall, and he sat against it, calm, wrapped in his thoughts, with his face to the window. Nobody but must have seen him. Janet could have seen him had I called her upstairs. It was like a picture, all the things I knew, and the same attitude, and the atmosphere, full of quietness, not disturbed by anything. I pulled Mr. Pitmilly's arm before I let him go. 'You see, you see!' I cried. He gave me the most bewildered look, as if he would have liked to cry. He saw nothing! I was sure of that from his eyes. He was an old man, and there was no vision in him. If I had called up Janet, she would have seen it all. 'My dear!' he said. 'My dear!' waving his hands in a helpless way.

'He has been there all these nights,' I cried, 'and I thought you could tell me who he was and what he was doing; and that he might have taken me in to that room, and showed me, that I might tell papa. Papa would understand, he would like to hear. Oh, can't you tell me what work he is doing, Mr. Pitmilly? He never lifts his head as long as the light throws a shadow, and then when it is like this he turns round and thinks, and takes a rest!'

Mr. Pitmilly was trembling, whether it was with cold or I know not what. He said, with a shake in his voice, 'My dear young lady, my dear . . .' and then stopped and looked at me as if he were going to cry. 'It's peetiful, it's peetiful,' he said; and then in another voice, 'I'm going across there again to bring your Aunt Mary home; do you understand, my poor little thing, my . . . I am going to bring her home—you will be better when she is here.'

I was glad when he went away, as he could not see anything: and I sat alone in the dark which was not dark, but quite clear light—a light like nothing I ever saw. How clear it was in that room! Not glaring like the gas and the voices, but so quiet, everything so visible, as if it were in another world. I heard a little rustle behind me, and there was Janet, standing staring at me with two big eyes wide open. She was only a little older than I was. I called to her, 'Janet, come here, come here, and you will see him —come here and see him!' impatient that she should be so shy and keep behind. 'Oh, my bonnie young leddy!' she said, and burst out crying. I stamped my foot at her, in my indignation that she would not come, and she fled before me with a rustle and swing of haste, as if she were afraid.

None of them, none of them! not even a girl like myself, with the sight in her eyes, would understand. I turned back again, and held out my hands to him sitting there, who was the only one that knew. 'Oh,' I said, 'say something to me! I don't know who you are, or what you are: but you're lonely and so am I; and I only—feel for you. Say something to me!' I neither hoped that he would hear, nor expected any answer. How could he hear, with the street between us, and his window shut, and all the murmuring of the voices and the people standing about? But for one moment it seemed to me that there was only him and me in the whole world.

But I gasped with my breath, that had almost gone from me, when I saw him move in his chair! He had heard me, though I knew not how. He rose up, and I rose too, speechless, incapable of anything but this mechanical movement. He seemed to draw me as if I were a puppet moved by his will. He came forward to the window, and stood looking across at me. I was sure that he looked at me. At last he had seen me: at last he had found out that somebody, though only a girl, was watching him, looking for him, believing in him.

I was in such trouble and commotion of mind and trembling, that I could not keep on my feet, but dropped kneeling on the window-seat, supporting myself against the window, feeling as if my heart were being drawn out of me. I cannot describe his face. It was all dim, yet there was a light on it: I think it must have been a smile; and as closely as I looked at him he looked at me. His hair was fair, and there was a little quiver about his lips. Then he put his hands upon the window to open it. It was stiff and hard to move; but at last he forced it open with a sound that echoed all along the street. I saw that the people heard it, and several looked up.

As for me, I put my hands together, leaning with my face against the glass, drawn to him as if I could have gone out of myself, my heart out of my bosom, my eyes out of my head. He opened the window with a noise that was heard from the West Port to the Abbey. Could anyone doubt that?

And then he leaned forward out of the window, looking out. There was not one in the street but must have seen him. He looked at me first, with a little wave of his hand, as if it were a salutation—yet not exactly that either, for I thought he waved me away; and then he looked up and down in the dim shining of the ending day, first to the east, to the old Abbey towers, and then to the west, along the broad line of the street where so many people were coming and going, but so little noise, all like enchanted folk in an enchanted place.

I watched him with such a melting heart, with such a deep satisfaction as words could not say; for nobody could tell me now that he was not there—nobody could say I was dreaming any more. I watched him as if I could not breathe—my heart in my throat, my eyes upon him. He looked up and down, and then he looked back to me. I was the first, and I was the last, though it was not for long: he did know, he did see, who it was that had recognised him and sympathised with him all the time. I was in a kind of rapture, yet stupor too; my look went with his look, following it as if I were his shadow; and then suddenly he was gone, and I saw him no more.

I dropped back again upon my seat, seeking something to support me, something to lean upon. He had lifted his hand and waved it once again to me. How he went I cannot tell, nor where he went I cannot tell; but in a moment he was away, and the windows standing open, and the room fading into stillness and dimness, yet so clear, with all its space, and the great picture in its gilded frame upon the wall.

It gave me no pain to see him go away. My heart was so content, and I was so worn out and satisfied—for what doubt or question could there be about him now? As I was lying back as weak as water, Aunt Mary came in behind me and flew to me with a little rustle as if she had come on wings, and put her arms round me, and drew my

243

head on to her breast. I had begun to cry a little, with sobs like a child. 'You saw him, you saw him!' I said.

To lean upon her, and feel her so soft, so kind, gave me a pleasure I cannot describe, and her arms round me, and her voice saying 'Honey, my honey!' as if she were nearly crying too. Lying there I came back to myself, quite sweetly, glad of everything. But I wanted some assurance from them that they had seen him too.

I waved my hand to the window that was still standing open, and the room that was stealing away into the faint dark. 'This time you saw it all!' I said, getting more eager. 'My honey!' said Aunt Mary, giving me a kiss; and Mr. Pitmilly began to walk about the room with short little steps behind, as if he were out of patience. I sat straight up and put away Aunt Mary's arms. 'You cannot be so blind, so blind!' I cried. 'Oh, not tonight, at least not to-night!' But neither the one nor the other made any reply.

I shook myself quite free, and raised myself up. And there, in the middle of the street, stood the baker's boy like a statue, staring up at the open window, with his mouth open and his face full of wonder—breathless, as if he could not believe what he saw. I darted forward, calling to him, and beckoned him to come to me. 'Oh, bring him up! bring him, bring him to me!' I cried.

Mr. Pitmilly went out directly, and got the boy by the shoulder. He did not want to come. It was strange to see the little old gentleman, with his beautiful frill and his diamond pin, standing out in the street, with his hand upon the boy's shoulder, and the other boys round, all in a little crowd. And presently they came towards the house, the others all following, gaping and wondering. He came in unwilling, almost resisting, looking as if we meant him some harm.

'Come away, my laddie, come and speak to the young lady,' Mr. Pitmilly was saying. And Aunt Mary took my hands to keep me back. But I would not be kept back.

'Boy,' I cried, 'you saw it too, you saw it, tell them you saw it! It is that I want, and no more.'

244

He looked at me as they all did, as if he thought I were mad. 'What's she wantin' wi' me?' he said; and then, 'I did nae harm, even if I did throw a big stane at it—and it's nae sin to throw a stane.'

'You rascal!' said Mr. Pitmilly, giving him a shake; 'have you been throwing stones? You'll kill somebody one of these days with your stones.' The old gentleman was confused and troubled, for he did not understand what I wanted, nor anything that had happened. And then Aunt Mary, holding my hands and drawing me close to her, spoke.

'Laddie,' she said, 'answer the young lady, like a good lad. There's no intention of finding fault with you. Answer her, my man, and then Janet will give ye your supper before you go.'

'Oh, speak, speak!' I cried, 'answer them and tell them! you saw that window opened, and the gentleman look out and wave his hand?'

'I saw nae gentleman,' he said, with his head down, 'except this wee gentleman here.'

'Listen, laddie,' said Aunt Mary. 'I saw ye standing in the middle of the street staring. What were ye looking at?'

'It was naething to make a wark about. It was just yon windy yonder in the library that is nae windy. And it was open—as sure's death. You may laugh if you like. Is that a' she's wantin' wi' me?'

'You are telling a pack of lies, laddie,' Mr. Pitmilly said.

'I'm tellin' nae lees—it was standin' open just like ony ither windy. It's as sure's death. I couldna believe it mysel'; but it's true.'

'And there it is,' I cried, turning round and pointing it out to them with great triumph in my heart. But the light was all grey, it had faded, it had changed. The window was just as it had always been, a sombre break upon the wall.

I was treated like an invalid all that evening, and taken upstairs to bed, and Aunt Mary sat up in my room the whole night through. Whenever I opened my eyes she was always sitting there close to me, watching. And there never was in all my life so strange a night. When I would talk in my excitement, she kissed me and hushed me like a child. 'Oh, honey, you are not the only one!' she said. 'Oh, whisht, whisht, bairn! I should never have let you be there!'

'Aunt Mary, Aunt Mary, you have seen him too?'

'Oh, whisht, whisht, honey!' Aunt Mary said; her eyes were shining—there were tears in them. 'Oh, whisht, whisht! Put it out of your mind, and try to sleep. I will not speak another word,' she cried.

But I had my arms round her, and my mouth at her ear. 'Who is he there? Tell me that and I will ask no more . . .'

'Oh, honey, rest, and try to sleep! It is just—how can I tell you?—a dream, a dream! Did you not hear what Lady Carnbee said?—the women of our blood . . .'

'What? What? Aunt Mary, oh, Aunt Mary. . .'

'I canna tell you,' she cried in her agitation, 'I canna tell you! How can I tell you, when I know just what you know and no more? It is a longing all your life after—it is a look-ing—for what never comes.'

'He will come,' I cried. 'I shall see him tomorrow—that I know, I know!'

She kissed me and cried over me, her cheek hot and wet like mine. 'My honey, try if you can sleep—try if you can sleep: and we'll wait to see what tomorrow brings.'

'I have no fear,' said I. And then, I suppose, though it is strange to think of, I must have fallen asleep—I was so worn out, and young, and not used to lying in my bed awake. From time to time I opened my eyes, and some-times jumped up remembering everything; but Aunt Mary was always there to soothe me, and I lay down again in her shelter like a bird in its nest.

But I would not let them keep me in bed next day. I was in a kind of fever, not knowing what I did. The window was quite opaque, without the least glimmer in it, flat and blank like a piece of wood. Never from the first day had I seen it so little like a window.

'It cannot be wondered at,' I said to myself, 'that seeing

it like that, and with eyes that are old, not so clear as mine, they should think what they do.' And then I smiled to myself to think of the evening and the long light, and whether he would look out again, or only give me a signal with his hand. I decided I would like that best: not that he should take the trouble to come forward and open it again, but just a turn of his head and a wave of his hand. It would be more friendly, and show more confidence—not as if I wanted that kind of demonstration every night.

I did not come down in the afternoon, but kept at my own window upstairs alone, till the tea-party should be over. I could hear them making a great talk; and I was sure they were all in the recess staring at the window, and laughing at the silly lassie. Let them laugh! I felt above all that now.

At dinner I was very restless, hurrying to get it over; and I think Aunt Mary was restless too. I doubt whether she read her *Times* when it came; she opened it up so as to shield her, and watched from a corner. And I settled myself in the recess, with my heart full of expectation. I wanted nothing more than to see him writing at his table, and to turn his head and give me a little wave of his hand, just to show that he knew I was there. I sat from half past seven o'clock to ten o'clock; and the daylight grew softer and softer, till at last it was as if it was shining through a pearl, and not a shadow to be seen. But the window all the time was as black as night, and there was nothing, nothing there.

Well: but other nights it had been like that; he would not be there every night only to please me. There are other things in a man's life, a great learned man like that. I said to myself I was not disappointed. Why should I be disappointed? There had been other nights when he was not there. Aunt Mary watched me, every movement I made, her eyes shining, often wet, with a pity in them that almost made me cry: but I felt as if I were more sorry for her than for myself. And then I flung myself upon her, and asked her, again and again, what it was, and who it was, imploring her to tell me if she knew? and when she had seen him, and what had happened? and what it meant about the women of our blood?

She told me that how it was she could not tell, nor when: it was just at the time it had to be; and that we all saw him in our time. 'That is,' she said, 'the ones that are like you and me.' What was it that made her and me different from the rest? but she only shook her head and would not tell me.

'They say,' she said, and then stopped short. 'Oh, honey, try to forget all about it—if I had but known you were of that kind! They say—that once there was one that was a scholar, and liked his books more than any lady's love. Honey, do not look at me like that. To think I should have brought all this on you!'

'He was a scholar?' I cried.

'And one of us, that must have been a light woman, not like you and me . . . But may be it was just in innocence; for who can tell? She waved to him and waved to him to come over: and yon ring was the token: but he would not come. But still she sat at her window and waved and waved —till at last her brothers heard of it, that were stirring men; and then . . . Oh, my honey, let us speak of it no more!'

'They killed him!' I cried, carried away. And then I grasped her with my hands, and gave her a shake, and flung away from her. 'You tell me that to throw dust in my eyes —when I saw him only last night: and he as living as I am, and as young!'

'My honey, my honey!' Aunt Mary said.

After that I would not speak to her for a long time; but she kept close to me, never leaving me when she could help it, and always with that pity in her eyes. For the next night it was the same; and the third night. That third night I thought I could not bear it any longer. I would have to do something—if only I knew what to do! If it would ever get dark, quite dark, there might be something to be done. I had wild dreams of stealing out of the house and getting a ladder, and mounting up to try if I could not open that window in the middle of the night—if perhaps I could get

248

the baker's boy to help me; and then my mind got into a whirl, and it was as if I had done it; and I could almost see the boy put the ladder to the window, and hear him cry out that there was nothing there.

Oh, how slow it was, the night! and how light it was, and everything so clear—no darkness to cover you, no shadow, whether on one side of the street or on the other side. I could not sleep, though I was forced to go to bed. And in the deep midnight, when it is dark, dark in every other place, I slipped very softly downstairs, though there was one board on the landing-place that creaked—and opened the door and stepped out.

There was not a soul to be seen, up or down, from the Abbey to the West Port: and the trees stood like ghosts, and the silence was terrible, and everything as clear as day. You don't know what silence is till you find it in the light like that, not morning but night, no sun rising, no shadow, but everything as clear as the day.

It did not make any difference as the slow minutes went on: one o'clock, two o'clock. How strange it was to hear the clocks striking in that dead light when there was no-body to hear them! But it made no difference. The window was quite blank; even the marking of the panes seemed to have melted away. I stole up again, cold and trembling, after a long time, through the silent house, in the clear light with despair in my heart.

I am sure Aunt Mary must have watched and seen me coming back, for after a while I heard faint sounds in the house, and very early, when there had come a little sun-shine into the air, she came to my bedside with a cup of tea in her hand; and she, too, was looking like a ghost. 'Are you warm, honey—are you comfortable?' she said. 'It doesn't matter,' said I. I did not feel as if anything mattered; unless if one could get into the dark somewhere— the soft, deep dark that would cover you over and hide you—but I could not tell from what. The dreadful thing was that there was nothing, nothing to look for, nothing to hide from—only the silence and the light.

That day my mother came and took me home. I had not heard she was coming; she arrived quite unexpectedly, and said she had no time to stay but must start the same evening so as to be in London next day, papa having settled to go abroad. At first I had a wild thought I would not go. But how can a girl say I will not, when her mother has come for her, and there is no reason, no reason in the world, to resist, and no right. I had to go, whatever I might wish or anyone might say. Aunt Mary's dear eyes were wet; she went about the house drying them quietly with her handkerchief, but she always said, 'It is the best thing for you, honey, the best thing for you!' Oh, how I hated to hear it said that it was the best thing, as if anything mattered, one more than another!

The old ladies were all there in the afternoon, Lady Carnbee looking at me from under her black lace, and the diamond lurking, sending out darts from under her finger. She patted me on the shoulder, and told me to be a good bairn. 'And never lippen to what you see from the window,' she said. 'The eye is deceitful as well as the heart.' She kept patting me on the shoulder, and I felt again as if that sharp, wicked stone stung me. Was that what Aunt Mary meant when she said yon ring was the token? I thought afterwards I saw the mark on my shoulder. You will say why? How can I tell why? If I had known, I should have been contented, and it would not have mattered any more.

I never went back to St. Rule's, and for years of my life I never again looked out of a window when any other window was in sight. You ask me did I ever see him again? I cannot tell: the imagination is a great deceiver, as Lady Carnbee said: and if he stayed there so long, only to punish the race that had wronged him, why should I ever have seen him again? for I had received my share. But who can tell what happens in a heart that often, often, and so long as that, comes back to do its errand? If it was he whom I have seen again, the anger is gone from him, and he means

good and no longer harm to the house of the woman who
loved him.

I have seen his face looking at me from a crowd. There
was one time when I came home a widow from India, very
sad, with my little children: I am certain I saw him there
among all the people coming to welcome their friends.
There was nobody to welcome me—for I was not expected: and very sad was I, without a face I knew: when
all at once I saw him, and he waved his hand to me. My
heart leaped up again: I had forgotten who he was, but
only that it was a face I knew, and I landed almost cheerfully, thinking here was someone who would help me.
But he had disappeared, as he did from the window, with
that one wave of his hand.

And again I was reminded of it all when old Lady Carnbee died—an old, old woman—and it was found in her
will that she had left me that diamond ring. I am afraid of
it still. It is locked up in an old sandal-wood box in the
lumber-room in the little old country house which belongs
to me, but where I never live. If anyone would steal it, it
would be a relief to my mind. Yet I never knew what Aunt
Mary meant when she said: 'Yon ring was the token,' nor
what it could have to do with that strange window in the
old College Library of St. Rule's.

WILLIAM WILKIE COLLINS

The Dream Woman

from THE QUEEN OF HEARTS

I

I HAD not been settled much more than six weeks in my country practice, when I was sent for to a neighbouring town, to consult with the resident medical man there, on a case of very dangerous illness.

My horse had come down with me, at the end of a long ride the night before, and had hurt himself, luckily, much more than he had hurt his master. Being deprived of the animal's services I started for my destination by the coach (there were no railways at that time); and I hoped to get back again, towards the afternoon, in the same way.

After the consultation was over I went to the principal inn of the town to wait for the coach. When it came up, it was full inside and out. There was no resource left me, but to get home as cheaply as I could, by hiring a gig. The price asked for this accommodation struck me as being so extortionate, that I determined to look out for an inn of inferior pretensions, and to try if I could not make a better bargain with a less prosperous establishment.

I soon found a likely looking house, dingy and quiet, with an old-fashioned sign, that had evidently not been repainted for many years past. The landlord, in this case, was not above making a small profit; and as soon as we came to terms, he rang the yard-bell to order the gig.

'Has Robert not come back from that errand?' asked

the landlord appealing to the waiter, who answered the bell.

'No, sir, he hasn't.'

'Well, then, you must wake up Isaac.'

'Wake up Isaac?' I repeated; 'that sounds rather odd. Do your ostlers go to bed in the daytime?'

'This one does,' said the landlord, smiling to himself in rather a strange way.

'And dreams, too,' added the waiter.

'Never you mind about that,' retorted his master; 'you go and rouse Isaac up. The gentleman's waiting for his gig.'

The landlord's manner and the waiter's manner expressed a great deal more than they either of them said. I began to suspect that I might be on the trace of something professionally interesting to me, as a medical man; and I thought I should like to look at the ostler, before the waiter awakened him.

'Stop a minute,' I interposed; 'I have rather a fancy for seeing this man before you wake him up. I am a doctor; and if this queer sleeping and dreaming of his comes from anything wrong in his brain, I may be able to tell you what to do with him.'

'I rather think you will find his complaint past all doctoring, sir,' said the landlord. 'But if you would like to see him, you're welcome, I'm sure.'

He led the way across the yard and down a passage to the stables; opened one of the doors; and waiting outside himself told me to look in.

I found myself in a two-stall stable. In one of the stalls, a horse was munching his corn. In the other, an old man was lying asleep on the litter.

I stooped, and looked at him attentively. It was a withered, woebegone face. The eyebrows were painfully contracted; the mouth was fast set, and drawn down at the corners. The hollow wrinkled cheeks, and the scanty grizzled hair, told their own tale of past sorrow or suffering. He was drawing his breath convulsively when I first looked at him; and in a moment more he began to talk in his sleep.

'Wake up!' I heard him say, in a quick whisper, through his clenched teeth. 'Wake up, there! Murder.'

He moved one lean arm slowly till it rested over his throat, shuddered a little, and turned on the straw. Then the arm left his throat, the hand stretched itself out, and clutched at the side towards which he had turned, as if he fancied himself to be grasping at the edge of something. I saw his lips move, and bent lower over him. He was still talking in his sleep.

'Light grey eyes,' he murmured, 'and a droop in the left eyelid—flaxen hair, with a gold-yellow streak in it—all right, mother—fair white arms, with a down on them—little lady's hand, with a reddish look under the finger-nails. The knife—always the cursed knife—first on one side, then on the other. Aha! you she-devil, where's the knife?'

At the last word his voice rose, and he grew restless on a sudden. I saw him shudder on the straw; his withered face became distorted, and he threw up both his hands with a quick hysterical gasp. They struck against the bottom of the manger under which he lay, and the blow awakened him. I had just time to slip through the door, and close it, before his eyes were fairly open, and his senses his own again.

'Do you know anything about that man's past life?' I said to the landlord.

'Yes, sir, I know pretty well all about it,' was the answer, 'and an uncommon queer story it is. Most people don't believe it. It's true, though, for all that. Why, just look at him,' continued the landlord, opening the stable door again. 'Poor devil! he's so worn out with his restless nights, that he's dropped back into his sleep already.'

'Don't wake him,' I said, 'I'm in no hurry for the gig. Wait till the other man comes back from his errand. And, in the meantime, suppose I have some lunch, and a bottle of sherry; and suppose you come and help me to get through it.'

The heart of mine host, as I had anticipated, warmed to me over his own wine. He soon became communicative on the subject of the man asleep in the stable; and by little and little, I drew the whole story out of him. Extravagant and incredible as the events must appear to everybody, they are related here just as I heard them, and just as they happened.

II

Some years ago there lived in the suburbs of a large seaport town on the west coast of England a man in humble circumstances, by name Isaac Scatchard. His means of subsistence were derived from any employment he could get as an ostler, and occasionally, when times went well with him, from temporary engagements in service as stable-helper in private houses. Though a faithful, steady, and honest man, he got on badly in his calling. His ill-luck was proverbial among his neighbours. He was always missing good opportunities by no fault of his own; and always living longest in service with amiable people who were not punctual payers of wages. 'Unlucky Isaac' was his nickname in his own neighbourhood—and no one could say that he did not richly deserve it.

With far more than one man's fair share of adversity to endure, Isaac had but one consolation to support him—and that was of the dreariest and most negative kind. He had no wife and children to increase his anxieties and add to the bitterness of his various failures in life. It might have been from mere insensibility, or it might have been from generous unwillingness to involve another in his own unlucky destiny—but the fact undoubtedly was, that he had arrived at the middle term of life without marrying; and, what is much more remarkable, without once exposing himself, from eighteen to eight-and-thirty, to the genial imputation of ever having had a sweetheart.

When he was out of service, he lived alone with his widowed mother. Mrs. Scatchard was a woman above the average in her lowly station, as to capacity and manners. She had seen better days, as the phrase is; but she never referred to them in the presence of curious visitors; and, though perfectly polite to everyone who approached her, never cultivated any intimacies among her neighbours. She contrived to provide, hardly enough, for her simple wants, by doing rough work for the tailors; and always managed to keep a decent home for her son to return to, whenever his ill-luck drove him out helpless into the world.

One bleak Autumn, when Isaac was getting fast towards forty, and when he was, as usual, out of place through no fault of his own, he set forth from his mother's cottage on a long walk inland to a gentleman's seat, where he had heard that a stable-helper was required.

It wanted then but two days of his birthday; and Mrs. Scatchard, with her usual fondness, made him promise, before he started, that he would be back in time to keep that anniversary with her, in as festive a way as their poor means would allow. It was easy for him to comply with this request, even supposing he slept a night each way on the road.

He was to start from home on Monday morning; and whether he got the new place or not, he was to be back for his birthday dinner on Wednesday at two o'clock.

Arriving at his destination too late on the Monday night to make application for the stable-helper's place, he slept at the village inn, and, in good time on the Tuesday morning, presented himself at the gentleman's house, to fill the vacant situation. Here, again, his ill-luck pursued him as inexorably as ever. The excellent written testimonials to his character which he was able to produce, availed him nothing; his long walk had been taken in vain—only the day before, the stable-helper's place had been given to another man.

Isaac accepted this new disappointment resignedly, and as a matter of course. Naturally slow in capacity, he had the bluntness of sensibility and phlegmatic patience of disposition which frequently distinguish men with sluggishly working mental powers. He thanked the gentleman's steward with his usual quiet civility, for granting him an interview, and took his departure with no appearance of unusual depression in his face or manner.

Before starting on his homeward walk, he made some inquiries at the inn, and ascertained that he might save a few miles, on his return, by following a new road. Furnished with full instructions, several times repeated, as to the various turnings he was to take, he set forth on his homeward journey, and walked on all day with only one stoppage for bread and cheese. Just as it was getting towards dark, the rain came on and the wind began to rise; and he found himself, to make matters worse, in a part of the country with which he was entirely unacquainted, though he knew himself to be some fifteen miles from home. The first house he found to inquire at was a lonely road-side inn, standing on the outskirts of a thick wood. Solitary as the place looked, it was welcome to a lost man who was also hungry, thirsty, footsore, and wet. The landlord was civil and respectable-looking; and the price he asked for a bed was reasonable enough. Isaac, therefore, decided on stopping comfortably at the inn for that night.

He was constitutionally a temperate man. His supper simply consisted of two rashers of bacon, a slice of home-made bread, and a pint of ale. He did not go to bed immediately after this moderate meal, but sat up with the landlord, talking about his bad prospects and his long run of ill-luck, and diverging from these topics to the subjects of horse flesh and racing. Nothing was said either by himself, his host, or the few labourers who strayed into the tap-room, which could, in the slightest degree, excite the very small and very dull imaginative faculty which Isaac Scatchard possessed.

At a little after eleven the house was closed. Isaac went round with the landlord, and held the candle while the doors and lower windows were being secured. He noticed with surprise the strength of the bolts, bars, and iron-sheathed shutters.

'You see, we are rather lonely here,' said the landlord. 'We never have had any attempts made to break in yet, but it's always as well to be on the safe side. When nobody is sleeping here I am the only man in the house. My wife and daughter are timid, and the servant-girl takes after her missuses. Another glass of ale, before you turn in? No! Well, how such a sober man as you comes to be out of place, is more than I can make out, for one. Here's where you're to sleep. You're the only lodger tonight, and I think you'll say my missus has done her best to make you comfortable. You're quite sure you won't have another glass of ale?—very well. Good night.'

It was half-past eleven by the clock in the passage as they went upstairs to the bedroom, the window of which looked on to the wood at the back of the house.

Isaac locked the door, set his candle on the chest of drawers, and wearily got ready for bed. The bleak autumn wind was still blowing, and the solemn surging moan of it in the wood was dreary and awful to hear through the night-silence. Isaac felt strangely wakeful. He resolved, as he lay down in bed, to keep the candle alight until he began to grow sleepy; for there was something unendurably depressing in the bare idea of lying awake in the darkness, listening to the dismal, ceaseless moan of the wind in the wood.

Sleep stole on him before he was aware of it. His eyes closed, and he fell off insensibly to rest, without having so much as thought of extinguishing the candle.

The first sensation of which he was conscious, after sinking into slumber, was a strange shivering that ran through him suddenly from head to foot, and a dreadful sinking pain at the heart, such as he had never felt before. The shivering only disturbed his slumbers—the pain woke him instantly. In one moment he passed from a state of sleep to a state of wakefulness—his eyes wide open—his mental perceptions cleared on a sudden as if by a miracle.

The candle had burnt down nearly to the last morsel of tallow, but the top of the unsnuffed wick had just fallen off, and the light in the little room was, for the moment, fair and full.

Between the foot of his bed and the closed door, there stood a woman with a knife in her hand, looking at him.

He was stricken speechless with terror, but he did not lose the preternatural clearness of his faculties; and he never took his eyes off the woman. She said not a word as they stared each other in the face; but she began to move slowly towards the left-hand side of the bed.

His eyes followed her. She was a fair fine woman, with yellowish flaxen hair, and light grey eyes, with a droop in the left eyelid. He noticed these things and fixed them on his mind, before she was round at the side of the bed. Speechless, with no expression in her face, with no noise following her footfall, she came closer and closer—stopped —and slowly raised the knife. He laid his right arm over his throat to save it; but, as he saw the knife coming down, threw his hand across the bed to the right side, and jerked his body over that way, just as the knife descended on the mattress within an inch of his shoulder.

His eyes fixed on her arm and hand, as she slowly drew her knife out of the bed. A white, well-shaped arm, with a pretty down lying lightly over the fair skin. A delicate, lady's hand, with the crowning beauty of a pink flush under and round the finger-nails.

She drew the knife out, and passed back again slowly to the foot of the bed; stopped there for a moment looking at him; then came on—still speechless, still with no expression on the beautiful face, still with no sound following the stealthy footfalls—came on to the right side of the bed where he now lay.

As she approached, she raised the knife again, and he drew himself away to the left side. She struck, as before, right into the mattress, with a deliberate perpendicularly downward action of the arm. This time his eyes wandered from her to the knife. It was like the large clasp-knives

259

which he had often seen labouring men use to cut their bread and bacon with. Her delicate little fingers did not conceal more than two-thirds of the handle; he noticed that it was made of buckhorn, clean and shining as the blade was, and looking like new.

For the second time she drew the knife out, concealed it in the wide sleeve of her gown, then stopped by the bedside, watching him. For an instant he saw her standing in that position—then the wick of the spent candle fell over into the socket. The flame diminished to a little blue point, and the room grew dark.

A moment, or less, if possible, passed so—and then the wick flamed up, smokily, for the last time. His eyes were still looking eagerly over the right-hand side of the bed when the final flash of light came, but they discerned nothing. The fair woman with the knife was gone.

The conviction that he was alone again, weakened the hold of the terror that had struck him dumb up to this time. The preternatural sharpness which the very intensity of his panic had mysteriously imparted to his faculties, left them suddenly. His brain grew confused—his heart beat wildly—his ears opened for the first time since the appearance of the woman, to a sense of the woeful, ceaseless moaning of the wind among the trees. With the dreadful conviction of the reality of what he had seen still strong within him, he leapt out of bed, and screaming—'Murder! —Wake up there, wake up!'—dashed headlong through the darkness to the door.

It was fast locked, exactly as he had left it on going to bed.

His cries, on starting up, had alarmed the house. He heard the terrified, confused exclamations of women; he saw the master of the house approaching along the passage, with his burning rush-candle in one hand and his gun in the other.

'What is it?' asked the landlord, breathlessly.

Isaac could only answer in a whisper. 'A woman, with a knife in her hand,' he gasped out. 'In my room—a fair, yellow-haired woman; she jabbed at me with the knife, twice over.'

The landlord's pale cheek grew paler. He looked at Isaac eagerly by the flickering light of his candle; and his face began to get red again—his voice altered, too, as well as his complexion.

'She seems to have missed you twice,' he said.

'I dodged the knife as it came down,' Isaac went on, in the same scared whisper. 'It struck the bed each time.'

The landlord took his candle into the bedroom immediately. In less than a minute he came out again into the passage in a violent passion.

'The devil fly away with you and your woman with the knife! There isn't a mark in the bed-clothes anywhere. What do you mean by coming into a man's place and frightening his family out of their wits by a dream?'

'I'll leave your house,' said Isaac, faintly. 'Better out on the road, in rain and dark, on my way home, than back again in that room, after what I've seen in it. Lend me a light to get my clothes by, and tell me what I'm to pay.'

'Pay!' cried the landlord, leading the way with his light sulkily into the bedroom. 'You'll find your score on the slate when you go downstairs. I wouldn't have taken you in for all the money you've got about you, if I'd known your dreaming, screeching ways beforehand. Look at the bed. Where's the cut of a knife in it? Look at the window —is the lock bursted? Look at the door (which I heard you fasten yourself)—is it broke in? A murdering woman with a knife in my house! You ought to be ashamed of yourself!'

Isaac answered not a word. He huddled on his clothes: and then they went downstairs together.

'Nigh on twenty minutes past two!' said the landlord, as they passed the clock. 'A nice time in the morning to frighten honest people out of their wits!'

Isaac paid his bill, and the landlord let him out at the front door, asking, with a grin of contempt, as he undid the strong fastenings, whether 'the murdering woman got in that way?'

261

They parted without a word on either side. The rain had ceased; but the night was dark, and the wind bleaker than ever. Little did the darkness, or the cold, or the uncertainty about the way home matter to Isaac. If he had been turned out into a wilderness in a thunderstorm, it would have been a relief, after what he had suffered in the bedroom of the inn.

What was the fair woman with the knife? The creature of a dream, or that other creature from the unknown world, called among men by the name of ghost? He could make nothing of the mystery—had made nothing of it, even when it was mid-day on Wednesday, and when he stood, at last, after many times missing his road, once more on the door-step of home.

<h1 style="text-align:center">III</h1>

His mother came out eagerly to receive him. His face told her in a moment that something was wrong.

'I've lost the place; but that's my luck. I dreamed an ill dream last night, mother—or, maybe, I saw a ghost. Take it either way, it scared me out of my senses, and I'm not my own man again yet.'

'Isaac! your face frightens me. Come in to the fire. Come in, and tell mother all about it.'

He was as anxious to tell as she was to hear; for it had been his hope, all the way home, that his mother, with her quicker capacity and superior knowledge, might be able to throw some light on the mystery which he could not clear up for himself. His memory of the dream was still mechanically vivid, though his thoughts were entirely confused by it.

His mother's face grew paler and paler as he went on. She never interrupted him by so much as a single word; but when he had done, she moved her chair close to his, put her arm round his neck, and said to him:

'Isaac, you dreamed your ill dream on this Wednesday morning. What time was it when you saw the fair woman with the knife in her hand?'

Isaac reflected on what the landlord had said when they had passed by the clock on his leaving the inn—allowed as nearly as he could for the time that must have elapsed between the unlocking of his bedroom door and the paying of his bill just before going away, and answered:

'Somewhere about two o'clock in the morning.'

His mother suddenly quitted her hold of his neck, and struck her hands with a gesture of despair.

'This Wednesday is your birthday, Isaac; and two o'clock in the morning is the time when you were born!'

Isaac's capacities were not quick enough to catch the infection of his mother's superstitious dread. He was amazed, and a little startled also, when she suddenly rose from her chair, opened her old writing-desk, took pen, ink, and paper, and then said to him:

'Your memory is but a poor one, Isaac, and now I'm an old woman, mine's not much better. I want all about this dream of yours to be as well known to both of us, years hence, as it is now. Tell me over again all you told me a minute ago, when you spoke of what the woman with the knife looked like.'

Isaac obeyed, and marvelled much as he saw his mother carefully set down on paper the very words that he was saying.

'Light grey eyes,' she wrote as they came to the descriptive part, 'with a droop in the left eyelid. Flaxen hair, with a gold-yellow streak in it. White arms, with a down upon them. Little lady's hands, with a reddish look about the finger-nails. Clasp-knife with a buckhorn handle, that seemed as good as new.' To these particulars, Mrs. Scatchard added the year, month, day of the week, and time in the morning, when the woman of the dream appeared to her son. She then locked up the paper carefully in her writing-desk.

Neither on that day, nor on any day after, could her son

induce her to return to the matter of the dream. She obstinately kept her thoughts about it to herself, and even refused to refer again to the paper in her writing-desk. Ere long, Isaac grew weary of attempting to make her break her resolute silence; and time, which sooner or later wears out all things, gradually wore out the impression produced on him by the dream. He began by thinking of it carelessly, and he ended by not thinking of it at all.

This result was the more easily brought about by the advent of some important changes for the better in his prospects, which commenced not long after his terrible night's experience at the inn. He reaped at last the reward of his long and patient suffering under adversity, by getting an excellent place, keeping it for seven years, and leaving it, on the death of his master, not only with an excellent character, but also with a comfortable annuity bequeathed to him as a reward for saving his mistress's life in a carriage accident. Thus it happened that Isaac Scatchard returned to his old mother, seven years after the time of the dream at the inn, with an annual sum of money at his disposal, sufficient to keep them both in ease and independence for the rest of their lives.

The mother, whose health had been bad of late years, profited so much by the care bestowed on her and by freedom from money anxieties, that when Isaac's birthday came round, she was able to sit up comfortably at table and dine with him.

On that day, as the evening drew on, Mrs. Scatchard discovered that a bottle of tonic medicine—which she was accustomed to take, and in which she had fancied that a dose or more was still left—happened to be empty. Isaac immediately volunteered to go to the chemist's, and get it filled again. It was as rainy and bleak an autumn night as on the memorable past occasion when he lost his way and slept at the road-side inn.

On going into the chemist's shop, he was passed hurriedly by a poorly dressed woman coming out of it. The glimpse he had of her face struck him, and he looked back after her as she descended the door-steps.

'You're noticing that woman?' said the chemist's apprentice behind the counter. 'It's my opinion there's something wrong with her. She's been asking for laudanum to put to a bad tooth. Master's out for half an hour; and I told her I wasn't allowed to sell poison to strangers in his absence. She laughed in a queer way, and said she would come back in half an hour. If she expects master to serve her, I think she'll be disappointed. It's a case of suicide, sir, if ever there was one yet.'

These words added immeasurably to the sudden interest in the woman which Isaac had felt at the first sight of her face. After he had got the medicine bottle filled, he looked about anxiously for her, as soon as he was out in the street. She was walking slowly up and down on the opposite side of the road. With his heart, very much to his own surprise, beating fast, Isaac crossed over and spoke to her.

He asked if she was in any distress. She pointed to her torn shawl, her scanty dress, her crushed, dirty bonnet—then moved under a lamp so as to let the light fall on her stern, pale, but still most beautiful face.

'I look like a comfortable, happy woman—don't I?' she said, with a bitter laugh.

She spoke with a purity of intonation which Isaac had never heard before from other than ladies' lips. Her slightest actions seemed to have the easy, negligent grace of a thoroughbred woman. Her skin, for all its poverty-stricken paleness, was as delicate as if her life had been passed in the enjoyment of every social comfort that wealth can purchase. Even her small, finely-shaped hands, gloveless as they were, had not lost their whiteness.

Little by little, in answer to his questions, the sad story of the woman came out. There is no need to relate it here; it is told over and over again in Police reports and paragraphs descriptive of Attempted Suicides.

'My name is Rebecca Murdoch,' said the woman, as she ended. 'I have ninepence left, and I thought of spending it at the chemist's over the way in securing a passage to the other world. Whatever it is, it can't be worse to me than this—so why should I stop here?'

Besides the natural compassion and sadness moved in his heart by what he heard, Isaac felt within him some mysterious influence at work all the time the woman was speaking, which utterly confused his ideas and almost deprived him of his powers of speech. All that he could say in answer to her last reckless words was, that he would prevent her from attempting her own life, if he followed her about all night to do it. His rough, trembling earnestness seemed to impress her.

'I won't occasion you that trouble,' she answered, when he repeated his threat. 'You have given me a fancy for living by speaking kindly to me. No need for the mockery of protestations and promises. You may believe me without them. Come to Fuller's Meadow tomorrow at twelve, and you will find me alive, to answer for myself. No!— no money. My ninepence will do to get me as good a night's lodging as I want.'

She nodded and left him. He made no attempt to follow —he felt no suspicion that she was deceiving him.

'It's strange, but I can't help believing her,' he said to himself, and walked away bewildered towards home.

On entering the house, his mind was still so completely absorbed by its new subject of interest, that he took no notice of what his mother was doing when he came in with the bottle of medicine. She had opened her old writing-desk in his absence, and was now reading a paper attentively that lay inside it. On every birthday of Isaac's since she had written down the particulars of his dream from his own lips, she had been accustomed to read that same paper, and ponder over it in private.

The next day he went to Fuller's Meadow.

He had done only right in believing her so implicitly— she was there, punctual to a minute, to answer for herself. The last-left faint defences in Isaac's heart, against the fascination which a word or look from her began inscrutably to exercise over him, sank down and vanished before her for ever on that memorable morning.

When a man, previously insensible to the influence of women, forms an attachment in middle life, the instances are rare indeed, let the warning circumstances be what they may, in which he is found capable of freeing himself from the tyranny of the new ruling passion. The charm of being spoken to familiarly, fondly, and gratefully by a woman whose language and manners still retained enough of their early refinement to hint at the high social station that she had lost, would have been a dangerous luxury to a man of Isaac's rank at the age of twenty. But it was far more than that—it was certain ruin to him—now that his heart was opening unworthily to a new influence at that middle time of life when strong feelings of all kinds, once implanted, strike root most stubbornly in a man's moral nature. A few more stolen interviews after that first morning in Fuller's Meadow completed his infatuation. In less than a month from the time when he first met her, Isaac Scatchard had consented to give Rebecca Murdoch a new interest in existence, and a chance of recovering the character she had lost, by promising to make her his wife.

She had taken possession not of his passions only, but of his faculties as well. All the mind he had he put into her keeping. She directed him on every point, even instructing him how to break the news of his approaching marriage in the safest manner to his mother.

'If you tell her how you met me and who I am at first,' said the cunning woman, 'she will move heaven and earth to prevent our marriage. Say I am the sister of one of your fellow-servants—ask her to see me before you go into any more particulars—and leave it to me to do the rest. I mean to make her love me next best to you, Isaac, before she knows anything of who I really am.'

The motive of the deceit was sufficient to sanctify it to Isaac. The stratagem proposed relieved him of his one great anxiety, and quieted his uneasy conscience on the subject of his mother. Still, there was something wanting to perfect his happiness, something that he could not realise, something mysteriously untraceable, and yet something that perpetually made itself felt—not when he was absent from Rebecca Murdoch, but strange to say, when he was actually in her presence! She was kindness itself with him; she never made him feel his inferior capacities and inferior manners—she showed the sweetest anxiety to please him in the smallest trifles; but, in spite of all these attractions, he never could feel quite at his ease with her. At their first meeting, there had mingled with his admiration, when he looked in her face, a faint involuntary feeling of doubt whether that face was entirely strange to him. No after-familiarity had the slightest effect on this inexplicable, wearisome uncertainty.

Concealing the truth, as he had been directed, he announced his marriage engagement precipitately and confusedly to his mother, on the day when he contracted it. Poor Mrs. Scatchard showed her perfect confidence in her son by flinging her arms round his neck, and giving him joy of having found at last, in the sister of one of his fellow-servants, a woman to comfort and care for him after his mother was gone. She was all eagerness to see the woman of her son's choice; and the next day was fixed for the introduction.

It was a bright sunny morning, and the little cottage parlour was full of light, as Mrs. Scatchard, happy and expectant, dressed for the occasion in her Sunday gown, sat waiting for her son and her future daughter-in-law.

Punctual to the appointed time, Isaac hurriedly and nervously led his promised wife into the room. His mother rose to receive her—advanced a few steps, smiling—looked Rebecca full in the eyes—and suddenly stopped. Her face, which had been flushed the moment before, turned white in an instant—her eyes lost their expression of softness and kindness, and assumed a blank look of terror—her outstretched hands fell to her sides, and she staggered back a few steps with a low cry to her son.

'Isaac!' she whispered, clutching him fast by the arm.

when he asked alarmedly if she was taken ill, 'Isaac! does that woman's face remind you of nothing?'

Before he could answer, before he could look round to where Rebecca stood, astonished and angered by her reception, at the lower end of the room, his mother pointed impatiently to her writing-desk and gave him the key.

'Open it,' she said, in a quick, breathless whisper.

'What does this mean? Why am I treated as if I had no business here? Does your mother want to insult me?' asked Rebecca, angrily.

'Open it, and give me the paper in the left-hand drawer. Quick! quick! for heaven's sake!' said Mrs. Scatchard, shrinking further back in terror.

Isaac gave her the paper. She looked it over eagerly for a moment—then followed Rebecca, who was now turning away haughtily to leave the room, and caught her by the shoulder—abruptly raised the long, loose sleeve of her gown—and glanced at her hand and arm. Something like fear began to steal over the angry expression of Rebecca's face, as she shook herself free from the old woman's grasp. 'Mad!' she said to herself, 'and Isaac never told me.' With those few words she left the room.

Isaac was hastening after her, when his mother turned and stopped his further progress. It wrung his heart to see the misery and terror in her face as she looked at him.

'Light grey eyes,' she said, in low, mournful, awestruck tones, pointing towards the open door. 'A droop in the left eyelid; flaxen hair, with a gold-yellow streak in it; white arms with a down on them; little, lady's hand, with a reddish look under the finger-nails. *The Dream Woman!* —Isaac, the Dream Woman!'

That faint cleaving doubt which he had never been able to shake off in Rebecca Murdoch's presence, was fatally set at rest for ever. He *had* seen her face, then, before— seven years before, on his birthday, in the bedroom of the lonely inn.

'Be warned! Oh, my son, be warned! Isaac! Isaac! let her go, and do you stop with me!'

269

Something darkened the parlour window as those words were said. A sudden chill ran through him, and he glanced sidelong at the shadow. Rebecca Murdoch had come back. She was peering in curiously at them over the low window blind.

'I have promised to marry, mother,' he said, 'and marry I must.'

The tears came into his eyes as he spoke, and dimmed his sight; but he could just discern the fatal face outside, moving away again from the window.

His mother's head sank lower.

'Are you faint?' he whispered.

'Broken-hearted, Isaac.'

He stooped down and kissed her. The shadow, as he did so, returned to the window; and the fatal face peered in curiously once more.

IV

Three weeks after that day Isaac and Rebecca were man and wife. All that was hopelessly dogged and stubborn in the man's moral nature, seemed to have closed round his fatal passion, and to have fixed it unassailably in his heart.

After that first interview in the cottage parlour, no consideration could induce Mrs. Scatchard to see her son's wife again, or even to talk of her when Isaac tried hard to plead her cause after their marriage.

This course of conduct was not in any degree occasioned by a discovery of the degradation in which Rebecca had lived. There was no question of that between mother and son. There was no question of anything but the fearfully exact resemblance between the living, breathing woman, and the spectre-woman of Isaac's dream.

Rebecca, on her side, neither felt nor expressed the slightest sorrow at the estrangement between herself and her mother-in-law. Isaac, for the sake of peace, had never contradicted her first idea that age and long illness had affected Mrs. Scatchard's mind. He even allowed his wife to up-braid him for not having confessed this to her at the time of their marriage engagement, rather than risk anything by hinting at the truth. The sacrifice of his integrity before his one all-mastering delusion, seemed but a small thing, and cost his conscience but little, after the sacrifices he had already made.

The time of waking from his delusion—the cruel and the rueful time—was not far off. After some quiet months of married life, as the summer was ending, and the year was getting on towards the month of his birthday, Isaac found his wife altering towards him. She grew sullen and con-temptuous: she formed acquaintances of the most danger-ous kind, in defiance of his objections, his entreaties, and his commands; and, worst of all, she learnt, ere long, after every fresh difference with her husband, to seek the deadly self-oblivion of drink. Little by little, after the first miser-able discovery that his wife was keeping company with drunkards, the shocking certainty forced itself on Isaac that she had grown to be a drunkard herself.

He had been in a sadly desponding state for some time before the occurrence of these domestic calamities. His mother's health, as he could but too plainly discern every time he went to see her at the cottage, was failing fast; and he upbraided himself in secret as the cause of the bodily and mental suffering she endured. When, to his remorse on his mother's account was added the shame and misery occasioned by the discovery of his wife's degradation, he sank under the double trial, his face began to alter fast, and he looked, what he was, a spirit-broken man.

His mother, still struggling bravely against the illness that was hurrying her to the grave, was the first to notice the sad alteration in him, and the first to hear of his last, worst trouble with his wife. She could only weep bitterly, on the day when he made his humiliating confession; but on the next occasion when he went to see her, she had taken a resolution, in reference to his domestic afflictions, which astonished, and even alarmed him. He found her dressed to go out, and on asking the reason, received this answer:

'I am not long for this world, Isaac,' she said; 'and I shall not feel easy on my death-bed, unless I have done my best to the last to make my son happy. I mean to put my own fears and my own feelings out of the question, and to go with you to your wife, and try what I can do to re-claim her. Give me your arm, Isaac; and let me do the last thing I can in this world to help my son, before it is too late.'

He could not disobey her; and they walked together slowly towards his miserable home.

It was only one o'clock in the afternoon when they reached the cottage where he lived. It was their dinner hour, and Rebecca was in the kitchen. He was thus able to take his mother quietly into the parlour and then pre-pare his wife for the interview. She had fortunately drank but little at that early hour, and she was less sullen and capricious than usual.

He returned to his mother, with his mind tolerably at ease. His wife soon followed him into the parlour, and the meeting between her and Mrs. Scatchard passed off better than he had ventured to anticipate; though he observed with secret apprehension that his mother, resolutely as she controlled herself in other respects, could not look his wife in the face when she spoke to her. It was a relief to him, therefore, when Rebecca began to lay the cloth.

She laid the cloth, brought in the bread-tray, and cut a slice from the loaf for her husband, then returned to the kitchen. At that moment, Isaac, still anxiously watching his mother, was startled by seeing the same ghastly change pass over her face which had altered it so awfully on the morning when Rebecca and she first met. Before he could say a word, she whispered with a look of horror:

'Take me back!—home, home, again Isaac! Come with me and never go back again!'

He was afraid to ask for an explanation; he could only sign to her to be silent, and help her quickly to the door.

As they passed the bread-tray on the table, she stopped and pointed to it.

'Did you see what your wife cut your bread with?' she asked in a low whisper.

'No, mother; I was not noticing. What was it?'

'Look?'

He did look. A new clasp-knife, with a buckhorn handle, lay with the loaf in the bread-tray. He stretched out his hand, shudderingly, to possess himself of it; but at the same time, there was a noise in the kitchen and his mother caught at his arm.

'The knife of the dream! Isaac, I'm faint with fear—take me away, before she comes back!'

He was hardly able to support her. The visible, tangible reality of the knife struck him with a panic, and utterly destroyed any faint doubts he might have entertained up to this time, in relation to the mysterious dream-warning of nearly eight years before. By a last desperate effort, he summoned self-possession enough to help his mother out of the house—so quietly, that the 'Dream Woman' (he thought of her by that name now) did not hear their departure.

'Don't go back, Isaac, don't go back!' implored Mrs. Scatchard, as he turned to go away, after seeing her safely seated again in her own room.

'I must get the knife,' he answered under his breath. His mother tried to stop him again; but he hurried out without another word.

On his return, he found that his wife had discovered their secret departure from the house. She had been drinking, and was in a fury of passion. The dinner in the kitchen was flung under the grate; the cloth was off the parlour table. Where was the knife?

Unwisely, he asked for it. She was only too glad of the opportunity of irritating him, which the request afforded her. 'He wanted the knife, did he? Could he give her a reason why?—No? Then he should not have it—not if he went down on his knees to ask for it.' Further recriminations elicited the fact that she had bought it a bargain, and that she considered it her own especial property. Isaac saw the uselessness of attempting to get the knife by fair means, and determined to search for it, later in the day, in secret. The search was unsuccessful. Night came on, and he left the house to walk about the streets. He was afraid now to sleep in the same room with her.

Three weeks passed. Still sullenly enraged with him, she would not give up the knife; and still that fear of sleeping in the same room with her possessed him. He walked about at night, or dozed in the parlour, or sat watching by his mother's bed-side. Before the expiration of the first week in the new month his mother died. It wanted then but ten days of her son's birthday. She had longed to live till that anniversary. Isaac was present at her death; and her last words in this world were addressed to him:

'Don't go back, my son—don't go back!'

He was obliged to go back, if it were only to watch his wife. Exasperated to the last degree by his distrust of her, she had revengefully sought to add a sting to his grief, during the last days of his mother's illness, by declaring that she would assert her right to attend the funeral. In spite of all that he could do or say, she held with wicked pertinacity to her word; and on the day appointed for the burial, forced herself—inflamed and shameless with drink—into her husband's presence, and declared that she would walk in the funeral procession to his mother's grave.

This last worst outrage, accompanied by all that was most insulting in word and look, maddened him for the moment. He struck her.

The instant the blow was dealt, he repented it. She crouched down, silent, in a corner of the room, and eyed him steadily; it was a look that cooled his hot blood, and made him tremble. But there was no time now to think of a means of making atonement. Nothing remained, but to risk the worst till the funeral was over. There was but one way of making sure of her. He locked her into her bedroom.

When he came back, some hours after, he found her sitting, very much altered in look and bearing, by the bedside, with a bundle on her lap. She rose and faced him quietly, and spoke with a strange stillness in her voice, a strange repose in her eyes, a strange composure in her manner.

'No man has ever struck me twice,' she said; 'and my husband shall have no second opportunity. Set the door open and let me go. From this day forth we see each other no more.'

Before he could answer she passed him, and left the room. He saw her walk away up the street.

Would she return?

All that night he watched and waited; but no footstep came near the house. The next night, overcome by fatigue, he lay down in bed in his clothes, with the door locked, the key on the table, and the candle burning. His slumber was not disturbed. The third night, the fourth, the fifth, the sixth passed, and nothing happened. He lay down on the seventh, still in his clothes, still with the door locked, the key on the table, and the candle burning; but easier in his mind.

Easier in his mind, and in perfect health of body, when he fell off to sleep. But his rest was disturbed. He woke twice, without any sensation of uneasiness. But the third time it was that never-to-be-forgotten shivering of the night at the lonely inn, that dreadful sinking pain at the heart, which once more aroused him in an instant.

His eyes opened towards the left-hand side of the bed, and there stood . . .

The Dream Woman again? No! His wife; the living reality, with the dream-spectre's face—in the dream-spectre's attitude: the fair arm up; the knife clasped in the delicate white hand.

He sprang upon her, almost at the instant of seeing her, and yet not quickly enough to prevent her from hiding the knife. Without a word from him, without a cry from her, he pinioned her in a chair. With one hand he felt up her sleeve; and there, where the Dream Woman had hidden the knife, his wife had hidden it—the knife with the buck-horn handle, that looked like new.

In the despair of that fearful moment his brain was steady, his heart was calm. He looked at her fixedly, with the knife in his hand, and said these last words:

'You told me we should see each other no more, and you have come back. It is my turn now to go, and to go for ever. *I* say that we shall see each other no more; and *my* word shall not be broken.'

He left her, and set forth into the night. There was a bleak wind abroad, and the smell of recent rain was in the air. The distant church clocks chimed the quarter as he walked rapidly beyond the last houses in the suburb. He asked the first policeman he met, what hour that was, of which the quarter past had just struck.

The man referred sleepily to his watch, and answered, 'Two o'clock.' Two in the morning. What day of the month was this day that had just begun? He reckoned it up from the date of his mother's funeral. The fatal parallel was complete—it was his birthday!

Had he escaped the mortal peril which his dream fore-told? or had he only received a second warning?

As this ominous doubt forced itself on his mind, he stopped, reflected, and turned back again towards the city. He was still resolute to hold to his word, and never to let her see him more; but there was a thought now in his mind of having her watched and followed. The knife was in his possession; the world was before him; but a new distrust of her—a vague, unspeakable, superstitious dread—had overcome him.

'I must know where she goes, now she thinks I have left her,' he said to himself, as he stole back wearily to the precincts of his house.

It was still dark. He had left the candle burning in the bed-chamber; but when he looked up to the window of the room now, there was no light in it. He crept cautiously to the house door. On going away, he remembered to have closed it; on trying it now, he found it open.

He waited outside, never losing sight of the house till daylight. Then he ventured indoors—listened, and heard nothing—looked into kitchen, scullery, parlour; and found nothing: went up at last into the bedroom—it was empty. A picklock lay on the floor, betraying how she had gained entrance in the night, and that was the only trace of her.

Whither had she gone? No mortal tongue could tell him. The darkness had covered her flight; and when the day broke, no man could say where the light found her.

Before leaving the house and the town for ever, he gave instructions to a friend and neighbour to sell his furniture for anything that it would fetch, and to apply the proceeds towards employing the police to trace her. The directions were honestly followed, and the money was all spent; but the inquiries led to nothing. The picklock on the bedroom floor remained the last useless trace of the Dream Woman.

．　　　．　　　．　　　．　　　．

At this part of the narrative the landlord paused; and, turning towards the window of the room in which we were sitting, looked in the direction of the stable-yard.

'So far,' he said, 'I tell you what was told to me. The little that remains to be added, lies within my own experience. Between two and three months after the events I have just been relating, Isaac Scatchard came to me, withered and old-looking before his time, just as you saw him today. He had his testimonials to character with him, and he asked me for employment here. Knowing that my wife and he were distantly related, I gave him a trial in consideration of that relationship and liked him in spite of his queer habits. He is as sober, honest, and willing a man as there is in England. As for his restlessness at night, and his sleeping away his leisure time in the day, who can wonder at it after hearing his story? Besides, he never objects to being roused up, when he's wanted, so there's not much inconvenience to complain of, after all.'

'I suppose he is afraid of a return of that dreadful dream, and of waking out of it in the dark?'

'No,' returned the landlord. 'The dream comes back to him so often, that he has got to bear with it by this time resignedly enough. It's his wife keeps him waking at night, as he has often told me.'

'What! Has she never been heard of yet?'

'Never. Isaac himself has the one perpetual thought, that she is alive and looking for him. I believe he wouldn't let himself drop off to sleep towards two in the morning, for a king's ransom. Two in the morning, he says, is the time she will find him, one of these days. Two in the morning is the time, all the year round, when he likes to be most certain that he has got the clasp-knife safe about him. He does not mind being alone, as long as he is awake, except on the night before his birthday, when he firmly believes himself to be in peril of his life. The birthday has only come round once since he has been here, and then he sat up along with the night-porter. "She's looking for me," is all he says, when anybody speaks to him about the one anxiety of his life; "she's looking for me." He may be right. She *may* be looking for him. Who can tell?'

'Who can tell?' said I.

EVELYN NESBIT

John Charrington's Wedding

No one ever thought that May Forster would marry John
Charrington; but he thought differently, and things which
John Charrington intended had a queer way of coming
to pass. He asked her to marry him before he went up to
Oxford. She laughed and refused him. He asked her again
next time he came home. Again she laughed, tossed her
dainty blonde head, and again refused. A third time he
asked her; she said it was becoming a confirmed bad habit,
and laughed at him more than ever.

John was not the only man who wanted to marry her:
she was the belle of our village *coterie*, and we were all in
love with her more or less; it was a sort of fashion, like
heliotrope ties or Inverness capes. Therefore we were as
much annoyed as surprised when John Charrington walked
into our little local Club—we held it in a loft over the
saddler's, I remember—and invited us all to his wedding.

'Your wedding?'

'You don't mean it?'

'Who's the happy fair? When's it to be?'

John Charrington filled his pipe and lighted it before
he replied. Then he said:

'I'm sorry to deprive you fellows of your only joke—
but Miss Forster and I are to be married in September.'

'You don't mean it?'

'He's got the mitten again, and it's turned his head.'

'No,' I said, rising, 'I see it's true. Lend me a pistol
someone—or a first-class fare to the other end of Nowhere.
Charrington has bewitched the only pretty girl in our

279

twenty-mile radius. Was it mesmerism, or a love-potion, Jack?'

'Neither, sir, but a gift you'll never have—persever-ance—and the best luck a man ever had in this world.'

There was something in his voice that silenced me, and all chaff of the other fellows failed to draw him further.

The queer thing about it was that when we congratulated Miss Forster, she blushed and smiled and dimpled, for all the world as though she were in love with him, and had been in love with him all the time. Upon my word, I think she had. Women are strange creatures.

We were all asked to the wedding. In Brixham everyone who was anybody knew everybody else who was anyone. My sisters were, I truly believe, more interested in the *trousseau* than the bride herself, and I was to be best man. The coming marriage was much canvassed at afternoon tea-tables, and at our little Club over the saddler's, and the question was always asked: 'Does she care for him?'

I used to ask that question myself in the early days of their engagement, but after a certain evening in August I never asked it again. I was coming home from the Club through the churchyard. Our church is on a thyme-grown hill, and the turf about it is so thick and soft that one's footsteps are noiseless.

I made no sound as I vaulted the low lichened wall, and threaded my way between the tombstones. It was at the same instant that I heard John Charrington's voice, and saw Her. May was sitting on a low flat gravestone, her face turned towards the full splendour of the western sun. Its expression ended, at once and for ever, any question of love for him; it was transfigured to a beauty I should not have believed possible, even to that beautiful little face.

John lay at her feet, and it was his voice that broke the stillness of the golden August evening.

'My dear, my dear, I believe I should come back from the dead if you wanted me!'

I coughed at once to indicate my presence, and passed on into the shadow fully enlightened.

The wedding was to be early in September. Two days before I had to run up to town on business. The train was late, of course, for we are on the South-Eastern, and as I stood grumbling with my watch in my hand, whom should I see but John Charrington and May Forster. They were walking up and down the unfrequented end of the platform, arm in arm, looking into each other's eyes, careless of the sympathetic interest of the porters.

Of course I knew better than to hesitate a moment before burying myself in the booking-office, and it was not till the train drew up at the platform, that I obtrusively passed the pair with my Gladstone, and took the corner in a first-class smoking carriage. I did this with as good an air of not seeing them as I could assume. I pride myself on my discretion, but if John were travelling alone I wanted his company. I had it.

'Hullo, old man,' came his cheery voice as he swung his bag into my carriage; 'here's luck; I was expecting a dull journey!'

'Where are you off to?' I asked, discretion still bidding me turn my eyes away, though I saw, without looking, that hers were red-rimmed.

'To old Branbridge's,' he answered, shutting the door and leaning out for a last word with his sweetheart.

'Oh, I wish you wouldn't go, John,' she was saying in a low, earnest voice. 'I feel certain something will happen.'

'Do you think I should let anything happen to keep me, and the day after tomorrow our wedding-day?'

'Don't go,' she answered, with a pleading intensity which would have sent my Gladstone on to the platform and me after it. But she wasn't speaking to me. John Charrington was made differently; he rarely changed his opinions, never his resolutions.

He only stroked the little ungloved hands that lay on the carriage door.

'I must, May. The old boy's been awfully good to me, and now he's dying I must go and see him, but I shall come

281

home in time for . . .' the rest of the parting was lost in a whisper and in the rattling lurch of the starting train.

'You're sure to come?' she spoke as the train moved.

'Nothing shall keep me,' he answered; and we steamed out. After he had seen the last of the little figure on the platform he leaned back in his corner and kept silence for a minute.

When he spoke it was to explain to me that his god-father, whose heir he was, lay dying at Peasmarsh Place, some fifty miles away, and had sent for John, and John had felt bound to go.

'I shall be surely back tomorrow,' he said, 'or, if not, the day after, in heaps of time. Thank heaven, one hasn't to get up in the middle of the night to get married nowa-days!'

'And suppose Mr. Branbridge dies?'

'Alive or dead I mean to be married on Thursday!' John answered, lighting a cigar and unfolding *The Times*.

At Peasmarsh station we said 'good-bye', and he got out, and I saw him ride off; I went on to London, where I stayed the night.

When I got home the next afternoon, a very wet one, by the way, my sister greeted me with:

'Where's Mr. Charrington?'

'Goodness knows,' I answered testily. Every man, since Cain, has resented that kind of question.

'I thought you might have heard from him,' she went on, 'as you're to give him away tomorrow.'

'Isn't he back?' I asked, for I had confidently expected to find him at home.

'No, Geoffrey'—my sister Fanny always had a way of jumping to conclusions, especially such conclusions as were least favourable to her fellow-creatures—'he has not returned, and, what is more, you may depend upon it he won't. You mark my words, there'll be no wedding to-morrow.'

My sister Fanny has a power of annoying me which no other human being possesses.

'You mark my words,' I retorted with asperity, 'you had better give up making such a thundering idiot of yourself. There'll be more wedding tomorrow than ever you'll take the first part in.' A prophecy which, by the way, came true.

But though I could snarl confidently to my sister, I did not feel so comfortable when late that night, I, standing on the doorstep of John's house, heard that he had not returned. I went home gloomily through the rain. Next morning brought a brilliant blue sky, gold sun, and all such softness of air and beauty of cloud as go to make up a perfect day. I woke with a vague feeling of having gone to bed anxious, and of being rather averse to facing that anxiety in the light of full wakefulness.

But with my shaving-water came a note from John which relieved my mind and sent me up to the Forster's with a light heart.

May was in the garden. I saw her blue gown through the hollyhocks as the lodge gates swung to behind me. So I did not go up to the house, but turned aside down the turfed path.

'He's written to you too,' she said, without preliminary greeting, when I reached her side.

'Yes, I'm to meet him at the station at three, and come straight on to the church.'

Her face looked pale, but there was a brightness in her eyes, and a tender quiver about the mouth that spoke of renewed happiness.

'Mr. Branbridge begged him so to stay another night that he had not the heart to refuse,' she went on. 'He is so kind, but I wish he hadn't stayed.'

I was at the station at half-past two. I felt rather annoyed with John. It seemed a sort of slight to the beautiful girl who loved him, that he should come as it were out of breath, and with the dust of travel upon him, to take her hand, which some of us would have given the best years of our lives to take.

But when the three o'clock train glided in and glided out

again, having brought no passengers to our little station, I was more than annoyed. There was no other train for thirty-five minutes; I calculated that, with much hurry, we might just get to the church in time for the ceremony; but, oh, what a fool to miss that first train! What other man could have done it?

That thirty-five minutes seemed a year, as I wandered round the station reading the advertisements and the time-tables, and the company's bye-laws, and getting more and more angry with John Charrington. This confidence in his own power of getting everything he wanted the minute he wanted it was leading him too far. I hate waiting. Everyone does, but I believe I hate it more than anyone else. The three thirty-five was late, of course.

I ground my pipe between my teeth and stamped with impatience as I watched the signals. Click. The signal went down. Five minutes later I flung myself into the carriage that I had brought for John.

'Drive to the church!' I said, as someone shut the door. 'Mr. Charrington hasn't come by this train.'

Anxiety now replaced anger. What had become of the man? Could he have been taken suddenly ill? I had never known him have a day's illness in his life. And even so he might have telegraphed. Some awful accident must have happened to him. The thought that he had played her false never—no, not for a moment—entered my head. Yes, something terrible had happened to him, and on me lay the task of telling his bride. I almost wished the carriage would upset and break my head so that someone else might tell her, not I, who—but that's nothing to do with this story.

It was five minutes to four as we drew up at the church-yard gate. A double row of eager onlookers lined the path from lynchgate to porch. I sprang from the carriage and passed up between them. Our gardener had a good front place near the door. I stopped.

'Are they waiting still, Byles?' I asked, simply to gain time, for of course I knew they were by the waiting crowd's attentive attitude.

'Waiting, sir? No, no, sir; why, it must be over by now.'

'Over! Then Mr. Charrington's come?'

'To the minute, sir; must have missed you somehow, and, I say, sir,' lowering his voice, 'I never see Mr. John the least bit so afore, but my opinion is he's been drinking pretty free. His clothes was all dusty and his face like a sheet. I tell you I didn't like the looks of him at all, and the folks inside are saying all sorts of things. You'll see, something's gone very wrong with Mr. John, and he's tried liquor. He looked like a ghost and in he went with his eyes straight before him, with never a look or a word for none of us: him that was always such a gentleman!'

I had never heard Byles make so long a speech. The crowd in the churchyard were talking in whispers and getting ready rice and slippers to throw at the bride and bridegroom. The ringers were ready with their hands on the ropes to ring out the merry peal as the bride and bridegroom should come out.

A murmur from the church announced them; out they came. Byles was right. John Charrington did not look himself. There was dust on his coat, his hair was disarranged. He seemed to have been in some row, for there was a black mark above his eyebrow. He was deathly pale. But his pallor was not greater than that of the bride, who might have been carved in ivory—dress, veil, orange blossoms, face and all.

As they passed out the ringers stooped—there were six of them—and then, on the ears expecting the gay wedding peal, came the slow tolling of the passing bell.

A thrill of horror at so foolish a jest from the ringers passed through us all. But the ringers themselves dropped the ropes and fled like rabbits out into the sunlight. The bride shuddered and grey shadows came about her mouth, but the bridegroom led her on down the path where the people stood with the handfuls of rice; but the handfuls were never thrown, and the wedding-bells never rang. In vain the ringers were urged to remedy their mistake: they protested with many whispered expletives that they would see themselves further first.

In a hush like the hush in the chamber of death the bridal pair passed into their carriage and its door slammed behind them.

Then the tongues were loosed. A babel of anger, wonder, conjecture from the guests and the spectators.

'If I'd seen his condition, sir,' said old Forster to me as we drove off, 'I would have stretched him on the floor of the church, sir, by heaven I would, before I'd have let him marry my daughter!'

Then he put his head out of the window.

'Drive like hell,' he cried to the coachman; 'don't spare the horses.'

He was obeyed. We passed the bride's carriage. I forbore to look at it, and old Forster turned his head away and swore. We reached home before it.

We stood in the hall doorway, in the blazing afternoon sun, and in about half a minute we heard wheels crunching the gravel. When the carriage stopped in front of the steps old Forster and I ran down.

'Great heaven, the carriage is empty! And yet . . .'

I had the door open in a minute, and this is what I saw:

No sign of John Charrington; and of May, his wife, only a huddled heap of white satin lying half on the floor of the carriage and half on the seat.

'I drove straight here, sir,' said the coachman, as the bride's father lifted her out; 'and I'll swear no one got out of the carriage.'

We carried her into the house in her bridal dress and drew back her veil. I saw her face. Shall I ever forget it? White, white and drawn with agony and horror, bearing such a look of terror as I have never seen since except in dreams. And her hair, her radiant blonde hair, I tell you it was white like snow.

As we stood, her father and I, half mad with the horror and mystery of it, a boy came up the avenue—a telegraph boy. They brought the orange envelope to me. I tore it open.

Mr. Charrington was thrown from the dogcart on his way to the station at half-past one. Killed on the spot!

And he was married to May Forster in our parish church at *half-past three,* in presence of half the parish.

'*I shall be married, dead or alive!*'

What had passed in that carriage on the homeward drive? No one knows—no one will ever know. Oh, May! oh, my dear!

Before a week was over they laid her beside her husband in our little churchyard on the thyme-covered hill—the churchyard where they had kept their love-trysts.

Thus was accomplished John Charrington's wedding.

DATE DUE

NOV 3 '96			
			PRINTED IN U.S.A.